Home to Trinity

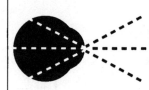This Large Print Book carries the
Seal of Approval of N.A.V.H.

Home to Trinity

Delia Parr

Thorndike Press • Waterville, Maine

LP
Parr

Published in 2003 by arrangement with
St. Martin's Press, LLC.

Thorndike Press® Large Print Americana Series.

The tree indicium is a trademark of Thorndike Press.

The text of this Large Print edition is unabridged.
Other aspects of the book may vary from the original edition.

Set in 16 pt. Plantin by Minnie B. Raven.

Printed in the United States on permanent paper.

Library of Congress Cataloging-in-Publication Data

Parr, Delia.
    Home to Trinity / Delia Parr.
      p. cm.
    ISBN 0-7862-5116-6 (lg. print : hc : alk. paper)
    1. Midwives — Fiction. 2. Women — Pennsylvania —
Fiction. 3. Mothers and daughters — Fiction.
4. Pennsylvania — Fiction. 5. Large type books. I. Title.
PS3566.A7527H6 2003b
  813′.54—dc21   2003041699

Dedicated to my mother and father,
Evelyn and John,
and all the sweet memories of you

Chapter 1

For most folks, a knock at the door meant company had come to call, but for midwife Martha Cade, the past ten years had taught her that each knock was a call to duty that might take her many miles from home to serve friends and neighbors, regardless of the hour or the weather or the state of her own affairs.

Just after dawn, a knock at the back door of the confectionery interrupted the day's baking. Martha glanced at her friends and benefactors and wiped her hands on her apron. "I'll answer. At this hour, it's probably for me," she suggested, anticipating her fourth call to duty in as many days.

Fern, the older of the two Lynn sisters, nodded and continued to twist and knot fresh dough into shape, but Ivy immediately stopped and waved away Martha's words. "Abner said he'd stop by early with cream and eggs," she countered and left to answer the door.

7

She returned with a stranger. The man was young, probably in his mid-twenties. His cheeks were red with cold, and it was the worried expression he wore that Martha recognized as the call to duty she had anticipated with the knock on the door.

Ivy offered Martha a knowing look. "This is Russell Clifford. Russell, this is Midwife Cade."

He removed his hat, revealing a thick head of brown hair almost the same color as his dark eyes. "I'm sorry to come to fetch you so early. I'm — I'm afraid I woke up Reverend Welsh, too. Didn't know where to find you, but he set me straight. Said you'd probably be up, anyway," he added, as if finding her at work eased his conscience a bit. "It's my wife. Nancy. She had a fall two days back, and she's worried about the babe she's carryin'. We were hopin' . . . that is, I was wonderin' if you could come home with me and see to her. I've got a homestead up on Double Trouble Creek. I'm afraid it's a good long ride from here with all the snow."

"Of course I will. Just how soon is the babe due?"

"Late April, best as she can figure."

"Tell me what happened," she prompted

as she began to remove her apron. "How did Nancy fall?"

He swallowed hard. "She . . . well, she was bringin' in some firewood from the barn when she musta tripped on her skirts. She's always been a tad clumsy."

"Any pains? Or bleeding?" she asked, without bothering to reprimand him for letting his teeming wife fetch firewood at all.

He shook his head. "Not before I left this mornin'. She's just bruised up a bit and worried somethin' awful. It's our first babe," he added.

Relief flooded Martha's spirit, and she set her apron aside. With God's grace, she would be able to set the couple's fears to rest and still be home before nightfall. "Nature protects her babes pretty well, but it won't do any harm for me to check and reassure you both. I'll just change and get my bag. Ivy, why don't you get this young man something to eat and a hot drink to warm him up, then send him over to Dr. McMillan's stable? I'll have Grace saddled by then."

Ivy nodded. "But what about your breakfast?"

"I'm not really hungry," Martha insisted for the second time that morning.

Fern rose from her seat. "Nonsense. You can't ride off on an empty stomach. I'll wrap up a honey bun. You can eat it on the way. Go on. Go get yourself ready," she suggested.

Without posing any argument, Martha went directly to the staircase while Ivy fussed over young Clifford. She mounted the steps and went straight to her room, where Bird, a wounded yellow warbler she cared for, chirped a greeting. She smiled and paused just long enough to add small pieces of molasses cookie to his seed bowl. "I'm off again. Behave yourself while I'm gone," she cautioned and quickly changed into her split skirt.

After donning a heavy woolen cape and sturdy riding gloves, she gathered her bag of simples, herbal remedies she prepared herself. On second thought, she retrieved the collapsible birthing stool she had inherited from her grandmother from beneath her bed, just in case she needed it.

She hurried from her room, followed the hall to the front staircase, descended, and continued through the shop foyer. Instead of worrying about the difficult ride ahead, she focused on the woman who needed her help.

Martha did not always know the women

10

or children she treated. She just wished she had seen Nancy Clifford before now, if only to have a better feeling about whether concern for the woman and her unborn babe was truly warranted.

Bitter cold air clouded in front of her as she took in deep breaths and exhaled while walking as briskly as she dared on the snow-covered ground. Carrying her bag and stool, one in each hand, actually helped her to keep her balance as she tried to keep her footing while walking into a stiff wind. Once she reached the protection of the covered bridge at the south end of West Main Street, which crossed Dillon's Stream, she let her shoulders relax and hurried through to the other side.

She reached Dr. McMillan's home and made her way to the stable located directly behind the house. Once inside, she set her bag on the ground, laid the birthing stool on top of it, and shut the door behind her. Grace greeted her with a snort and stomped the ground with a forefoot. Half draft horse and half saddle horse, she was quite sturdy, with a gray coat mottled by splotches of black and white. "Good morning to you, too. And you," she added when she spied her brother's former stable cat, Leech, perched on Grace's back.

He was one nasty cat who much preferred horses to humans, and Martha had a scar on her forearm to prove it.

Leech responded with a customary hiss, then promptly exchanged his sleeping place for one on the back of the doctor's horse in the next stall.

She gave Grace a good portion of oats, which she ate while Martha got the mare saddled and strapped on the birthing stool and bag. After leading the horse outside, she resecured the barn door. "If we hurry, and if we're all truly blessed this day, you and I will be home in time for supper," she murmured.

She mounted the horse, tightened the fastening on her hood, and tucked her cape around her as the wind whipped at her split skirt. She leaned forward and patted Grace on the neck. Instead of waiting for Russell Clifford, however, she urged Grace forward toward the confectionery.

A howling, incessant wind and snow-covered terrain demanded all of Martha's attention and made conversation nigh impossible during the lengthy trek to the Clifford homestead. Long frozen, her breakfast lay untouched in her cape pocket.

Once inside the rustic, isolated log cabin, Martha set her bag and birthing stool just inside the door and removed her cape. As she struggled to ease the frozen gloves from her hands, she glanced around the room. The furnishings in the great room were meager and crudely constructed, but the wooden floor had been swept clean and the room was neat.

Two chairs nestled against a small table near the hearth, where a large black kettle hung over ashes nearly gone cold. The hooked rug beneath the table provided the only splash of color in the room. Cookware, plates, and utensils sat together on yet another rickety table. No curtains adorned the two windows on either side of the door. A door to her right, apparently to the bedchamber, was closed.

Russell went directly to the hearth and stoked the fire back to life. "We're just startin' out," he apologized. "It's frightful cold in here. Nancy should have kept this going," he murmured. "She's probably still restin' in bed. Been sleepin' a lot since she fell," he explained when Martha cocked a brow.

She warmed her hands in front of the fire. Although eager to see to her patient, she knew better than to go near Nancy with hands numb with cold. Apparently, Russell had also left his wife alone, instead of having one of the neighbor women stay with her. She found that odd, if not troubling. "Where do you come from?" she asked as the warmth from the fire began to bring life back to her hands.

He stood up and slapped away splinters of wood and ash from his trousers. "We left New Jersey early last fall when Nancy and I got married."

"I suppose you haven't met many neighbors."

He blushed. "Not yet. But I try to take good care of my wife. When she said she needed help, I went straight to town to fetch you. Are . . . are you gonna see her now or not?" he asked, clearly anxious about his wife as well as his unborn child.

"Right away." Martha secured her bag and headed directly to the bedchamber. "Wait here. I shouldn't be long," she informed him, entered the room, and closed the door behind her. She glanced quickly around the room. A single trunk anchored one wall. A small table with a pitcher and washbasin sat on the other wall below a single, curtainless window that cast garish light into the room.

Her patient was lying in a double bed

14

with the bedclothes in disarray. Nancy appeared to be quite young, perhaps even as young as Martha's daughter, Victoria, yet here she was, married and already expecting her first child. Strands of limp brown hair lay matted against her thin, pale cheeks. Martha could see no sign of bruising on the woman's face, but there looked like a bump on her head that would account for her sleeping so much.

Her eyes were closed, and for the moment, she appeared to be resting comfortably. As Martha approached the bed, Nancy groaned, clutched her abdomen, and rocked from side to side. Martha's heart began to pound as she raced forward. "Nancy, I'm Martha Cade. I'm a midwife. Russell brought me here to help you."

Nancy let out a whelp and began to cry. "T-too early. T-too early. P-please help me. Make the pains stop," she pleaded.

Martha took Nancy's right hand into her own and stifled a gasp. In addition to the deep scrapes on the heel of the palm, the middle finger curved up at the middle knuckle and did not lie flat. The small finger jutted out at the knuckle in an odd angle, but neither finger carried any bruises to indicate the woman's hand had been injured in her fall. Martha had seen

15

enough poorly set, broken bones to know that Nancy had broken each of her fingers at one time, but she had no time to waste on anything other than the woman's current distress.

Martha placed her other hand on top of the woman's swollen abdomen and tried to hide her concern. "How long have you had the pains?"

"Since . . . since just after Russell left," she managed, then gritted her teeth together.

Martha felt the young woman's abdomen go rigid with another contraction that edged Martha's concern up another notch. All told, Russell had been gone for several hours, which did not bode well for anything Martha might attempt to do to stop the pains. "How long have they been this close?" she asked, but her patient was unable to answer. Both the quick timing and the intensity of the contractions led Martha to believe the pains had shifted from groaning pains to forcing pains, which meant birth was imminent.

When the pain subsided, Martha took a fresh cloth from her bag, moistened it with rose water, and bathed Nancy's face. "How long have your pains been this close?" she repeated.

Soulful brown eyes filled with tears. "I don't know. An hour. Maybe two." She clutched one of Martha's hands hard. "Make them stop. Please. It's too soon. My babe's not due till April. Please help me."

"I'll see what I can do. First, I'll need to examine you. Then . . . well, we'll see," Martha promised. She worked quickly, rolling the quilt and sheet up from the bottom of the bed to form a small mound that rested on the woman's chest. When she eased Nancy's nightdress up from her ankles to her knees, she noticed the bruises on each of her shins, evidence she must have tripped and fallen forward, just as Russell had said. She feared the girl's abdomen, perhaps, had taken the brunt of her fall, which may have caused the premature pains.

Martha rinsed her hands, dried them, and lubricated her right hand. "I'm just going to see how far you've gotten," she explained. Before she could begin her examination, however, Nancy cried out and doubled up with yet another pain. A gush of bloody fluids flowed from her loins and drenched the bedcovers.

Martha caught her breath. Birth was indeed imminent, but the joyful anticipation she normally felt was replaced by sorrow.

Born this early, the babe would be too small to survive, and there was nothing Martha could do now to prevent the tragedy about to unfold. There would be no groaning party, no celebration of new life for Nancy and Russell. Only grief that faith and time would one day heal.

"Russell — come quickly. Bring the birthing stool. Now!" she barked.

Dismayed that she had no assistants to help her, Martha eased her patient into a sitting position. She slid the younger woman's legs over the side of the bed until her feet rested on the floor, then sat down on the bed and put her arm around the suffering woman's shoulders while Russell struggled to set the birthing stool into proper position. "It's too late to stop what nature has begun. I'm sorry. But I'll do what I can to make this easier for you."

"My babe!" Nancy cried before she slumped forward and clutched her abdomen. "My babe. My poor, dear babe."

"We can't question the Lord's plans for your babe. He's probably too small to survive, but we don't know that. Not yet," she added. It was not uncommon for a woman to misjudge when her babe was due, especially the first, but the small size of Nancy's distended abdomen did not offer

18

much hope. "Pray, sweet girl, and trust Him to take care of both of you."

"No. It's too soon. I can't have my babe yet," she wailed.

Martha held the girl through another pain before guiding her to the stool. "You sit down on the stool first, Russell. That's right. Nancy, sit right on his lap. There you go. Now hold on to your wife, Russell, while I get my things."

Within moments, Martha had her scissors and a small towel that would have to serve as a blanket. After she tied her birthing apron into place, she yanked a sheet from the bed to use as a birthing sheet. She put it into place as best she could, knelt down in front of her patient, and tried to offer her a reassuring smile. Tenderly, she eased her hands beneath the nightdress and placed one hand against the soft, moist flesh near the birth canal. "When the next pain begins —"

She never got to finish her instructions. The next pain hit with a vengeance. Nancy screamed, and Martha felt the baby's head emerge. Another pain, and she held a little body in her hands. Within a heartbeat, Martha had the baby boy cradled in her lap. His whole body was tinged a pale blue, but he bore no bruises or any other injuries from his mother's fall.

He lay perfectly still. So very, very still. She wiped his little face and rosebud lips with a corner of the towel before cutting the cord.

"Russell? What's happening, Russell? Why can't I hear the babe cry?" Nancy cried.

"Sh-h-h," he whispered. "It's all right. Everything is going to be all right."

While Russell tried to comfort his wife, Martha worked gently, but firmly, to remove the cord that had wrapped not once, but twice, around the boy's tiny neck. She blinked back tears. In the midst of tragedy, Martha had found a blessing. This baby would have strangled to death during birth, whether that was now or later. She offered a prayer of thanksgiving that this fact would help to relieve any guilt Nancy might bear for the fall that hastened her son's entrance into this world.

Martha massaged his little body and prayed she could bring life back to his form, if only to have his mother hear him cry. Just once. To give them a few moments of life to share together — moments that would have to last Nancy a lifetime.

But to no avail.

She held his lifeless body, so very small,

yet so perfectly formed, in the palm of her hand. "Your sweet little angel boy has already gone Home," she whispered before wrapping him in the towel and placing him into his mother's trembling arms. Choking back her own sobs, she prayed as she delivered the afterbirth. For Nancy. For Russell. And for their little angel son.

Profound sadness enveloped her spirit, and she struggled to embrace this little one's loss as his mother wept. In nearly ten years of practice, she had lost only four babies to stillbirth, and each still lived vividly in her memory. Still, nothing could ever prepare her for this experience, and she tried with all her might to accept this baby's death as an opportunity for all of them to receive even greater blessings.

Later, she would record today's tragedy in her diary and pray it would be a very long time before she had to do it again.

"I'm sorry, Russell. I'm so sorry. It's all my fault. Please forgive me. Please."

Startled by Nancy's plea, Martha looked up. Nancy cradled her dead child against her bosom with her deformed hand. She began crying uncontrollably, but it was Russell who garnered all of Martha's attention.

With his lips pressed together in a firm

21

line, he held his body stiff. His gaze was hard and unforgiving. Instead of answering his wife, instead of reassuring her that he did not blame her for this accident of nature, he eased her from his lap, stood up, and handed her over to Martha.

"I have a grave to dig," he mumbled and quickly left the room without ever holding his son or offering a single word of comfort to his wife.

Stunned, Martha embraced the young woman. With the tiny boy's body pressed between them, they wept together. Childbearing was indeed a woman's lot, her cross as well as her greatest blessing, creating bonds of sisterhood between all women — bonds most men could scarcely begin to understand. Memories of her own two babies, now resting next to their father in the cemetery, still ran deep.

For many men like Russell, the shock of losing a babe unleashed emotions they would bury deep in their hearts and hide from the world, but in time, she prayed, Russell and Nancy would be able to grieve together, accept their loss as God's will, and forgive the accident that had led to this early, tragic birth.

Nancy was far from home and family, with no mother to console her, no familiar friends or neighbors to help her. For now, Martha would have to be the anchor that held Nancy and her faith steady. "Give a good cry, sweet Nancy. You are not alone. You are never alone," she crooned. "I'm so sorry, so very sorry."

Later, there would be time to offer hope, to speak of the children Nancy would someday carry and welcome into the world with great joy and celebration, but now was not that time. Although this baby had never drawn a single breath or suckled at his mother's breast, to his mother, he had been real. He had been her baby for many months — months filled with dreams that now would never be fulfilled.

Now was a time for grieving his loss, for forgiving, and for healing, both in body and soul. She cried with Nancy for all that could have been and prayed for healing for this couple — a healing that would bring them closer together, united as one, in faith and in love.

Chapter 2

Martha was emotionally drained and physically spent by the time she had Nancy back in bed, washed, and gowned in a fresh nightdress. It was no simple accomplishment since Nancy refused to let go of her dead newborn for a single moment. All visible signs of the birthing had now been removed, and Martha's work, for now, was done.

An eerie silence engulfed the room with sadness, broken only by the rhythmic echo of a pick attacking frozen earth or the scraping of a shovel as Russell prepared a final resting place for his son.

Martha sat at the foot of the bed. She studied the young mother as waning afternoon sunlight cast gentle shadows onto the bed. Even in sleep, her face was haunted by grief and the ordeal of childbirth. Her eyelids were still puffy and dried tears stained her cheeks. Her crooked hold on her silent angel was firm, and he lay, silent and still, in the crook of her neck.

Martha moistened her lips and steepled her hands together. She was far from content that all would soon be well for Nancy, even though the tragic birth had proceeded quite normally. Still, she could not account for the variety of bruises she had discovered on Nancy's body while applying the traditional wrappings and bathing the young woman after the birth.

Some bruises, like those on her shins and abdomen, were clearly fresh and caused by the fall that triggered the premature birth of her son. Others, tinged with telltale yellow, were much older, like those on her upper arms and the one on the side of her neck.

Adding the multiple bruises to the crooked fingers on Nancy's hand made Russell's comment at the confectionery about Nancy being clumsy appear to ring true. Most farm women suffered physical injuries from hours of long, hard work, but not nearly to the extent Nancy did. Was she just naturally clumsy and prone to injury as Russell suggested? Instead, was there a medical condition responsible for the abnormal extent of bruising Martha had detected? Perhaps Nancy suffered from an impairment in her vision. Or some kind of brain defect that affected her equilibrium, which would account for her apparent clumsiness?

Martha could not be sure. As well-versed as she might be in women's ailments, pregnancy, and the birth process, she was not trained to diagnose or treat more serious conditions, something the young Dr. McMillan would be quick to point out.

With years of experience, Martha pondered these questions, even as her heart began to race with yet another, more awful possibility. It was entirely possible Nancy was neither clumsy nor ill, but married to a man who was not the loving husband he presented himself to be. And the bruises could be evidence of his brutal treatment. If that were the case, there was no way Martha could leave Nancy here alone with him, especially after what had happened today.

Before she could begin to think of a way to approach the subject with her patient, Nancy stirred and opened her eyes. She blinked several times, then tightened her deformed hand around her babe as fresh tears fell. "I . . . I was so sure this was just a bad dream. Just a horrible dream," she whimpered.

Martha reached out and rubbed one of the girl's feet. "How I wish I could tell you it were true."

Nancy sniffled and wiped her face with the sleeve of her nightdress. Fear paled her complexion. "Where's Russell?"

"He's still outside. The ground is frozen hard, so it may take him some time. . . ."

Nancy's bottom lip began to quiver. "He must be so angry with me."

Martha cocked a brow and grabbed the very opening she needed to answer her concerns. "Does Russell get angry with you very often?"

Nancy's eyes widened as she obviously absorbed the implications in Martha's question. When she shook her head, tears escaped and trickled down the sides of her face. She pressed her lips together and tilted her chin. Her gaze sparkled with defiance. "Russell is a fine man and a good husband. He's patient and understanding, and —"

"I didn't mean to imply otherwise," Martha insisted. Most definitely rebuked, she was taken aback by the younger woman's adamant defense of her husband. Loath to be responsible for upsetting her patient, Martha regretted even suggesting there was trouble in this young couple's marriage.

"It's not his fault I'm just naturally clumsy, but this time . . ." Nancy paused and wiped the tears from her face. "This time I'm afraid he'll never forgive me for being such an oaf. I know I never will. It's all my fault this happened. I should have waited for him to get the firewood, then I wouldn't have fallen, and my babe . . . my poor babe. . . ." She dissolved into tears.

"You won't help matters by blaming yourself," Martha insisted. She briefly explained the double-wrapped cord around the baby's neck. "So you see, perhaps ending your pregnancy now is God's mercy at work. You can mourn your babe's loss as nature's accident, not yours."

Nancy brushed away new tears with the back of her hand and looked back and forth from the door to her swaddled babe. "Why did this have to happen? Why?" she wailed.

Martha moved closer to sit alongside the grief-stricken young woman. "We don't know why," she murmured. "All we can do is trust the good Lord to help us through tragedy. I know your heart is broken, but God's power to heal —"

"God should have used His power to save my babe," Nancy countered before she turned her back to Martha and began to sob.

Martha let her cry herself back to sleep.

When the world outside once again grew silent, she gathered her bag and birthing stool, tiptoed from the room, and gently closed the door just as Russell returned to the cabin.

He placed a small wooden box onto the table and emptied out the contents, an odd collection of nails and screws. "Don't need to bother makin' a coffin. This should do," he murmured.

Martha swallowed the lump in her throat and set her things down by the bedchamber door. "I'm so sorry, Russell. I wish I had been able to do more."

"You did what you could. There's no need to apologize or waste any more time here. Figure you'd want to head back to town and get home before nightfall."

His words were clipped, his expression hard.

Her heartstrings tightened. "I should stay awhile longer. To check Nancy and make sure she doesn't have any complications. I'd also like to stay and pray with you when you bury your son."

He tightened his jaw, and a tic dimpled one of his reddened cheeks. "I can bury my son without troublin' you further, and I can tend to my wife."

She softened her gaze. "You don't have

to do it alone. Nancy's resting now. At least let me help you get the babe's coffin ready and make something for you to eat. Then when Nancy wakes up, I'll check her again and leave, if that's what you want. The two of you should spend some time together with your son. Nancy needs you, Russell, more than she needs me right now. She's plagued with guilt —"

His eyes filled with tears, but he held them back and balled his hands into fists. "If she had waited for me, instead of bein' impatient and goin' out for that firewood herself, God knows none of this would have happened. None of it!"

"You can't blame Nancy," she argued. "Her fall triggered the birth, but the cord was wrapped tight around that babe's neck not once, but twice. I've seen it a few times before, unfortunately. Whether that babe entered this world today or next week or in April, I'm afraid the end result most likely would have been the same. What happened to your son was an accident of nature, and it won't help bring him back to blame Nancy."

He relaxed his hands, drew in deep gulps of air, and swallowed hard as he visibly struggled to accept her explanation. When the echo of her words faded away, he nodded toward the bedchamber door. "Have you told her this?"

"Yes, but she's still very upset and frightened you'll be angry with her. She's weak from childbirth, and her heart is broken. Sit with her until she wakes up again and reassure her. In the meantime, I'll see what I can do about fixing up that box for your son. Did Nancy have any blankets ready for him? Anything at all I could use to make a soft bed for him?"

He shook his head. "We were supposed to go to the general store and get some wool, but . . ."

"Don't worry. I'll think of something. Go on. Sit with her. And with your son."

"Peter. His name is Peter," he whispered before he left her standing all alone.

Feeling guilty for thinking he might have struck his wife, when he so clearly cared for her, Martha waited until he closed the door behind him before she glanced about the room. No curtain covered the window. No cloth adorned the table. There was nothing, simply nothing she could use to line the box, but she refused to allow Peter's resting place to be nothing more than a coarse, wooden box.

She caught her lower lip with her teeth, thought hard, and came up with a solution.

Selfishly, she rejected it for a heartbeat before accepting the sacrifice she must make. "Dear Lord," she prayed, "I know Hannah went to great lengths to make this special petticoat for me to wear with my split skirt, but I think she'd want me to do this. It's just . . . well, sometimes it's hard for me to give up something I especially like, so I ask You to please forgive me for coveting this petticoat and hesitating to use Hannah's gift for little Peter."

With her prayer done, she went to the far corner of the room, turned her back to the bedchamber door, eased out of her split skirt, and slid her petticoat free. Her hands shook as she tugged her split skirt back into place, and she let out a sigh of relief that she had managed the first part of her task without being caught half-dressed.

She carried her petticoat back to the table, retrieved her scissors from her bag, and got straight to work. She cut several squares of white cotton from one leg, laid them on top of one another inside the box, and tucked under the unfinished edges. Content with her efforts to create some semblance of a little mattress, she cut off another larger square with the wide bank of embroidery at the hem from the same leg. She had no needle or thread; instead, she finished the edges of the make-do coverlet by cutting a scallop design.

With the inside of the wooden box transformed into a suitable little coffin, she kept busy by adding a few logs to the fire and starting a kettle of potato soup. Her stomach growled, reminding her she had not eaten yet today. She retrieved the honey bun from her cape pocket and nibbled it away in no time.

When Russell finally emerged from the bedchamber, the soup was bubbling. "If you're hungry —"

He waved away her suggestion. "Not now. I want to bury Peter before dark." He walked over to the table and retrieved the box.

She answered the surprise in his expression with a smile. "It's not much, but Nancy will feel better if —"

"It's fine. Thank you. Nancy . . . Nancy asked if you'd help her with Peter and say a prayer with her now. She's in no condition to go outside and pray at his grave."

Martha nodded and followed him back into the bedchamber. Nancy was sitting up in bed now and held the babe in the crook of her arm. Her eyes were red and swollen from crying, but she appeared to be composed.

Until Russell placed the coffin onto her lap.

Fresh tears spilled down her cheeks. When Martha reached for little Peter, Nancy flinched and tightened her hold on him.

"There's no rush. We can wait a bit. Until you're ready," Martha crooned.

"Nancy, give her the babe."

Nancy looked up at him, pressed one last kiss to her baby's face, and handed him to Martha, before she dissolved into tears.

Ever so gently, Martha wrapped Peter in his little coverlet and placed his tiny body into the box. While Russell stood stoically at his wife's side, Martha led them all in prayer. "We commend thee, Peter Clifford, into the loving arms of your heavenly Father. Sweet angel boy, as you look down on us from above, you can see that you were much loved. Know that you will remain in your mother's heart and your father's heart forever. Always their darling son. Always their sweet babe. We wait for the day you will be reunited when you welcome your parents Home."

Martha took a deep breath.

Nancy sobbed.

Her husband remained stoic.

Martha continued. "We pray, dear Lord, that You will comfort Nancy and Russell in this, their hour of great sorrow, and ease their grief with Your endless love and generous mercy. We ask for Your blessing now and in all the days and nights that follow. Amen."

Russell cleared his throat. "Amen."

Nancy's voice whispered an echo of a response as she stared at her baby as he lay in his little coffin. Without further comment, Russell slid the cover into place and carried his son away. Nancy followed them with her gaze until Russell disappeared from view. When the cabin door opened and then slammed shut, she began to tremble. "I can't believe he's gone. My little Peter," she cried.

Martha did her best to console the grief-stricken woman, and they listened together as Peter buried the little boy. Eventually, after Martha checked Nancy to make sure there were no complications from the birthing, the young woman cried herself to sleep yet again, and Martha returned to the outer room.

When Russell finally came back inside, his expression remained frozen with determination. Exhaustion aged his face. He held up a lantern. "It'll be gettin' dark soon. I used this to get to town earlier, but there's plenty of oil left. I saddled your mare and strapped on your things so you can take your leave now."

"I wouldn't mind staying with Nancy for the night. The soup's ready. I could fix you some supper."

He squared his shoulders. "I appreciate everythin' you've done for my wife, but I can tend to her now."

"Most women need an afternurse for the first week or so. If you won't let me stay the night, at least let me send someone tomorrow to stay with Nancy."

He frowned. "That won't be necessary."

Unaccustomed to having her recommendations rejected out of hand, she stiffened her spine. Her heart began to pound, and she tried to understand why he was being so adamant. Granted, he was battling emotions that were understandably difficult. He was angry and bitter over the death of his son, and his grief was so raw and so deep he just could not be thinking clearly.

There was nothing she could do to force him to let her stay the night or to compromise and to allow her to arrange for an afternurse to come in the morning. She had to hold true, however, to her responsibility to her patient and pressed her case.

"I think it is necessary, and unless you want to risk your wife's health, you'll do as I suggest. Millicent Fenway lives just a few miles away. I could stop and see her on my way home. I'm sure she'd be willing to come to stay with Nancy tomorrow, just for a few days."

He raked one hand through his hair. "I don't know how I'm goin' to pay your reward, let alone one for anyone else."

Martha's heart constricted. "We can work something out for my reward. Millicent won't come because she wants to earn a reward. She'll come because that's what we womenfolk do for one another. We help one another."

His shoulders sagged, and he glanced at the bedchamber door. "Nancy's been real lonely since we left Newark. I guess . . . I guess it would help her to have another woman with her. If you'll give me directions, I'll ride over and speak to Mrs. Fenway myself in the mornin'. You can go home tonight. Unless . . . unless you think somethin' might go wrong during the night."

"No, I think Nancy will be fine till morning," she assured him and accepted his offer as a fair compromise.

"Thank you."

"You're welcome. Now, set yourself down and get some soup into you, young man, while I give you those directions. Later, when Nancy wakes up, see if you can get her to eat some, too. And if she has any trouble during the night, you're to get Mrs. Fenway to stay with her and fetch me back. Agreed?"

He grinned. "Yes, ma'am. I will."

With the crisis passed, she took her leave and started for home within the hour. Except for an occasional break in the heavy clouds overhead that promised more snow and allowed a gentle moon to guide her home, she truly appreciated the lantern Russell had insisted she take with her. The air was still frigid, but still, and Grace's steps were steady.

As Martha passed sleeping homesteads, a familiar yearning stirred in her heart. She would be forever grateful for the life she had been able to create for herself and for her children, but there was still a part of her that hungered for what might have been if her husband, John, had not died some ten years ago. Companionship. A home. A real home of her own, instead of a room in someone's else's home.

She sighed and hoped the Lord would forgive her for being selfish and ungrateful.

Life was not supposed to be perfect, but sometimes, it surely seemed that she had been given more than her own fair share of burdens.

Despite her sorrows, Martha had received many blessings. Fern and Ivy had become such good friends, she sometimes forgot they had only been in Trinity for four years; in fact, she thought of them as family — the only family she had had in Trinity for several long months now.

Her brother, James, and his wife, Lydia, were now living temporarily with their married daughter in Sunrise, some thirty miles east. Martha's son, Oliver, now lived in Boston where he was practicing law with his grandfather. Her daughter, Victoria, had . . .

She sniffled and blinked back tears. Rather than focus on all the grief and worry that had troubled her the past seven months, she tried to concentrate on the joy tomorrow would bring when her runaway daughter finally came home to Trinity.

When she passed through the covered bridge at the north end of town and rode toward Dr. McMillan's home, she looked about the town and smiled. But Trinity was not the same sleepy little town Victoria had left behind when she ran off with a traveling theater troupe seven months ago.

Martha passed the barren plot of land at the north end of East Main Street where Poore's Tavern, once the family's mainstay, had stood for over sixty years. Fire had claimed her brother's tavern and the separate quarters Martha had shared with Victoria only last fall, but nothing could erase the memories of happier days.

So much had changed. So much remained the same. So much needed to be resolved when Victoria returned.

Martha had Aunt Hilda to thank for giving her the courage to face tomorrow's reunion with honesty and a real commitment to clear up the misunderstandings that had driven Victoria from home. As the last surviving original settler, Hilda Seymour was more than the town matriarch. She had been Grandmother Poore's closest friend, and Martha claimed her as family, too, as her aunt-by-affection.

Aunt Hilda was now her dearest friend, her confidante, her inspiration, and the very lifeline that kept her grounded to her faith, her family, and her calling. She was also the best afternurse for miles. Although Millicent Fenway would be more than competent, Martha would have felt a whole lot better leaving Nancy with Aunt Hilda by her side. Unfortunately, Aunt Hilda was already on duty at the Goodman homestead, and Martha made a mental note to check on Aunt Hilda's cottage in the morning as she had promised to do.

With Victoria's homecoming so close at hand, after seven long months of worry, she marveled that Aunt Hilda could still be so certain she would one day be reunited with her long-lost husband, Richard, who had left home some thirty years ago and never returned.

No one, not even Aunt Hilda, had ever heard from him again. Most folks, Martha included, had had him planted under six feet of ground for years, but not Aunt Hilda. She remained convinced he would come home to her someday, triumphant, with his pockets full of the fortune he had left to find.

Now nearing fourscore, Aunt Hilda still refused to move from the cottage that had been their home for fear he would not be able to find her when he did return. Martha smiled and let out a sigh. Aunt Hilda was nothing less than a living lesson in faith, and Martha was humbled by her feeble attempts to follow her example.

Lost in her own musings, Martha was

surprised when Grace suddenly halted and Martha found herself back at the stable behind Dr. McMillan's house. Within minutes, she had the mare fed and content in her stall. " 'Twas a sad call today," Martha murmured as she patted the horse's neck. "Thank you, dear friend, for carrying me safely home."

She left the stable and made her way to the bridge. As she approached the confectionery, she noted the light in the kitchen and smiled. Bless their hearts, Fern or Ivy must be waiting up for her, which meant there was also a good fire in the hearth and a bit of supper warming on the cookstove.

She hurried to the back of the confectionery, let herself in the door, and left her bag and birthing stool in the storage room before she entered the kitchen. To her surprise, neither Fern nor Ivy were sitting at the table.

She did not recognize the young matron who looked back at her, but she surely knew the woman's younger companion. Stunned, Martha stared at the petite young woman, unable to speak as her heart fluttered in her chest. She rushed forward into open arms, and managed to speak in spite of her tears. "Welcome home, child. Welcome home."

Chapter 3

"Victoria! My sweet girl. My girl! Sweet Saviour, it's really you. You're home!" Martha gushed.

Her entire body tingled with joy and excitement. She hugged her daughter and held her close. Her heart beat so fast she grew dizzy.

She placed a hand on either side of Victoria's head and pressed several kisses to her forehead. "Sweet Saviour!" She hugged the girl again. "Mercy, it's so good to have you home again." She squeezed her in another embrace, as if to make sure she was not an illusion that would try to fade away.

With her head pressed against Martha's shoulder, Victoria chuckled. "Yes, Mother, I'm home. But if you don't give me room to breathe —"

"Oh, I'm sorry." Martha set Victoria back from her and held her by her shoulders. "Let me take a look at you."

Through blurred vision, Martha stared at her daughter and shook her head as she

43

sighed with relief. "You look well. You look just wonderful!"

And she did. She truly did.

Despite all Martha's fears that Victoria would return home ill or thin and emaciated after struggling to survive on her own, her daughter was the picture of good health. Still youthfully slim, like her father had been all his life, she wore her dark hair in a fashionable style that made her appear older. Instead of wearing her dark curls long, country-style, she had parted her hair in the middle and piled her curls high, with small tendrils framing the sides of her oval face.

Beneath finely arched brows, her hazel eyes, the same color as her father's, shimmered with tears and relief. Her cheeks were rosy, her lips full. "You're even lovelier than ever," Martha murmured before she pulled her daughter back into an embrace. "You're home. You're really home. I've been so worried about you. So frightened something would happen to you."

Victoria snuggled closer, laid her head on Martha's shoulder, and wept softly. "I know. I'm — I'm so sorry. I never meant to cause you worry. Forgive me, Mother. I never should have left without talking to you first or at least writing sooner to let you know —"

"You're forgiven, darling girl. You're forgiven." Martha pressed a kiss to the girl's temple and rocked her from side to side until her tears were spent. All traces of anger had eased from Martha's heart months ago; she offered a silent prayer of gratitude for the faith that had sustained her during Victoria's absence, and for the ever-protective Lord who had watched over Victoria and kept her safe.

The past seven months, though difficult, had also given her new insights. She vowed to treasure this child for her gifts, even if that meant accepting Victoria's preference not to continue family tradition and follow Martha into her calling as a midwife.

Out of the corner of her eye, she caught a glimpse of the young matron who sat at the table quietly observing the reunion between Martha and her daughter. She edged Victoria to her side and placed her arm possessively around the girl's shoulders. "Introduce me to your friend," she urged.

Victoria wrapped her arm around Martha's waist. "Oh, I'm sorry. Mother, this is Mrs. Morgan. She traveled home with me." She nodded toward the woman who rose from her seat. "This is my mother, Martha Cade."

The woman approached and extended her hand. An obvious woman of means, Mrs. Morgan was the same height as Martha, but more than a few pounds lighter. She was a good ten years younger, probably in her early thirties. Her light brown hair was pulled back severely into a bun at the nape of her neck, which accented her finely chiseled, almost classical features. The pale silk gown she wore shimmered with elegance, and Martha noted the slightly distended abdomen that indicated Mrs. Morgan was probably expecting her babe in late spring.

Her doe brown eyes glistened with warmth. "I'm June. June Morgan. I'm so very happy to finally meet you."

Martha caught the woman's hand, and they briefly embraced. Curious about the relationship Victoria shared with this woman, Martha smiled. "I'm so grateful that Victoria did not travel alone."

June smiled back. "I couldn't let her come alone. Fortunately, my husband is as fond of Victoria as I am and insisted we make the trip together."

Martha cocked a brow, but resisted the urge to pepper either Victoria or June with questions that simply begged for answers. Instead, she nuzzled her daughter's head with the tip of her chin and kept a tight hold on her. "I thought you weren't coming until tomorrow. I so wanted to be here when you arrived."

"It's all right, Mother. Truly. Once we left the coach behind in York and rented a sleigh, we traveled much faster. I'd forgotten how much snow winter brings. We only arrived just before dark. When I saw the tavern gone, I — I didn't know where to find you so I stopped at the general store. Wesley told me you were staying here at the confectionery. Miss Fern and Miss Ivy told us you'd been called up to Double Trouble Creek."

Martha sighed, truly disappointed that she had not been home when Victoria arrived. "It was a sad case, I'm afraid, but I can tell you about that later. Trinity has changed a great deal since you left. You must have so many questions."

June chuckled. "A host of them, I'm afraid, but Fern and Ivy were good enough to answer most of them for her. They kindly offered me a place to stay as well." She smiled. "You and Victoria have much to talk about so I'll leave you two together now. We can talk in the morning, after we've all gotten some rest." She patted her extended tummy. "It's my third. Thaddeus and I have two sons. Luke is four. John is almost two. I'm hoping for a daughter this time."

Martha nodded. "Thank you. Thank you, again, for bringing Victoria back to me."

"You're very welcome," June murmured. She and Victoria exchanged a look, which triggered concern that Martha quickly dismissed.

Once June left, Victoria sighed deeply, turned to give her mother a hug, and ushered Martha to the table. "Sit. Miss Ivy left a platter for you. We can talk while you eat."

With their roles oddly reversed, Martha did as she was told. Victoria moved with a new sense of grace and self-assuredness, which was not lost on her mother while she secured a platter warming on the cookstove and utensils that she sat in front of her mother. She added a jug of honey, a plate of cookies, a cinnamon stick, and a mug of cider to her offering before taking a seat across the table from Martha.

The vision of warm corn bread and thick slices of ham made Martha's stomach growl, but it was the sight of fresh oatmeal cookies that made her mouth water. She eyed the cookies again, hesitated, then sampled one before starting on her supper.

Victoria chuckled. "Some things don't change," she teased.

"I suppose not," Martha admitted. Her hankering for sweets was almost legendary, which must have provided townspeople with plenty to gossip about after she moved into the confectionery.

Famished, she made quick work of devouring every bite of her supper before taking another cookie. She stirred the cider with a cinnamon stick and carefully tried to sort out her questions, deciding which one to voice to Victoria first.

As if sensing her mother's dilemma, Victoria moved to a seat next to her mother and caught her hand. "I know how much I've disappointed you and upset you. It was selfish of me to leave without telling you where I was going, and I'm sorry. I never meant to hurt you."

Martha swallowed hard and kept the promise she had made to herself to express all of her feelings to Victoria openly. She gently squeezed Victoria's hand and held on tightly. "You did hurt me, Victoria. I was so scared and confused and . . . and shamed by what you'd done. I tried to find you," she admitted. "I followed the theater troupe for months, but I was always a day or two behind. When the troupe split into two groups and left New York City, I was exhausted. I barely had any funds left, so I came home. To wait. To worry. And to read and reread your note, wondering why you left, with only a note. . . ."

Tears coursed down Victoria's cheeks. "I'm so sorry, Mother, but I — I knew that if I waited for you to come home, you wouldn't understand why I was so unhappy. You wouldn't have let me go, either."

Martha brushed the tears from her daughter's face. "You're right. I wouldn't have. Not then. But I've had a long time to think about you. About us. You are so precious to me. I wish I'd been able to tell you that more often while you were growing up."

When Victoria opened her mouth to speak, Martha shook her head. "No. Let me finish."

Victoria nodded.

"I love you, Victoria. You're my child. My daughter. I only ever wanted what I thought was best for you." She paused and swallowed the lump in her throat. "You're home. That's all that matters. I know you have no desire to follow me into my calling. I accept that now, and I'll do whatever I can to support you in whatever you choose to do until you decide to marry and begin a family of your own."

Victoria's eyes widened for a moment before she dropped her gaze. "I wish I could be a midwife like you, so you'd be proud of me like Great-grandmother Poore was of you, but I can't. I just can't."

Martha put a finger under Victoria's chin and tilted her face so they could look directly into each other's eyes. "I know you can't, but that doesn't mean I love you any less. The good Lord gives each of us different gifts. I understand that now. Mine is very like your grandmother's, although I don't have her patience and Lord knows how I still struggle with my temper. Now you, child, you are blessed with a different gift and other challenges. You're a scholar, like your father. You can put words together better than I can grow my herbs. You're headstrong, like me, I suppose, but you're also kinder and more honest that I can ever hope to be."

"Mother, I —"

"No, let me finish," Martha insisted. "I know that whatever I did, whatever you felt that made you think that you had to run away, is in the past. We can't dwell on that now, except to try very hard not to repeat the same mistakes. You're no longer a child, Victoria. You're a young woman now. We must always be honest with each other. Respect and love one another, despite our differences, now that you're home, praise God."

Victoria sniffled and took out a handkerchief to wipe her tears. "I want so much for you to be proud of me."

"I am very proud of you," Martha crooned. "It wasn't easy for you to decide to run off, and I know it was hard for you to come home. But you're here now. That's all that matters. We have plenty of time to talk about where you've been and what you've been doing."

Victoria managed a smile. "I do have something to show you. I . . . I think you'll like it," she gushed as she rose. She went over to the cupboard in the corner and brought back a periodical she handed to Martha. "There's so much I want to tell you, but I want you to see this first."

Curious, Martha looked at the cover and read the title page aloud: "Blessings of Home and Hearth," she murmured. "Volume thirty-three, February, 1831. Dedicated to the virtues of womanhood. Published monthly by T. J. Morgan, New York City." She paused to look at Victoria while her mind connected the publisher's name with the woman who had brought Victoria home. "It's a ladies' magazine?"

Victoria nodded, and her eyes lit with excitement. "It's an early copy of next month's issue. Turn to page seventeen."

Martha thumbed to the page.

"At the bottom. In the right column. There's a poem," Victoria prompted.

Martha found the poem and read the title to herself: " 'A Tribute to a Midwife' by V. J. Cade." She choked back tears. Her hands began to tremble, and she had to lay the magazine on top of the table so she could read the entire poem:

*By day or by night, she answers His call
    and travels,
Through downpour or blizzard, warm
    sunshine or windblown terrain
With no thought for herself, she rides for
    miles and miles,
To help women give birth or heal those sick
    and in pain*

*She follows His word and brings hope
    to all of His children,
When grief or sorrow arrive in one form
    or another.
She is a woman of faith, a good friend
    and neighbor,*

But to me, she is more. She is love.
She is . . .
Mother.

By the time Martha finished, tears completely blurred her vision. "You wrote this?"

"For you," Victoria responded. "It's my first published poem. I have several more that have been accepted, too, and one by another magazine, but this is my very first. I'm glad it was this one."

Touched beyond measure, Martha's heart filled with pride. "I'm so happy for you. And proud," she added. Unable to completely express herself in words, she embraced her daughter. "Thank you, Victoria. Your father would be proud of you, too. Just wait till I show everyone. My daughter — a real poet!" she gushed. "We'll have to have a welcome home party. I'll speak to Fern and Ivy about it in the morning. We'll ask Mrs. Morgan to stay, of course. She should rest before traveling home anyway. We'll write to Uncle James and Aunt Lydia. They'll want to come back to see you. Why, we'll invite the whole town. Then when everyone is here, we'll show them the magazine and have you read the poem. It'll be great fun. And perfectly exciting. We'll have to live with Fern and Ivy until the tavern is rebuilt, which I'm sure is what Uncle James will decide to do, then we'll have our very own quarters again. You can continue to write of course, and send your poems to New York by post —"

"I'm afraid I'm not staying in Trinity, Mother." She tilted her chin. "I'm only home for a few days to visit, then I'm returning to New York City with Mrs. Morgan."

Chapter 4

Stunned, Martha looked into the depths of her daughter's eyes. Her heart pumped so fast she clapped her hand to her breast to keep her heart from exploding.

Determination stared back at Martha.

"You're not . . . staying? What do you mean, you're not staying? Of course you're staying!"

Victoria moistened her lips, adding a sheen that made the tiny scar on her bottom lip more prominent. "I love you. I hope my poem helps you to understand how very deeply I respect you and appreciate everything you've done for me, and the sacrifices you've made, especially since Father died." She paused, lowered her gaze, and took several breaths. When she looked up again, she took Martha's hands in her own and clasped them tightly. "I have a position in New York City with the Morgans, and they've opened their home to me as well. I want to go back to New York, and I'm asking for your blessing."

"My blessing? How can I possibly give

you my blessing and allow you to live in a city so far from home?"

Victoria squared her shoulders. "You gave Oliver your blessing when he wanted to move to Boston with Grandfather Cade to become a lawyer."

Martha's eyes widened with disbelief, and she had a difficult time keeping her temper in check. "That's a completely different issue. Oliver was a young man, and your father wasn't here. Oliver went to Boston to live with your grandfather so he could give Oliver the proper guidance and provide an apprenticeship in his firm for your brother. But you're . . . you're a young woman. You need your mother."

"Mrs. Morgan is very strict with me. You'd approve —"

"I approve of having you here. With me. With friends and neighbors who have watched you grow up. In Trinity. That's where you belong. This is your home, not some city teeming with vices and dangers you can't possible avoid."

Victoria's eyes glistened with tears. "My home. You mean here? In the confectionery?"

"That's only temporary. We'll have our own quarters again in a few months."

"With Uncle James and Aunt Lydia?"

Martha nodded. "I hope so."

"A room isn't a home. We haven't had a home of our own since Father died and the farm was sold. We live on people's charity. We have no home."

Martha huffed and brushed away the echo of her own similar sentiments as she was returning home earlier tonight. "That's not true! The rewards I earned, I shared with your uncle. Fern and Ivy won't allow me to do that, they're so generous, so I help them with the baking and tend to customers whenever I'm here."

Victoria pulled her hands free, rose, and began pacing in front of the fire. "How often is that, Mother? You're always at everyone's beck and call, traveling miles to tend to others. I grew up never knowing when you'd be home and spent my days working in the tavern, alone, wanting you to be home with me, all the while listening to everyone tell me what a blessed saint I had for a mother. Wasn't I a lucky girl?"

The bitterness that laced Victoria's words sliced through Martha's heart and underscored the very anxiety her calling had inspired. Her daughter's resentment cut even deeper. "I had no other choice. I still don't," she murmured.

Victoria stopped and faced her mother.

"I know that. Truly, I do. But I want . . . I need more now. Mr. and Mrs. Morgan have taken me into their hearts as well as their home. They've become like family. I have a real home now and an opportunity to pursue my writing. They're good people. Fine people," she whispered.

Martha's temper finally slipped out of her control. "*Fine* people don't take in a runaway girl and allow her mother to wonder if she's dead or alive. *Fine* people," she snapped, "don't come between a mother and her daughter! Now I'll hear no more nonsense about your going back to New York City. Not tonight. Not to-morrow. Not ever again! You're staying right here. In Trinity. And that's final."

With her chest heaving and her cheeks burning, she set her lips in a firm line and silently dared her daughter to challenge her.

Tears coursed down Victoria's cheeks. Her shoulders slumped, and she toyed with the handkerchief in her hands. Her gaze, however, was steady. "Some things don't change, do they, Mother? You still won't listen to me, but I've already made my decision about where I want to live and what I want to do. Since you won't even consider my wishes, then I suppose there's nothing left for me to do but leave in the morning," she whispered before she walked from the room and started up the stairs.

Martha closed her eyes and listened to the sound of the girl's footsteps. When she heard a bedchamber door open and close, she leaned forward and pressed her hand against her forehead. Her head pounded and her mind ached with the echo of her daughter's harsh words, and she took long measured breaths of air until her heartbeat returned to some semblance of normal.

She was angry. Upset. Too upset to think beyond Victoria's vow to be disobedient: "I'll be leaving in the morning."

The loving, joyful reunion Martha had anticipated had disintegrated into a disaster. A total disaster. How had that happened? "How?" she asked aloud.

Her heart was so heavy with disappointment her chest ached. After all these months of daily worry, after all the sleepless nights, how could Victoria come home, only to break her mother's heart again?

Resentment flared, and all the questions she had wanted to ask Victoria clamored for answers. If Martha had not lost her temper, she might have had a chance to get those answers. Instead, she had alienated her daughter, and she was not sure how to change that.

She directed all of her ill-feeling, however, toward June Morgan. She was the adult, not Victoria. But what kind of woman stole the affection of another woman's child? Exactly how had she accomplished that? What kind of woman would have the sheer audacity to come here, into Martha's home, and expect Martha to simply hand over her only daughter into the hands of a stranger?

Not a good woman.

Not a God-fearing woman.

Martha rose from her seat and stiffened her spine. No wealthy, spoiled, city-bred woman was going to lure Victoria away from her mother. Not while Martha drew a single breath.

In time, Victoria would learn to accept Martha's decision. In time, when Victoria had married and had children of her own, she would understand a mother's duty. Until then, Martha would simply have to keep a strong hold on her faith — faith in God and faith in herself.

Resolved, but still numb with disappointment, Martha cleared her supper dishes from the table and pumped water into a basin. She washed and dried the dishes, placed them back into the cupboard, and wiped the table clean. After she banked the fire in the hearth, she doused the oil lamp and wearily mounted the staircase.

The day had begun with great sadness she had shared with Nancy Clifford, and Martha's heart ached anew for the young woman. The day was ending, however, with yet more troubles, this time waiting for Martha at home. Her legs felt heavy, like they were made of lead. Heart-weary and physically exhausted, she approached her bedchamber door. Muted light from the hall window guided her steps. Even though all was quiet, Victoria was probably still awake, and Martha was not quite sure what she would be able to say to her daughter to salvage what she could from their disastrous reunion.

She paused, took a deep breath, and reached for the door handle. She heard a door down the hall open and then close; Martha turned, ready to apologize to Fern or Ivy for waking them.

To her surprise, June Morgan approached her. She wore a loosely belted robe over her nightdress and her hair fell in waves on either shoulder. She pressed one finger to her lips. "I've gotten Victoria to sleep," she whispered. "Come. Let's go downstairs. I'll fix us some tea."

"Victoria's in your chamber?" Martha asked and immediately regretted not softening her voice.

"She was very upset, as I suppose you are, too. If you'd prefer to talk in the morning . . ."

Distraught anew, Martha welcomed the opportunity to put this woman in her place. Now. "No, we should go downstairs and talk."

She followed June back down the staircase. When they reached the kitchen, Martha went ahead and relit the oil lamp. June filled the teakettle with water and set it to boil on the cookstove while Martha set out two cups. She secured a good measure of chamomile tea leaves she put into a ball and carefully placed into the teapot.

Chamomile tea. Good for settling the nerves. Good for prompting sleep. Sleep would be a blessed release from this nightmare, but Martha knew sleep this night would be impossible. Whatever nerves she had were raw, and perhaps the tea would help ease the sheer animosity toward this woman that had Martha's mind a quagmire.

June stoked the fire back to life and set two chairs in front of the hearth. "Why don't we sit here until the water boils?"

Martha took a seat. She stared at the glowing embers and prayed her anger would subside long enough for her to speak her mind. Coherently. Firmly. And without the bitterness that soured her mouth.

When June sat down beside her, Martha studied the woman out of the corner of her eye. June was the epitome of grace and gentility, and the picture of understated elegance. She was about as opposite from Martha as a woman could be, even granting the apparent ten-year difference in their ages. She folded her hands over her stomach. Her nails were short, but neatly sculpted. They looked soft, with no hint of the calluses or heavy veins Martha had in her work-lined hands.

She hid her hands in the folds of her skirts.

June let out a deep sigh. "I'm not sure where to begin."

Martha closed her eyes for a moment. "My daughter ran off with a theater troupe. You can begin by explaining just how you came to know her."

June nodded. When she spoke, her cultured voice was soft. "My husband, Thaddeus, was one of two investors in the troupe. When the members returned to New York City, the other investor took his share of the profits and decided not to back another tour. Thaddeus followed suit, and the troupe disbanded. Some members went to —"

"To England. The rest went to Charleston. I know," Martha interjected. "I followed the troupe for months trying to find Victoria and bring her back. I got to New York City the day after the members of the troupe sailed off in two different directions. Apparently, Victoria didn't leave with either one as I had assumed."

June caught her lower lip and held it for several heartbeats. "No. She didn't. The troupe's manager, Dayton Willis, had taken her under his wing. *After* he discovered she had stowed herself away in the wagon used to transport the costumes. By then they were only miles from the city, and he thought it would be better for Victoria, safer, if he allowed her to stay with the troupe, rather than send her home alone. It's not wise to allow a young woman as attractive and as . . . as inexperienced as Victoria to travel alone. He brought her with him to his meeting with the investors. Thaddeus brought her home to me," she murmured.

Martha wanted to lash out, to let loose her contempt for this woman, but June had spoken earnestly, from her heart, and Martha was loath to voice complaint. It was apparent, at least for now, that the Morgans' concern for Victoria's well-being had protected the girl, but that did not excuse them from their obligations to contact Martha. "Why didn't you write to me at once? You have children of your own. You must have known how worried I would be."

June caressed her stomach, but kept her gaze on the fire. "I wanted to write, but Victoria would never tell us exactly which town she had left behind. There were dozens. Mr. Willis suspected she had come from half a dozen, including Trinity, but all these rural towns look alike when you're on the road for months. He couldn't be sure. And . . . and I was afraid."

"Afraid?" Martha challenged.

"Yes, afraid. It was obvious from the moment we met Victoria that she had come from a loving home where she'd been raised well. Educated well. But she was certainly not able to survive on her own. Not in the city. I was afraid that if we pressed her, if we demanded that she write home, she would simply run away again." She smiled. "For all her good qualities, for all her talents, she is a stubborn, strong-willed young woman. And very determined," she added.

She glanced at Martha. "Apparently, she's a lot like her mother?"

Highly offended, Martha opened her mouth to protest. Honesty made her clamp her lips together and think carefully before she responded to June's question. When she eventually spoke, her voice was even, although it grated to admit June had hit a nerve. "Victoria may favor her father in looks, but you're right. She's just as stubborn and determined and strong-willed as I am."

"Truly her mother's daughter."

"Truly," Martha admitted. "But she's *my* daughter. Mine alone," she insisted. She turned and looked directly at June, silently daring her to argue the point.

Chapter 5

June flinched. Her eyelids batted back tears as she drew in short gulps of air. Her distress was genuine. She finally appeared composed, but when she spoke, her voice quivered. "I know Victoria is your daughter. She's subject to your will and your authority, as she should be. That's why I insisted she come home."

Her hands curved protectively over her abdomen. "I would never do anything to come between a daughter and her mother. Please believe me."

Moved by the woman's plea, Martha softened her gaze. Her resolve remained firm. "Then convince Victoria she must stay here. Her place is with me. Here in Trinity. I simply can't allow her to traipse back to New York City and live with . . . with strangers. I mean no offense, but I know nothing about you or your husband. I don't know exactly what position she has in your household. I didn't raise my daughter to become someone's . . . servant."

June's eyes widened. "A servant? Is that

what you think she is? My servant?"

"Most likely, just one of many," Martha quipped.

"I have three," June admitted. "A nanny for the children, of course, a housekeeper, and Mrs. Paulson, our cook. We also have a gardener and a young man who keeps the stable." Her gaze hardened. "Instead of hiring our servants through an agency, I suppose you think we find it more convenient to lure runaways from the streets and never encourage them to contact their families."

She paused and tilted her chin. "If that's true, why in heaven's name would I travel all this way in abominable weather to chaperone Victoria? Because I wanted the girl to have your blessing so she could be a mere servant?"

Properly chastised, Martha struggled to find her voice. "I just assumed —"

"You assumed incorrectly," June countered. "Victoria is a member of our staff, a valuable contributor to the magazine my husband and I publish. Did she show you next month's issue?"

Martha blushed. "Yes. She did."

"Thaddeus handles the advertising and the actual printing at his office. I work from our home, editing submissions, organizing the content of each volume, and corresponding with our authors and subscribers. The magazine has been surprisingly successful. By last summer, the volume of work had grown so much I was literally up to my throat in paperwork. When Victoria arrived, she was an answer to my prayers. She was able to take over almost all of the correspondence, and I've even been able to let her begin editing."

June paused and caressed her abdomen. "I want to spend more time with my children, even if that means I have to give up my duties with the magazine. I can always return to those tasks later, perhaps when the children are older."

She turned in her seat so she faced Martha. "I know it's selfish of me to ask, but I will anyway because it's so important to me. And to Victoria. Let her come back to New York City with me. Just until fall, at the very latest. By then, the baby will be born and I can have my permanent replacement fully trained. It would be so much easier for me if I could have Victoria there to help me. I really need her," she murmured.

"I need her, too," Martha challenged. She did need her daughter. She did. But she could not argue against the fact that

June Morgan did, too. She could not find fault with June's goals. Indeed, she lauded the woman's decision to spend more time with her children, but it did not seem fair that Martha would have to sacrifice her needs for the sake of someone else's needs. Again.

While Martha weighed her own needs to have Victoria home against June's needs, the other woman rushed ahead and continued to plead her case. "It's only for a few months. We'll see she eats well, gets plenty of rest, attends meeting every Sunday, saves a good portion of her wages, never leaves the house without a chaperone, and writes to you at least once a week. I — I brought references with me. They're right upstairs. I have a letter from our pastor, Reverend Blackstone, and another our housekeeper dictated to me since she's never been schooled in her letters."

Overwhelmed, Martha suspected she had been outtalked and outmaneuvered, if not outwitted. June had cleverly addressed almost every concern in Martha's heart, and she just wanted to . . . to hate her.

But she could not.

She just could not.

June Morgan had not prompted the crisis tonight.

If Martha had let Victoria explain about her life in New York City, if she had treated Victoria like a young woman instead of a child, if she had only listened to her daughter, Victoria would not have left the kitchen in tears or issued her own ultimatum.

Martha herself and her all-fired pride and strong maternal emotions had driven her child straight to another woman for comfort tonight, just like she had driven her from home last June.

Truth be told, there was much more at the root of her turmoil that nourished her determination to keep Victoria in Trinity. Her late husband, John, had turned his back on both family and social standing when he quit his studies at Harvard and moved west. He had built a good life for them all as a yeoman farmer, and it was only after his untimely death that his father, Graham Cade, had entered Martha's life.

She had steadfastly refused all of his efforts to have her move to Boston so he could see to his grandchildren's welfare, but when Oliver turned sixteen, she could not argue with his decision to go to Boston to begin studying law under his grandfather. Today, he practiced in his grandfather's law firm.

The irony never ceased to confound her. Oliver now had the life his father had rejected, but to lose Victoria to a city, too, was almost too much to bear. Her eyes filled with tears, and her heart ached with every heavy beat that pounded in her chest.

Had God blessed Martha with these two children, only to have them reject the life both she and John had wanted for them here in Trinity?

Was she being completely selfish?

Probably.

That thought did not sit well, any more than the next thought. At least she and Oliver remained close. He visited at least once a year and always left with her promise she would come to Boston to see him. If she totally alienated Victoria, if she forced Victoria to disobey her and return to New York City without her mother's blessing, could Martha ever hope to see her again?

The answer cut to the very essence of her spirit.

And if she were honest and fair, she would realize that this was an opportunity for Victoria that Martha could never give to her. She could not ever hope to match the Morgan's wealth or station. She could not help Victoria to pursue her talents, any more than she could have done for Oliver. Not without Graham Cade.

She could, however, offer Victoria what no one else could — a mother's love and understanding and encouragement to nurture the gifts the Creator had given to her.

Martha let out a deep sigh and knew what she must do. "I think the water is ready now. If you could fetch those references, I'll fix the tea. But be careful not to wake Victoria. Not just yet," she added, just in case June thought Martha was completely ready to give in.

With a relieved and hopeful smile on her face, June rose from her seat. "I think there are some oatmeal cookies left from supper. Do you think Fern and Ivy would mind if we had some? I simply can't resist sweets."

Martha chuckled, in spite of herself. No, she could not harbor any ill-feelings for this younger woman. Jealousy, perhaps. Even a little envy that a woman who hankered for sweets like June said she did could remain so trim, even when she was teeming.

Loving sweets might be all they really had in common, save for one seventeen-year-old girl who was precious to them both.

★ ★ ★

Martha finished her third cup of tea and read through all the references again. She reached for another cookie and found it hard to believe the plate was empty. Empty? She groaned and found little solace in what she had read, either.

If she believed only half of what each person had written, she would be forced to put a halo around June Morgan's head. No one could possibly be that saintly. Or kind. Or generous.

Being skeptical, even with all the references that lay before her, was being cautious, not unfair, and Victoria was too precious, too priceless to risk.

She looked at June and pointed to the letters. "All this is well and good, but references can be . . ." She almost said "forged," but caught herself. It would serve no purpose to offend the woman, especially if she were all the references claimed her to be. "The references can be considered, but I'll have to confirm them, of course. Since we're so far from New York City, it will take time."

"Of course. Write to any or all of the people who provided the references. Except for Mrs. O'Malley. She relies on me to do that for her."

75

"Beyond that, I still have reservations," Martha countered.

June wiped the corner of her lips with a napkin. "Please. Go ahead. I'd be happy to answer any questions you have."

Did the woman have to be so . . . so sweet?

Martha folded her hands and laid them on top of the table and decided to cut right to the vortex of her concern. "How can I be certain you won't hire Victoria as your permanent replacement so she'll want to stay in New York instead of returning home to Trinity in the fall?"

"I give you my word," June responded. "Victoria shows great promise, but she's still relatively inexperienced. It would be several years before she would be qualified —"

"But she might want to stay on as an assistant, like she is now," Martha argued.

"I'll make it clear that staying in any capacity is not an option." She smiled. "You and I are very much alike, you know. I don't think Victoria truly realizes that yet."

"We are," she insisted when Martha's mouth dropped open. "We're both capable, efficient women with a strong sense of duty and faith. We're both blessed with good constitutions and a strong will that's both blessing and curse."

Martha huffed. "Nevertheless, our worlds couldn't be more different."

"True, but it's what we each do with the gifts we have been given that matters. I was raised to believe that wealth and position are gifts that should be used to benefit many. That's why I started the magazine. I admire the work you do. Helping sick women and children or delivering babies are gifts, but they're not mine. And they're not Victoria's. They're yours. But each of our gifts is equal in His sight because He chose to give them to us, and we must all use our gifts to His glory. That's the message I hope my magazine carries to women everywhere."

It was a message that touched Martha's heart and eased some of her reluctance to admit June might be all she had presented herself to be. And more.

An urgent series of knocks at the back door interrupted their conversation, reminding Martha that only that morning, Russell Clifford had knocked at that door, summoning her to duty. Fearful that Nancy might have taken a turn for the worse and Russell had returned to summon Martha again, she rushed to the door. Much to her relief, she found young

Dr. McMillan shivering outside.

"I s-saw the light and hoped it was y-you. S-still up," he chattered. "I . . . I hope I'm not disturbing you."

An uncommonly short man with a wide girth, he must have been out in the cold for some time to have gotten so chilled. His plump cheeks were chafed from the wind and cold, and his nose was the color of ripe, summer cherries. He bore a few scars on his face from scratching at the chicken pox, a recent, embarrassing malady, although he had resented Martha's nursing more.

At least at first.

"Come in. Come in. You sound half frozen and you look even worse. Come in, but get that snow off your boots, first. I'll get you some hot tea to warm you up. I think we still have some oatmeal cookies around." She stepped aside to let him enter.

"Nothing to eat. Just something hot, then we need to talk," he responded. He stomped his boots to knock off the snow, then came inside.

Concern quickened her heartbeat. He had come to her before with concerns about his patients, but he had never turned down something to eat before, especially some of Fern and Ivy's treats. She followed him into the kitchen and prayed whatever errand had brought him here so late could either be settled quickly or resolved later.

After she had resolved her dilemma about what to do with Victoria.

As she followed him, she remembered that June was in the kitchen, dressed in her nightclothes. Before Martha could ask him to wait so June could slip upstairs, the doctor was already in the kitchen.

He took one look at June and braced to a sudden halt.

Martha nearly collided with him. "I'm sorry. I forgot to tell you —"

"June? Is that really you?"

She chuckled. "Benjamin! I almost didn't recognize you. I'm . . . I'm afraid you've caught me in my nightclothes. You look frightfully cold. Come. Warm yourself by the fire."

Absolutely confused, Martha peeked around him, glanced from one to the other, and clamped her gaping mouth shut. Again. Of all the people she expected to be able to confirm June Morgan's identity and attest to her character, Dr. McMillan would be last in line.

Dead last.

Chapter 6

Dr. McMillan spun around, and his face was flushed a deeper shade of crimson. He nearly knocked Martha over. Again.

Fortunately, she was a bit lighter on her feet than he was. She managed a quick side step and eased around him. She grabbed her cape from the peg on the wall and handed it to June. "Here. Put this on. Apparently, you two know one another so there's no sense bothering to introduce you."

Still, the air was wrought with embarrassment for all. Even though the man was a doctor, he rarely, if ever, tended to a woman in her nightclothes. Martha treated most women when they were ill. For very serious cases that required a doctor, propriety demanded that he examine his female patients as they lay in bed fully dressed and covered by the bedclothes.

With her cheeks flaming, too, June donned the cape and sat down again. "You can come in now, Benjamin."

He hesitated, then turned around and

approached the hearth. When he was close, he turned his back to the fire and warmed his hands behind him. "I'm sorry. I didn't know Widow Cade had a guest, let alone . . . I mean, whatever are you doing here in Trinity?"

June chuckled. "It's a long tale, I'm afraid. I could ask you the same question, though. The last time I saw Charles, he said he'd lost touch with you and hadn't heard from you in ages."

Basically ignored and excluded from the exchange, Martha watched and listened to the conversation. Her expression, apparently, prompted June to pause and explain. "Benjamin and my brother, Charles, were friends."

The doctor nodded. "I've gained a few pounds since then, I'm afraid. We went to school together in Boston, and I went home with Charles for several holidays."

June laughed out loud. "Holidays indeed! Father never quite got over one visit before Charles brought you home for another." She winked at Martha. "Wealthy, young stallions. Both of them. Scouring the herd of equally wealthy young mares, looking for just the right one to claim. For the night," she teased.

The doctor puffed out his chest, but

Martha still found it hard to imagine this rotund young man as a stallion of any sort. "That's a bit of an exaggeration, but I daresay we didn't find the city boring. Not once. Of course, we always had to bribe a certain someone's big sister not to give away all our secrets. Till she up and married. Then our secrets were quite safe and certainly cheaper," he quipped.

"Indeed," June murmured. "I thought for certain you'd practice in New York when you returned from France after finishing your training there. What changed your mind?"

He dropped his gaze. When he looked up, his sad smile tugged at Martha's heartstrings. "I married in France. Claudine. She was so young, so very beautiful . . ." He paused to clear his throat. "She died quite suddenly soon after we were married. Somehow, I managed to finish training. When I went home . . . it was a difficult time. I went into seclusion. I knew if I contacted Charles or other friends, I would only have to explain. . . ."

He paused and cleared his throat. "Grandfather told me his friend in Trinity, Doc Beyer, had passed on. He thought I might try to start my practice here. He was right."

June paled. "I'm so sorry. I had no idea."

He waved away her expression of sympathy. "It's been awhile now. I have a new life. A satisfying one. At least I can think back to our short time together and be grateful for the time we did have and . . . and pray that one day I'll find another woman as special as she was."

Martha held very still. She could feel the rapid beating of her heart in her fingertips. She never ceased to marvel at how often men and women kept their tragedies private, tucked deep within their hearts, safe from prying gossipers.

Until the past caught up with the present.

No one in Trinity had an inkling of this young man's apparent wealth or that he was a widower. She stored his secret next to all the others she had learned over the years, so necessary if she were to keep the trust of the folks she treated.

While June and the doctor reminisced about mutual friends, Martha fixed a new plate of cookies and poured a fresh cup of tea for him. "Come. Sit at the table," she suggested.

June yawned and covered her mouth with her hand. "I'm sorry. It's been a long day full of surprises. I think I'll take to my bed and let you two talk privately. At this hour, I assume there's something urgent you need to discuss. We'll talk more tomorrow."

While Dr. McMillan went to the table and started to eat, she rose from her seat and adjusted the cape around her shoulders. "I'll bring this down first thing in the morning, unless . . ."

"No. That's fine. If I'm called out before then, I can always knock at your door."

June headed toward the staircase, then paused and turned around. "What about Victoria? Do you want me to wake her and have her move to your room?"

Martha swallowed hard. As much as she wanted to be near Victoria and see her face the moment she opened her eyes in the morning, she shook her head. "Let her sleep. I'll speak to her in the morning and let her know my decision. You can . . . you can tell her we talked."

With a grateful smile, June bid them good night and proceeded up the stairs. Dr. McMillan polished off a cookie and cocked his head. "Did she say Victoria? Your daughter's home?"

Martha sat down across from him and quickly recounted her tale. "So you see, it appears my girl has come home only to ask

84

my blessing to go back to New York City and live with the Morgans."

He reached across the table and covered her trembling hands with one of his own. His tender touch and the genuine concern in his eyes caught her off-guard. "They're very fine people."

"So I've been led to believe. From the references she brought with her," she murmured.

"Sometimes we must remember to love deeply enough to let those we care about most in this world find their own way. It's too late after they're gone."

Martha gently removed her hands and lay them on her lap. His poignant words hinted at yet another element in his tragic loss. The idea that this young man, scarcely older than Oliver, could offer her such wise counsel was unsettling, especially since she had always been the one to offer advice to him in the past. His words, however, brought comfort and would help to make her decision about whether to let Victoria return to New York City all the easier to consider. She was not quite ready to make that decision. Not quite. "You said we needed to talk?" she asked, changing the direction of their conversation.

He leaned back in his chair and rubbed

his forehead with the tips of his fingers. "Before I begin, I'll ask for your confidence about my late wife. I'm not ready to share —"

"Of course," she whispered.

He let out a long sigh. "Thank you. Now . . . I'm afraid I have some troubling news." He looked her straight in the eye, then let out a deep breath. "There's no easy way to say this, so I'll be blunt. Samuel's vision is gone. He's completely blind, and I'm afraid there's nothing more to be done for him."

Martha's heart leaped in her chest. Her mind raced with questions that tumbled out in a rush. "Blind? Are you certain? When did this happen? Why wasn't I summoned? What happened?"

She paused to drag in several long breaths as her mind tried to sort through her thoughts about Samuel. A recluse since moving to Trinity some years back, Samuel Meeks lived in an isolated cabin in the woods behind the cemetery. With a raised tattoo of a serpent covering one cheek, and other tattoos hidden by shirt-sleeves, he had a vocabulary worthy of his former trade, a seaman. He frightened most folks. Except for Martha and Will, a displaced young orphan from New York who made his home with Samuel now.

She had been secretly treating the recluse for nearly a year, but nothing she had tried had cured the ailment that had been slowly claiming his eyesight, and Dr. McMillan's news was truly disturbing.

The idea of pairing Samuel and Will together some months back, in an effort to keep the boy from running off to sea, had been nothing short of divine inspiration. Martha had been as surprised as anyone else by the depth of the bond that quickly developed between Samuel and the boy. Despite his advanced years, Samuel had just the right spirit and disposition to be able to handle the seven-year-old who could match Samuel's salty vocabulary, if not surpass it.

Will's yearning to follow Samuel's footsteps into a life at sea had inspired a sort of hero worship that gave Samuel an edge when it came to molding the boy's character. While watching the reclusive curmudgeon nurture the boy, Martha had seen Samuel evolve into the kind, generous man she knew existed behind the gruff exterior he presented to the rest of the world.

Separating the two of them now would be disastrous, but necessary, if Samuel had truly lost his vision completely.

"What happened?" she repeated, sorely disappointed that Samuel had apparently waited too long before seeing the doctor, as she had begged him to do for months.

"Will came to fetch me just after supper. I hadn't been home all day, and he'd been to the office three times earlier. Anyway, according to Will, Samuel woke up this morning and his vision was gone. Simply gone. He hasn't any sense of shadows anymore. Only total darkness."

Martha clapped her hand to her heart, and all the fears about what would happen if Samuel lost his vision jumbled together and formed a lump in her throat. She swallowed hard. "Mercy. I can't believe it's finally happened. Poor Samuel. He must be devastated. What will he do now? And . . . and Will. What will happen to our Will?"

"I don't know. That's why I came directly to you. Something will have to be done for both of them. Just what that will be — I'm open for ideas," he prompted. "It's not going to be easy."

Already overburdened with the troubles of the day, Martha sighed. "Nothing ever is, but that's neither here nor there. Samuel won't be able to live in that cabin by himself, let alone care for a young boy.

Something has to be done, but that 'something' is troublesome. No matter what we suggest, we're going to have to contend with one very stubborn, old fool and a boy ready to find the first ship ready to sail."

"He's too young. No one would hire him on as a mate, no matter how skilled he is with those knots he's learned," the doctor countered.

"He's old enough to be a cabin boy and willful enough to do it. No, I can't let that happen, even if I have to tie that boy to a tree until he listens to reason. Since neither one of them has any family, we'll just have to find a home for them. That's all."

The doctor sputtered and choked on his tea. "That's all? It'd be easier to find a home for a pair of rattlesnakes than those two. There isn't a family for fifty miles that would take them both in."

She frowned. "Maybe not. But we might be able to find them separate homes."

"Separate homes?" He chortled. "They're bonded together like bark to a tree. Whether you're looking for one or separate homes, there's not going to be a long line of folks anxious to take them in."

Her frown deepened. Her resolve stiffened. "We don't need a long line of folks. Only two will suffice." Her mind raced with possibilities. As a midwife and healer, she knew most folks in the surrounding area, and she reviewed them all in her mind.

He watched her closely. The skepticism in his gaze only made her more determined to prove him wrong. She cast him a disapproving glance and he held up one hand. "Maybe you can find a family for Will. Maybe. He's young and hard-working, but he's a far cry from —"

"He's a boy with great promise. Only folks who recognize that will be good enough for that child," she murmured. She was sorely tempted to take Will in herself, but with no home of her own and with no husband to provide the stern guidance Will required, she rejected that idea, even as an image of a family took shape in her mind.

"Suppose you find such a family for the boy," he countered. "I'll even admit you might just be able to do that. But Samuel is a different matter. The man's at least seventy. He's blind, and he won't be able to contribute anything to his care. He's also scary enough to give most children nightmares. He'll have to become a ward of the town, and he's just ornery enough to hear the word 'charity' and storm off into the woods, get good and lost, and freeze to death."

Try as she might to disagree, she simply could not. She almost admitted to herself that there was nothing she could do for Samuel . . . until she remembered something she had read earlier that night. She closed her eyes and knitted her brows together. She thought long and hard until she very clearly remembered reading something that might well prove to be the perfect solution.

When she opened her eyes, she looked at Dr. McMillan and grinned.

He narrowed his gaze. Disbelief etched his expression. "Tell me you've thought of an answer to this whole dilemma, and I'll . . . I'll give up sweets for a month of Sundays."

She rose and reached across the table to pat his arm. "In that case, I'll be right back. There's a cherry pie in the shop just begging to be sampled. If I'm right, as I suspect I am, tomorrow you'll be forced to eat your own words."

She chuckled at her own pun.

He glowered.

"I'd better get that pie and cut you a big piece," she teased.

Her steps were light, and she hummed to

herself as she made her way to the shop in the front of the confectionery. Despite the tragedy that had befallen both Samuel and Will this day, despite the disappointment that clouded Victoria's homecoming and the heart-wrenching decision Martha would be forced to make, despite the grief Nancy and Russell Clifford now embraced, there were blessings to be found.

True blessings.

Now all she had to do was take those blessings and put them to good use.

Come morning, she intended to do just that.

Chapter 7

Drat! Martha had overslept again. Not just a few hours this time. By half a day!

She charged into the kitchen. Empty. She glanced around the room. Brilliant sunshine danced through the openings in the curtains. A hearty chicken stew bubbled on the cookstove. The worktables were wiped clean of any evidence of the day's baking. She could hear the chattering of voices coming from the shop.

"It must be after ten," she muttered. With so much to do, she could ill-afford to waste half the day abed. She needed to see Victoria first and set her own house in order before she tackled the problem of finding a home for Samuel and Will. With her mind made up about Victoria's future, she was anxious to see her daughter.

She proceeded directly into the shop where she hoped to find Victoria helping Fern and Ivy. Along each side of the room, checkered cloths covered tables laden with what was left of the day's offering of breads and sweets. Straight ahead, she saw the two sisters, but there was no sign of Victoria or her benefactor.

Fern stood on top of a stool in front of a narrow window. Ivy stood below, holding the other end of a freshly laundered and ironed curtain they were trying to rehang.

Ivy grinned, and her blue eyes twinkled. "Thought you might sleep through till tomorrow morning."

Fern turned her head and studied Martha for a moment. "You look rested," she quipped before getting back to her task.

"I don't think I've ever slept this late in my life! I'm so embarrassed to have to apologize to you both again. Here, let me help," she insisted as she approached them.

Ivy waved her back. "We're almost finished. Did you get yourself some breakfast?"

"No. I wanted to talk to Victoria. I thought she might be in here with you."

Fern sniffled and took the rest of the curtain from her sister. "She's with Mrs. Morgan helping her settle in at Dr. McMillan's. Thought she'd be back by now."

"June moved to Dr. McMillan's?"

Ivy clucked. "Such a refined lady. So

considerate. We tried to tell her it wasn't an imposition to have her here with us, but she insisted. It'll be nice for the doctor to have the company of an old friend, don't you think?" Her eyes widened. "Did she tell you that her brother went to school with him and that —"

"She did," Martha quipped, reluctant to hear the tale repeated.

Fern finished her task and climbed down from the stool. "It's probably best if she stays with him. Rosalind's there. So's Burton, so people won't be able to gossip."

Martha nodded. Her friend and her husband lived with Dr. McMillan, just as they had with Doc Beyer, with separate quarters on the third floor. Rosalind Andrews tended house and cooked for the doctor. Burton, who had only just returned after legal charges against him had been dropped, worked at the sawmill during the week, but handled the heavier household chores.

"You and Victoria need some time together. Alone. Without anyone trying to interfere," Fern added and cast a harsh glance at her sister.

Ivy ignored the warning. "Don't be absurd. Mrs. Morgan has no intention of interfering. She came all this way, even in her delicate condition, just to make sure Victoria arrived safe and sound."

Martha wanted to ask Ivy if she wanted a halo to hang over June's head, but thought better of it. Ivy always did see the best in people. Fortunately, Fern's pessimism was a healthy counterbalance, at least most of the time. "I think I'll venture over and see if Victoria's ready to come home, unless you have something you'd like me to do first."

Fern and Ivy shook their heads in unison. "Nothing," Fern insisted. "Go on. When you both come back, it'll almost be time for dinner."

"I sent a few things over with Victoria for the doctor and the Andrews. You could bring the plates back," Ivy suggested.

Martha agreed, found her winter cape hanging on the peg in the kitchen as June had promised, and went out the back door. Several piepans had been returned, by custom, and lay stacked on the steps. She put the pans into the storage room, closed the door, and tugged her cape a little tighter.

The sun seemed unnaturally bright today, but the air was nippy. She walked around the back of the building and went directly to the covered bridge. Relieved that no one seemed to be out and about, she hurried. It took a few steps for her eyes to get adjusted to the shadowy walkway, and she was halfway through when an all-too-familiar figure came out of Dr. McMillan's and headed straight for the bridge.

Her heart did a flip-flop, and conflicting emotions tumbled through her spirit. Thomas Dillon was definitely not a complication she needed today.

She slowed her steps, waiting for him to take notice of her. She had ended their first courtship twenty-five years earlier. In the ensuing years, each of them had married someone else and had families. Each of them had endured the pain of losing a beloved spouse. Each of them had followed callings — Martha as a midwife, Thomas as mayor and town leader, heir to his father's fortune and the legends surrounding Jacob Dillon's founding of Trinity some sixty years earlier.

For the past few months, Thomas had seemed determined to restore the affection they had once shared, and she had let him. Faithful and ardent, he had stopped just short of asking her to marry him. As much as she cared for him, however, she was not sure exactly how she would respond if he did ask her.

She was cautious. And uncertain. She

was also forty-two years old and set in her ways. She had a life and a calling that demanded most of her energies, if not her time, as her problem with Victoria could attest. She had absolutely no intention of abandoning her calling.

Not for Thomas.

Not for anyone.

Still, part of her yearned for his companionship, to ease the loneliness she felt whenever she left a household and headed home where she knew no one she could call her own was waiting for her. Another part of her, quite to her embarrassment, longed for physical intimacy, a touch, a gentle kiss. . . .

She shook her head to clear those shocking ideas, just as Thomas entered the bridge, apparently so lost in his own thoughts he had yet to notice her presence. He was tall and lean, and as handsome as no man had a right to be at his age, which only made her feel a little more self-conscious about her curves, which had become even rounder since she had moved into the confectionery.

Her heart raced like a schoolgirl's. Again. A reaction that unfortunately had been repeated all too often these past few months.

The moment their eyes met he broke into a smile and quickened his step. "Martha! Just the woman I wanted to see on this glorious day!"

"Glorious indeed," she responded, although with all she had to do today, glorious was not quite the word that came to mind, unless the good Lord decided to add a few extra hours for her benefit.

Thomas stopped only inches in front of her. Close. Too close.

She took a step back.

"You're looking well, Martha. I heard the news. You must be overjoyed to have Victoria home to stay. I'm so happy. For both of you."

She smiled. News about Victoria's plans to return to New York City had not yet spread, but she was not about to lie to Thomas. "Victoria is only hoping to be home for a short visit," she responded, and briefly explained the situation. Before he asked any question, however, she turned the focus back to his own family. "I take it Eleanor is well?"

His smile broadened at the mention of his daughter's name. After Martha's intervention, Eleanor had returned to Trinity with her husband and would be presenting Thomas with his first grandchild in early spring. "Very well, thanks to you. We've both been blessed, haven't we?"

"We have," she murmured. She could not help envying his blessing more than her own. With his son, Harry, away at school, Thomas had been left alone after Eleanor had married and moved to Clarion, some thirty miles away. Temporarily, Eleanor and Micah now made their home with Thomas while they made plans to settle here permanently.

"Take a sleigh ride with me," Thomas urged. "I have something I want you to see."

"A sleigh ride? Now?"

He grinned, adding extra warmth to his gray eyes. "Now. The horses are hitched. The bricks are warming. The blankets are stacked on the seat. And Mrs. Clark is packing a picnic for us, even as we speak."

She laughed. "A picnic? It's the dead of winter, and we have half a foot of snow on the ground!"

"All the more reason to have a picnic. It's . . . it's unconventional. Unexpected. It'll be an adventure. And I promise to have you home before dark."

His enthusiasm was contagious. She was sorely tempted, and disappointed to have to decline. "I can't. I'm on my way to fetch

Victoria. She's at Dr. McMillan's with —"

"Actually, I just left there. It seems she left more than an hour ago with Dr. McMillan and a Mrs. Morgan. Rosalind told me it was Mrs. Morgan who brought Victoria home."

Martha's eyes widened. "They left? Left for where?"

"Just a sleigh ride. Maybe," he added, "maybe they went for a picnic."

She pursed her lips.

He took her arm, turned, and led her through the bridge. "Rosalind said they wouldn't be back for several hours so before anyone else makes demands on your time, I'm packing you into the sleigh and stealing you away. I'll tell Mrs. Clark to take a walk over to the confectionery to let Fern and Ivy know you're with me."

Martha held her temper in check. She was annoyed that Victoria had gone off without even bothering to return home to see her mother, let alone ask her permission. She was angry at June for spiriting Victoria off and mad at Dr. McMillan for being their accomplice. She was put out that she had slept late, and perturbed with Thomas for being so all-fired sure of himself. For starters.

"A picnic," she grumbled. "I must be

101

out of my mind for letting you talk me into this. A picnic!"

He laughed and leaned close. His very nearness melted all of her anger and disappointment and set her blood to simmer with emotions that spelled pure trouble. "Yes, a picnic. Among other things. Along the way, you can tell me all about Victoria and her adventures."

Candle Lake lay frozen solid, stilling the waters that fed the three creeks that joined together and cascaded together as Crying Falls and pooled into a pond at the north end of town. Snow-draped, barren trees and occasional stands of evergreens, still deep with the color of life, formed a natural horizon that stretched as wide as she could see and high, nearly touching the few winter clouds overhead. Chimney smoke from nearby homesteads gently twirled upward.

Martha snuggled deeper beneath the blanket, chilled but content. "It's so peaceful," she murmured. Her spirit relaxed, despite all the worries that troubled her. This was a place she would like to visit again, if only to recapture the feeling.

Thomas smiled. "Peace and quiet. True balm for the weary and the troubled."

She shivered again, certain he could see straight into her heart and mind. Just like he always had. An annoying habit, one of only a few that had prompted her to end their courtship so long ago.

"You're cold." He clicked the reins. "We're almost there. Once we're inside, I'll get a good fire going to warm you up."

She looked at him askance. "Inside? I thought you said we were going on a picnic?"

"We are. Of sorts. No questions," he cautioned when she opened her mouth. "Not yet. Just observe."

He turned the horses down a path nearly hidden by a stand of tall evergreens and guided the sleigh toward a two-storied log cabin situated on the shores of the lake. When he stopped the sleigh and helped her down, she had so many questions she could not quite decide which one to ask first.

He placed a finger to her open lips and hauled the basket out of the sleigh. "Inside with you. First, the fire. Second, we eat. Then you get to ask your questions."

She braced her feet and refused to take a single step before she had at least one question answered. "Just who happens to own this cabin?"

"Does it matter?"

"Yes. It matters." Just why Thomas was being so secretive triggered alarms that kept her feet planted firmly on the snow-packed earth. She was not about to let him rush her into anything because she knew only too well that he could sweet-talk her into making a big mistake.

"I'm not putting a toe inside that cabin until you tell me what you're up to, Thomas Dillon."

He frowned, put the basket down, and crossed his arms over his chest. "You're a stubborn woman, Martha Cade."

She huffed. "I don't like secrets, and I'm especially not fond of being ordered about."

"Ill-tempered, too."

"Only when I'm cold and hungry and treated like a . . . a child."

He eyed the basket, then glanced at the door. "Well, I'm cold and hungry, too." He picked up the basket and took out a key to unlock the door. "I'm going inside to get warm and have my picnic. Are you going to join me or not?"

She swallowed hard. "Considering you still won't answer my questions, give me one good reason why I should."

His gaze softened. "Because I asked," he

murmured. "Because it's important to me. Because it's my cabin. And because . . . I'm leaving Trinity tomorrow, perhaps for a very long time, and this is the only chance we'll have to be alone together before I do."

She followed him into the cabin.

Chapter 8

Martha glanced around the main room of the cabin to keep her thoughts from dwelling on Thomas's surprising admissions. The furnishings were substantial, not as luxurious or ostentatious as those in his home in town, but a stark contrast to the rustic, spare furniture in the small cabin Nancy and Russell Clifford called home. Thoughts of Nancy inspired a quick prayer that she was recuperating well before Martha studied the sitting area facing a massive stone fireplace where Thomas was busy starting a fire.

A plump settee and two chairs, upholstered in forest green fabric, sat atop a thick wool rug. Directly to her right, an oak rolltop desk and a daintier lady's desk sat on either side of a large front window, which provided a striking view of the lake. A grandfather clock, its hands stilled, stood sentry in the corner, as if waiting for a family to arrive and order time to begin.

To her left, an unusually wide doorway gave her a full view of a kitchen. In addition to a modern cookstove on the outer wall and a round pine table in the center of the room, two corner cupboards were bursting with cookware and tableware.

The home had a feeling of sturdiness and comfort that made her feel as if she had, indeed, come home. This cabin beckoned to her, tugging at her heartstrings, stirring alive her strong feelings for Thomas, and rekindling the yearning to have a home of her own, here, with the man who had just told her he was leaving, possibly forever.

An overwhelming sense of loss and confusion threatened to consume her. Just yesterday, Victoria had come home, only to announce she intended to leave again. Now, Thomas announced he was leaving Trinity, too. Fearful that she was destined to spend her life watching everyone she ever cared about move away, Martha struggled against the temptation to merely curl up on the settee, close her eyes, and simply fade away into sweet, peaceful oblivion.

Before she could slide headlong into self-pity, Thomas joined her, helped her to remove her cape and gloves and placed them near the fire to warm. Once he had finished, he returned and escorted her to the sitting area. To her surprise, she found more than much-welcomed heat from the fire he had started.

He had spread a brown tweed blanket on top of the rug. In the center, the picnic basket lay open and a magnificent feast had been set out. Sandwiches made with thick slabs of ham cushioned between slices of wheat bread, a handful of boiled eggs, a large bowl of custard, and a plate of sugar-crusted doughnuts lay near table-ware and crisp, white napkins.

"There's enough food here to feed half the town," she gushed.

He chuckled. "I promised you a picnic, and you deserve only the finest. Now, if you'll take your seat. . . ."

When she hesitated, he touched her elbow. "Are you worried someone will find out we're here?"

"Not . . . not overmuch," she whispered. Truth be told, she was concerned. She prized her status in the community, and it would not do to have her character be-smirched by having people gossip about her being here alone with a man who was not her husband.

When he cocked a brow, she sighed. "Perhaps a little. Then again, we're not ex-actly youngsters. We're both middle-aged adults. We've both been married be-fore. . . ."

"And still, people will gossip and judge you poorly for being here alone with me. I'm sorry. I never meant to compromise your reputation. Never," he murmured. "They already have enough to talk about where I'm concerned. I shouldn't involve you."

She held silent. Gossipers had had plenty to chew on lately where Thomas was concerned. His recent betrothal to Samantha, a woman half his age, had been broken before it was officially announced. Soon after, his ardent attentions to Martha had not gone unnoticed. He was not, however, a man who would let anyone force him out of town, and she was loath to let the possibility of gossip steal this last chance to be with him. "I suppose we shouldn't let all this food go to waste."

He smiled and helped her down to the blanket where she sat, Indian-style, with her back straight and her skirts carefully arranged to cover her crossed legs as she faced the fire.

Thomas assumed a similar position next to her.

After holding out her hands to warm them over the fire, she passed him a plate and napkin before taking one of each for herself. He piled two sandwiches and three eggs onto his plate and started eating immediately. She paused, then selected one of the doughnuts and spooned out a good serving of custard for herself.

His eyes widened, and he gulped down a bite of his sandwich. "Do you always skip straight to the desserts?"

She savored a glorious spoonful of custard, then shrugged her shoulders. "If you can plan a picnic in the dead of winter, I can have dessert first, don't you think?"

His gray eyes twinkled. "That sounds fair enough." He glanced around the room. "So what do you think?"

"It's heavenly, but Eva Clark always did make the creamiest custard."

He feigned a wounded look.

She nibbled at the doughnut, then chuckled. "Oh? You meant the cabin! It's very nice. Very comfortable." She turned to look over her shoulder. "I love the view of the lake. Look," she whispered. "There's a moose. No, two of them!"

He watched them with her, silently, until the animals finally disappeared back into the dense woods surrounding the lake. He smiled and turned back to his meal. "They're massive animals, but they have a certain grace about them," he suggested.

She nodded and tackled the rest of her

custard. "How long ago did you buy the cabin?"

He grinned. "I bought it several years ago, but I only remodeled it last summer while you were gone."

She nearly choked on a piece of the doughnut. "*You* did?"

Another wounded look. "I've never been useless when it came to tools."

"I didn't mean you were. I'm just . . . surprised," she admitted. "Actually, I'm more surprised I haven't heard anything about it."

He chuckled, peeled one of the boiled eggs, and polished it off. "Most folks still don't know about it. Those who do just assume I plan to sell it after I finish remodeling. All for a hefty profit, I might add, if I were to sell it. The place was pretty run-down."

She wiped her lips with her napkin and wrapped her hands around it. "What changed your mind about selling it?"

He stared into the fire. "There wasn't one pivotal moment that changed my mind. It happened gradually. After Sally died last year, I started taking a good, long look at my life."

Memories of the difficult first year after John died swept over her. "It's always hard when you lose a spouse."

He drew in a deep breath and shook his head. "Like a fool, I thought I could start over with Samantha. Between that near-disaster and the difficult time Eleanor was having, I realized I didn't want to start over and live the same life I'd had before. I wanted a new one."

She cocked a brow. "So that's why you're leaving? To start a new life? You should know by now you can't run away from your past, Thomas. It will just follow you wherever you go."

He turned and gazed at her with such tender affection he nearly stole every thought in her head, save those for him. "I'm not running away from the past. I'm leaving to create a new future for myself. Once I do, that's when I'll be able to decide if I want to return here to live permanently or just keep the cabin for when I come back to visit."

The idea that Thomas might move away permanently now, after his daughter and her husband had decided to move back to Trinity, made no sense to Martha at all. "But what about Eleanor? Her babe is due in February. Honestly, Thomas, I can't believe you'd be so willing to leave and be gone so long without regard for your own daughter. Why not stay for the birth . . . then leave if you must?"

"I intend to come back for a visit after the babe is born," he countered.

"For a visit." She narrowed her gaze. "Then you'd be leaving again."

He nodded.

She let out a sigh. "I wish I could say I understood what you're doing, but I don't."

He took her hand and held it, but stared into the fire. His grip was warm and comforting, and held the promise of strength. "Let me see if I can explain this better. As you probably know, my father had many business interests that I inherited after his death. Along with Anne, of course."

She nodded. His sister, Anne Sweet, lived in Harrisburg with her husband, George, a state representative, when the legislature was in session. They were expected back in Trinity by the end of the month, when they would return to the mansion next to Thomas's. It was their son, Wesley, who operated the general store.

"Some of those interests are here in Trinity," Thomas continued. "Father kept a good bit of the land surrounding the town to lease to homesteaders. He had other interests in New York and Philadelphia — tracts of land, a few mercantile establishments, several factories, even a small interest in a shipping line, all of which provide a sizable income, which allow me to devote most of my time to civic matters, just like he did."

She was amazed at the true extent of his holdings, as well as his willingness to discuss such private matters with her. "Civic matters. Like being mayor?" she asked.

"Exactly." He turned and gazed at her. "George has agreed to take over my duties as mayor until the next election in April, with the consent of the town council, of course. Obviously, I won't be seeking re-election."

Shocked that he could give up his position so easily, she tightened her hold on his hand. "How long do you expect to be gone before you decide what you're going to do?"

He exhaled slowly and stared back into the fire. "Six months. Perhaps a year. I'm not really certain."

"Do you know where . . . you're going?"

"Philadelphia, at first. Then New York for a spell."

When he let out a sigh, she locked her gaze with his, still searching for more of an explanation — one he seemed reluctant to give her. "But why? Why must you leave?"

He squared his jaw and entwined his fingers with hers. "Because I'm tired, Martha. I'm tired of running businesses from a distance and constantly traveling back and forth to attend meetings with lawyers and bankers. To be perfectly frank, I'm tired of being mayor, too. Without Sally to consider now, I only have the children. Eleanor has happily settled down with Micah and Harry's decided to spend a year traveling through Europe after graduating in the spring. I can finally think about what I want."

He turned to face her. "I might not know exactly what my life will be, but it'll be mine. Not my father's and not the one he planned for me. That's why I understand Victoria and what she's asking to do."

Comparing his apparent unhappiness with Victoria's did not sit well with Martha. "You're an adult. Victoria is still a child," she countered. "If you aren't even sure about what you want, how could she be so certain?"

When she tried to tug her hands free, he refused to let go. "Don't turn this into a discussion about your daughter, Martha.

This is about me and you."

Her temper snapped. "Me? This has nothing to do with me, especially after you've just told me you're leaving Trinity, perhaps for good."

A challenge sparkled in his eyes. "But it is about you. Tell me you're not tired, too. Tired of traipsing cross-country in all kind of weather. Tired of not knowing when you go to bed whether you'll be able to get a good night's sleep. Tired of being alone, of not having a home of your own."

His charges struck several chords of truth, all tucked deep in her heart so she would not have to face them often or admit to anyone else how tired she truly had become. In truth, there had been little she could do to change her situation after John died. She was a widow with no one to support her and she had enough pride to insist she support herself and her children for as long as she was physically able to do so.

As usual, however, Thomas could see right into the deepest recesses of her mind. Her backbone stiffened. "Of course I get tired," she admitted and held her voice soft and low. "Sometimes I'm very, very tired. Then I realize I have no other choice. I carry on because I must . . . and because other people depend on me to help them. Even if I wanted to change the life I lead, I couldn't. But you can. You can change your life because you have options I don't have. That I've never had," she snapped.

"You did once," he murmured, "but your interest in being a midwife came first. Before me. Before —"

"How unfair of you to dredge up the past," she protested.

He raised a brow. "What's so unfair about being honest? You made it perfectly clear when you broke our betrothal years ago that you weren't willing to give up being a midwife and working with your grandmother."

"And you agreed with me!"

"I don't remember it quite that way."

She huffed. "Well you did. You agreed that if I became your wife, I wouldn't have the time I needed to devote to my responsibilities to others who needed me. You told me I had to choose, so I did."

His gaze softened, melting any protest she might have raised. "I don't fault the decisions we each made in the past, any more than I can change them. We've each had good marriages, but we're both alone now. If you'd stop huffing long enough to really listen, you'd realize that I'm simply saying I don't want all the same things now that I wanted twenty-five years ago. Only some of them."

She swallowed hard. "And just what might they be?"

He smiled and tucked an errant lock of hair back behind her ear. "I want to love you, to take care of you, to give you a home of your own. I want us to be together. As husband and wife."

Her heart began to pound. Her cheeks burned. He had never spoken so openly about his feelings for her, at least not since that day so long ago when he first asked to court her. "Thomas, I . . . I don't know what to say."

He turned and tilted her chin. His eyes glistened with affection and longing so startling, he nearly stole her breath away. "Say yes. Say you'll marry me and come with me. Reverend Welsh can marry us today. I'm the mayor. I can convince him to waive the banns."

Martha's head was spinning. "M . . . marry you? Go with you?"

"Marry me," he repeated. "These past few months, I've come to think you felt the same affection for me as I have for you. Have I been wrong?"

All the affection she had tried to deny

for so long silenced her intended denial. "No, you haven't. I . . . do care for you, Thomas."

He caressed her cheek with the knuckles on one of his hands. "Then marry me. Today. We can leave for Philadelphia first thing in the morning. We'll stay in the finest hotels. You can shop while I wrap up my business affairs during the day. At night, we'll dine in candlelit restaurants, go to the theater, whatever you want. Together, we can decide exactly how we want to spend the rest of our lives."

"I can't leave today," she said, ignoring the greater issue of marriage. "What about Victoria? Heavens, she just got home. There's still so much to resolve —"

"I thought you decided —"

"No, I said I was *considering* letting her go back to New York. Oh, bother!" She tugged her hands free.

"Bring her with us," he offered. "Then there wouldn't be any reason you have to stay in Trinity."

"I have my duties to think about," she reminded him. "If I marry you and leave, who will tend to my patients?"

He frowned. "Dr. McMillan is here. I know he's young, but he's well-educated and very committed to his profession. He's also more than a little anxious to take over your duties. He's made that clear from the start. And you've gone out of your way to help him, or have I just imagined the sketches and essays you've made for him to describe the herbs and simples you use?"

She instantly regretted showing her work to Thomas. "He hasn't any idea about how to treat teeming women," she quipped. "That's my duty and my calling. I have the experience he lacks and my patients need. I can't abandon these women. Not again," she whispered. The memory of abandoning her patients last summer while she searched in vain for Victoria was still painful.

Disappointment doused the affection in his gaze. "Can't? Or won't?"

She squared her shoulders. Apparently, her dedication to her calling was an obstacle that would stand between them now, just as it had so long ago. "Both," she said firmly.

She had secretly hoped Thomas might have grown to accept her calling as a midwife and respect her for her commitment to her patients. Based on her conversation with him now, however, whatever secret hope she carried in her heart that she might someday marry this man suffered a very sudden death.

Until he cupped her cheek with one hand and looked deep into her eyes.

"You're still so stubborn, so strong-willed," he whispered. "I didn't think I had a prayer of convincing you to say yes, at least not today, but I had to try. It's going to be a very long time until we're together again, but when I return, I intend to convince you to embrace the life we could have together. I won't ask you to give up all of your duties, but I would hope you could curtail them so we can spend time together."

His proposal hit a nerve, inciting her fears that sooner or later, most women would call for the doctor instead of her, sharply reducing her patients to relatively few. Tears welled. Her throat constricted. Her calling was the one constant in her life that kept her firmly rooted in this community, if not her faith, and she simply would not know how to live without her work as a healer and midwife. Even with all its blessings and rewards, her calling had exacted a heavy price. First, her daughter. Now, her last chance at happiness? "I . . . can't promise to marry you," she murmured.

He pressed a kiss to her forehead and

pulled her into a warm embrace. "You've worked so hard. You've been alone for so long. Let me take care of you. Just promise you'll think about me while I'm gone. Think about how different your life would be if you accepted my proposal."

She nuzzled into his strength and weakened. "I promise," she whispered. Her heart ached, almost more than it had twenty-five years ago when she had ended their courtship, but she knew, in the end, that no matter how deeply she might be tempted by the life of ease he offered, her calling would always stand between them.

The sooner Thomas accepted that reality, the better off he would be.

And so would she.

Thomas nearly broke his promise to have her home before dark. Twilight had but a few last moments of life when he finally delivered her to the back door of the confectionery.

"Home delicious home," he teased, breaking the awkward silence that had ridden back to Trinity with them. He helped her down from the sleigh, and his hands lingered overlong at her waist. "If I write, will you promise to write back?"

She nodded. "Of course."

He took one of her hands and kissed the back. "Good. And you'll take good care of Eleanor and the babe?"

"You know I will. I . . . I should get inside. I need to talk with Victoria," she said, grateful to have had the opportunity to continue their discussion about her daughter on the way home, if only to divert any further talk about his proposal.

"You're making the right decision," he offered.

She swallowed hard and gently removed her hand. "I hope so. Godspeed, Thomas. Be safe and well in your journey."

"I'll be home to visit my new grandchild. Perhaps you'll have changed your mind by then, and —"

"No," she countered, refusing to let him leave with false hopes, if only to make their next meeting easier for both of them.

He smiled. "We'll see. I'm a patient man. A lot can happen between now and then."

She took her leave without commenting. She was almost too afraid to think about the prospect of any more change. She had had enough in the past seven months to last a lifetime. She stomped the snow from her feet and entered the storage room. Moist heat and tantalizing aromas from the chicken stew simmering in the kitchen were a welcome that lightened her steps.

When she entered the kitchen, she found Fern and Ivy sitting at the table with their backs to her. Victoria sat on the other side facing Martha, an empty place setting beside her.

Victoria met her mother's gaze and smiled a bit awkwardly. She patted the back of the chair next to her. "Mother! We've just started supper. Sit down and have something hot," she suggested. She rose and poured hot cider into a mug, which she set in front of Martha's place.

Fern and Ivy each turned around. Fern frowned. Ivy grinned. Martha took her seat.

"How's Thomas?" Ivy asked. "Lovely day for a sleigh ride."

"He's well. Pass the honey, will you, Fern?"

She added a hearty dollop to her cider the moment she had the jug of honey in her hands.

Victoria chuckled. "You're the only one I've ever seen do that."

"What?"

"Add honey to your cider."

Martha paused, glanced down at her cider, and shrugged her shoulders. "This batch was a little tart," she commented.

She carefully sipped the cider and let it warm her throat.

Victoria chuckled again. "*Every* batch is tart. At least every batch you ever tasted."

Martha huffed.

"We all have our little foibles," Ivy suggested as she spread a thin layer of butter on top of several chunks of chicken. She swatted Fern's hand away when she tried to take the butter away. "My sister should mind her own plate, or I'll simply have to insist we make another batch of apple taffy using that recipe she was so set on trying last fall."

Fern pulled her hand back and pursed her lips.

Victoria looked from one sister to the other, clearly puzzled.

Martha took a long sip of cider before she explained what had happened. Fern had a penchant for trying new recipes and doctoring up old ones, which invariably led to disaster more often than not. On this particular occasion, her attempts to try a new taffy recipe with apple flavoring had failed miserably. Instead of soft, pliable taffy, they had bowls and bowls of a concoction that hardened like a rock nearly faster than they could roll it out and cut it into small squares. At Martha's suggestion, the sisters had presented the results as Lynn's Lozenges, along with a direct warning that anyone who tried to chew them would likely break a tooth.

By the time Martha finished recounting the episode, they were all laughing. "There is a moral to the story," she added.

"Never give up," Ivy suggested.

"Never admit defeat," Fern added.

Victoria looked at Martha with hope glistening in her eyes. "Never let mistakes go undone."

Touched, Martha placed her hand on top of Victoria's. "And never forget that life's troubles or disappointments always contain blessings. They are His gifts to us, His children."

Victoria squeezed her mother's hand.

Fern stood up and tapped her sister on the shoulder. "Come along. I need you in the shop."

Ivy shrugged her shoulders. "The shop's been closed for an hour. I've not finished my supper."

Fern tapped Ivy's shoulder again. "That curtain we hung this morning is crooked. I need you to help me fix it."

Ivy rolled her eyes. "Now? Can't it wait for morning? Martha and Victoria —"

"Need time together. Alone," Fern insisted as she urged Ivy from her seat and nodded toward Martha and Victoria. "We'll be a while, but just leave the dishes. We'll do them later," she promised and led Ivy from the room.

Martha took in a deep breath and looked directly at her daughter. "I'm sorry I overslept. I wanted to speak to you first thing this morning. I was on my way to Dr. McMillan's to fetch you when I met Mayor Dillon. He said you'd gone out with the doctor and Mrs. Morgan so I didn't think it would do any harm to spend some time with him. We had some matters to discuss."

Victoria blushed, as if she knew her mother had attracted a suitor. "Miss Fern and Miss Ivy told us how busy you've been these past few days. You needed your rest." She dropped her gaze. "I should have come home first, to see if you were awake. I'm sorry."

"I wasn't up. Not when you left," Martha admitted. As curious as she was about where the trio had gone, she was more anxious to end the estrangement with her daughter. "I assume Mrs. Morgan told you we talked."

Victoria nodded, but kept her gaze focused on her lap where her hands lay, trembling.

"Well, there's nothing to be gained by waiting. I may as well tell you I've made my decision about your future. All I expect is that you will abide by my decision and respect my authority, whether or not my decision is to your liking. I'll also have no more ultimatums or tantrums. And no threats to run away again, either. Whatever problems you have with my decision, we'll discuss here and now and settle, once and for all."

Chapter 9

Martha waited with bated breath. Her mouth went dry. Her heart began to race faster. Victoria's willingness to accept Martha's authority was crucial and would spell whether the path their relationship would follow would be rocky or smooth. She would have felt a much lot better if she had been able to talk this over with Aunt Hilda first, but Martha could not wait and simply had to rely on her own ability to handle this as best she could.

Victoria toyed with a curl that draped over her shoulder. Pale pink blushed her cheeks. She lifted her gaze, moistened her lips, and nodded ever so slightly.

Heartened, Martha took a deep breath and tried to remember all she had written in the daybook she had been preparing for Victoria before the fire at the tavern rendered the book a pile of ashes. It had been easier to write down her feelings. Expressing them face-to-face was so much harder.

But necessary.

"First," she began, "I don't approve or in any way condone what you did, running off with that band of misfits."

Victoria paled.

"What you did was wrong. Pure and simple. You put yourself at great risk, young lady, and only the grace of God protected you. I was more frightened than you will ever know, until you have babes of your own."

Victoria's bottom lip quivered. "I think I know. Now. And I'm . . . I'm sorry. I told you that."

"You did. And now that I've had some time to think everything over, I want you to know I accept my share of responsibility for your running away. I haven't always been home for you, and when I was, I was either too tired or too busy helping Aunt Lydia to notice how unhappy you'd become. The good Lord knows how different it could have been if your father hadn't passed on, but even if he'd lived, I probably wouldn't have faced even the remotest possibility you weren't going to follow me into my calling like I followed your great-grandmother Poore."

She paused and took another deep breath. "Family tradition is important, a link to both the past and the future that binds us all together. I was so certain you'd embrace our family tradition, and it was tradition, rather than your needs, that blinded me. But you're not the first to want to take another path," she admitted.

Confusion darkened Victoria's gaze.

"You know my parents died when I was very young. My grandparents raised me," Martha explained. "I was taught that my mother embraced the calling to be a midwife, and I wanted desperately for you to embrace it, too. It was only after you'd left, when I was so hurt and so distraught, that Aunt Hilda set me straight."

Victoria leaned toward Martha.

"Contrary to what my grandmother had told me, and I, in turn, told you, my mother had no gift for healing or growing herbs or tending to teeming women and their babes. She was very talented with the needle, though. To hear Aunt Hilda tell it, my mother made the finest quilts this side of heaven."

"Those were her quilts we had on our beds, weren't they?" Victoria asked.

Martha nodded. "We lost them in the fire. We lost so much that night. If you'd been here working in the tavern, I might have lost you, too," she whispered.

Victoria laid one hand on top of Martha's.

Martha turned her hand and entwined their fingers together. "All I wanted, all I ever prayed for while you were gone, was to have you back home with me. I still want that. Desperately. And I had so hoped you'd want that, too."

Victoria's eyes flashed with disappointment. She bowed her head.

"I'm not so unusual," Martha argued. "All mothers have dreams for their daughters. We watch them grow up and pray they'll find good men to love them. That they'll have healthy children and teach them to be faithful to the Word. That they'll embrace the very traditions that bind us all together as families and as neighbors, so the rhythm of life, like the seasons, continues here in Trinity. Where I hope you'll one day have those dreams, too."

Victoria's shoulders sagged. Martha put her arm around her daughter. When she stiffened, Martha felt the girl's resistance and the difficulty she had in accepting Martha's words.

Martha continued, speaking quickly for fear the girl would close her mind and her heart to what Martha had to say. "I've had moments of great worry and sorrow while you were gone, but I've also experienced great joy. I've had time to reflect on our life together, and I've learned many lessons. Traditions are important. To all of us. But no matter how important tradition is to me, I can't put that tradition before my own child. I must learn to trust you and to trust your instincts, to allow you to make your own mistakes.

"You're a talented, bright young woman. You've proven yourself to be responsible to me and to the Morgans. I must let you develop your gifts and follow your own dreams and pray, pray so very hard that your dreams will one day lead you back home to Trinity and to me."

Victoria eased from her mother's embrace. When she looked up at her mother, tears welled. "But I thought . . . you're . . . you're really going to let me go back to New York City? Truly?"

Martha wiped away a single tear that escaped and trickled down Victoria's cheek. "Assuming you'll agree to several conditions."

Victoria hugged Martha tightly enough to nearly squeeze the breath out of her. "Thank you! Oh, thank you! You won't be sorry. I promise. I'll do anything you wish. Anything!"

Martha gave her a squeeze and set her

back so she could look her square in the eye. "Don't be so quick to get all excited. You haven't heard my conditions yet."

Victoria nodded so hard Martha thought the girl's neck might snap.

"First thing in the morning," Martha said, "I want the three of us to sit down. You, Mrs. Morgan, and me. I don't want any misunderstandings between us."

Victoria grinned.

"Second, you're to tell no one, absolutely no one about your plans until the three of us have come to an understanding, just in case we fail. And that includes Miss Fern and Miss Ivy."

Victoria's cheeks flushed with youthful enthusiasm and excitement. "It's not very late. Couldn't we both go to see Mrs. Morgan now?"

"The morning will be soon enough," Martha countered, coveting at least one night alone with her daughter before she had to share her with June Morgan again. She also kept some worries about her decision to herself, but vowed to speak to Victoria about them before she left. "I have other business with the good doctor, and I'm not sure there would be time to do that, too, at least not without imposing on his bedtime. Now, be a good girl and heat up some of that chicken for me. I'm famished. While you're working, you can tell me everything that happened from the instant you left Trinity with that theater troupe to the moment you landed at the Morgans."

Victoria launched into her tale before she even rose from her seat. Martha listened to every word. Time and time again, when Victoria was in a position where she could have been hurt or victimized, good fortune had intervened.

No. Luck had nothing to do with it. Only the good Lord and a host of His angels could have been responsible. Some overworked angels, Martha conceded, and prayed they might have earned some extra measure of eternal reward for doing their job so well.

On second thought, she prayed they might agree to keep a strong watch over Victoria in the coming months, provided all went well in the morning. And if Martha prayed even harder, there might just be one angel who would offer to watch over her and reassure her she had made the right decision.

As dawn broke and argentine light filtered into her bedchamber, Martha was awake, but still abed. Her thoughts traveled back to a small cabin on Double Trouble Creek, and she prayed that Nancy was finding some sense of peace and acceptance after the loss of her son, Peter.

Closer to home, Thomas would soon be on his way east to begin forging a different path in his life journey. If all went well later this morning, Victoria would be set to travel back to New York City to follow her own dreams, leaving Martha behind, still content with being here. In Trinity. Staying true to the course she had chosen so many years ago.

She lifted herself up and leaned on her elbow to gaze at her sleeping daughter. To her surprise, hazel eyes stared back at her. "I thought you'd still be asleep," she whispered.

Victoria grinned. "I've been awake awhile. Watching you. Why . . . why are we whispering?" she asked.

Martha pointed to the cage where Bird was still asleep. Victoria grinned again, then Martha patted her mattress. "When you were very little, you used to sneak into our bed once in a while during the night. We'd never even know you were here until morning."

Victoria grinned. "Actually, I used to

sneak into your bed most every night. You or Father only caught me when I didn't wake up early enough to get back into my own bed." She paused and toyed with the corner of her blanket. "Do you still miss him?" she asked, perhaps echoing her own sentiments.

Martha laid back down, then turned on her side so she could still face her daughter. "It's easier now than at first, but I still think of your Father. Very often," she admitted. "Time heals our hurts. Faith sustains us. But the heart always remembers. You were only seven when he died. So innocent. You hardly knew what was happening."

Victoria snuggled against her pillow. "I try to think about Father, but I don't remember him very clearly. Except that he was very, very tall."

Martha chuckled. "You were very little then. Your father was no taller than most men, but he was very gentle and a man of few words." Bittersweet memories surfaced, and she embraced them. "He always said his actions spoke well enough for him, and I suppose they did. He worked very hard everyday to provide for all of us. He attended meeting every Sunday and helped his neighbors. He never complained, even after my grandmother passed on and I assumed all of her duties."

"Aunt Lydia used to tell me not to question God's plan for us, but I did. I didn't want my father to die."

Martha felt her chest tighten. She and Victoria had not really spoken about John's passing for many years, and it troubled Martha to think her daughter harbored any guilt associated in any way with his passing. "Aunt Lydia meant well, but she was wrong. It's only natural to question God when He takes someone we love, especially when he's so young, but it's our faith that gives us the strength to eventually accept His will and to look for the blessings He always showers upon us when troubles come our way."

"Blessings?" Victoria's eyes widened with disbelief. "What blessings could there be when a family is broken and they lose their home?"

"We were blessed more than most," Martha argued. "We still had each other. We had Uncle James and Aunt Lydia to help us, along with countless friends and neighbors, and I had my work to provide for us. Otherwise, I'm not sure what we would have done."

Victoria curled her knees up to her

chest. "Oliver and I used to wonder. Did you ever think to marry again?"

Martha heard the echo of Thomas's proposal yesterday until it faded, only to be replaced by the softer echo of another proposal she had tucked deeper in her memory bank. She sighed. "There weren't too many men willing to marry a widow with two children, especially when she's called from home so often. There was one man who offered," she admitted.

Victoria blinked several times. "Truly? Who?"

"His name was Jeremiah Pound. You wouldn't remember him, I'm sure. He was a trapper by trade and stopped in Trinity only two or three times a year for supplies. Until your father died. As I recall, Mr. Pound followed us home from the cemetery after the service for your father, knocked on the door, and proposed. I hadn't even had time to note your father's passing in the family Bible."

"He didn't!"

"He surely did. I sent that man packing right quick." She chuckled. "I guess he was tired of living in shanties and thought he could get himself a good farm and the poor, grieving widow would be forever grateful to have him rescue her and her children from certain ruin."

Victoria chuckled, too. "He didn't know you at all, did he?"

"As I recall, he had a rather queer expression on his face when I told him I expected to provide for myself and my children. I don't blame him for trying, though. Most widows are hard-pressed to survive on their own. I suppose . . . that's partly why I'm going to let you go back to New York, assuming we all agree on the conditions. So someday, should the need arise, you'll be able to provide for yourself and not be forced into accepting someone like a Jeremiah Pound. So you can wait for the right man, a good man."

"Did you . . . do you think that might happen for you, even now?"

Martha sighed. Thomas's image flashed in her mind's eye, and her heart began to thud in her chest. "No, child. Not anymore," she whispered. "Not so much anymore."

Chapter 10

By the time Martha and Victoria finally slipped away from the confectionery and arrived at Dr. McMillan's, the town had yawned awake.

Familiar sounds. Familiar sights. Workmen were busy at the sawmill. A few groups of townspeople hustled along the planked sidewalk to complete the day's errands. A sleigh, several saddled horses, and a mule were tethered to the hitching post outside the general store.

Rosalind Andrews, the doctor's housekeeper, ushered Martha and Victoria inside and quickly closed the door to shut out the cold. "Mercy! It's worse than any winter I can remember." She clucked and fussed over them until they were standing in front of the hearth. "Let me take your capes. Warm up a bit. The doctor's gone out, but I hope you'll stay for a visit with me. I have a whole pan of cinnamon rolls left from breakfast."

Martha handed over her cape with a groan and tried not to feel guilty about having a second helping of biscuits with honey for breakfast. "We're not hungry. Is Mrs. Morgan up yet?" she asked.

"She's upstairs in the sitting room. She said something about writing a letter home. Lovely, lovely lady. It's so good for the doctor to have company."

Martha nodded to Victoria. "Why don't you go up and tell her we're here? There's no hurry. While you're waiting, you can tell her about the talk we had last night. I need to talk to Mrs. Andrews first, but I'll be up shortly."

Victoria practically skipped her way to the staircase, mounted the steps, and disappeared. When Martha heard the murmur of voices overhead, she joined Rosalind at the kitchen table where Rosalind had a basket of socks ready for mending.

"We can talk while you work," Martha insisted.

Rosalind smiled, inserted a wooden darner into the heel of the sock, picked up a knitting needle, and began mending a hole the size of a plump bean. "Imagine throwing away good socks like this. The man's got no sense for thrift. He's generous, though. Said I could mend them and give them away," she explained.

As Rosalind proceeded to list a number of families who could use the socks to good advantage, Martha studied her friend. Rosalind looked years younger than only a few months ago. The bitterness and desperation that had lined her face and deadened her gaze was gone now that her husband, Burton, had returned home.

Only last spring, shortly before Victoria ran away, a bitter feud between Burton Andrews and Webster Cabbot, the local gunsmith, had escalated when Cabbot filed theft charges against Andrews, claiming he had stolen Cabbot's missing heirloom watch.

Though innocent, Andrews had fled, leaving his wife to deal with the scandal and shame all alone. Instead of turning to her friends, like Martha, or leaning on her faith, Rosalind had become embittered and isolated herself. By sheer chance, Samuel Meeks had found the watch near the town trash pit, unaware of the controversy. At Martha's request, he gave it to her to return.

Only Webster Cabbot knew the role Martha had played in resolving the dispute. In return for his dropping the charges, prompting Burton's return, Martha had protected Samuel's involvement for fear Cabbot might charge the recluse with the theft. She had also reconciled with Rosalind.

Another secret.

Another homecoming.

Another reconciliation, between husband and wife, between friends, although Andrews and Cabbot remained estranged.

Martha smiled and handed Rosalind another sock.

"You must be so happy now that Victoria's back home where she belongs. That was a terrible thing she did, running off like that. She's very lucky to have found the Morgans. You're lucky, too."

Martha knew her friend was thinking about her only child, Charlotte, who had died some years ago.

Rosalind laid down her mending and lowered her gaze. "Sometimes my arms just ache to hold her again. Just once."

Martha patted her hand. "I know how much you miss Charlotte."

Rosalind sniffled. "A mother's lot is never easy. If we'd only had another child, not that I would miss Charlotte any less, I think it'd just be . . . easier somehow." She shook her head and straightened her shoulders. "But Providence saw fit to give us only one."

Martha caught her lower lip with the tip of her teeth. Prompted by the idea that had popped into her head two nights ago, which was precisely why she wanted to speak to Rosalind today, she took a deep breath. "Sometimes we have to keep our hearts open to love another child."

Rosalind looked at Martha like she had grown another pair of ears. "Another child? Now? At my age? That would take a miracle! As much as I didn't deserve it, I got my miracle when Burton was able to come home an innocent man."

Martha grinned. "The last I heard, there were as many miracles still waiting to find a home as there are children who need one."

Rosalind's eyes widened, then she narrowed her gaze and stared at Martha. "I know that look in your eyes, Martha Cade. It's the same look you had when we were schoolgirls and you tied that . . . that dead critter to my pigtail."

Martha clapped her hand to her heart and feigned a wounded look. "How unfair of you to bring that up. I've apologized any number of times — "

"Don't you go acting all hurt," Rosalind challenged. "I've known you all my life. You're up to something. I know it as surely as I know you're going to try to sweet-talk me into doing something."

Martha laughed. "There's no friend like an old one, is there? Here. Darn another sock. While you mend, I'll tell you about a miracle that's hanging right over your head, just waiting to be claimed. Then I've got to get upstairs to see Mrs. Morgan."

"I suppose you've got a miracle in mind for her, too?" Rosalind quipped.

"She'll be part of it," Martha murmured, praying she could work not one miracle today, but two.

They spoke for nearly half an hour. By the time Martha started up the stairs to the sitting room, she had Rosalind's promise to think about Martha's idea. Praise God, Rosalind had not rejected the idea outright, although Martha had not expected a definitive answer right away. Burton had to be consulted, and so did Dr. McMillan, but with every step Martha took, she had the feeling she just might have planted the seeds of hope that would give life to miracle number one.

Miracle number two was even easier to set into motion. No surprise there, although Martha could not count this as a true miracle until Samuel and June

146

Morgan both agreed. Actually, discovering that June Morgan and Dr. McMillan were old friends convinced Martha this was no coincidence, any more than June's unique position to be able to help Samuel might be construed as luck.

Just another blessing given as a result of Victoria's running away, and she was quick to give credit to the good Lord for whispering both ideas into her ear.

When Martha arrived in the upstairs sitting room, she quickly outlined her proposal to provide for Samuel's future. To her relief, June agreed to help and offered assurances that her husband would also be willing to lend his support.

"Then I'll speak to Samuel later today," Martha promised June. "Now that that's settled, we need to talk about Victoria. I assume she told you about the talk we had last night," Martha said.

June sat across from Martha and Victoria in a lady's chair upholstered in a blue fabric almost the identical color as the daydress she wore. It was hard to tell where the daydress ended and the chair began, but there was no mistaking the woman's genuine smile that provided the answer to her question. Out of the corner of her mind, a memory flashed, reminding

Martha of the prayer she had offered, asking God to provide someone to watch over Victoria after she had run away. He had given her June Morgan. Of that, Martha had no doubt.

She took her daughter's hand, noted the difference that age and hard work had made in her own, and continued. "I hope Victoria didn't forget to mention several conditions I have. Unless we all agree to them, I'm afraid Victoria will have to remain here with me."

"Of course. I understand. Completely."

Martha kept her shoulders as straight and steady as her gaze. "First, I want you to know that a mutual friend will be verifying the references you provided. Even though Dr. McMillan has spoken so highly about your family, he hasn't been in contact with you for several years. If anything appears amiss, my friend will arrange for Victoria to come directly home."

"Mother! Really!" Victoria protested.

"Mayor Dillon agrees with me," Martha argued back. She was ever grateful for Thomas's promise to help, in spite of her refusal to accept his proposal. Perhaps he thought if he helped, he could use that to strengthen his position when he came home next month and tried to change her mind.

He should know her better.

Her conscience echoed perhaps that she should know him better, too.

"No. It's all right," June countered. "I have no objection. I'd probably want to do the same thing if our positions were reversed."

Martha chose not to respond. "There's also the issue of her Uncle James and Aunt Lydia. They were caring for Victoria when she ran away, and they've been wracked with guilt ever since. They're living temporarily in Sunrise. I'd like you to take Victoria to Sunrise on your way back home. It's only a few miles out of your way."

"Certainly."

Martha turned to her daughter. "You need to apologize to your aunt and uncle. A letter simply won't do. Ask them to write to me after your visit to let me know all went well."

"I will, Mother. I promise."

Martha let out a sigh. So far, she had encountered no resistance. "There's also the matter of your wages," she suggested. "I'll expect you to save the greater portion, young lady." She turned and focused on June. "I'm sure Mr. Morgan will be able to help Victoria establish an account at his bank."

"That's easy enough," June agreed.

Victoria nodded. "I will. I promise."

"Good." Martha paused, then looked at June again. "Victoria has always attended meeting every Sunday. I expect no less when she's living with you."

June's cheeks reddened. She stiffened her backbone. "We're faithful worshipers. Victoria has always gone with us. I see no reason why she wouldn't continue."

"I will," Victoria promised. Her hazel eyes fairly glistened with excitement. "Is there anything else?"

"I also expect you to be properly chaperoned if you leave the house, even on small errands. I won't have you gallivanting around New York City."

Victoria chuckled. "Mr. Morgan is even stricter than you are."

"I sincerely doubt that," Martha grumbled. "There's only one last condition. From what Mrs. Morgan has told me, she and her husband expect to hire a permanent replacement for her with the magazine so she can spend more of her time with her children."

Victoria's gaze was as steady as her mother's. "She and Mr. Morgan have explained their plans to me."

"They need your help only until the replacement is found and trained to their satisfaction. Then, they'll be looking for another assistant, one to do the work you're doing now. Contrary to any plans you might have, remaining as a member of the staff for the magazine is out of the question. I want you back here in Trinity by the end of September."

Victoria stiffened and pulled her hand away. "But what if the Morgans can't find anyone else? What if I want to stay?"

June intervened before Martha could answer. "I'm afraid what you may or may not want is not the issue. Your mother wants you to come home by the end of September, and she still has the right to ask for your obedience. It's a just compromise, Victoria. Considering your mother doesn't have to let you return with me at all, I think it would be most unfair of you to question your mother's wishes. And considering how selfish you were to run away and cause your mother so much heartache, it would be unconscionable to refuse."

Victoria blanched, looked from Martha to June and back again, clearly disappointed both older women seemed to be in alliance on this issue, too. "I . . . I suppose. Yes, all right."

"We'll have time to discuss your future

beyond that when you come home," Martha promised. "By then, you may find you've had your fill of the city. If not, you'll have a fair nest egg saved to secure any new adventures you decide to take, instead of relying on the good character of perfect strangers to protect you. As much as I'd hate to lose you to Boston, too, at least I could let you visit there for a spell and know your brother would be there to help keep you safe."

Hope and optimism overcame the girl's disappointment. "I probably don't deserve you," she gushed and leaned in to her mother's embrace.

Martha hugged her daughter. Hard. "You deserve so much more," she whispered and prayed she had made the right decision to let her daughter leave again. She prayed harder she would not regret it.

Before her emotions went beyond her control, she pressed a kiss to Victoria's forehead and sat her back down. "Today's Thursday. I'd like it if you'd both stay for meeting on Sunday. It'll give you a chance to see everyone. By then, I should know for sure whether Samuel will agree to our plan. Speaking of Samuel, I should probably be on my way." She rose and rearranged her skirts. "I assume you'd like to stay here awhile?" she asked Victoria.

"Unless you want me to come with you."

"No. I'd probably better do this alone. I'll stop by on my way home to pick you up."

June walked Martha to the top of the staircase. She took Martha's hand and pressed it between her own. "Thank you. This means so much to me. And to Victoria. I know how hard this must be."

Martha swallowed a lump in her throat. "No, I don't think you do. But you will. Someday," she whispered.

She descended the steps slowly. Deliberately. She knew, in her heart, she had made the right decision. If so, she wondered why her mother's heart was still trembling.

Chapter 11

Martha was ready for battle and summoned none other than the Archangel Gabriel himself as her compatriot.

Armed with two pair of mended socks for Will and a pan of cinnamon rolls for Samuel that Will would also claim as booty, Martha headed away from town toward the southern end of East Main Street en route to Aunt Hilda's cottage. With all that had happened, she had not had an opportunity to check on the cottage before now. While she was there, she decided to get a bottle of Aunt Hilda's famous honey wine for Samuel, too.

She hunched her shoulders and lowered her face when a gust of wind showered her with snow and quickly chilled her. When she finally approached the front door of the cottage, she was more than anxious to just check the house, get the bottle of honey wine, and be on her way. She had a long walk ahead of her to get to Samuel's cabin, which was located at the opposite end of town in the woods behind the church cemetery. By the time she got there, she would probably be frozen to the bone.

Quickly, she let herself into Aunt Hilda's cottage. She had no need for a key. Aunt Hilda never locked a door or window, just in case her errant husband returned and had lost his own key somewhere in his travels.

Shivering, she stood just inside the door in the sitting room. She paused and listened, on the remote possibility Aunt Hilda had returned unexpectedly. She heard no sound, other than her own breathing and the pounding of her heart in her ears. "Aunt Hilda?" she called, just to be sure she was right, rather than risk startling the older woman if she had come home.

No answer.

She looked around the sitting room. Nothing seemed amiss, but she would have welcomed a fire to warm herself. She went directly to the kitchen and sat her basket on the table. When she opened the pantry door, she was surprised. The contents of the pantry were in disarray, yet Aunt Hilda was a stickler for neatness.

As she began to search for the smallest bottle of honey wine, primal instinct flashed through her body, stilled her hands, and raised the hair on the back of her neck. Her heartbeat charged into double time, and she held perfectly still. She listened hard, but heard nothing, only the shrill sound of the wind whistling through barren trees and the whisper of her own conscience chiding her for being foolish and letting her imagination run wild.

Shaken, she moistened her lips. She snatched the closest bottle of honey wine and shut the pantry door. When she turned around, she gasped and clapped both hands to her chest. The bottle of wine crashed to the floor. Splinters of dark green glass flew hither and yon. Amber wine puddled at her feet, which was just about where her heart had fallen, and stained the hem of her cape.

She blinked several times, but the startling apparition remained, standing in the doorway between the sitting room and the kitchen. Her mind toyed with what her eyes beheld. Common sense rejected one explanation after another. Until the ghost held up both hands.

"I'm sorry. I didn't mean to startle you."

The voice was familiar, but age had bowed the man's frame, claimed nearly all of his hair, and whitened the scraggly beard he still wore. Spectacles did not shutter the dark blue eyes behind them, but age had dulled their luster. Dressed in a flannel shirt and denim overalls, he looked like he had just come in from working at his hives.

It may have been thirty years, but Martha still recognized this man and realized she was looking straight into the face of another miracle.

She let out a sigh of relief and struggled to find her voice. "Welcome home, Mr. Seymour."

He smiled and rubbed the top of his left arm. "Is that you, Rena? Rena Fleming? I thought for sure you'd passed on before I left."

Martha returned his smile. "She did. I'm Martha. Rena's daughter."

"Little Martha? Landsakes, you're the spittin' image of your mama. Sorry, gal. Didn't mean to frighten the freckles off your face." He shivered. "I got here right before dawn, waitin' to surprise my Hilda. Didn't even want to start a fire. It'd ruin the surprise. I've been samplin' some of her honey wine to keep warm. Still the best I ever tasted. I can't believe she's still keepin' the hives. Thought you mighta' been her. Didn't hear ya come in. Just heard somebody rattlin' about in the kitchen."

"I . . . called out when I came in. I just stopped to check on the cottage and to get a bottle of honey wine for a friend," she gushed, trying to explain her presence here when Aunt Hilda was not at home.

"I don't expect Aunt Hilda to be back for a couple of weeks," she informed him. "She's at the Goodman farm helping Miriam with her fine new baby boy. You might remember Sean, her husband. He was Frederick Goodman's youngest boy."

He nodded, but his smile had drooped into a frown. "I do. But several weeks? I don't think I'd survive waitin' that long. Not without a fire, and I don't want her findin' out I was back from anyone but me." He paused, and his expression filled with anxiety. "You wouldn't know . . . I mean, I wouldn't blame Hilda if she'd had a headstone put up with my name on it so she could stop every Sunday after meeting to yell at me for leavin' her here alone for so long . . . anyway, if you've got any notion how she'll react when she sees me, I'd be beholdin' —"

"She'll be thrilled. Utterly thrilled,"

Martha assured him. "She never once doubted you'd come home to Trinity."

He straightened his shoulders. His gaze became wistful. "I surely wish I could take back all those years and live them over with Hilda, but I can't. I'd settle for spendin' the few years I have left with her, though. I don't suppose there's any way you could get her home sooner than a few weeks?"

She chuckled. "I think that can be arranged."

"Don't spoil my surprise though. Just in case . . ."

She cocked a brow.

He swallowed a lump in his throat that was large enough to make his Adam's apple bob up and down. "Just in case she decides not to let me stay."

His gaze grew troubled, but she did not encourage him to explain further. Any and all explanations he had about where he had been and why he had been gone for so long belonged to Aunt Hilda, and Martha prayed her aunt-by-affection would be able to forgive whatever transgressions her husband thought might be reason for her to send him away.

Martha pointed to the mess on the floor. "I'll have to clean this up first and get another bottle of honey wine, then I'll see what I can do about securing a replacement for Aunt Hilda. Actually, I have several people in mind, but I have another errand to tend to first. It'll be a few hours, I'm afraid, before Aunt Hilda could come home."

His frown immediately disappeared. "After thirty years, a few hours is like the blinkin' of an eye."

She started picking up the broken shards of glass. He got a broom to help and asked one question after another, catching up on the thirty years of progress he had missed in Trinity. She had no trouble supplying any of the information, except when he asked about the four children he and Hilda had had together.

None were still living, and when she finally left him alone in the cottage, she almost wished she believed in ghosts, if only to have four of them come to comfort the man who had been their father. Perhaps their spirits could get a temporary pass from eternity to do that, an image that better matched her faith.

As she made her way to secure a replacement for Aunt Hilda, a sudden burst of inspiration lightened her steps. She had not drawn any connection between some of the events of the past few months, but re-counting them to Richard Seymour had given her a new perspective — one that restored hope for the future.

With Victoria running away, returning, and now planning to leave Trinity again and Thomas's departure only this morning, a sense of loss and confusion had swirled around Martha like a gray mist, preventing her from seeing things clearly, preventing her from believing they would both return one day.

But Burton Andrews had come home, even though most folks had wagered against it. And now Richard Seymour had come home, once again proving folks wrong. If these two men could come back to Trinity, then Victoria and Thomas surely would.

Her heart filled with gratitude. Perhaps the greatest blessing this day had been saved for her.

On her very first call, Martha had found a replacement for Aunt Hilda. Lucy Palmer was the oldest of five children and inexperienced, but she showed great promise. Even though Lucy had never served as an afternurse before, she was steady and reliable, with enough good common sense to know if Martha should be fetched. Since Miriam Goodman had already borne three children without complication, Martha was quite satisfied Lucy could handle the role.

Riding double on Grace, they arrived at the Goodman farm by midafternoon. While Lucy made herself useful by watching the other children, Martha went to the bedchamber to check on Miriam and her newborn son. She found them in bed, with young Robert nursing at his mother's breast. Aunt Hilda sat knitting by the window.

"You're all looking well," Martha offered.

Miriam's eyes widened. "Martha! I didn't expect you back."

Aunt Hilda set her knitting aside and rose to meet her. "What brings you all this way?"

Martha swallowed hard. Lying, even for a good purpose, did not come easily. "Good news. Victoria is home! She's healthy and happy and very anxious to see you, which is why I'm here."

Aunt Hilda cocked her head. "I'd love to see her, too, but I'll be here with Miriam for another week or two —"

"Actually, I brought Lucy Palmer with

me. She's offered to stay with Miriam so you can come home. The girl's so anxious to prove herself, I thought this might be a good opportunity for her." She glanced at Miriam. "Assuming you'd agree, of course. If you'd rather, I'm sure Lucy wouldn't mind if it was only for a day or two, just so Aunt Hilda and Victoria can get reacquainted."

Cuddling her son, Miriam smiled. "Let Lucy stay for the week or so. Unless Mrs. Seymour would rather not —"

"Let the girl stay. I don't want to discourage her, especially since she seems so interested."

Twenty minutes later, reassured that Miriam was indeed recovering well, Martha left her patient and went into the parlor where she found Miriam's husband, Sean, and Aunt Hilda engaged in a war of words.

At first glance, the battle appeared to be a huge mismatch. Sean Goodman topped six feet and had thick muscles on his sturdy frame while Aunt Hilda was a full foot shorter. With her hair wrapped in a braided white crown atop her head, she looked positively regal. As the undisputed town matriarch, she could intimidate anyone, especially when an occasion called for it.

Like right now.

Aunt Hilda put hands to hips and glared up at him. "Lucy rode out here with Martha, and there's no good reason why I can't ride home with her. And that's all I'm going to say on the matter."

He puffed out his chest. "There's no way I'm going to let a woman of your age ride double on horseback. I'm hitching up the wagon and taking you home."

"Balderdash! I didn't help Sarah Poore bring you into this world over forty years ago to have you order me about." She poked his chest and he took a step back. "I shouldn't have to remind you to show your elders a little respect. I have a good mind to stop in to see your mama on the way home and tell her what a self-righteous bully you've become."

He looked over to Martha, his gaze pleading for help.

She shook her head and held up her hands, reluctant to intervene on his behalf when she agreed with Aunt Hilda.

He let out a deep sigh. "Suit yourself. Ride home with Widow Cade. Just don't blame me if you fall off."

Aunt Hilda turned to face Martha wearing a triumphant smile. "I'm all set to go. Lucy already took my bag out and strapped it to Grace."

Moments later, Martha knew better than to argue when Aunt Hilda refused to ride sidesaddle in front of her. She set off for town with Aunt Hilda seated behind her. While they rode, Martha answered all of Aunt Hilda's questions about Victoria and discussed the girl's plans to return to New York City. They were just outside of town when Aunt Hilda squeezed Martha's waist. "Slow down for a moment. I've got to shift again. I don't want anyone to see me half falling off this horse."

Martha caught a smile and tugged Grace to a halt.

Panting, Aunt Hilda nudged herself around a bit, and Martha felt her nearly totter off as she tried to rearrange her cape and skirts. "Mercy, this is a big horse! I feel like last fall's turkey wishbone ready to be split in half. My ankles are frozen solid, which means I'll be hobbling around like an old woman for days. I don't know how you do it," she grumbled.

"I told you to ride sidesaddle in front of me," Martha gently reminded her. "I do perfectly fine with Grace, especially since I wear split skirts."

"Harrumph! Get along. We haven't far to go now. And if you mention one word of my grumbling and whining to anyone, especially Sean Goodman, I'll never make you another cherry pie for the rest of your life, Miss I-love-my-sweets."

Martha chuckled and clicked the reins. For all her good qualities, Aunt Hilda made terrible desserts, but Martha would never hurt her feelings and tell her. Besides, how bad could anything really taste when it was topped with gobs of honey? "I won't breathe a word," she promised.

Aunt Hilda leaned forward and laid her head against Martha's back. "I know you wouldn't. That's one of the reasons I love you like my own. You're a good woman. You haven't had it easy, have you? I know it's been hard for you with Victoria, but I'm so proud of you. You're making the right decision, Martha. A hard one, but right," she murmured.

Martha's heart swelled. She had valued Thomas's opinion, but it was Aunt Hilda's approval that meant even more.

"Now you bring that girl over and let me have a good talk with her. That Mrs. Morgan, too. It won't hurt to let them both know you're not alone being concerned."

"I will. Sometime tomorrow. After you've had a chance to . . . to thaw out and get a good night's sleep in your own bed," Martha suggested as they approached

Aunt Hilda's cottage. She pulled up, turned in her seat, and helped Aunt Hilda to get down. She held on to the elderly woman until she was steady on her feet before dismounting herself.

"Come inside. We'll get a good fire going —"

"I have an errand I have to tend to, but I'll be back with Victoria tomorrow," Martha promised, determined that the reunion between Aunt Hilda and her husband would be conducted in private, even if Martha had to stretch the truth a little to make that happen.

She waited until Aunt Hilda had entered the cottage and closed the door before taking Grace back to her stall and feeding her an extra portion of oats for being so good about carrying extra weight today. She proceeded directly to Samuel's cabin on foot, carrying her gifts with her in a basket.

With a little luck, she would be back home just in time for supper, and she looked forward to spending a quiet evening at home with Victoria. Lord knew there were precious few of those left to her.

Martha tried knocking on Samuel's cabin door a third time and paid extra attention to using the signal knock she used to let Samuel know who was at the door.

Still no answer.

She glanced at the windows on either side of the door, but didn't bother with them. The shutters were latched closed. She muttered under her breath. She had slipped on ice and fallen twice and landed on her bottom in thick banks of snow. She had dropped her basket both times. How the bottle of honey wine had survived intact was a mystery, but Will's socks looked like four sorry snowballs. The cinnamon rolls were smashed and looked fit for hogs.

She could barely feel her toes. Her fingers were practically numb. Drat!

Both impatient and irritable, she pursed her lips, formed a fist, banged hard, and then again. "Samuel? Will? I know you're in there! Let me in, or . . . I'm going to get the sheriff and have him break down the door."

No response.

She kicked the door, letting out a shrill scream as pain shot from her toes to her knee and back again. She looked down at her foot to make sure she had not actually kicked her toes right off. "Temper! When are you going to learn to control your temper?" she grumbled.

She closed her eyes and waited for her foot to stop throbbing before making one last attempt to see the troublesome pair inside. Surely they had to be here. Where could Samuel go now? He was blind, and Will would not have any reason to set out by himself.

She knocked the signal one last time.

Silence.

She had no other recourse but to leave. She was simply too cold to wait them both out, but she was also confused. They had never refused to see her before, which did not bode well for her plans. There was simply no way Samuel and Will could stay here now, and refusing to see her would not prevent the inevitable.

"They must know that," she murmured. She sat the basket down in front of the door.

Samuel was too old and stubborn and Will was too young and ornery to admit it. That's all. The bond between the crusty recluse and the streetwise orphan was as amazing as it was strong, and Martha had no one to blame but herself for pairing the two. She had given divine inspiration all the credit at the time, but nothing short of divine intervention would be able to resolve the crisis that would now force the two apart.

Resigned the battle would have to be postponed for another day, she turned to leave. Straight ahead, emerging from the woods, the life images of stubborn and ornery appeared. Relief flooded through her veins. A smile tickled the corner of her lips.

As they drew closer, she realized they had carried trouble home with them. She rushed to meet them with a shout to wake up that sleepyhead archangel who just might earn a demotion if he did not wake up and get back to work.

Chapter 12

Unfortunately, trouble often came in pairs, but that archangel could not have picked a better time to guide both Samuel and Will back home.

Martha glanced at both of them, turned sideways, and pointed to the cabin. "Don't stop to explain. Just get inside. Both of you," she ordered.

She could not tell which one looked worse. Both were a ghastly shade of blue with their cheeks stained crimson. Their clothes were frozen stiff. She did not dare go ahead of them for fear they might fall and she would not be able to drag either one of them very far.

Will tugged on Samuel's hand. "C-come on. C-coupla more steps. C-cabin's just ahead. Hold 'er steady on c-course," he barked, with all the authority of a ship's captain triple his own size and age.

"Y-you g-got no b-b-business here," Samuel bellowed to Martha.

She forgave his rude welcome. She even managed to ignore it, followed them inside

171

the cabin, and set her basket to the side. "Don't get comfortable, Samuel. You, either, young man," she warned as Will steered them toward the chairs in front of the Franklin stove in the middle of the room. She removed her cape and gloves and set them aside.

"D-don't go m-meddlin', w-woman," Samuel countered. His teeth were chattering so hard she half expected to see them crack and drop out of his mouth like yellow kernels of corn. He bristled with indignation.

She glared at him, and she felt better, even though she knew he could not see her expression. But Will could, and he squared his thin shoulders. "W-we d-don't n-need no help."

"I can see that. You're both the picture of health and good sense." She shut and bolted the door behind her. "I'll be sure to tell folks that when they're staring at your corpses wondering how on earth a grown man and a boy could both be so half-witted as to go swimming in the pond at this time of year."

Her flippant guess hit closer to the truth than she might have expected.

"We b-bloody well d-didn't go s-swimmin' on purpose," Will snapped. "We was

. . . we was ice fishin', and the d-damn ice just c-cracked open. D-dumped us both in. G-good thing we was c-close to shore."

"You're lucky you both didn't drown," Martha snapped, too shocked by what had happened to reprimand the boy for his atrocious language. Only last fall, both Will and Thomas had wound up in that same pond after he tried to rescue the boy from an ill-fated attempt to build a raft upstream, only to have the craft break apart when he guided it over the falls. She just might have to fence the pond off to protect Will from himself, then realized he would just scale the fence anyway, the stubborn scamp. "Now strip, both of you, down to the skin while I find some blankets."

Samuel's purple lips sputtered. "Y-you've gone lunatic if you th-think I'm gonna —"

"I've had the same suspicions about my sanity more than once today," she countered.

Shudders shook Will's body. Beneath spiked lashes and brows dusted with snow and ice, his dark eyes snapped. "I ain't barin' my ass in fronta no girl!"

"You'll both strip. Now," she repeated. "I'll get some blankets, then keep myself busy in the galley looking for some fresh horseradish to grate for that wise mouth of yours."

Either they were both too cold or too much in shock to argue further. After she dropped some blankets on the floor at their feet, she went straight to the corner of the cabin Samuel referred to as the galley. His stores were meager.

She passed over the horseradish and found several soft and wrinkled turnips and carrots. She diced them for soup. There was only one potato, but it was large. She diced that, too, and tossed everything into a pot. There was not a single herb to add for flavor or meat to provide strength, but the soup would be filling and hot. She got a fire going on the cookstove, covered the vegetables with water, and set the pot to boil.

By then, the grumbling and complaining behind her had stopped, and she judged it safe to turn around. Sure enough, both Will and Samuel were parked in front of the Franklin stove, each with a blanket draped around their shoulders and another that covered them from their waists to their feet. They huddled together, their chairs side by side, like two old squaws, with their wet clothing lying in a heap on the floor.

"You two look a little better," she murmured. She added more wood to the stove and draped the wet clothing around the cabin to dry.

Will sneezed and wiped his nose with the corner of the blanket. "Coulda done this ourselves," he spat.

Samuel swatted at the boy's head. "Mind your manners, boy. The woman can't help herself. She's got to meddle. Just born to it, I suppose."

"You could have both drowned," she argued. "And you would have, but for the grace of God."

Or one very alert archangel.

"If God had a mind to, he coulda helped us off the ice before it cracked." He sniffed the air. "What's that you got cookin'?"

"Soup. Not that you deserve any," she remarked as she approached him.

"Smells good. We thank you," Samuel murmured.

"It should warm your insides. The stove should warm the rest. There's not much more we can do now. Just wait and see if you both come down with lung congestion. Whatever were you thinking? Why on earth would you decide to go ice fishing?"

Samuel let out a sigh. "Old fool that I am, I was thinkin' about catchin' some fish for supper. The falls are frozen silent. The ice shoulda held. Will said it was good and thick, but I couldn't see for myself . . ."

She pressed her hands together. "I'm sorry. Dr. McMillan told me what happened."

"Young know-nothin'! He's got no right tellin' my business to nobody."

"I'm your friend," she insisted.

"Then be one. Leave me and the boy to work this out. We got through worse than this before."

Martha's heart trembled. Samuel clearly had no concept of the difficulty he and Will would face now that blindness had rendered Samuel so helpless. "I'd like to help," she suggested.

He put his arm around Will's shoulders. "Then help this mate into his hammock so he can rest. Now that my bones are thawin' out, I'd like to get into some warm clothes, if you'd get them for me."

Will yawned. "I ain't tired."

Martha urged him to his feet. "Maybe not, but you'll be all toasty and warm in the hammock while you're waiting for the soup to cook. Samuel and I need to talk."

Will rolled his eyes, a habit she thought he had broken.

He did not protest further, and she led

him to one of two hammocks in the corner of the cabin opposite the galley. He got into the hammock on his second attempt. Martha tucked the two blankets around him and added a third to cover him from head to toe. "Get some rest." She nudged the hammock until it began to rock.

He yawned and closed his eyes. "You gonna be here when I wake up?"

"Probably."

"Figured as much," he grumbled and promptly drifted off to sleep.

Will was fast asleep. So far, he showed no sign of fever. Samuel had dressed and polished off two large bowls of soup, rather neatly considering his handicap. Martha sat with him in front of the Franklin stove, wondering how to broach the subject that would cause both Samuel and Will great pain.

Samuel broke the silence that stretched like a taut rope between them. "I know the boy's got to go. Problem is, I got no place to send him. That boy needs a firm hand, and I know I can't wield it. Not like I am now," he murmured.

Surprised that he would openly admit his own weakness, as well as relinquish all claims to Will, she did not know how to respond.

He leaned an elbow on his lap and covered the raised serpent tattoo on his cheek with the palm of his hand. "Expect that's why you came. To take him."

"No, I . . . not yet. Soon, perhaps, but not today, especially after that spill into the pond. He'll need plenty of rest and good hot food. So will you," she cautioned.

He straightened up and gripped the arms of his chair. "I been on my own most of my life. Don't see that changin' now. I might have two eyes that are plumb useless, but I still got my sturdy constitution and my wits."

"Yes, you do. As for Will, let me tell you what I have in mind." She gave him a brief description of the home she thought might be best for Will and answered all of his questions. "Nothing is set in stone quite yet, so I wouldn't say anything to Will."

"He won't like it, but he'll do it," Samuel promised.

She wanted to take him at his word, but she knew Will well enough to be skeptical. He had run off several times in the past, though never from Samuel. "How can you be so sure?"

She thought she saw a flash of pain in eyes that no longer held any sign of life. "Because I'll tell him it's an order. He'll obey. Taught him to," he responded.

Martha caught her breath and held it for several long heartbeats. Why the good Lord had seen fit to bring these two together, only to tear them apart made no sense. No sense at all.

"You'll give me a good bit of warnin', though? I have things to discuss with the boy before I send him away."

"I will. Of course," she promised. Until she remembered that June and Victoria would be leaving in four or five days. "Maybe you should talk to Will over the next few days while he's recuperating. Just in case things happen faster than we suspect."

Samuel tipped his chin up a notch and cocked his head. His eyes might be clouded forever now, but she could still see he was puzzled.

"Just in case you're . . . you're not here for much longer," she explained.

He laughed out loud. Not an ordinary laugh, either. A full, belly-shaking laugh that colored his cheeks. "One dang slip into the pond, and you got me dead and buried, is that it? I've been keelhauled twice, shipwrecked more than half a dozen times, and I've faced the wrong end of a pirate's sword more than you'd probably believe. It's gonna take more than a pond of ice to do me in."

He laughed again, then his emotional pendulum swung wide and fast to the opposite end of the spectrum. He paled and gripped the arms of his chair so hard his knuckles whitened. He struggled, visibly, as anger flared, then slipped behind despair. "After all I've fought against and won, don't seem fair to lose my eyesight to some cowardly, sneaky ailment nobody can cure." He shook his head. "Can't say the prospect of bein' a helpless, useless old man is all that appealin'."

Martha swallowed hard. "You're helpless, perhaps, and not up to living on your own anymore, but you're certainly not useless. God has plans for all of us, though we may not like them. There's so much —"

He slapped his thigh and silenced her. "Don't go gettin' all spiritual and start proselytizin' like some preacher. Got no time for that."

Her backbone stiffened. "I have no intention of preaching to you. I came to offer you a position, if you have to know the truth."

He sniffed the air. "You're tipsy. Knew there must be some reasons for you sayin' somethin' so ridiculous. I'm blind, woman!

The only position I could get is sittin' in this chair."

She huffed. "I am not tipsy!"

"I smell it. Wine's my guess. Maybe honey wine."

Her gaze dropped to the bottom of her skirts. Sure enough, the hem was stained just like her cape. "I didn't drink any honey wine. I dropped the bottle. It broke, and the wine splashed the hem of my skirts."

"Waste of good wine," he grumbled. "Well, if you're not tipsy, I must have been right earlier. You've gone lunatic on me. Shame. You're mighty young —"

"I have not gone mad," she snapped, "but I am getting mad, and if you don't let me tell you about the position, I will lose my temper. *I* don't want to lose my temper. *You* don't want me to lose my temper. If Will were awake, he'd tell you *he* doesn't want me to lose my temper, either."

Panting, she paused to grab a breath and realized she sounded just like Anne Sweet. No wonder the woman got her way. Folks just gave in to her to get some peace and quiet. "Lord, spare me," she whispered, although she admitted to having a new respect for Anne's tactics.

He chuckled. Again and again. "You got the spirit of a true sailor! You shoulda been a man. I'da been proud to serve with ya. Now, tell me about this so-called position. Just what are you plannin' for me?"

She took a deep breath and hoped the archangel had a flock of assistants nearby for reinforcements. "A home. A perfectly lovely home. For aging sailors, and —"

He leaped to his feet and balled his hands into fists. Splotches of anger stained his cheeks. "A home? You want to lock me up in some kind of institution? You best be thankful you're not a man," he bellowed, "or I'd cut out your tongue and feed it to the sharks before I put that head of yours on a spike and mounted it on the top mast!"

Chapter 13

Praise heaven, winged reinforcements held Martha's temper in check, kept her from quaking in her skirts, and even managed to whisper an idea into her ear.

She took a deep breath and let the words pour out so fast Samuel would be shocked silent, if only long enough for him to realize he had turned into a bully. "Sit down, Samuel, and make up your mind. One minute you tell me I should have been a man. In the next breath, you're spewing nonsense about how grateful I should be for *not* being a man. Seems to me you've lost more than your vision. You haven't gone lunatic on me, now, have you? Of course not. Maybe you struck your head on the ice. Or you're simply confused. Or in shock. I don't think you're still cold. Not after a second helping of soup. Not that the soup had any flavor. I tried to warn you the soup wasn't ready —"

"Enough! Be silent, woman!" Deflated as though her words had been pins that poked holes in his harangue against her, just as she had hoped, he dropped back into his seat. "I'm not sure what's happened to you. Never used to chatter like a magpie. Take a deep breath, girl, and explain yourself in three sentences. Three. Use one more and I'll be tempted to overlook you're a woman."

Martha grinned. "All right. Let's see," she began. "There are several philanthropists in New York City who are funding the building of a home for aging sailors who have retired from the sea. That's one sentence, right?"

He nodded.

She gathered and rearranged her thoughts. "The home is nearly ready and though they've hired an administrator and most of the staff, they would like, no, they need someone to be a sort of resident captain, someone who could talk with the men as they arrive and see that they adapt to living in a . . . a home, and you know you could do that, Samuel."

"I knew you'd have to take a breath eventually. That's two sentences, and I'm bein' mighty generous."

"They would be willing to consider you for the post, provided you leave for New York within a few days and . . . provided you'd agree not to frequent the tavern next to the home after the gates are locked at ten o'clock and provided —"

"That's three," he snapped. He ran a forefinger along the length of the serpent tattoo on his cheek. "I might be awful sorry I asked, but how in tarnation did you manage to find out about this?"

Martha's heart began to race. At least he was considering her words and not rejecting her idea outright. "Through a friend from New York, June Morgan, who's visiting." Without embellishing the facts, she explained about Victoria's return home and her impending departure. "Thaddeus Morgan, June's husband, is one of the directors of the home. He can arrange for you to meet with the others to discuss the position."

In truth, there had been no position. At least not until she had presented the idea to June, who, in turn, agreed the idea made such perfect sense she felt confident her husband would not only agree, but would make sure the others endorsed the idea as well. The major stumbling block would be getting Samuel to New York, unless he agreed quickly enough to leave with June and Victoria.

"I'll consider it."

"You will? You'll actually consider it?"

she asked, surprised he would acquiesce so easily.

"I said I'd consider it. I didn't say I'd do it," he snapped. "Man's gotta think carefully before he alters course."

"Yes. I understand. It would be a dramatic change and the position would carry a lot of responsibility. If you weren't up to traveling or felt perhaps you were a bit too old —"

"Martha Cade, you start chatterin' again and I'll . . . I'll toss you outta here and don't think I won't. I can still find my way to the door, so don't think you can take advantage of me."

She frowned. "I wouldn't do that," she insisted, although she did harbor some guilt for not being completely honest and telling him she had made his position one of her conditions for allowing Mrs. Morgan to take Victoria back home with her.

"No, you wouldn't," he admitted. "You've been a good friend to me, and I don't want you feelin' all bad for not findin' some cure for these eyes of mine. You tried your best," he murmured. "Some things just can't be fixed."

Unaccustomed to seeing Samuel speak so openly, Martha held in a sigh. She was going to miss this old man. A lot. With all her heart, she wished she had been able to help him. Dr. McMillan had been her last hope, and Samuel's as well. Perhaps it was a blessing that the old seaman had lost his vision gradually. Nothing else could account for his seeming acceptance of what he must have known was inevitable.

Her own acceptance would take longer. "I'll come tomorrow to check on both of you," she suggested. She donned her cape and gloves, then spied the basket sitting by the door. "I've got some socks for Will. They're damp, so I'll set them by the stove to dry. There's a pan of cinnamon rolls for you both. They're a little squashed, but they should taste good."

She put the pan of rolls on his lap and laid all four socks on the chair she had been using while he sampled one of the rolls. "I suppose that's everything. Except for this." She wrapped his hand around the bottle of honey wine. "When you're considering the offer, I want you to keep something in mind."

He cocked a brow, but a smile tickled the corner of his lips as he embraced the honey wine with both hands.

"I don't want to impose, and I wouldn't want you to feel obligated in any way," she insisted, "but if you do go to New York, I'd be forever grateful if you could be there if Victoria has need for a friend. I don't expect anything to go wrong, but if it did, I'd rest easier knowing there was someone I trust she could turn to for help. She's coming back to Trinity next September, like I said. If you don't like the home, you could come back with her, and I'll think of something else."

He nodded. "If I do go, and mind you, I said *if,* I'd ask you to return the favor and keep a close watch on that boy of mine. Make sure he's treated well."

Martha glanced at Will. His normal color had returned, and he was sleeping peacefully. "He's not going to be happy about all this," she warned. "Not at first. He loves you very much, and he's going to miss you."

"Maybe."

Martha leaned down and pressed a kiss on the old man's forehead. "I'll see you tomorrow." The sight of the tears welling in the corner of each of his opaque eyes silenced the rest of the words and captured her heart. Without prolonging her departure any longer, she left him there sitting by the stove with a pan of cinnamon rolls on his lap and the bottle of honey wine in his hands, while the heart he tried so hard to keep hidden from the world was breaking.

She left the angels behind to comfort him and sent a few to stay with Nancy Clifford to help her as she grieved the loss of little Peter.

Finding her way back through the woods in the dark without falling again was no easy accomplishment. Once Martha reached the cemetery, lights in one of the two mansions on either side of the meetinghouse grounds provided all she needed to head home feeling more secure in her steps.

Inside the Sweet home, all would remain dark and quiet for several more weeks until Thomas's sister and her husband returned home. In the other home, Thomas's daughter, Eleanor, had her husband to help her now that Thomas had left town, and Martha made a mental note to stop to see the girl tomorrow. Eleanor's pregnancy had been difficult, and she hoped Thomas's departure had not complicated matters.

Thinking about Aunt Hilda, at home reuniting with her husband in their small cottage at the far end of East Main Street, lifted Martha's spirits. She hurried home, anxious to find one more place today that was not troubled. It was so late she had probably missed supper, which meant she owed an apology to all. Her stomach growled, reminding her she had missed dinner at midday.

More important, she had not spent much time with Victoria today, but there was nothing to be done about that now. To her chagrin, her duties today had once more come at great personal cost, an ever-present difficulty she had balancing her responsibilities as a mother with her duties as a midwife, friend, and neighbor.

She passed Dr. McMillan's home and glanced up. The second floor was well lit. He was no doubt spending the evening with his old friend. Martha still needed to talk to him about several issues, but they would have to wait. The third floor, where the Andrews' had their own quarters, was dark, save for light coming from the front room they used as a sitting room. Hopefully, Rosalind was discussing Martha's idea with her husband this very minute.

Martha whispered a prayer, made her way through the covered bridge, and approached the confectionery. The second floor was not lit. The shop was dark. Another day's business was done, although she wondered how the two sisters managed to make a profit. They gave away almost as much as they sold, charged a pittance for their baked goods, and gave credit without bothering to make any attempt to have folks settle up.

Just where the sisters had lived before they landed in Trinity four years earlier remained a mystery. Their utter goodwill and generosity, however, had stilled gossip about them long ago. Folks simply accepted Fern and Ivy for what they were — good, honest women who loved the Word and practiced it. And made scrumptious confections.

As soon as Martha cut to her left to walk alongside the building to get to the back door, light from the kitchen gave her hope. Supper, though later than usual, must still be in progress. She quickened her steps and formulated a proper apology. If supper was late, it was because Fern and Ivy had held it hoping Martha would make it home in time to join them.

Martha stomped her feet clean, slipped inside, removed her cape and gloves, and set them aside. She entered the kitchen. "I'm so sorry for being late," she said. "I had so much to do, but I truly thought I'd —"

Her apology died on her lips. She stared at the scene before her and glanced from one figure to another trying to make sense of it all. Shock rendered her speechless and immobile. Alarm sent her pulse pounding at her temples. She blinked several times, but the scene remained the same.

Thomas stood in front of the hearth. Exhaustion and worry etched his features. Fern and Ivy stood across from each other at the table. Between them, bloodied cloths lay next to a basin of water and an assortment of salves and ointments. Martha's bag of simples lay open. Victoria was nowhere to be seen.

Ivy rushed over to Martha and clasped her hand. "Thanks heavens you're finally home! We practically searched the entire town looking for you."

"Victoria. Where's Victoria?" Martha croaked. "She's been hurt, hasn't she? What happened? How badly is she hurt?" Without waiting for answers, she swirled, about to head upstairs to find Victoria.

Ivy yanked her back. "Victoria is fine. She's not hurt at all. She's right upstairs."

Relieved, Martha blinked back tears. "She's fine? Then what happened here? Someone's obviously been hurt."

Thomas rubbed his forehead. "There's

192

been an . . . an accident," he offered.

Fern snatched up the cloths from the table and bunched them into a ball. "You've got to be dumb and blind to think that what happened was some sort of accident!" she snapped. "It was deliberate."

"You don't know that," Ivy protested.

When Fern glared at her, Ivy dropped her gaze.

Martha looked at Thomas and felt her heart leap. "An accident? You've been hurt! Why didn't you go to see Dr. McMillan?" she cried. She rushed to him, visually searching for any sign of injury, but braced to a halt when he held up his hand.

"I'm fine. I just happened to be at the right place to be able to help. As for the doctor, the fewer people involved right now, the better."

When Martha cocked a brow, he sighed. "We've only been here an hour or so. If you hadn't come home soon, we would have sent for him."

Martha looked from Fern to Ivy to Thomas and back again. "Will somebody please tell me what's going on?"

Fern and Ivy clamped their mouths shut and looked to Thomas.

He nodded, took Martha's arm, led her

to the table, and packed the salves and ointments back into her bag. "Let's go upstairs. Fern and Ivy did the best they could, but I think you should look in on your patient."

"My patient? I still don't know who my patient is, let alone what happened."

"I'll explain everything later," he assured her. "First, I want you to see your patient. Assess the injuries. Then we'll talk. You can decide for yourself if this was an accident or not."

Martha was still mystified, but too concerned about the patient waiting for her upstairs to waste time arguing. Thomas led her up the steps to the guest chamber where June had stayed. He handed Martha her bag and knocked softly.

When Victoria answered the door, dim light inside the chamber gave Martha the opportunity to see for herself that her daughter was all right. She was pale and obviously distressed, but unharmed. Her eyes widened with relief when she saw her mother. She put her finger to her lips and stepped aside.

Martha stepped into the chamber and glanced at the figure of the woman sleeping in the bed. Unsure of the woman's identity, she took a few steps closer and felt her heart skip a beat. With all the injuries to her face, the woman was barely recognizable, but Martha knew exactly who had been brought to her for help.

She turned and hugged Victoria. "Go downstairs with Mayor Dillon," she whispered. "I shouldn't be long."

"I'd like to stay to help, if you'll let me."

Martha eyed her daughter, saw determination staring back at her, and smiled. "I'd like that." She turned to Thomas. "We'll be down in a bit. Have Fern or Ivy set some water to boil, just in case I need it," she murmured.

As soon as he left, she shut the door. Gently. She went straight to the task at hand. "I need more light," she said. "Are you sure you want to stay?"

Victoria nodded. "I promised her I wouldn't leave."

"Then let's get to work. Fern and Ivy have probably done what could be done, but I'd like to make sure."

With her bag in one hand, she approached the bed while Victoria turned up the lamp. As soon as Martha had a clear view of the woman's face, she gasped. Her pulse quickened. Her hand tightened on her bag.

The word "accident" ricocheted in her mind, leaped over "clumsy" and "illness" and crashed headlong into another word: "impossible."

Chapter 14

"You'll rue this day, Russell Clifford!" Martha vowed. She unclenched her fists and drew in a deep gulp of air before she lost all sensibility and sight of her responsibility to her patient. Nancy Clifford might be clumsy, either due to natural awkwardness or some sort of disorder, which could account for the other bruises Martha had seen, perhaps even the fall that triggered the premature birth of poor Peter.

But this . . . this was an abomination no woman deserved. Ever.

Feeling guilty for leaving Nancy, Martha studied the woman's battered face and assessed the treatments Fern and Ivy had applied. A thin sheen of ointment on the bruises glistened, but there was no telling what the ointment was for sure. Both Nancy's eyes were swollen shut. Red and purple streaks mottled the lids and the half-moon of flesh beneath the sockets. Her nose was red at the tip, but did not appear to be broken. Parted in sleep, her lips fared worse. Fresh blood oozed from a small slit in the center of her bottom lip. Her upper lip had swollen to twice normal size.

No fall, no accident could cause this much damage. Only a man's hands or fists.

Martha swallowed hard and turned to Victoria, fearful of what other unseen injuries Nancy might have sustained, as well as possible complications the poor girl might have while recovering from the stillbirth. "I need you to go downstairs. Tell them to add more wood to the stove if they have to, but —"

"But I promised I'd stay."

"I need to examine her further. While I do, you have to go outside. Get Mayor Dillon to help you. Fill several pails of snow. Then bring them inside and pack some towels with the snow."

Victoria's eyes widened. "Snow?"

"To stop the swelling," Martha explained. "Hurry, dear. And get Miss Fern to get me some clean cloths and dry towels while Miss Ivy gets the teapot ready." She opened her bag and handed Victoria some peppermint. "Tell Miss Ivy this needs to steep for ten minutes. I want the tea hot and strong so it's ready for Mrs. Clifford when she wakes up."

Victoria glanced at the woman she had

been watching. "She's . . . she's going to be all right, isn't she?"

"I believe she'll recover nicely, but I need to examine her now to be sure. Go on, child. If she wakes up, I'll tell her you'll be right back."

Victoria touched the small scar on her bottom lip, a memento from infancy she still carried, and glanced at Nancy again. "She'll have a scar, too, won't she?"

"She will, and she'll likely carry others no one will be able to see," Martha murmured.

Victoria tiptoed from the room, and Martha went straight to work. Despite a careful, but thorough examination, Nancy did little more than moan from time to time, which told Martha the girl had been given some sort of drug.

Laudanum came to mind, but Martha never, ever carried it, used it, or approved of it for treating her patients. Any illness or injury that required laudanum was well beyond her realm of expertise. As far as she knew, there was no laudanum in the confectionery, and she could not imagine either Fern or Ivy having any call to need laudanum, let alone keep it on hand.

Stymied, she took heart knowing Nancy did not have many other injuries beyond those to her face, only a few bruises on her hands and fingers. Her bleeding from the birth appeared normal.

Martha sat in a chair while she waited for Victoria to return and searched her mind, replaying her stay at the Clifford homestead over and over again, but she could not imagine Russell as the kind of man who would ever beat his wife, especially after the tragedy of losing Peter.

Or had that tragedy triggered yet another?

Had the man become enraged and blamed his wife for their son's premature birth and death, despite Martha's assurances the child would probably have strangled to death during birth whenever that had taken place? Or had she been right to suspect what was now obvious to Martha — that Russell routinely hit his wife?

Images flashed through her mind that sent tremors through her body. Guilt lay heavy on her heart. Had she simply accepted his claims, as well as Nancy's, that she was uncommonly clumsy because he seemed so young and so devoted to his wife? Was there anything she could have done to prevent this tragedy?

She had stayed in scores of homes during the past ten years and many before that as she learned her trade. She had lived intimately with her patients' families and had observed husbands and wives together. Most men treated their wives with respect, if not affection. Only a precious few, thank heavens, had overstepped their God-given authority and defied both God's laws and the laws of man by physically harming their wives.

From experience, she knew the image of rural life, with bountiful harvests, healthy children, and affectionate marriages, was an ideal most folks did not achieve. Irregular weather, crop failures, illness, or injury were inevitable, but more often frustrating than devastating, whether personally or financially.

For most, faith provided hope and the courage to carry on. For some, faith was as shallow and useless as Dillon's Stream, which dried up during frequent droughts. That old stream could not carry more than a light raft when it ran high, which destined Trinity to forever remain a mere crossroad in the backcountry.

At best, the stream provided a quirky atmosphere to Trinity, quaint covered bridges at either end of town, a skating spot during winter, and a place for children to skip stones in summer. Memories of the townspeople who had formed a brigade and passed up buckets of water in a fruitless attempt to save her brother James's burning tavern flashed through her mind's eye.

Suddenly, the chamber door opened, and Victoria entered. Martha set her musings aside and went to work. Victoria proved to be a valuable assistant, and she followed Martha's directions well. First, Martha lifted Nancy's head so Victoria could slide several towels below to cover the pillow. Next, Martha used the fresh cloths and some pokeweed to prepare cold poultices she placed over the bruises. She finished by laying the snow-packed towels along either side of Nancy's face and across her lower face.

Nancy moaned. She began thrashing about, and tried grabbing at the towels, but it was apparent the girl was not fully conscious.

"Hush, now. It's Widow Cade. I'm trying to help your bruises and slow the swelling. I know it's cold. There now," she crooned. She caressed the girl's hands until they went limp. When she tucked Nancy's hand beneath the blanket, she noted the crooked fingers on her right hand, further evidence of a previous beating?

Eventually, Nancy's breathing became even. Her body relaxed, and she slipped, once more, into a deep, restful slumber.

Satisfied for now that she had done all she could, Martha straightened the bedclothes and tucked the quilt just below Nancy's chin.

Victoria remained at the foot of the bed. "It wasn't an accident, was it?" she whispered.

Martha let out a heavy sigh. There would be little good that would come from this whole affair, but there was nothing Martha could do to protect her own daughter from learning that all marriages were not ideal. "No, I'm afraid not. Did she . . . did she tell you anything about what happened?"

"No. She fell asleep pretty quickly after Mayor Dillon carried her to bed."

"And before that?"

Victoria shrugged her shoulders, but her eyes flashed with indignation. "I was upstairs when I heard some commotion in the kitchen. I went down to find out what was happening, but Miss Ivy shooed me right back up the steps and told me to put fresh linens on the bed, that you had a patient who would be staying with us awhile." She paused and took a deep breath. "I'm not a child," she protested. "I could have helped. She was . . . she just kept crying and crying. I could hear her."

Victoria shuddered. Her eyes filled with tears. "She wouldn't let go of my hand. She kept squeezing and squeezing, begging me not to leave her."

Martha went straight to her daughter and embraced her. "Don't fret. It's the reassuring touch we give to others that means the most of all, but it's not always easy to give comfort, is it?"

Victoria wept softly. Martha rocked her from side to side until she quieted. "What's going to happen to her now?"

"She'll need time here to mend. After that, I'm not sure. I need to talk to Mayor Dillon for a moment to find out exactly what he knows about this. Do you think you could stay with Nancy while I go downstairs?"

Victoria sniffled and wiped her teary face with her hands. "I can stay with her all night, but what do I do if she wakes up?"

"I won't be very long. I have to come back to change the dressings. If you'd feel better, I'll send Miss Ivy or Miss Fern up to keep watch with you until I can come back."

With a quick lift of her chin, Victoria

smiled soberly. "I'll be fine by myself."

Martha slipped from the room. She was so proud of her daughter. She must remember to tell her.

When Martha reached the kitchen, she found the room tidy. The pot of peppermint tea was steeping, filling the room with a fresh aroma. Fern and Ivy sat together in front of the fire, talking quietly. Oddly, Fern had a rolling pin on her lap. Ivy held the poker for the fire in her hand. There was no sign of Thomas, so she would have to rely on the two sisters to provide the details surrounding Nancy's "accident."

Martha approached the two women, and they stopped whispering. "Nancy is resting now. Very soundly. Perhaps too soundly. Which one of you would care to tell me where you found the laudanum you used?" she asked gently.

No response.

Two pairs of blue eyes feigned ignorance, but guilt blushed cheeks on both pale faces.

Martha held out her hand. "Give it over."

Fern pursed her lips.

Ivy tilted her chin.

"I know you must have some laudanum.

There's nothing in my bag to account for how deeply Nancy is asleep. I know you meant well, but I don't approve of using something so strong."

Ivy narrowed her gaze and tightened her grip on the poker. "The girl needed something strong to help her heal faster. And to forget."

Fern shook her head. Her eyes glistened with compassion, even as she ran her hands over the rolling pin. "That sorry excuse for a husband beat his wife with his fists. She'll never forget what he did, but she needs time to heal and get her strength back. Before she has to stop making excuses for him and face the truth. Before she has to stop forgiving him for being a brute." Her gaze hardened. "If that man tries to put one toe near that girl. . . ."

The longer Fern talked, the more her gaze hardened and the shriller her voice became. Martha felt a shiver run the length of her spine. Fern sounded as if she had firsthand knowledge of how Nancy might feel and react, but that was impossible.

Fern, as well as Ivy, had never been married before. Since that was the case, Martha assumed Fern had witnessed a woman being brutalized by her husband or perhaps she and her sister had grown up in a household where her father had beaten their mother. Since Martha had no knowledge of their past, she could only speculate, but she had no doubt that both Fern and Ivy recognized the real cause of Nancy's injuries — a beating.

Nevertheless, Martha still needed more facts as well as an explanation about Thomas's involvement, and it would serve no purpose to have Fern and Ivy complicate matters by dwelling on painful childhood memories that had no bearing on Nancy's difficulties.

Ivy patted her sister's arm. "Russell wouldn't dare show his face here. But if he does, we're ready for him!" She brandished the poker like a sword and nearly knocked Fern in the head.

How had these two sweet, docile women turned into such firebrands? Martha grabbed the poker and snatched the rolling pin away as well. "Whatever's gotten into you two?"

Ivy plucked her poker out of Martha's grasp. "I'd use a shotgun if I could, but I don't have one. Nancy can't protect herself, can she?"

Martha rolled her eyes. "So you two will? With a poker and a rolling pin?

Where's Thomas? He's obviously not here. He wouldn't have left if he thought Nancy was in any danger."

Fern grabbed her rolling pin back. "Mayor Dillon said he'd be back, but that won't make any difference. Men stick together. They say they wouldn't allow a man to beat his wife. They pass all sorts of laws against it, too, but they don't enforce them. They protect each other."

Martha gasped. "Do you honestly believe Thomas will protect Russell if Nancy admits he did this to her?"

"He's the mayor, not the sheriff," Ivy murmured. Her gaze was troubled. "Enoch Myer is a good man, but he'll be like the rest. He'll want to keep everything all quiet, so folks don't gossip. He'll talk to Russell and make him promise never to hit his wife again. Then he'll talk to Nancy and make her promise to be a better wife so Russell doesn't have any reason to lose patience with her. Even Reverend Welsh will step in. He'll counsel both of them with platitudes about the sacred nature of marriage and use the Bible to remind Russell to be a just husband and Nancy to be an obedient wife. Then the young couple will go home together and everything will be all right."

"For a while," Fern interjected. She stared into the fire. "That wife will spend every moment of every day in fear and pray he'll never hurt her again. Then one day, she'll do something wrong. Forget to sweep in the corner. Overcook his biscuits. It doesn't matter. He won't need much of an excuse to beat her. Then he'll apologize. She'll forgive him again. And again. Until one day. . . ." She let out a sigh.

Ivy stood up, put her arm protectively around Fern's shoulders, and gazed directly at Martha. "Until one day, he kills her. Unless somebody talks some sense into that girl and gets her to leave him."

"Or somebody stops him," Fern whispered.

Martha's throat constricted. Her heart began to pound. She looked from one sister to the other, confused and shaken by their words.

Finally, Fern rose from her seat. Ivy laid her hand on her sister's arm. Fern shrugged her away, turned, and faced Martha. "That girl's all alone. She's got no family here. She needs somebody to help her, somebody to talk some sense into her," she argued as she held the rolling pin close to her side.

Martha swallowed the lump in her

throat. No matter how well-intentioned Fern and Ivy meant to be, they were both overwrought and not thinking clearly. "We don't know all the facts yet. How can you be so sure about what happened? How can you be sure about what Russell will or won't do? How can you be so sure about what Nancy needs?"

Fern took her sister's hand. Before she could open her mouth to speak, Ivy leaped to her feet. "Please, Fern. You don't have to explain. You don't have to say another word."

Fern pressed her lips together and they stopped quivering. She drew in a deep breath, then smiled. "It's time," she whispered. "I'm tired of always running away. I'm tired of hiding. I'm tired of living a lie." She looked directly into Martha's eyes. "I know. I'm sure. I only survived the nightmare Nancy is living right now because I had someone who loved me enough to sacrifice her future happiness for me. When no one else would come forward. Ivy did. For me."

Chapter 15

Martha froze in place. Beyond shocked, she could only stare at Fern as her mind tried to comprehend the unthinkable and juxtaposed images of Fern as a wife who had been mistreated and a God-fearing, good-natured spinster.

The opening and closing of the back door, followed by heavy footsteps, broke through the momentary hush that had settled in the kitchen.

Ivy stood and aimed her poker at the doorway. Fern raised her rolling pin and rested the pin in the palm of her other hand. Martha turned, her nerves aflutter. What on earth would happen if Russell Clifford appeared, asking for his wife?

Thomas strode into the room, took one look at the armed sisters, and rocked back on his heels. "Ladies? Any particular reason you're angry at me and armed for battle?"

"Thought you might be that scoundrel," Ivy explained as she waved the poker through the air.

Fern ducked, barely in time. She patted

the palm of her hand with the body of the rolling pin. "Are you still set on staying the night?"

He nodded. "Now that I'm back, maybe you should store your weapons and think about getting some rest. It's been a long day for both of you."

Martha had to give the man credit. Mocking either woman right now would have been a big mistake, but there was not an iota of condescension in his words.

Ivy turned and started to put the poker back on the stand near the hearth, hesitated, then returned to her sister's side. "We'll take them upstairs with us."

Fern squared her jaw. "Just in case he tries to sneak in through a window."

Thomas's eyes widened. "On the second floor?" he asked as he took a few steps forward.

Ivy huffed and raised the poker again.

He stopped dead in his tracks.

"He might catch you dozing and slip past you," she argued.

Fern nodded in agreement. "Or break through the shop and use the front stairs. He'd find that poor girl before you even —"

"That's not going to happen," he countered. Wisely, he stayed put, but looked to Martha for help.

Martha found her voice, although her heart was still racing. "No. Thomas will stay awake and make sure nothing happens. I'll be up awhile yet, too," she promised. "You've both had a difficult day. You should try to get some sleep. You have to be up early for tomorrow's baking, and it won't go well if you're not well-rested."

After many long, pounding heartbeats, Martha saw Ivy lower her poker. "Maybe she's right," she said to her sister. "Martha won't let anything happen."

Fern caught Martha's gaze and held it. A plea to keep her revelations about her past in confidence glistened in her eyes and tugged at Martha's heartstrings.

Martha nodded, ever so slightly.

Relief flooded Fern's gaze. A small smile tickled the corners of her lips.

"Perhaps you can check on Nancy and Victoria for me," Martha suggested. "The dressings probably need to be changed soon. And you should take the tea upstairs, just in case Nancy wakes up."

"I can do that," Fern murmured. "I'll spell Victoria for a bit, too. The girl's too young to have to see all this. Come along, Ivy."

When they left, side by side, they also carried their weapons with them, apparently much to Thomas's chagrin. Wisely, he did not challenge them, but as soon as their footsteps rained overhead, he turned on Martha. "What's gotten into those two? I know the whole affair has been unsettling, but . . . but they'd be no match for Clifford if he somehow managed to show up here."

Thomas rubbed one of his temples. "Ivy's plumb dangerous with that poker. She's lucky she didn't put out somebody's eye the way she was waving that blasted thing around. Did you see how close she came to hitting Fern? Foolish women. I told them Sheriff Myer would keep watch on Clifford. I've never known them to be so . . . so unreasonable."

Mindful of her obligations to keep the sisters' motivation secret as well as their fears that nothing would be done, in the end, to protect Nancy, Martha tried turning his attention to herself. "They're just upset, and they're alone without a male protector. They're not used to seeing anyone hurt so badly. It's my fault, actually. I knew it would be an imposition for me to stay here, but until now, it's never been more than calls in the middle of the night that disturbed them. If I'd just been here —"

"Well, you weren't. Just where were you?" he asked.

"With Samuel and Will."

He sobered. "Dr. McMillan told me about Samuel's problem. What are you going to do with them now?"

She sighed, pointed to the two chairs by the fire, and took one of them for herself. He joined her there.

"What makes you think I'll be doing anything for either one of them?" she asked.

"Because I know you. Because once you've taken an interest in something or somebody, you never let go. You're like a beaver, constantly at work, either building something, patching holes, or looking for weaknesses. It's part of your charm. You took an interest in me some years ago. I suppose that's what gives me hope you'll weaken and accept my proposal. You will. Eventually."

"A beaver? That's the best comparison you could come up with?" Highly insulted, she huffed. "I'd never marry a man who told me I reminded him of a beaver! Seems to me you're a bit too sure of yourself, Thomas. A beaver indeed!"

He grinned. "Your cheeks get all pink when you're flustered. Did you know that?"

She went to touch her cheek, then dropped her hand back to her lap. "Embarrassing a lady is ungallant. Given all the day's troubles, perhaps you'd better content yourself with telling me what happened and how you got involved. The last time we spoke, you said you were leaving at first light for Philadelphia."

He stretched out his legs and leaned back in his chair. "Actually, I was on my way when I passed by the Fenway farm. Mrs. Fenway flagged me down. She told me she thought there might be some trouble at the Cliffords'."

Martha nodded. "She was at home? Russell was supposed to fetch her to stay with Nancy."

"To hear her side, Clifford sent her home at the end of the first day. He said his wife didn't need any more help."

"I told him she'd need someone for a few weeks," Martha argued.

"Mrs. Fenway tried. He wouldn't let her stay. Apparently, she'd seen enough to be concerned about that poor young woman, and he knew it."

Martha smiled. "He just didn't know Millicent Fenway."

"No, he didn't. She was concerned enough to insist I head right there to check things out and save her husband from heading to town for the sheriff. Seemed to be the right thing for me to do. Mrs. Fenway isn't a woman prone to hysterics without good reason."

He paused to stare into the fire, and Martha did not rush him. Judging by the set of his jaw and the hardening of his gaze, he was remembering what must have been a difficult scene. "Once I got to the Clifford cabin, he wasn't too pleased to see me. I guess when I told him I was the mayor, he thought twice about slamming the door in my face. I didn't want to tell him about Mrs. Fenway's concerns, just in case she was wrong. I . . . I almost didn't get to see Nancy. I spent some time talking with Russell, encouraging him to join the congregation, especially after he told me about the son he'd just buried in the yard."

He shook his head. "He was amiable enough. Spoke highly of you. Seemed worried about his wife. Till she started moaning and calling for him from the bedchamber. He tried really hard to get me to leave."

Thomas turned to face Martha.

She smiled. "But you wouldn't leave."

"No. When she wouldn't give up crying out for him, he had no other course but to go to her. When he opened the door and tried to slip inside, I got enough of a glimpse of her to know Mrs. Fenway had been right. There was big trouble at the Cliffords'. Unfortunately," he added, "Nancy disagrees."

Martha leaned toward him. She kept her fingers entwined and her hands on her lap to keep them from trembling. "How could she possibly explain the injuries she sustained?"

His gaze grew troubled. "She kept babbling about how clumsy she was by nature and how weak she was from childbirth." His hands balled into fists. "She claims she merely fell out of bed and landed flat on her face."

Martha snorted. "That's hogwash! Women weak from childbirth don't fall out of their own beds! Even if they did, they'd be able to break their fall with their hands! As for Russell Clifford, the only help he could have given her came *after* he pummeled her with his fists."

Chest heaving, she could barely pull a breath deep enough to fill her lungs. Images of Russell repeatedly striking his wife collided with images of some man brutalizing Fern. Martha's cheeks flamed. Her blood boiled, melting the reins on her temper as well as her self-control. She hissed. "That bas— monster!"

Thomas flinched. "Martha! I've . . . I've never heard you utter a single nasty word, let alone part of a profane one!"

She shook and offered heaven a quick prayer for forgiveness. She could not remember thinking of a profanity or ever contemplating using one. Her cheeks felt like they had burst into flames, fueled by the fire of indignation still raging in her body. She bowed her head. "I'm sorry. Please forgive me."

He took her hands and covered them with one of his own. "You're forgiven. I let loose more than a few profanities myself today."

She closed her eyes for a moment. "There's no excuse for what I almost said. None," she murmured, certain the quicker she changed the subject, the sooner she could try to forget her grievous blunder. "How did you manage getting Nancy here, away from her husband?"

He gave her hands a squeeze before folding his arms over his chest and staring back at the fire. "It wasn't as hard as I expected it would be. I sent Russell's own words praising you right back at him, but I had to stretch the truth a bit, too. I told

219

him you'd have my hide and his, too, if I didn't get his wife straight to town so you could tend to her."

Given her current state of mind concerning Russell Clifford, Martha was not sure if Thomas had stretched the truth, but she chose not to think about it. "But didn't he just insist that I come there instead?"

Thomas cocked his head and looked at her sideways. "I can be very persuasive. Oddly enough, Nancy fought harder against coming here than her husband did."

She swallowed hard. "He must have insisted on taking her back home when I wasn't here."

"It was precisely because you weren't here that I was able to get him to leave her and go home. I told him there was nothing he could do here to help and there was no sense wasting his time waiting for you. With Fern and Ivy huddled together fussing over Nancy, all he could do was get in the way."

He glanced overhead. "Considering the armed guards I found waiting for me just now, the young man was probably wise to put some miles between himself and the Lynn sisters."

"Indeed," Martha murmured. "But I still don't understand how Sheriff Myer got involved."

He took in a long drag of air. "After Russell left and his wife was being tended to, I rode over to Enoch's and told him my suspicions." He chuckled. "That's when my language became spirited and . . . salty. He agreed to go see Russell Clifford right away and told me he was going to stop to see if Reverend Welsh would go, too. I came back here to wait for you. I doubt Russell will simply confess, in which case Myer wants a statement from you before he'll pursue the matter officially. That's assuming Nancy tells the truth and stops lying to protect her husband. If she doesn't, I'm afraid there's nothing more to be done. I'll stay put for a few days, but there's not much else I can do. Will you help?"

Martha stared down at her lap. As a midwife, she had only been summoned to a birthing on two occasions where one of her duties had been to get the unmarried woman to identify the father of her babe. If her family could not convince the man to marry her, the law would force him to support his own bastard child rather than letting moral, God-fearing taxpayers carry the burden.

Martha did not like taking advantage of a suffering woman. She liked the prospect of a man abandoning his responsibilities even less, so on both occasions, she had done her duty.

Both women had married the fathers of their babes within days, sparing Martha the ordeal of testifying in court. She recalled Grandmother Poore telling her about testifying herself only once, but it was so long ago, Martha could not remember the people involved.

As a healer for women and children, Martha had never been asked to gather information and to be prepared to testify before now. She assumed her word would carry the same weight as in bastardy cases, but it placed a heavier burden on her shoulders.

With childbirth, there was no question. There had to be a father. With illness or injuries, there could be any number of causes. In this case, it would be Martha's assessment of those injuries that would determine whether the law became involved, since no jury of men would likely take the word of a man's wife against him without corroboration of some kind.

The echo of Fern and Ivy's warning about the futility of getting men to take action against a brutalizing husband rang loud and clear, clanging against Thomas's words that suggested otherwise. Despite the sisters' vehement position, Martha had no doubt Thomas would keep his word.

Right now, however, everything depended on what Martha would do and say, as well as her ability to get Nancy to admit to the truth: Her husband had beaten her. If Martha gave any credence to Fern and Ivy's claims that women who had been brutalized by their husbands would not be cooperative in making allegations against them, Martha had to have greater faith in her own ability to get Nancy to admit the truth — first to herself, then to others.

Even so, Martha had to act quickly. Before the law could take any action, some people in the community might be tempted to take matters into their own hands and give Russell Clifford a sampling of his own brutality.

For the first time in all her days as a midwife and healer, the task at hand seemed overwhelming and at odds with her usual role. Normally she saw herself as a mediator between God and man. The Creator had given her a gift to help Him bring new life into the world and to use her knowledge and experience to heal those who suffered from the ills of the world.

As always, according to His will.

When she succeeded, families were made whole and faith was rewarded. When she failed, she continued to minister to her friends and neighbors, comforting the grief-stricken and helping them to keep a strong hold on faith that was being tested.

This time would be different.

This time, if she used her gifts, she would help to separate a couple joined together as one.

Or save a life?

Given a choice, Martha would have turned to Aunt Hilda for advice and support, but her aunt deserved time to reunite with her husband without any distractions or interruptions to dampen her joy. Martha would just have to make a decision without her.

The path Martha had to take, however, suddenly appeared very clear, and she made up her mind about what to do. With no firsthand experience to guide her, she steepled her hands and prayed for strength, wisdom, and courage. As she prayed, she heard Fern's words again, reinforcing her decision as the only one she could live with: "She has no one to help her."

When she finished her prayer and looked

up, Thomas was still watching her, waiting patiently for her to answer him.

"I'll help," she whispered. "I'll have to help. I have no other choice."

Chapter 16

Upstairs in the sickroom, Victoria had fallen asleep in her chair next to Nancy's bed. Martha checked her patient again, tucked a blanket over her daughter, and doused the lamp. Whatever dose of laudanum the sisters had given to Nancy would likely keep the young woman sleeping till morning. If she woke before then, Victoria would be there, so Martha headed to her own chamber to get some sleep.

The day had been trying. The morning would bring new troubles of its own, she feared. She slipped out of the room into the dark hall and stopped to cock her ear. All was quiet downstairs where Thomas was keeping guard as he had promised, though he did so only to satisfy the sisters' fears that Russell Clifford would appear. At the other end of the hall, Fern and Ivy were probably sleeping with their weapons within arm's reach.

Martha shook her head and tiptoed back to her room. Heart-weary and nearly numb with exhaustion, she stepped inside.

226

She turned to close the door, then decided to leave it halfway open so she could hear Victoria better if she called for her mother.

When Martha turned around, she spied a figure sitting in the chair in the corner near her bed and gasped. It was too dark to tell who it was, but the silhouette was impossible to miss.

"It's only me. I didn't mean to startle you," Fern whispered. "Shut the door. We need to talk."

With her heart pounding, Martha eased the door closed. "I thought you'd be sleeping by now," she admonished as she made her way to her bed.

"I couldn't sleep."

Martha sat down on her bed, faced Fern, and saw the shadow of the rolling pin sitting on her lap. "You should try to get some rest. Thomas is downstairs. He won't let anything happen during the night."

Fern caressed the rolling pin with her hands. "Perhaps."

Unsure of what to say next, Martha held silent. It was rather awkward trying to have a conversation like this, and she could not see Fern's face to tell what she might be thinking or feeling.

Finally, Fern took several long breaths, then sighed. "I'm sorry we misled you.

227

We've had to mislead everyone here, but we had no other choice. Or so it seemed."

"You don't have to apologize," Martha insisted. "And you don't have to explain anything. Not to me. Not to anyone else."

Fern sighed again. "We do love it here. Of all the places where we've tried to settle since . . . since running away, we've liked it best here. We never stayed this long before," she offered. "He always managed to find us."

"Your . . . your former husband?" Martha asked.

"Unfortunately, I believe he's still my husband. Bartholomew Randall Pennington III. Entrepreneur. Philanthropist. Civic leader. He was quite dashing and utterly charming. He swept me off my feet and carried me straight to the gates of hell." Her voice broke, and she paused. "I won't shock you with all the horrid details. Only this."

Fern opened her robe and placed Martha's hand at the base of her neck. Martha could not see the thick band of scars, but she traced it with her fingertips and shuddered.

"When I'm tempted to think I made a mistake by running away, tempted to believe he would have changed, that he truly loved me, the scars are always there to remind me that he would have loved me. To death."

"I'm so sorry," Martha crooned. Fern's tears dampened Martha's fingertips. She could feel her friend trembling and longed to take away her painful memories. When she cupped Fern's cheek, her friend leaned into the caress.

"Ivy lived with us after Father died," she explained. "We were originally from Delaware. She saw what was happening and tried to convince me to leave my husband, but I wouldn't listen. I loved him so, and he was always so ashamed of himself. After. He'd promise never to hurt me again, and he'd buy me some outrageously expensive piece of jewelry as a peace offering. Not that I wanted or needed any. I already had a box full of his family's heirlooms. All I ever wanted was his love and affection."

Fern sniffled. "I don't recall much of that last night. All I truly remember is the belt around my neck. He wrapped it round and round, pulling it harder and harder as he dragged me across the floor, forcing the necklace I was wearing into my flesh. He was screaming at me for . . . for something I'd done. The room started spinning. I

thought I was going to die. I don't remember much after that. I must have
swooned. When I roused, there was blood
everywhere. Ivy was standing over him
with a bloodied poker in her hand. Fortunately, she hadn't killed him, but she had
managed to knock him unconscious. She
told me later she had first given him a
good bash to his head. When he turned
around and tried to attack her, she belted
him in the face. Broke his nose and split
his lip open. She forced me out of that
house right then and there. We've been
hiding from him ever since. It's been
nearly fifteen years now. Fifteen years.
Sometimes it seems like a lifetime ago.
Other times, like now, it's as if it happened
yesterday."

Martha let her own tears run freely. Her
heart trembled with compassion for Fern,
leaving no room for anger at the brute who
had mistreated her. Only room enough for
relief, that Fern had escaped and that Ivy
had had the courage to act, that they had
each survived. "Surely he's given up by
now," Martha suggested. "You're safe here
in Trinity."

Fern took Martha's hand from her neck
and squeezed gently. "We thought we were
finally safe four years ago when we were

living in Mountain View. It's a fairly large town in New Hampshire. We'd been there a little over a year. We had a little house on the edge of town, but we were thinking about opening a confectionery like we have here. We'd gone to look at a storefront and decided to treat ourselves to supper at the tavern. One of the guests had a city newspaper. The paper was a few months old, but that's where we found it. Again."

"Found what?"

"The advertisement: 'Runaway wife. Prone to madness.' He had those two lines set in big print right at the top. The rest was my description along with Ivy's." She chuckled. "I don't know what made my sister angrier. That he claimed I was mad or that he described her as half-witted. But in either case, we knew it was only a matter of time before someone recognized us from the advertisement, contacted him, and told him where we were."

Martha huffed. "They were your neighbors! Why would they do that?"

"For the 500 dollar reward. It had happened before, you see, but each time we had the good Lord watching over us. We got wind of what was happening and managed to leave one town or another before he arrived. We left that very night."

"So then you came here. To Trinity."

"Exactly. Living in a city with its own newspaper was out of the question, so we had already given up thinking we could live in a large town. We wanted someplace small and remote, someplace that didn't look like it would grow too fast or attract too many newcomers, and someplace without a confectionery," she added.

Martha recalled the very day Fern and Ivy had arrived in Trinity and smiled. "Folks here haven't been the same ever since." She patted her lap. "I know I haven't."

Fern chuckled. "That's mostly Ivy's doing, you know. We weren't raised to lift a hand to work. Father was quite wealthy. We had a lovely home in Delaware overlooking a river and so many servants! Once Ivy was old enough to stand on a stool by herself, you couldn't get her out of the kitchen. Not when Mrs. Pugh was baking. Mercy! I haven't thought of her in ages. It's a good life we have now, but we still wait and watch, wondering when we'll have to move at a moment's notice. . . ."

"But that's so unfair!" Martha protested.

Fern snorted. "Fair or not, that's the way it is."

"But it's been four years now. What

makes you think he'll find you here?"

"Because I know he'll never give up looking. Not till the day he's called Home to account for himself," Fern spat.

"Maybe he has been called Home," Martha suggested, mystified as to why any man would spend years of his life searching for a woman he had brutalized. "Besides, you haven't had any contact with him for fifteen years —"

"Don't forget about the newspaper advertisements," Fern cautioned.

Martha waved her hand. "Even so, what if he has passed on? If he hasn't, he's surely given up searching for you by now. It's hard to believe he searched for you as long as he did. What would ever possess him to do that?"

Fern sat up straighter. "Pride. Family honor. And . . . and something else."

Martha cocked her head. "Something else?"

"The night we left, Ivy and I only took the clothes on our backs and . . . and my box of jewelry. I barely had the strength to walk. I was so frightened he would wake up and try to stop us that I . . . I never bothered to sort through the jewelry and separate mine from his family's. I just grabbed that box and ran. So . . . so you see, it's not me he wants. It's the family jewelry I stole."

"You took his mother's jewelry?"

"And his grandmother's," Fern whispered. "I've managed to hold on to a few of my own pieces. For an emergency," she explained. "I still have every single one of his family's pieces. I've always intended to return them. I just never figured out how to do that."

"Just send them," Martha cried.

"And take a chance they'd all be stolen? The post isn't secure."

"Then take them back yourself and . . . and leave them on his doorstep."

"And risk being caught? I'd rather not spend the rest of my life in prison, thank you."

"He wouldn't have you arrested!"

"Oh, yes he would. And I can't send anyone with the jewelry, either. If they didn't run off with the jewelry, they'd wind up telling him where to find me, and I don't want to take the risk he'd show up here and cause trouble. You see? Believe me, I've thought this through. There's nothing to be done about this now, but . . . but when I've passed on, and Ivy, too, would you see that it's returned? You're like my own sister. I trust you, Martha.

Please. Will you do that for me?"

Martha patted her friend's knee. "You know I will, but . . . but what will you do if he does find you? I don't think he will, but what if he does? What will you do?"

Fern collapsed against the back of her chair. "I'm too tired to run anymore. If the good Lord sees fit to let that man find me, I'll just have to deal with it then. He can have the jewelry back, but only if he agrees to leave Ivy and me in peace. If not, I'll make sure he never sees a single piece. Not even Ivy knows where it's hidden."

Thoroughly overwhelmed, Martha could scarcely unscramble all the thoughts swirling in her head. The day had been too long and the events too difficult, but Fern's confession had shocked Martha beyond any chance of sustained, rational thought. "We'll think of something," she promised and silently vowed to make sure Fern and Ivy would not spend the rest of their days living in fear.

"We have to think about Nancy. She's more important right now," Fern insisted. "We can't let her go home with her husband. Next time, he could kill her."

"I'm afraid you might be right."

"Then you agree with me? You understand why this is so important?"

Martha helped her friend from her chair and embraced her, ignoring the pinch of the rolling pin caught between them. "I'll help. We'll both be able to help her. Tomorrow. Now get yourself some rest."

Arm in arm, they walked to the door. Fern started toward her own chamber, then returned. "I'm ashamed to have to ask you this, but what I shared with you tonight —"

"Remains here," Martha whispered and pressed Fern's hand to her heart.

Fern sighed and turned about. The rolling pin swung at her side. Her steps were heavy. Her shoulders were sagging. Until she reached Nancy's door. Martha could not see more than just the shadow of her silhouette, but she clearly saw the woman's shoulders straighten a bit before she continued to her room.

Martha found little sleep waiting for her in her bed. She tossed and turned, slipped from a dream into a nightmare and woke up drenched with sweat and her heart slamming against the wall of her chest. She curled into a ball and found release waiting for her.

In prayer.

Chapter 17

Answers to prayer often took time. They required patience and faith, along with a willingness to accept God's wisdom when the answer finally came in an unexpected form.

The following afternoon, Martha took one step into the confectionery shop and knew the instant she saw the two men coming through the door that they were not the answer she had expected or could easily accept.

She tightened her hold on the tray of bread she was carrying, plastered a smile on her face, and wondered how on earth she would get these two out of the shop before Fern or Ivy returned.

At the moment, Fern was upstairs helping Victoria bathe Nancy. Ivy had gone to the general store on an errand. As far as Martha could see, the sisters' absence from the shop was perhaps the only answer to prayer Martha had received.

"Reverend Welsh. Mr. Clifford. Good morning to you," she murmured.

Young Russell halted a good two steps

behind the minister, removed his hat, and twirled it in his hands while he kept his gaze glued to the floor.

Reverend Welsh, hatless in all kinds of weather by custom, smiled warmly. "It's always a blessed day when I see you, Martha. I heard Victoria finally came home. As soon as I did, I started writing a special sermon for the occasion. I expect I'll see you both at meeting?"

"You will." She set the tray down and started lining up the loaves on the table, which stretched along the outer wall. Reverend Welsh was a man of uncommon faith and a gentle shepherd for his flock. His talent for preaching, however, fell far short of gifted, but he had the wisdom to keep his sermons brief.

"The bread is still hot from the oven. Last batch of the day. Would you like a loaf to take home?"

"Actually, I was wondering if we could talk for a spell. The three of us," he suggested.

Talking to Russell Clifford was the last thing Martha wanted to do, especially since she had yet to speak to Nancy about the incident that had landed her in Martha's care. The laudanum had worn off by midmorning, and Martha had done no more than change the woman's dressings, offer reassurances that she would recover well, and listen to Nancy's slurred, pitiful excuses for her injuries.

With time, Martha would be able to question her patient closely about the incident, but certainly not before the girl got past the painful job of healing. And most certainly not at her husband's insistence, even if he did have the minister's support.

Fern's warning that the minister would intervene and try to reconcile the young couple rang loud and clear. Curious to know precisely what role Reverend Welsh intended to play and cautious about prejudging either man, Martha could hardly refuse to listen to what both had to say.

She could not invite them into the kitchen for fear either Fern or Ivy would interrupt, and offering to take them upstairs to the sitting room would put both men too close to Nancy. Instead, she nodded toward the side room in the shop where day-old offerings at reduced prices and tins of hard pretzels and cookies were displayed. "I'm keeping an eye on things this afternoon. Perhaps we could talk for a moment in there," she suggested.

Without waiting for either of them to argue, she led them straight to the side room. After the minister and Russell entered and stood side by side in front of the colorful tins, she took a place in the center of the archway to block anyone's view. "Nancy is resting as comfortably as can be expected," she offered.

Russell paled. His hands trembled, but he remained mute.

Reverend Welsh put his arm around the younger man's shoulders. "I met Russell only yesterday, but we spent the good part of the day together. Tragedy takes a heavy toll at times, especially when we feel . . . alone. Losing a child, a son, is never easy, but God's mercy and His love can sustain us if we turn to Him and when we have other followers to help us through our sorrows."

When he paused to take a breath, Martha held silent.

"When that tragedy is compounded by another, and we try to continue alone, we often fail. And young Russell has failed," he murmured. "He has failed his Creator. He has failed himself. And he has failed his wife, the woman he vowed before God to love and protect."

Martha's heart began to race. Had Russell actually confessed? Was that what Reverend Welsh meant? It was impossible to even think Russell would simply admit his guilt and expect all to be forgiven so quickly and so easily.

In the next heartbeat, the impossible became reality. "Russell has fallen from grace," the minister continued. "He's broken God's law, but he has confessed his sins and sought forgiveness from his Maker. He's come to ask his wife to forgive him as well, so he can take her back home where she belongs."

Martha shook her head, as if to make sure she had heard Reverend Welsh correctly. She refused to accept a word of the minister's claims until Russell as least spoke for himself. "Forgiveness? You've come to ask for forgiveness for . . . for your wife's accidental fall?" she asked. "Or are you taking responsibility for her injuries?"

Russell paled. His eyes welled with tears. His hands, cupped as if in prayer, trembled. "I . . . I take responsibility," he whispered. His voice was hoarse and his gaze was penitent. "I can offer no excuses for what I did. I was wrong. I hate what I did. I love my wife. I never should have hit her, but . . . but I did. God forgive me, I did."

The young man's tears fell freely now, and his lips quivered as he visibly struggled for control. "I love her so much. I need her. I know what I did was wrong, but I swear I'll never lay a hand to her again. Please, you must believe me," he pleaded. "It's just been so hard since we moved here. Then when we lost Peter, I . . . I just don't know what came over me."

Moved by the man's honesty as well as his plea, Martha kept a tight hold on her compassion. "It wasn't the first time you hit her, was it?"

Surprise flashed in his eyes, followed by just the barest glint of anger, which he extinguished so quickly she almost missed it. His cupped hands briefly clenched into fists, and he dropped his gaze. "No. It wasn't."

"And you've squeezed her hands so hard, two of her fingers have broken."

His shoulders shook. "I never meant to —"

"And the day she bore your son, she didn't trip of her own accord, did she?" she charged, pressing him hard.

When he looked up again, deep sorrow filled his gaze. "Yes, I have hit my wife. But this time will be the last. By all that's holy, I swear it will be the last time. All I want to do is see my wife and beg for her forgiveness. On my knees if that's what it takes, and I'll spend the rest of my life treating her properly. But I need to see her today. I have to convince her to let me prove I can be the loving husband she deserves."

Reverend Welsh had been nodding as the younger man pleaded to see his wife and spoke before Martha could fully comprehend the enormity of what she had just heard. She would not have believed it if she hadn't witnessed it herself.

"As Christians, we must be people of compassion," the minister urged. "We must all do our share to help Russell and Nancy," he admonished, as if he sensed Martha's reluctance. "Under the circumstances, Sheriff Myer has agreed not to pursue the matter. I'll continue to counsel both Russell and Nancy, of course. And they'll both be joining the congregation, too. With their prayers and faithful attendance at meeting, along with the congregation to provide guidance and support, I'm convinced this young couple can overcome their difficulties and remain together, united as one by faith and fellowship."

Stunned by the minister's support and Sheriff Myer's reluctance to intervene, Martha was momentarily speechless. Any relief she felt for not having to testify and give an official statement was short-lived. The whole scenario had unfolded almost precisely as Fern and Ivy had predicted it would. Did Thomas know what had transpired? Did he approve?

Regardless of Thomas's involvement, Martha had to be ever mindful that her responsibility was first and foremost to her patient. She also needed time to be sure of what to do. "You may see your wife, of course, but not today. She's still groggy from medications," she cautioned.

Russell stiffened. His eyes flashed once more, and this time Martha recognized his anger as a challenge she was ready and willing to meet, if only to give herself time to talk to Nancy and decide how to proceed. "Nancy needs to regain her strength. At least wait until Sunday after meeting. By then, her lip should be better healed so she can actually talk to you without causing further damage. I'm sure you'll agree to wait a few days . . . if you truly have your wife's best interests at heart."

Russell's shoulders drooped a bit lower. His gaze was troubled. Clearly disappointed, he looked to Reverend Welsh to support him against Martha.

To the minister's credit, he patted the young man's shoulder, then released him. "He can wait. If there's one thing I've learned over the years, it's to trust your judgment, Martha."

A modicum of guilt shadowed her conscience. She nudged it aside.

Though the minister started forward to leave, Russell held his place. He locked his gaze with Martha's, and she could see he was torn between roles. The domineering man determined to get his own way battled with the penitent one, while his sense of natural superiority as a man reared against her place as a woman, his inferior.

Martha hardened her gaze to one she reserved for situations that demanded one and all to accept the authority that her status gave her.

Reverend Welsh paused and turned to the young man. "Come along, Russell. We'll go back to the house. I know I have an extra Bible or two somewhere. Mrs. Welsh can help me find one you can keep. We'll look at some Bible verses together till supper. I have a meeting with the church elders tonight. Perhaps you'd like to come along."

Russell covered his reluctance to leave well. "I don't want to impose —"

"Nonsense, son. Mrs. Welsh enjoys having someone to fuss over besides me, and the elders will be anxious to meet the newest member of our congregation."

Apparently, Russell realized he had nothing to gain by antagonizing either the woman who stood between him and his wife or his earnest intermediary who supported her. He donned his hat. "You'll tell her I was here, won't you?" he asked Martha.

The minister answered for her. "Of course she will."

They approached Martha together. "We thank you for your time," the minister murmured. "If Nancy is able to see her husband before Sunday, just send word to my house. Russell will be staying with us until he can take his wife home."

She stepped aside to let them pass. Long after she heard the shop door close behind them, she was still standing there, so lost in dark, troubled thoughts, she never heard the door open again.

"Oh, there you are! I was hoping you'd be here. I have such news! And you simply have to be the first to hear it!"

Hearing Aunt Hilda's voice at that moment was as joyous as hearing a babe cry for the first time in this world. Martha swung around, barely in time to ready herself for a bone-crushing embrace.

"He's come home. He's here!" Aunt Hilda whispered. "Come. I want you to —"

"Who's here?" Martha asked. Obviously, Richard Seymour had not told his wife of Martha's complicity in his scheme to surprise her, and she had enough control of her wits to feign ignorance about his return.

Beaming, Aunt Hilda looked up at Martha. Her eyes danced with a gentle reprimand. "Who's here? Why, my Richard, of course."

Martha's eyes widened. "He's here? In Trinity? He's really come home?" she asked. She did not want to spoil her aunt's enthusiasm with a confession about the role she had played in summoning Aunt Hilda home. Later, she would have to confess, but not now. Judging by the level of her aunt's excitement, whatever fears Richard Seymour had harbored about being well-received had been for naught.

"He's here. Back in his very own house. Just like he promised. Now get your cape. I want you to see him for yourself, but you can't tell everyone else he's here. They're just going to have to wait till Sunday when we both show up for meeting. That'll be some surprise!"

She shook her head. "Poor man's as thin as a sapling. While I'm waiting for you, I'll just wrap up a few goodies. I did manage to get a good stew to pot, though. We've just been so busy. Talking and . . . and such, I haven't had a moment to bake a thing."

Martha gazed down at the elderly woman. Her cheeks were stained pink, but not from the cold. She was blushing! "And such," Martha repeated.

Aunt Hilda gave Martha's shoulder a playful swipe. "We're old, but we're not so old we've forgotten how to . . . to . . . ," she sputtered and mumbled something under her breath. "Go get your cape. If you think Victoria could keep a secret, you could bring her along. We'll have a double re-union."

Rather than tell her that Victoria was up-stairs with Nancy, which meant Martha would have to explain the entire situation, she decided nothing should dampen Aunt Hilda's joy. "I think we should surprise Victoria on Sunday, too," she suggested.

"Then get your cape!" her aunt-by-affection repeated.

Chuckling, Martha did as she was told. Sunday's meeting was going to be one the town would never forget. First Victoria. Now Richard Seymour. Prodigal daughter and prodigal son. The folks here would have quite a bit to say about their both coming home to Trinity. Perhaps enough to overshadow another homecoming of sorts, especially if Russell Clifford had come home to his faith and planned to attend meeting, hoping to garner the congregation's support. That possibility merely strengthened Martha's resolve to see that did not happen.

Not until Martha was able to fully make up her mind about whether to support Russell in his attempt to reconcile with his wife or to support Nancy and convince her she might lose her life if she returned home with her husband.

Martha would find her decision only through prayer. With patience and with faith, and with an answer that would sit comfortably with her conscience.

She grabbed her cape, then proceeded up the stairs to tell Victoria and Fern about visiting with Aunt Hilda. Each step Martha took only made her more determined. If Russell Clifford thought he could rush her into making a hasty decision, he would quickly learn that when confronted with choosing between her duty to God and her patient and her duty to acquiesce to any man's authority, Martha Cade was one woman he could not bully or intimidate, even if he did have every single official in town on his side.

And she would not be alone.

The image of Fern and Ivy standing on either side of Martha, each with their weapons at the ready, was very real. Real enough for her to decide to keep Russell's startling confession and Reverend Welsh's intervention to herself, at least until she had time to think of how she would tell the sisters that their fears had come to fruition. Russell Clifford was staying with the minister and his wife, far closer to Nancy than anyone had imagined.

Chapter 18

Joy and happiness had virtually transformed Aunt Hilda's cottage from a shrine devoted to the past into a living, breathing home again.

A fire blazed in the sitting room that for years had sat cold and abandoned. Delicate lace doilies, long relegated to a trunk, once again decorated the faded upholstery on three chairs in the center of the room. The stew bubbling in the kitchen added tantalizing aromas, but they were not quite strong enough to keep Martha from detecting the subtle scent of lavender when Aunt Hilda came close and took Martha's cape.

"I'll just hang this up with mine and tell Richard you're here. Have a seat. I'll be right back."

Martha had scarcely sat down when Aunt Hilda accompanied her long-gone husband, hand in hand, into the room. If Aunt Hilda glowed any brighter, Martha suspected the woman's face might burst into flames.

"Here she is, Richard. You probably don't recognize Martha," Aunt Hilda gushed. "She was so young when you left, but you should remember her mother, Rena Fleming. She favors her, don't you think?"

He winked at Martha. "I most certainly do. Fact is, I already told her so myself."

Aunt Hilda looked up at her husband, then at Martha. The confusion in her gaze quickly gave way to understanding. "You knew! That's why you got young Lucy to replace me. It wasn't Victoria you brought me back to see at all!"

Martha looked to Richard for help. "Well, I —"

"And you!" Aunt Hilda elbowed her husband's stomach playfully. "You didn't tell me you'd seen Martha! Of all the things you had to tell me, how could you forget —"

He grinned and silenced her protests by smooching her lips. Eyes twinkling, he finally set her back before she swooned from lack of air. "Forgiven?" he asked.

She blushed and swatted his arm. "Forgiven." She turned to face Martha and shook her finger at her feigning disappointment, which did not match the merriment in her eyes. "As for you, young lady . . ."

Martha surrendered by raising both hands. "I apologize. I had only come to check on the cottage and to get some honey wine when I accidentally discovered he was here waiting for you to come home. He made me promise I wouldn't spoil his surprise."

"That's exactly what happened," he admitted. "Now that that's settled, suppose we all have a seat. I'm still tuckered out. . . . Long journey," he explained.

"Thirty years long, but I'm not complaining. Not one bit. Especially now that I know. . . . Well, you tell it, dear. It's your tale, not mine," his wife suggested before they all sat down together.

The couple, Martha noted, still held hands.

Richard Seymour toyed with his wife's fingers and rubbed the back of her hand with the pad of his thumb. "Before I do, there's something I should say to you, girl. Hilda tells me you've been very good to her all these years, as good as our Charity would have been if she had lived past girlhood. I thank you for that."

Martha swallowed the lump in her throat. "Aunt Hilda is easy to love."

He smiled and pressed a kiss to the back of his wife's hand. Aunt Hilda's blush deepened, and Martha began to fear the stain might become permanent.

He sobered and let go of his wife's hand to rub his left arm a bit before entwining his fingers with hers again. He met Martha's gaze and held it. "I want you to know that I expect folks will be mighty surprised come Sunday when I show up at meeting."

When Martha opened her mouth to agree, he raised his other hand. "Let me speak."

She nodded.

"I've made my peace with my Shepherd and He led me back home. Now that I've made my peace with Hilda and she's forgiven me for what kept me from her side for so long, the only one who deserves to know the truth is you. Since that's what Hilda wants, that's what she'll get. Everyone else can wag their tongues till they fall off, but they don't have a right to know nothin'. I can't change what happened, but I won't have this good woman sufferin' from gossip for a single moment for somethin' she didn't do herself."

Moved by his honesty and devotion to Aunt Hilda and touched by his willingness to share an obviously painful tale with her and trust her to keep their confidence, Martha blinked back tears. She was curious beyond measure, and even though she would have no trouble keeping the secret he was about to reveal, she loved and respected Aunt Hilda too much to question her decision to welcome this man back into her life.

She leaned forward and gazed at them both. "I'm so happy you're finally home. Wherever you've been and whatever you've done all these years concern only the two of you and have no bearing on my thoughts. Just seeing you together, seeing how happy Aunt Hilda is, well, that's good enough for me."

His eyes widened. He cocked his head and tugged on his beard. "You're sure?"

She smiled. "As sure as I've ever been."

Aunt Hilda tugged on her husband's hand. "I told you she was special," she murmured. "Just wait till you meet Victoria on Sunday. She's mighty special, too."

Before Martha could say a word, Aunt Hilda rose and nodded toward the kitchen. "I have to check that stew. While I'm gone, you can tell him all about Victoria and where she's been and what she's got planned for herself now that she's home."

Martha barely got to describe what Victoria looked like when Aunt Hilda returned. "Stew's fine. Just needed a little more salt. Go ahead. I don't mind hearing again about how that girl of yours landed after she ran off."

Martha held nothing back. She detailed Victoria's adventure exactly as she had told Aunt Hilda yesterday, as well as her daughter's plans for the immediate future. When she concluded, Aunt Hilda smiled. "You've learned some hard lessons along the way, but you're still amazing. I'm proud of you. I know I already told you that, but I am. I'm proud of Victoria, too. She's proven what I knew all along," she suggested.

Martha cocked her head.

Aunt Hilda chuckled. "After all is said and done, Victoria truly *is* her mother's daughter, isn't she?" When Martha could not find her voice to protest, Aunt Hilda scowled at her. "Don't look at me like you're all confused. Just think about it. You'll see it for yourself. I don't suppose you'd like to stay to supper?"

"No," Martha said absently. "I promised Victoria I'd be home for supper." With her aunt's words still begging for an explanation, Martha made her way home, wondering if this time Aunt Hilda had not gone too far.

Martha could not imagine a mother and daughter who were more different than she and Victoria were. Or had Martha yet more lessons to learn about her daughter as well as herself?

More joy awaited Martha at the confectionery.

Supper was just about to begin, and they had saved a place for her at the table. No easy task, not with June Morgan, Dr. McMillan, and Thomas there, too. With Nancy resting upstairs, Victoria had come down. Fern and Ivy had even stored away their weapons.

Supper was delicious and the desserts too-tempting, as usual. Conversation had been interrupted by laughter more than a few times. Whether by chance or choice, the topic of Russell Clifford and his wife had never surfaced. The mood around the table was as festive and gay as any Martha could recall, and she accepted this supper as a blessing indeed.

While Fern and Ivy took June on a tour of the shop, with Dr. McMillan tagging along to snag a few goodies for himself, and Victoria upstairs to see if Nancy was awake and willing to try a little supper, Martha and Thomas had a moment alone. "How long will you be staying before you leave?" she asked.

"I'm set to leave sometime tomorrow afternoon. I spoke to the sheriff and Reverend Welsh. They seem to have everything under control. Actually, I have to admit I was as surprised by Russell Clifford's admission as I was relieved you won't have to get involved. The issue is pretty much settled, from what I've been told."

Rather than protest and admit her continued interest in the situation or attempt a well-intentioned lie, which he would sense immediately, she dropped her gaze and toyed with the frayed hem on the tablecloth.

"I'm not sure what's so fascinating about the tablecloth. Would you care to enlighten me?"

When she ignored him, he sighed and tilted up her chin. "Tell me you're not getting involved. No, don't bother. You *are* getting involved. I can see it in your eyes."

She huffed and moved her chin far enough away that he was forced to drop his hand. Thomas had known her intentions simply by looking at her, and she bristled. "Of course I'm involved. Nancy is my patient. Are you suggesting she'd be better tended by . . . by Dr. McMillan?"

"That's not what I meant, and you know it!"

She met his gaze and held it. "Exactly what did you mean? That I should simply patch her up and send her back to that man and simply accept his promise he'll never beat her again? Or bow to Sheriff Myer, who hasn't yet ever held a man accountable on charges like this when I suspect he should have? Or maybe you think I should have the same faith as Reverend Welsh and just trust Russell Clifford to follow the Word and act like a responsible husband instead of a brute. Do I look that naive? Doesn't my experience count for anything? Do you honestly think I would endanger any of my patients, just to keep the town officials happy? I thought you knew me. I thought you were different from how you were twenty-five years ago. Kinder. More supportive."

He flinched. "I didn't mean to be unkind or to imply that I'm questioning your judgment. I'm concerned about you, that's all. I know you'll do what's right."

Indeed, he had changed. She barely caught a grin before it escaped, as her heart well-knew. Now if she could only get him to agree to stay for just a few more days. . . .

Chapter 19

The shift from joy to concern took Martha only as long as it took her to carry Nancy's supper tray upstairs and convince Victoria that she needed some time away from her nursing duties.

She found Nancy sitting up in bed. The snow-cold towels had done their job and greatly reduced the swelling in the young woman's face, but only time would gently fade, then erase the bruises. "You must be feeling better," Martha suggested as she set the tray on top of a chest of drawers. "You're hungry, I hope."

Nancy's eyes lit up, adding a sparkle to the center of the dark hues that blackened her face. In the next heartbeat, she lifted her hand and gingerly touched her lips. The sparkle disappeared.

"I know it won't be easy for you, but you need some nourishment. We'll just take our time about it."

Nancy's gaze never left Martha as she pulled the chair a little closer to the bed and covered Nancy's chest with a large towel. She smiled. "I expect we'll spill a good bit, but don't you worry about making a mess," she said and returned the lopsided smile she got with a tender one.

Martha settled the tray on her lap. "Everything is cool to the touch so you won't burn your mouth. I'll help you, if that's all right."

A relieved glance. A quick nod.

"We'll start with some of Miss Ivy's chicken broth." She offered a spoonful to Nancy, being careful to avoid touching her swollen lips. Most trickled out of the corner of Nancy's mouth. Martha chuckled. "Half in. Half out. That's pretty good!"

For the next half hour, Martha worked patiently, offering spoonfuls of nourishment and even bigger doses of encouragement. When the bowl of broth and the small cup of custard she had thinned with milk was empty, she wiped Nancy's chin, removed the towel, and set the tray on the floor. "You did very well. It'll get easier, I promise."

Nancy's eyes welled with tears, and she gripped Martha's hand. "Th-thank you."

The girl's words were slurred, since she had to talk as best she could without moving her lips, but Martha had nursed enough patients to be able to understand her perfectly. "You're very welcome."

Nancy glanced at the door. "-ussell?"

Martha took a deep breath and prayed for wisdom. "Russell came to see you today. He's staying in town with Reverend and Mrs. Welsh."

A raised brow. Beneath, a flicker of fear flashed through dark brown eyes glistening with fresh tears.

"I told him you were still recuperating. If you want, we can send for him in a few days when you're feeling stronger."

Nancy closed her eyes for a moment. Her breathing became quick and shallow. She trembled.

Martha squeezed the girl's hand. "You don't have to see him at all. He's told me what really happened. You don't have to be afraid. He can't hurt you here."

Nancy's eyes snapped open. Tears coursed down her cheeks. She stared at Martha, shook her head, and tugged on Martha's hand. "He'll come. He'll hit me. Again."

"No. He won't ever hit you again. Not here. Not anywhere," Martha assured her.

Nancy pulled her hand free and curled into a ball. She sobbed so deeply, Martha thought her heart would break. Clearly, the girl was frightened, but was she frightened enough to want to leave her husband forever? Or would she vacillate and change her mind the moment her injuries had healed? How much influence would Reverend Welsh have in the matter? More important, could Russell truly change or was his brutish behavior too ingrained?

Martha had no answers to her questions, but she did take comfort in knowing that her decision to keep Russell from seeing his wife had been a good one. Until Nancy recovered fully and could make a clear and rational choice, Martha had every intention of making this sickroom off-limits to anyone other than herself, Victoria, and the two women who had given this young woman a safe haven.

Martha got out of her chair, sat down on the bed, and urged Nancy into her arms. "We'll find a way through this. Together," she promised. She caressed the girl's head and crooned words of encouragement until Nancy fell asleep.

Gently, Martha laid Nancy back on her pillow, dampened some clean cloths, and sponged the girl's face to remove the tearstains and the fresh blood that was still oozing from her bottom lip. Martha looked down at her bodice and sighed. There was nothing to be done now for the bloodstains; instead, she sat back down in her chair, watching. Waiting. Ready to offer comfort as soon as Nancy awoke, even as her mind replayed all that had just occurred.

If Nancy was able to admit being afraid of her husband, Martha counted that as an important first step toward resolving the question of Nancy's future. Martha was not quite sure how to proceed, but she certainly knew two women who could offer practical advice, assuming they would put their weapons aside long enough to talk.

When Victoria slipped back into the sickroom a few hours later, Martha put a finger to her lips and rose from her seat. Exhaustion had added a few years to her daughter's youthful face. "I thought I told you to rest yourself tonight," she admonished in a whisper. "You can sit with Nancy tomorrow."

Victoria knitted her brows together. "Then who is going to sit with her during the night?" she asked, keeping her voice soft.

Martha feigned a hurt look. "I hope you aren't suggesting I'm too old for the task!"

Victoria chuckled. "I know better. I'd just like to be with Nancy tonight. I can sleep in the chair. Otherwise I'll be afraid I won't hear her if she wakes up and needs something."

Martha studied her daughter's earnest expression. Although Victoria was a caring, sensitive girl, she had always been uncomfortable helping Martha with her duties, whether the patient was a woman who was ill or about to give birth. Perhaps witnessing others suffering was simply too much for her, and Martha did not want to force Victoria to remain for fear her daughter might become too distressed. "You don't have to stay. I know how hard it is for you."

Victoria chewed on her lower lip. "I know, but . . . but I really want to stay." She looked at Nancy and sighed. "Did you know she only just turned nineteen? We're almost the same age."

Taken aback, Martha skewed her gaze. "Are you sure?"

"She told me today."

Martha sensed her daughter had made a personal connection to this patient. Perhaps because they were so close in age, Nancy would be more open with her, rather than Martha. "Her husband told me they were from somewhere in New Jersey and that she missed her family. Did she mention any family to you?"

Victoria snorted. "Such as it is. Nancy told me she lost her parents years ago. She lived with a relative, an uncle or cousin, I'm not sure which." She blushed. "It's a little hard to understand her, and I didn't want to keep asking her to repeat herself."

Martha nodded.

"Anyway, she said this relative was very good to her, at first. Then he got sick. The sicker he got, the nastier he became." She shook her head. "She said it was her fault. Why would she say that?"

Mindful of the similarity between Nancy's relationship with her husband and her relative, Martha shrugged her shoulders. "I'm not sure," she murmured, certain now that sending Nancy back to her relative was not a good option.

"Well, it couldn't have been her fault," Victoria argued, clearly mystified by Nancy's attitude. "She was teaching school when she met Mr. Clifford. She thought her life would get better when they married. But it didn't, did it?"

Martha briefly embraced her daughter. "No, sweetheart, it surely doesn't appear so."

Victoria sniffled. "You told us he came to see her today, but you wouldn't let him.

Not until Sunday. What will happen then? Miss Fern and Miss Ivy said they won't let him —"

"If Nancy wants to see her husband, we shouldn't stop her," Martha cautioned. "Right now, though, she seems very afraid of him."

"He can't force you to let him see her, can he?"

Reluctant to let Victoria know how worried Martha was about just such a possibility, she chuckled. "With Miss Fern and Miss Ivy on guard duty?"

Victoria grinned and leaned toward Martha to whisper in her ear. "They look rather silly carrying that poker and rolling pin around with them all day."

"Never underestimate the power of a determined woman or a pair of them," Martha teased. "Which reminds me. Is there anything special you want to do before leaving on Monday? I'm sure Miss Fern or Miss Ivy wouldn't mind staying with Nancy for a few hours. I have a few errands to take care of tomorrow morning, but after that. . . ."

Victoria's face lit up. "Can we go back to see Father's farm? I haven't been there for so long."

Martha cupped her daughter's cheek.

She was not surprised. The farm was the only home of their own they had ever known as a family. "Neither have I. We can leave right after dinner and be home before dark. We could even ride double, like we used to do when you were little. I'll get Miss Fern to pack some sweets. We'll have a picnic," she suggested, remembering Thomas's invitation only days ago.

Victoria giggled. "A picnic, Mother? With only sweets to eat? And it's winter. There's snow on the ground!"

"I have just the place in mind. If you think hard enough, you'll know right where I mean and since we have plans now, you'll really need your rest tonight. Are you sure you won't let me stay with Nancy?"

Victoria marched her mother to the door. "Stay here," she ordered. She retrieved the supper tray, handed it to Martha, and turned her around to face the door. "Good night, Mother."

Martha looked over her shoulder, back at Victoria. "Are you sure?"

Victoria kissed her mother's cheek. "If Nancy needs you during the night, I'll get you. Don't worry. I'll be fine."

Martha's throat constricted. "Yes, I believe you will, sweet girl. I believe you will."

As Martha made her way back downstairs, she could not help but wonder at the difference in her daughter. She was much more self-assured and confident than before she ran away, and she certainly seemed much more comfortable in the sickroom.

When Martha reached the kitchen, so many lamps were lit, the room was as bright as midday, even though it was well past seven at night. She found Ivy, poker and all, at the worktable where clothing lay sorted into piles sitting on either side of an open sewing basket.

Ivy lay down a petticoat she had apparently been mending. "How's our patient?"

"Better." Martha set the supper tray down near the sink. "Where's Fern?"

"Upstairs. In bed."

"Already?"

Ivy picked up the petticoat and started restitching the hem. "I'm staying up until one, then Fern will keep watch."

Martha sat down across from Ivy, took a pair of lady's drawers, and inspected them. She found a split seam along the side. "You really don't have to worry about anything happening."

Ivy pursed her lips. "He's right here in town. That should make you worry, too."

Ivy did not have to use Russell's name for Martha to know exactly who she was referring to. "He promised to wait until Sunday."

Ivy cocked a brow. "And you believed him?"

Martha tossed the drawers aside. "He promised in front of Reverend Welsh. Of course I believe him."

Ivy's gaze softened. "That's your first mistake," she murmured. "The next one may cost Nancy Clifford her life."

Both hurt and confused, Martha felt the blood drain from her face. "Mistake? How can you say that? You don't know Russell Clifford. How can you be so sure he won't keep his promise?"

"Because I made the same mistake! I believed Bartholomew Pennington when he promised never to hurt my sister again. I know it's hard to believe, but men like Fern's husband and Russell are almost too easy to love."

Martha nearly dropped her sewing. "Easy to love?"

"Too easy. After an episode, they're utterly devoted. Charming. And so remorseful, they make women fall in love with them all over again. Then one day, without warning, they strike again. Just like Russell did to Nancy. Just like Bartholomew did to Fern. The last time, he nearly killed her."

She paused to blink back tears. "And he would have killed her if I hadn't been there to stop him."

Martha moistened her lips. "You must have been very frightened."

Ivy sighed and leaned against the back of her chair. "I was petrified, but I was also outraged. I vowed Fern would never spend another night in that house. Ever."

"Fern told me you both ran away that night."

Ivy looked off into the distance, as if she could see the past unfold. "Yes, I know. She told me you'd talked, but I'm quite sure she didn't tell you that days later, after she started healing, she begged me to take her home again."

"Back home? Why on earth would she have wanted to go back to her husband?"

Ivy leaned forward and placed both elbows on the table. "Because she was afraid."

On the verge of total frustration, Martha threw up her hands. "Afraid? You're talking in riddles! If she was so afraid of her husband, she wouldn't have wanted to go back. She'd have wanted to run away. Which she did."

Ivy picked up the poker and wrapped her fingers around it. "She was afraid of him, but she was more afraid of being without him. She would have gone back to him, too, but I wouldn't let her. We'd been through it too many times before. It was only a matter of time before he finally killed her. I just couldn't stand by and let that happen."

Martha narrowed her gaze. "How did you stop her?"

A blush stained Ivy's cheeks. "I put a whole ocean between them. I just took that sister of mine straight to England and kept her there a good two years until she could think rationally. That's where we sold most of her jewelry. Pennington may have been a brute and a fiend, but he had exquisite taste in gems."

"Fern told me you'd moved a lot, but I had no idea you'd gone overseas."

Ivy grinned. "It's the one place he never suspected we'd go. Poor Fern. She got terribly seasick when he took her to Europe and swore she'd never set foot on a ship again. The trip had been his wedding gift to her. Should have been an omen," she muttered. "Nevertheless, off we went. I'd never used laudanum before. The poor dear slept for three days. I thought I'd killed her. When she finally woke up, she got so seasick, she didn't have the strength or the wits to be too mad at me."

Martha's eyes widened. "You kidnapped her?"

"And I'd do it again. I was determined to get her head out of the clouds." She glanced overhead and sighed. "We were fortunate. We had her jewelry to sell, so we didn't have to worry about surviving, but in a way, the best gift that husband of hers ever gave her were those scars on her neck. Every time she tried to tell me how much he loved her, I'd make her look at those scars. It took time. Nearly two years and more than a few buckets of tears, but she finally came to her senses."

Martha furrowed her brow as she tried to reconcile Ivy's account with the one Fern had given. The more she thought about it, the more confused she became.

"What's wrong?" Ivy asked. "You look confused."

"Actually, I am," she admitted. "By your account, Fern was reluctant to leave her husband, but she spoke as if she had been anxious to escape him."

Ivy smiled. "Fern wasn't reluctant to leave her husband that last night. She was reluctant to leave him permanently. It took time for her to realize there was nothing she could do to change him. Once she accepted the fact that he would always find fault with her, no matter how hard she tried to please him, and that he would ultimately express his displeasure with physical violence, that's when she knew she could never go back."

She paused to take a deep breath. "Nancy's arrival here, I'm afraid, brought back a lot of bad memories for Fern. The old fears and anger never really go away. They just stay tucked asleep until something rouses them. It'll happen like that for Nancy, too."

"I suppose," Martha murmured. She threaded a needle and started mending the drawers, and they worked together in companionable silence. She believed Fern and Ivy were sincere in their concern for Nancy. Martha could even acknowledge that their experience, even if their accounts were not identical, made them far more competent on this issue than Martha was. She just had never been confronted with a husband who had brutalized his wife so badly.

Until Nancy actually declared her intention to leave her husband, or Russell proved he was incorrigible, Martha was hesitant to intervene and reserved final judgment about her course of action. For now, Nancy was safe here while Reverend Welsh had watch over Russell. Over the next few days, Martha had others, namely Will and Samuel, who needed her immediate attention. At least she felt fully competent and positive her ideas for each of them would come to fruition.

More important, she and Victoria had a special afternoon planned for tomorrow, and she prayed she might be granted that one afternoon without her other duties interfering.

After she got Ivy to turn over that bottle of laudanum.

Chapter 20

Saturday morning dawned bright, clear, and uneventful — a good omen, Martha thought as she looked forward to finding out if her tentative plans for Samuel and Will could be finalized today.

She knocked on Dr. McMillan's door. At her feet, buried beneath several heavy blankets, Bird squawked and fluttered in his cage. "Mind your manners, Bird," she scolded. "This is for your own good."

She had never managed to come up with a proper name for him, but by now, Bird seemed to fit just right and she had finally given up any attempts to rename him.

When Rosalind answered the door and saw it was Martha, her smile drooped. "I meant to come see you yesterday. About that issue we discussed."

Martha bent down and lifted up her noisy cargo. "No matter. We can talk as soon as I deliver this patient to the good doctor. Is he in?"

Wide-eyed, Rosalind stepped aside to let Martha enter. "He's out with Mrs. Morgan."

Martha strode right to his office anyway. "I'll just set him right here," she announced and put the cage smack in the middle of the doctor's desk. "He'll need fresh seeds and water every morning. I have some seeds right here." She retrieved a small canvas sack from her cape pocket and handed it to Rosalind. "If you have a crust of bread, let him have a small piece in the afternoon. He prefers pie crust, though."

While Rosalind stared, open-mouthed, Martha unwrapped the cage, refolded the blankets, and set them aside. Bird squawked a few meager protests, but quieted the moment she dropped in a few small pieces of a molasses cookie. "He loves sweets, too," she explained. Of course he loved sweets. Every pet she had ever owned had loved sweets, come to think of it, except for Leech. Technically, he was James's cat, but she liked to think the tomcat would be much nicer to people if he ate a few sweets.

Rosalind backed away from the cage. "Does Dr. McMillan know about this?"

Martha chuckled. "He didn't know I'd be bringing Bird today, but he'll remember what he's supposed to do, especially after I remind him." She pulled a note written on a piece of brown paper she had taken from the shop out of her pocket and slid it halfway under the cage. "I wrote this just in case he wasn't here. If he has any questions, he knows where to find me."

Rosalind cocked a brow. "You're sure he agreed to treat this . . . creature?"

"Has Dr. McMillan still got a few pox scars on his face?" she asked, knowing full well he did. She was just as sure he would not forget agreeing to fix Bird's wing in exchange for Martha's care when the young man suffered from an embarrassing case of chicken pox.

Rosalind nodded.

"Then he'll remember his promise. He needs to take care of this soon, or I won't be able to set Bird free in the spring. Now, let's you and I chat before I head over to see Samuel and Will," she suggested and led her friend back to the kitchen. "Did you have a chance to talk with Burton and Dr. McMillan?"

Rosalind twisted her hands in front of her. "I did. Several times. I even spoke to Reverend Welsh."

Heartened, Martha smiled. "What did you decide?"

The look of pure distress that suddenly pained Rosalind's face provided a clear hint that the answer that was forthcoming would be a great disappointment. "You don't want to adopt Will, do you?" Martha asked.

"Dr. McMillan said it didn't matter to him. He's out so much, he probably wouldn't notice the added noise and activity, but Burton felt it would be an imposition on the doctor." She paused and took a deep breath. "It's not that we don't want to do our duty and help an orphaned child, but Burton thinks . . . he thinks we're just too old to start over with a young boy so set in his ways, especially since we don't even have our own home."

"What did you think?" Martha asked. She had no intention of trying to change the Andrews's decision, if only because Will deserved a mother and father who truly wanted him. Martha sensed, however, that her friend was disappointed, too, and needed someone to listen.

Rosalind tilted her chin. "I think it's probably wise if you try to find him a different home. With a younger couple. It's going to take a firm hand and lots of patience to mold that boy into something decent, assuming it can be done at all."

Rosalind's words were clipped, as if she had been parroting her husband's refusal instead of talking out her own feelings. "I understand. Truly," Martha murmured. "You would have been a good mother to Will, just like you were to Charlotte."

When Rosalind caught Martha's gaze and held it, her dark eyes misted. "I think so, too, but it's . . . it's probably best for all concerned if we don't take him."

Martha embraced her friend. "Thank you for thinking it over. I'm sorry if —"

"Don't be sorry. It makes me proud to know you asked us first."

Martha gave Rosalind another hug. "As much as I'd like to stay and chat, I'd best leave. I need to check on Samuel and Will, then Victoria and I are riding out to the old farm."

They talked their way back to the front door. "I hear the Pratt's have kept the farm up nicely."

"I hope so," Martha admitted. "We'll see you at meeting?"

"We'll be there," Rosalind assured her as she opened the door. "Wait! I almost forgot!" She hurried away and returned with a large wrapped package. "It's not much. Just a few more pairs of socks and an old shirt of Burton's I cut down for the boy. Will you take it to him?"

Martha tucked the package under her

arm and stepped outside, even more certain that Rosalind would have loved to have taken Will into her home, as well as her heart. When Martha reached the end of the front walkway, she turned, gave Rosalind a final wave, and headed straight down East Main Street on her way to Samuel's cabin.

Rather than take a chance of running into anyone, which might delay her, Martha turned around, retraced her steps to enter the woods behind Dr. McMillan's house, and took a trail few even knew about. Oddly enough, someone else had already traveled on the path and packed down the snow. It was a tad slippery underfoot, but it was a lot easier than traipsing through a half foot of virgin snow.

Though disappointed in the Andrews's decision, which put a quick end to her plans for Will, Martha had no qualms anticipating Samuel's answer. He had come close enough to consider taking the position in New York the last time they spoke that Martha was fully confident he would agree. At least half of her plans for the two of them would work out. Two days from now, when June and Victoria left Trinity, Samuel would go with them. What other choice did he have?

None, she decided, although she would have to take Will home with her until she found a family for him. The closer she got to the cabin, the more convinced she was that Samuel would agree to her plans. He might be stubborn, strong-willed, and independent, but he had survived a lifetime at sea by being realistic and accepting Nature's authority over all of mankind.

When she reached the cabin, she shifted the package to her other arm and carefully knocked the signal.

No response.

She tried again, knocking heavier this time, and felt the door move. When she pressed her palm to the door and applied pressure, the door swung completely open. The moment she stepped inside, she knew she had been totally and unquestionably wrong.

There was no sign of Samuel or Will and nothing indicated they expected to return. No fire warmed the one-room cabin. No kindling or logs had even been stacked inside. Beneath the hammocks still tied in place, trunks once brimming with treasures Samuel had collected in his travels were lying open, the half-contents in visible disarray.

When she spied the note nailed to the

back of one of the chairs in front of the Franklin stove, her heart began to pound. She walked toward the chair. Her steps were unsteady, and her mind kept trying to argue against the impossible as her gaze kept scanning the room, as if miraculously, Samuel and Will would appear.

With her hand trembling, she removed the note and read it silently:

Martha,

The boy and I are together. That's what he wants. That's what I want. We're obliged for your kindness to us both. Don't worry about Will. I took some horseradish with me.

Samuel J. Meeks

She read the note again. The spelling was perfect, the grammar was flawless, but the penmanship, though bold, was shaky, as if penned by a young hand, but the message still made no sense.

Samuel and Will had run off together? Impossible. How on earth could a blind man of advanced years and a seven-year-old boy run anywhere? How far did Samuel think they could go? Where would they go?

No. There had to be another explanation. Samuel could not have taken that boy and just left. Not after the long talk she had had with the man. Samuel had admitted he could not care for the boy any longer. Mercy, the man could not take care of himself now that he was blind. He had even talked about how important it was for Will to have a real family. He had . . .

She paused as the light of truth shined on her thoughts and then she knew. Samuel must have been preparing for this very possibility for months, knowing that his blindness was inevitable. He had said everything she had wanted to hear the other day because he knew her well enough to anticipate she would insist that Will be put out to another family for adoption.

"That sly, manipulating, conniving . . . ," she snorted. At this moment, she wondered if she had really known Samuel at all, or if he had only played the role of a reclusive old seaman for her benefit, just as he had done for the townspeople. The words themselves did not come from a man barely literate, as Samuel had claimed to be, yet he must have dictated the note for Will to write down.

Assuming he had used his real name,

just who was Samuel J. Meeks? Truly?

She crumpled the note and sank into the chair, thoroughly defeated. She set her package on the floor. How had her plans come undone so completely? How could she have failed Samuel and Will so badly?

She had never felt so thoroughly incompetent. Discovering that she had forced Samuel and Will to run off only added to the frustration and uncertainty she had been experiencing these past few days with Nancy and her situation, undermined her confidence, and made her question whether she could do anything right.

Maybe Thomas had been right. Maybe it was time to withdraw from the public role she had treasured and retire to a quieter, more private life, if only to keep from making another series of blunders that could spell disaster for people who depended on her for help.

Images of Thomas and his cabin on Candle Lake brought a smile to her lips. The temptation was so sweet — just not sweet enough to eradicate the bitter taste of failure and disappointment in herself that rankled her very nature.

She squared her shoulders and stiffened her spine. She was not ready to pass her bag and birthing stool to another. Not yet.

Not until she mended the mistakes she had made with Samuel and Will and helped Nancy Clifford resolve her predicament.

Though feeling daunted, Martha rose and strode from the cabin, letting anger build just hot enough to incinerate self-doubt, and — in the ashes — letting sparks of determination rekindle her faith in herself.

She marched down the path and headed straight home to change before going to Thomas's house. Since he was not set to leave until later in the day, he would have to stay long enough to notify Sheriff Myer about Samuel and Will's disappearance. The sheriff could then raise the alarm so folks would be on the lookout for one ornery cuss of a seaman and his equally ornery young partner.

Even though Samuel and Will were not exactly town favorites, folks would be willing to help. She just knew they would. For her part, she had her plans with Victoria for this afternoon — plans Martha refused to change. Just alter. She and Victoria were heading up Reedy Creek anyway, so they could search there while the sheriff searched elsewhere.

She had talked to Samuel on Thursday, which meant he could have at least a two-day start. He and Will were probably long gone, but she could not take the risk they had somehow gotten lost and might be freezing to death in the woods.

She almost wished they would. It would serve them right for frightening her like this. She shook her head. For a day that had begun so well, things had soured pretty quickly, and she could hardly imagine how the day could get any worse.

Until she arrived back at the confectionery and found disaster waiting to greet her with open arms.

Chapter 21

Martha walked into the kitchen where the two men were so preoccupied, they didn't notice her arrival. Dr. McMillan was standing in front of Thomas, who was seated with his back to the table. She could not see either man's face, but the moment she spied the splatters of blood on Thomas's coatsleeve, she bolted into the room. "Whatever happened?" she cried.

Dr. McMillan looked over his shoulder and smiled before turning back to his work. "Just a minor accident."

"Ouch!" Thomas growled. "I thought you said you were finished! This was not minor, and it was not an accident!"

"Be still, or I'll have to start over," the doctor warned.

"Not a chance," his patient muttered.

When Martha reached Thomas's side, she saw he had both hands wrapped around the poker on his lap. He ignored her. Dr. McMillan, meanwhile, tied off and cut the last stitch of three, which created an inch-long crease that ran through the center of Thomas's right eyebrow.

The doctor eyed his handiwork and stepped back. "That should do it. Stop by the office in a few days so I can make sure it's healing well. A week after that, I should be able to remove the stitches."

"A week after that? By then I hope to be well on my way east," Thomas spat. He glared at Martha. "Unless one of your friends kills me before I can get out of town. I thought you, of all people, could have convinced them to stop acting like . . . like hysterical women!"

He brandished the poker. "Couldn't you at least have hidden this away from her? She could have killed me, and she darn near killed herself!"

"Who?" Martha asked, thoroughly befuddled. The only person she had seen with the poker lately was Ivy, but she had no reason to attack Thomas.

Thomas rolled his eyes. "Miss Ivy, of course. She swung at me so hard the second time that she lost her balance and almost fell down the staircase headfirst. She would have, too, if I hadn't caught her."

Martha was still confused. "Why on earth would she hit . . . oh, no. She didn't want to hit you, did she? She thought you were —"

289

"Russell Clifford," he snapped.

Martha narrowed her gaze. "You're twenty years older than he is, and you look nothing like him at all. How could Ivy have possibly mistaken you for Russell?"

Dr. McMillan snapped his bag shut. "It might have something to do with the fact he was sneaking up the back staircase —"

"I wasn't sneaking," Thomas argued, but his expression had turned sheepish. "I was being cautious."

The doctor grinned. "I'd love to stay to hear the rest, but I have a patient waiting for me. He's particularly fond of molasses cookies, I understand. I'll see myself out," he announced and promptly left.

Martha cocked a brow. "You were being cautious because . . ."

Thomas sighed. "I'd been to see Reverend Welsh, and he told me Russell had gone back to his farm to check on things. Naturally, I thought I'd better stop in here to make sure he hadn't decided to try to visit his wife before I left."

"Naturally," Martha repeated. "Even though you told me you didn't think Fern and Ivy had anything to worry about, that Russell would not be back before Sunday at the earliest."

His cheeks reddened. "I just . . . all

right, let's just say I haven't been completely convinced by Clifford's rather quick claim of redemption. In any case, when I got to the confectionery and entered the shop, I didn't see either of the Lynn sisters, so I called out for them. I got no answer. I checked the kitchen. It was empty. That's when I heard it."

"Heard what?"

"Loud voices. I thought maybe it was an argument. All coming from upstairs." He dropped his gaze and stared at the poker. "I thought maybe Russell had come and forced his way upstairs, but I didn't want to charge upstairs and make a fool of myself, so —"

"So you snuck up the stairs, quietly, hoping no one would hear you, knowing full well how upset Fern and Ivy have been and how they were guarding Nancy? It never occurred to you they just might think you were Russell Clifford, so maybe you should call out and identify yourself? Or just call out their names so they could recognize your voice?"

He looked up and his gaze pleaded him guilty. "I didn't want to alarm anyone, but I certainly didn't expect to find myself at the receiving end of this poker!" he complained.

"Poor Ivy," Martha murmured. "She must have felt absolutely awful when she realized she'd hit you instead of Clifford."

He winced. "It wasn't her fault. Not really. She'd seen Russell heading down West Main Street and got frightened. She thought he was headed here. Apparently, she raised the alarm upstairs, which caused the commotion I heard, and I just happened in during the middle of it." He looked up at the ceiling. "She's still crying. Can't you hear her?"

Martha nodded. "I should go see her. Maybe she'll have some chamomile tea and lie down. She should feel better in a few hours. You did apologize for scaring her, didn't you?"

"Twice. But I don't think she heard me. She was wailing pretty loud."

When Martha rose to leave, Thomas handed her the poker. "See if you can't find a safe place for this, and try to get the ladies to relax. Nothing is going to happen to Nancy while she's here, and the sooner they believe that, the safer we're all going to be."

She took the poker and let out a sigh. "I will. I've been meaning to get that bottle of laudanum, too, but I doubt I can confiscate Fern's rolling pin. She uses it every morning."

"Fair enough," he murmured.

When he stood to leave, she suddenly remembered what had sent her rushing home. Quickly, she explained what had happened with Samuel and Will. Minutes later, Thomas was on his way to Sheriff Myer's, and Martha had set a kettle of water on the cookstove to boil.

She headed up the stairs. "It's only me. Martha," she cried as she neared the landing. Just in case. The way this day was headed, she wished she could go back to bed and start over. Almost. She had the sinking feeling it probably would not make a difference. She would just have to deal with the same troubles all over again.

Less than an hour later, Martha escaped from the confectionery with Victoria and left town with utter disaster still behind her.

Miss Ivy had been inconsolable. Nancy had been anguished by the whole event, and Miss Fern had closed the shop early to remain upstairs. June Morgan was the only rational soul in the bunch, and she had promised to stay with them all until Martha and Victoria returned.

Victoria rode behind her mother on Grace, with a basket of cookies strapped in front. They had stopped at half a dozen homesteads already and searched for miles along the western shores of Reedy Creek for Samuel and Will, all in vain.

After an hour in the peaceful quiet Martha remembered only too well from her days as a farmer's wife, she could almost feel the tension of the day slipping away. As they neared the property where Martha had lived all of her married life, Victoria leaned closer. "I'm getting excited. Are you?"

"I am. The day your father came to see your great-grandfather Poore to ask to court me, we came out here. All four of us."

"You did? Why?"

Martha chuckled. "Your father insisted on showing me and my grandparents that he intended to take good care of me, so out we came. I had only broken my betrothal to Thomas some months before, and I think your father was worried whether the house he'd built would be grand enough to suit me."

"I guess he was wrong," Victoria commented.

Fond memories rushed to be embraced. "Oh, indeed," Martha whispered. "We were married as soon as the banns could be announced, and I went to housekeeping the same day your father gave me his name."

Victoria tightened her arms around Martha's waist and laid her head against her mother's back. "Did you ever regret marrying Father instead of Mayor Dillon?"

Martha shifted the reins to her left hand so she could take her daughter's hand. "Not for a single moment. Besides, if I hadn't married your father, you and Oliver wouldn't be here."

"True. But . . . but what made you decide Father was the one you wanted to marry? Why not Mayor Dillon? He's old now, but he was probably passably handsome years ago."

Martha huffed. "Very much so. But I thought your father was very handsome, too."

"Mayor Dillon was well-educated. Probably the wealthiest man for miles."

"He wasn't the mayor then, but the rest is true."

"Then why didn't you marry him?" Victoria asked.

Martha was unaccustomed to having such an intimate discussion with her daughter, but sensed the girl was not so much searching for answers for curiosity's sake, but for guidance. Now that Victoria was on the verge of womanhood, the day was fast approaching when she would have to choose her future husband.

Perhaps the Clifford fiasco had prompted Victoria to be worried about making a wise choice, to avoid the same mistake that Nancy had apparently made. "Thomas is a good man," Martha explained, shoving aside the memory of his more recent proposal. "He would have treated me well. To be honest, his wealth made me uneasy. We were very young, and Thomas had certain ideas about . . ."

She paused to reframe her thoughts. Some things were private and better left unsaid. "As Jacob Dillon's son, Thomas had his place in this community preordained, and there was a role his wife would be expected to play. I didn't see that as something I wanted."

"Because of your work?" Victoria prompted.

"That was part of it," Martha admitted. "I didn't devote myself fully to being a midwife until after Great-grandmother Poore died, but I always knew I would. Someday. I just didn't think Thomas would be happy if I did. As it turned out, I married your father and Thomas married, too. The best advice I can give you is to know yourself very well before you begin to consider marrying anyone. Then stay true to yourself."

Victoria nuzzled closer. "You're both alone now," she said, apparently still focused on Martha and Thomas. "Mrs. Andrews told me he's been very attentive for the past few months, 'rekindling the old spark,' I think she said."

Martha stiffened and tugged the reins so Grace would turn down a narrow roadway to her right. Thomas's recent proposal echoed in her mind again, but she was unprepared and unwilling to discuss the matter with anyone right now, especially her daughter. "Rosalind Andrews should know better than to spread gossip," Martha quipped. "Now . . . look around and see if you can tell me where we are."

Victoria sat up. Martha brought Grace to a halt and looked around herself. A narrow band of snow-freckled pine trees lined either side of the road and filled the cold air with a heady scent. Snow blanketed the earth, obliterating any sign of the trail Victoria and Martha were hoping to find.

"There! Over there!" Victoria cried. She scrambled down from the horse and trudged to the left. When she reached a blue spruce tree with a double trunk, she stopped and waved to Martha, then pointed to the ground. "The trail starts here!"

Martha dismounted and led Grace, trailing the reins behind her. "You're sure?"

"Positive. I remember the tree. Oliver used to tie my boot laces to each trunk, then run away and leave me there to try to undo the knots."

Martha scowled. "I never knew he did that!"

"I got even. I —"

"I don't want to hear this," Martha protested. She tethered Grace to the tree, patted her neck, and removed the basket of cookies. "We'll be right back. Don't get into any trouble."

Martha followed Victoria through the woods, grateful both she and Victoria had worn heavy boots. Gradually, the forest thinned, but Victoria never faltered and made her way unerringly. When they reached a break in the trees, Martha spread out the blanket well back from the edge of a low cliff. She and Victoria sat down, with the basket of cookies in front of them, and surveyed the farm below, snuggled on the banks of Reedy Creek.

Ribbons of smoke from the chimney decorated a gray winter sky above a white clapboard farmhouse. Now barren, a wide, front porch that extended around to the side of the house waited for summer and pitchers of mint tea and rocking chairs. A few yards in front of the steps, a snowman sported a bright yellow scarf.

Memories wrapped around Martha's heart. She handed Victoria a sugar cookie. "The Pratts added the porch some years back. Your father always talked about doing that." She nibbled on her own cookie and pointed to several outbuildings. "He built that barn all by himself. The smokehouse, too. It looks like they've added an icehouse. See how it's built into the side of that low hill?"

Victoria nodded. "The house looks different with the porch," she whispered.

"It's natural for things to change. Even the land changes over time. So do people. They come into our lives and sometimes, sadly, they leave far too soon. But our memories — of our loved ones and our lives together — are ours to keep. Sometimes they fade a bit and we lose little details, or we might even forget whole incidents. Until something prompts us to remember. But the goodness, the warmth, the love our memories contain — that's what will always stay in our hearts so we can carry our memories wherever we go. And there's always room to add more," she whispered.

Victoria stared at their old home for several more moments, then bowed her head. When she finally spoke, her voice was low and soft. "I need to apologize for all the hurtful things I said that first night I was home. I know it was hard for you to leave here and take us to live with Uncle James."

"Come here." Martha urged her daughter into an embrace. "We can't let the past shadow any of the days we have together or fill our hearts with bitterness about what might have been or sharpen our tongues. I love you, girl. And I know you love me, too."

They held one another for endless moments, letting a full reconciliation heal old wounds.

When Martha finally looked overhead, she set Victoria back. "I don't like the looks of that sky. There's more snow coming. We should get home. We've got enough word spread about Samuel and Will, and I have an idea they didn't head this way anyway," she murmured as she suddenly remembered that snow-packed path that led to Samuel's cabin. Knowing of Will's fascination with the sea and Samuel's former life as a seaman, she thought it more likely they had gone to Clarion, a small port on the Faded River.

"Maybe we'll find them both in town when we get there," Victoria suggested.

Martha did not bother contemplating that wishful thought. Not on a day like today when everything had gone wrong.

They retraced their steps, mounted Grace again, and rode back to the main road. Grace wound up with several molasses cookies, much to Victoria's delight, and Martha urged Grace into a quicker pace as the clouds thickened overhead.

Fortunately, Grace was heavy and strong enough to handle most anything winter could produce. In the distance, Martha spied a rider heading their way. Once they drew closer to one another, Martha recognized the rider as Alexander Stern.

The harried expression on his face told her she would not be going directly home, and she feared she might be headed into yet another failure for the day.

Chapter 22

Alexander Stern was a large-boned man with muscles brawny from a life of farming. As he drew up next to Martha and Victoria, she saw her bag and birthing stool strapped behind him. "Widow Cade! I went to town to fetch you for Lena. Miss Fern said you'd come up this way. She said to take your bag and stool with me to save time." He nodded to Victoria. "Good to see you back home."

"Lena's a good month away from her time. Are you sure you need me?" Martha asked, although the women attending Lena would not have sent for her unless they were certain the pains were not going to stop, as they often did with this much time left before the actual delivery was expected.

He laughed. "Early or not, Lena's set her mind on havin' this one on her mother's birthday. Since that's today, looks like she's gonna get her way. Miss Dorie said to tell you to hurry, though. This one's comin' faster than the last."

Mention of Dorie Fisk's name gave

added credence to his request. As well, slightly more than a year ago, Lena had given birth to her fifth child with a mere three hours separating the first from the last pain. Martha's heart began to pound. "Mercy! Faster? How long ago did her pains start?"

He grinned. "By now? 'Bout two hours. Give or take."

Martha turned at the waist to speak to her daughter. "I'm sorry. There's no time to take you home first."

"It's all right. Hurry. We don't want to be too late."

"I'll follow you," Martha told him.

As they started off together, he hunched his shoulders against the wind. "I saw Sheriff Myer on my way out of town. He said to tell you not to bother about searching up here for that old recluse and the boy."

Martha leaned back and stared at him. "Not bother? Why?"

"Apparently, Stan Pitt, down at the mill? He saw the pair of them buildin' some sorta sailin' raft in the pond behind the mill for the past coupla weeks."

"A sailing raft?" Martha snorted. "Every stream and creek for miles is frozen solid. They can't sail a raft on ice."

Stern cocked his head. "Pitt claimed it wasn't like any raft he'd ever seen. It was flat with small logs lashed together like you'd expect, but he swore he saw wooden runners underneath, like you'd see on a sleigh."

Martha was tempted to roll her eyes, but resisted. "You're telling me the two of them made a sailing sleigh? I never heard of such a thing."

He shrugged his shoulders. "Guess that's about what you'd call it. Pitt said whatever it was, he noticed it was gone a few days back."

She sighed. If her instinct was right, Samuel and Will had been testing the sailing sleigh last Thursday when something went wrong and they wound up taking a dunk in the pond. When she showed up unexpectedly, Will had concocted the ice-fishing tale to cover up what they'd really been doing, an easy task for the former street orphan from New York City who was quite talented at deception.

In all likelihood, the quirky vessel was now resting on the bottom of the pond.

Martha, however, suspected otherwise. If she closed her eyes, she could almost see Captain Samuel and Will, serving as first mate and Samuel's eyes, as they pushed the craft below the covered bridge before raising the mast and sailing out of town, right down Dillon's Stream. They would end up, eventually, on the Faded River, where future possibilities were only as limited as Samuel's blindness would make them. Given his amazing ability to forge an escape, Martha could only pray his luck would hold and he would find a haven for himself and Will. She prayed he would one day write and let her know they were safe and well.

In the meantime, she had a more urgent prayer to offer for Lena and prayed hard the woman's pains would stop. Although her babe was closer to being born at full term than little Peter Clifford had been, Martha knew only too well the dangers attached to an eight-month babe. More often than not, they were blue babies, unable to take in any air, and they usually died within a few days of birth.

The sad prospect of losing two babes in a row wrapped around her troubled heart. Her confidence wavered again, but sheer determination kept her riding tall in the saddle, straight to the woman who depended on Martha's skill and experience to make this a day of joy for them all.

If anyone deserved a miracle today, it

was Lena Stern and by sheer association, Martha prayed she might receive a blessing or two for herself.

Lena Stern was short by any standards, matched her husband in weight, and had an earthy sense of humor that blessed everyone she knew.

Victoria volunteered to take the five Stern children out to the barn so they could show off the litter of kittens, a rarity at this time of year. Alexander Stern, who once again declined to participate in the birthing, busied himself with stabling the horses. Neighbors Isabel Fallon and her sister, Louisa Terwell, were in the kitchen working on the food for the groaning party that would take place after the birth.

Martha stopped in the kitchen only long enough to remove her cape and gloves, wash her hands, and make sure there was water on the cookstove.

"Is that you, Martha? For mercy's sake, get in here! I feel like an overripe melon about to split wide open!" Lena cried.

Martha chuckled, in spite of her concern, and carried her bag and birthing stool into the small room behind the kitchen. Most of the time, the room was used for storage, but once a year, for six of the past eight years now, the room had been converted into a birthing room. She found Lena pacing about, with Dorie Fisk and Melanie Biehn on either side of her. Food stored in barrels and tins, along with sacks of staples, lined all four walls, leaving only a narrow walkway. In lieu of birthing sheets, a square of canvas had been set on the floor in front of a single bed at the far end of the room, which had been cleared out to make room for the birthing stool, the expectant mother, and her assistants.

Lena's face lit up the moment she saw Martha. "Hurry and set up that stool before I drop this baby girl right where I'm standing," she teased. "I thought you would have been here every few days to check on me."

"You're a good month ahead of schedule," Martha countered as she squeezed past the three women.

"Doesn't matter. Little Lavinia has her mind set on to- . . . today."

While Lena gritted through another pain, Martha positioned the stool in the center of the canvas square. "Dorie? Melanie? Let's get her seated so I can check on how things are progressing. I'd sure feel better if those pains would stop."

Lena's eyes widened. "Stop? They'd better not!"

The two women helped Lena to sit down. Dorie knelt in front, to her left. Melanie took her place standing behind Lena. Martha knelt down and eased Lena's nightdress up to her knees as another pain hit. By the time it was over, Martha had her bag open and her birthing apron tied into place.

Martha positioned her hands at the birth canal and Lena yelped. "Your hands are freezing!"

"I'm sorry. You didn't give me enough time to warm up."

Lena groaned and clasped Dorie's hand hard. "Oh . . . oh, here she comes! Get ready, Martha."

Martha immediately felt the baby's head emerge. It was too late to stop now. "Good work. Another push —"

"Now!" Lena cried and pushed the rest of the baby out.

Martha leaned back on her haunches and brought the baby out from behind the curtain of her mother's nightdress. She held her breath and laid the squalling newborn on her lap. To her amazement, the baby looked full-term. "Your baby girl is plump and pink and perfectly formed," she whispered. Both surprised and relieved, she cut the cord and wiped the baby clean with the towel. The baby could not possibly be a full month early, which meant Lena's calculations must have been off. The tragedy Martha feared had been averted, and her heart nearly sang with joy.

Lena bent forward and glanced down at her new daughter. "Darn if she doesn't look like all the rest."

Martha chuckled. "Your babes all look so much alike, folks think you must use a mold or something."

Lena winked. "Wouldn't be half as much fun if we did." She held out her arms, and Martha gave the baby to her mother. "Come to Mama, little Lavinia. There, there," she crooned.

Within moments, Lavinia was quiet, suckling at her mother's massive breast. After Martha delivered the afterbirth, her assistants helped Lena into bed. The new mother was nearly as wide as the mattress, and the babe seemed much smaller now that she was engulfed in her mother's arms.

Martha remained behind while her two assistants carried all evidence of the birth away and went to fetch Lena's husband and other children.

"We'll have to fatten you up, little one," Lena crooned, apparently oblivious to

Martha's ministrations. Once Martha had Lena's wrappings in place, she carefully re-arranged the bedclothes and propped several pillows behind Lena's back so she could sit up just a bit.

Alexander arrived and led his three sons and two daughters into the room. Each had the Stern large build, cow-brown eyes and pale blond hair. He lined them up around the bed. Isabel, Louisa, and Victoria joined them, as soon as Dorie and Melanie returned. They linked their hands together to form an unbroken human chain. Martha acknowledged Stern family tradition and let Alexander lead them all in prayer instead of doing it herself.

"Lord of all, our heavenly Father, we lift up our hearts this day to praise You and thank You for the precious gift You have given us." He took the sleeping baby from her mother's breast, supported her little body with the palm of his hand, and raised her up to the heavens. "Lavinia Faith Stern, we dedicate your life to your Creator, who has entrusted us with your care. We promise to love you and teach you to follow His Word every day we are blessed to have you. Amen," he whispered and pressed a gentle kiss to her forehead.

One by one, starting with Lena and then

Lavinia's brothers and sisters, each of them whispered "amen" to seal their vow and kissed the baby. Martha went last. "Amen," she whispered and let reverent tears fall freely. When she glanced at the others, she could see she was not alone. Tears were aplenty. No one had been left unmoved.

"Now we can really celebrate," Lena announced. "I'm celebrating with a little nap. The rest of you, go on. There's plenty of food. Children, mind your manners," she urged. She yawned, cuddled her newborn, and curled on her side.

While the others left to begin the groaning party, Martha stayed behind to pack her things. With her faith refreshed and her spirit renewed, she checked on Lena one last time, found her resting well, and returned to the kitchen.

After celebrating by devouring several pieces of fruitcake, Martha learned Louisa would be staying on as an afternurse and gave her the necessary instructions. Anxious to return home before dark, given the brewing storm, Martha dressed for the ride home and got Victoria to do the same.

With several new coins in her bag, a rare, but welcome reward, Martha tied her stool and bag in place, mounted Grace, and helped Victoria to sit astride behind her. When they got out of the barn into the twilight, Martha looked up at the ominous sky and groaned.

"Wait! Miss Victoria, wait! Papa said yes!"

Eight-year-old Tillie Stern, the oldest of the brood, ran from the house with her little hands cupped in front of her. When she got a few yards from Grace, she paused and kept a good distance between them. "Papa said you could have this one," she said proudly.

She opened her hands, and a tiny white kitten meowed pitifully.

Martha looked over her shoulder at Victoria. A guilty blush stained her cheeks. "I didn't tell her I would take one of the kittens for sure. I just said I would love to have one, if I could."

Martha chuckled. "And you expected an eight-year-old to understand the difference?"

"It's an adorable little kitten," Victoria noted.

"Adorable or not, you're leaving in two days," Martha argued.

"I don't want to hurt Tillie's feelings. I'm sure Mrs. Morgan wouldn't mind if I took the kitten along. If she does, then I'll . . . I'll think of something." Before

Martha could prick a hole in that argument, Victoria reached down. "I'd love to have the white one. Bring it a little closer, Tillie."

The little girl took a few steps and rose on tiptoe. Victoria took the kitten and promptly tucked it beneath her cape. "Thank you. I'll let you know what I name him."

Tillie giggled. "It's not a boy kitten. It's a girl. Like me!"

"Oh! Then I suppose I'll have to give her a girl's name, won't I? Hurry now. Go back inside. It's too cold for you to be outside without your coat."

After Tillie skipped her way back into the house, Victoria put one of her arms around her mother's waist. Martha clicked the reins and urged Grace to start for home. "Don't say a word, Victoria Jane. Just listen. So help me, I will not, I repeat not, take care of that kitten for you. Not once. And if Mrs. Morgan has the sense I credit her with having, she'll make sure you give that kitten back or find it another home. Make sure you keep her tucked in tight. We've got to hurry or we're going to get caught in a snowstorm."

Chapter 23

The snowstorm broke quietly at twilight. Small, delicate snowflakes began to dance gently to earth with hardly a breeze to scatter them, just as Martha and Victoria, along with a still-nameless kitten, arrived back in town.

With Grace groomed, fed, and settled back into her stall, Martha led Victoria home. As they emerged from the covered bridge, just ahead and to the right, Martha saw two familiar figures leave the confectionery shop. Instinctively, she braced to a halt and put out her hand to stop Victoria. "Let's wait a moment," she whispered, reluctant to confront the two men who might very well have been waiting for Martha to return.

Not that she lacked the will to confront either of them. She just needed a moment to garner her thoughts.

Victoria took a step closer to her mother. "What do you think Reverend Welsh and Mr. Clifford were doing at the confectionery?"

"They couldn't have been making a purchase. The shop should have closed up an hour ago. They were probably trying to see Nancy. Let's hope Miss Fern and Miss Ivy held their ground peacefully." Thankfully, Martha had been able to confiscate both the poker and the bottle of laudanum from Ivy, which left only Fern's rolling pin to worry about. Unless Ivy had rearmed herself, which was not likely. Not after the misadventure she had had with Thomas.

Martha and Victoria watched together in silence as the two men started off in the opposite direction down the planked sidewalk, which was quickly being covered with a fresh layer of snow. Thank Providence, neither man appeared to be injured, which was reassuring. They also did not appear to have taken notice of the two women, perhaps because they were too busy talking.

Martha could not hear what they were saying because they were too far away. The sharp, agitated tone of Russell's voice, however, left no doubt in her mind that his attempt to see his wife had either failed completely or had been disappointing. Whether the minister had been allowed to visit with Martha's patient was unclear.

Once the men were a good square away

and disappeared behind a misty curtain of snow, Martha nodded toward the confectionery. "I think it's safe for us to proceed," she said and started out from the cover of the bridge with her birthing stool in one hand and her bag in the other.

Victoria hesitated, then quickly caught up. "Why didn't you want them to see us?"

Martha ignored the implication that she had acted cowardly, lowered her head, and turned her face away as the wind began to gust. "I'd rather wait and talk to Miss Fern and Miss Ivy first."

Victoria slipped on an icy patch. With her hands beneath her cape holding the kitten, she had no way to regain her balance. She gasped, and the kitten began to meow frantically as they toppled to the side.

Martha caught her daughter by the shoulders, but nearly hit her with the bag in the process. "Easy does it," she cautioned.

Victoria panted. "I . . . I almost dropped her."

Martha chuckled. "You almost dropped yourself. Come along. Hold on to my elbow. We're almost there."

Together, they managed to get to the back door of the confectionery and stepped inside the storage room without either of them losing their footing. Martha had scarcely shut the door and set down her stool and bag when Ivy came charging into the room. Her heavy bosom was heaving. Her cheeks were flushed. Her eyes snapped with frustration. "Thank heavens you're home! You won't believe the afternoon we've had!"

Martha eased out of her cape and gloves, handed them to Ivy, and started helping Victoria remove her cape. "I take it Reverend Welsh and Mr. Clifford were too anxious to see Nancy to wait until after meeting tomorrow."

Ivy's eyes widened. "How did you know they'd been here?"

"We saw them leaving," Victoria responded and held up the kitten. "Isn't she sweet? Tillie Stern gave her to me. She needs a name. Maybe you can help me to think of one."

"I helped Lena deliver a fine baby girl this afternoon," Martha explained and quickly detailed the rest of the day's events.

Ivy's gaze softened. She reached out and patted the kitten's head. "She's darling. She looks just like a little loaf of sugar. With fur," she added. Oddly, her gaze took on a worried look.

"Sugar's a perfect name, isn't it?" Victoria asked as she nuzzled the kitten, apparently unaware of the change in Ivy's demeanor. "I know it's an imposition having her here, but it'll only be for a few days. I'm taking her back to New York with me."

Martha cocked a brow. "Assuming Mrs. Morgan gives her permission. Traveling that far with a kitten won't be easy."

"If not, I'll just find her a good home," Victoria countered. "Maybe you'd like to keep her," she suggested to Ivy.

The older woman shook her head. "I'd love to take her, but Fern can't be around cats. They make her sneeze like the dickens. Her eyes get all red and scratchy, too. Maybe you'd better take the kitten right up to your room and keep her there. That way, Fern won't —"

"I won't what?" Fern asked as she joined them. She took one look at the kitten, paled, and started backing straight out of the room. "Get that . . . critter out of here!"

Victoria paled. "I'm so sorry. I didn't know you couldn't tolerate cats."

Ivy put her arm around Victoria and led her past Martha and Fern. "Of course you didn't. We can't put that little thing out in this storm, so we'll just take her right up-stairs. I have an old basket we can line with something to make her a proper bed. Then I'll come down and get her some milk. You'd like that, wouldn't you, Sugar?" she crooned.

While Ivy took Victoria upstairs, Fern led Martha into the kitchen. "I thought the kitten was a bad idea all along. I feel simply awful," Martha offered. "I'm sorry. I didn't know you were sensitive to cats, either."

Fern sneezed twice. "As long as the kitten stays upstairs in your room, it shouldn't be too much of a problem. I can heat up some supper for you and Victoria, if you like."

"Thank you, but we've eaten. I'd love a hot mug of cider, though."

While Fern set the cider to heat, Martha put out two mugs and made sure the honey crock was on the table. While they worked, Martha repeated the news of the day she had already shared with Ivy. "I saw Reverend Welsh and Mr. Clifford leaving the shop," she added, hoping Fern would be able to explain.

Fern's hand trembled as she mopped her brow. "I wouldn't let that sniveling liar anywhere near that girl! Naturally, I reminded him of his promise to wait until after meeting tomorrow."

Martha exhaled slowly. "I assume you mean Russell?"

Eyes wide, Fern huffed. "I might not trust Reverend Welsh completely on this matter, but he is a man of the cloth. I'd never refer to him that way."

"I'm sorry. I didn't —"

"Never you mind." Fern waved her hand in the air, took a thick towel, wrapped it around the handle of the pot, and poured the steaming cider into the mugs. At that moment, Ivy returned, got a saucer of milk for the kitten, and went back upstairs.

Fern shook her head, as if she could not understand her sister's interest in the kitten, and put the pot back onto the cookstove. "I wound up letting Reverend Welsh see Nancy. Ivy insisted it was the only way we could get those two men to leave." She joined Martha at the table and wrapped her hands around her mug. Her gaze grew troubled. "He's got that girl so confused now, she's talking about going back to . . . to that fiend of a husband."

She snorted. " 'What the Lord has joined together, let no man separate,' " she said, mimicking Reverend Welsh. "I was so mad I wanted to scream!"

Martha cocked her head. "It sounds to me like you're still angry," she commented before adding a spoonful of honey to her cider. She took a long sip and relished the warmth that slid down the length of her body.

Fern took a sip of her cider. "I'm afraid I am. It's just so frustrating to have to stand by and watch the whole sorry scene, knowing in my heart what's going to happen, and yet I can't get anyone to listen!" She paused and shook her head. "Why can't I get anyone to listen to me? If Nancy goes back home with that man, she's going to wind up in the cemetery."

Martha put her hand on top of Fern's. "We have to make sure that doesn't happen."

Fern's eyes lit with surprise. "Then you agree with me that she can't ever go home with him?"

"I think we shouldn't rush Nancy into anything, whether it's a reconciliation or a separation. To start with, I think we have to let Russell see her tomorrow, even if meeting is canceled due to the storm."

Disappointment doused Fern's enthusiasm. "How's that going to help?"

"If you and I are both present for their reunion, which I'll insist upon, we can judge for ourselves whether Nancy truly wants to return home with him, and if he seems sincere about changing the way he treats her. You have more experience at this than I do, so I'm going to depend on your opinion a great deal. It may be that we'll have to let them go home together, if that's what Nancy insists upon doing, but we'll visit them frequently to keep him on guard. He might keep a better hold on his temper if he knows one of us is likely to stop by unexpectedly."

Fern shook her head, obviously unconvinced. "I don't care how sincere he appears to be. That man's brutalized her more than once, and he'll do it again. Even if one of us literally moved into their home, it wouldn't guarantee her safety. Ivy lived with me, but that didn't stop my husband, remember?" She paused and gently massaged the base of her neck. "I'll be there with you when he meets with her tomorrow. If he waits until then."

Martha's pulse began to race. "What do you mean? Did he say he was coming back tonight?"

"Not in so many words, but I saw that look in his eye. He'll be back tonight to try to sneak in to see her, but I'll be there when he does. If you'll excuse me, I'm going to get ready now."

Before Martha could offer any sort of response or caution her friend about not repeating the same mistake as Ivy had made when she mistook Thomas for Russell Clifford, Fern retrieved her rolling pin from the counter and headed up the stairs.

She stopped halfway up the stairs, turned, and called back to Martha. "I almost forgot. Thomas left on his trip shortly after you went out with Victoria. He dropped something off for you. It's in your room," she offered, then promptly continued on her way.

Curious, Martha cleared the table first before she followed Fern upstairs. As tempted as she was to go to her room to find out what Thomas had left for her, she knew she needed to see Nancy first. Fern was just too emotional to be objective, but with good reason, given her past. Martha had not even begun to think about how to resolve Nancy's situation, which made her feel a bit guilty.

Rather than rely on Fern's opinion about what Nancy intended to do about her marriage, Martha decided it would be better to talk to the young woman directly, especially if Martha were to have any chance of judging the impact of Reverend Welsh's visit.

She started down the hallway and went directly to Nancy's room. The chair outside her door was empty, which meant Fern either decided to stand guard inside the room or she had not finished getting ready yet. Martha knocked once, slowly opened the door, and stepped inside. Fortunately, Fern was nowhere to be seen. She found Victoria and Nancy sitting together on the bed with the kitten snuggled on Nancy's lap.

Martha chuckled. "It looks like you've met Sugar."

Nancy offered her a crooked smile. Although the bruises around her eyes and on her cheek were turning deep purple, a sure sign of healing, her eyes were clear and sparkling. "Cute, isn't she? Her name is Snowball, though."

Martha chuckled. Lucky little kitten. Scarcely half a day after leaving her mother, she had already been given two names, whereas poor Bird still had none. Martha wondered how he was faring with Dr. McMillan and made a mental note to speak to the doctor about the bird tomorrow after meeting.

Victoria grinned. "Nancy loves the kitten so much she wants to keep her! I told her yes, of course. It wouldn't be fair to expect

Snowball to sit still in a basket for the long journey to New York," she said, echoing the very argument Martha had used on the way home, an argument that Victoria had summarily dismissed at the time.

Victoria pointed to the floor near the corner of the room. "Look! Miss Ivy made up a little bed for her."

Sure enough, there was an oval basket, lined with the same yellow gingham that covered the tables in the shop below. Martha smiled. "I have a feeling she'll be one spoiled kitten, but if she stays here with Nancy, that means Miss Fern won't be able to visit. She's sensitive to cats, remember?"

Victoria frowned.

Nancy lifted a brow. She caressed the sleeping kitten. "I'm feeling so much better. Miss Fern and Miss Ivy have been very kind to let me stay here, but I was wondering if . . . if maybe I could go home soon."

Martha cast a warning glance at Victoria who rose immediately. "It's been a long day. I'll leave you two to talk," she suggested and promptly took her leave after giving Snowball a pat on her head.

Nancy lifted the kitten and held her against her chest.

Martha sat down beside her. "Are you sure you want to go home?"

The young woman's bottom lip, still split, but not quite as swollen, began to quiver. "Reverend Welsh says it's a wife's duty to be faithful to the vows she pledged before God and remain with her husband through good times as well as bad."

Martha nodded. "And according to the Word, a man must love his wife as he loves himself. It's also his duty to honor and respect his wife. I don't believe Russell has done that."

Tears welled in Nancy's eyes. "It's not all Russell's fault. It's mine, too. He . . . he wants me to forgive him and start again," she whispered. She pulled out a wrinkled piece of paper from her pocket and handed it to Martha. "Russell wrote this note to me. Reverend Welsh brought it with him today."

Martha swallowed hard. "Do you want me to read it?"

A slight nod. "I don't know what to do," Nancy whimpered. "I was so frightened at first, I thought I could never go home again. Now . . . now that I've talked with Reverend Welsh and read Russell's note, I believe I must. Miss Fern and Miss Ivy told me you help people all the time. Victoria even told me how understanding you've been, even though she ran away from home. Will you read Russell's note and help me to decide what to do?"

Martha swallowed hard. "I'll try," she murmured. She closed her eyes for a moment and silently murmured a prayer for guidance. Whatever message the note contained must have been a powerful one to have Nancy on the verge of relenting and going back home with her husband. If she encouraged Nancy to go home, Martha would have to be prepared to carry the guilt if anything happened to that young woman. On the other hand, what right did Martha have to encourage Nancy to leave her husband? Could she carry the burden of knowing she had helped to end a marriage that could have been saved?

The mantle of responsibility lay heavy on Martha's shoulders, but she opened her heart as she prayed, knowing He would help her follow the right path.

Chapter 24

Martha flattened the note from Russell Clifford and read it silently to herself:

My dearest wife,

I long to see you, if only to tell you how much I grieve for the wrong I have committed against you. Though I have sinned against God and broken my vows to you, through grace I have been forgiven. Now I am begging for your forgiveness and remind you of your vow to be a dutiful wife.

If at first you think you can never forgive me, I ask you this question. How many times must we forgive others? According to the Word, seven times seventy.

As soon as you are able to travel, I want to take you home where you will once again take your rightful place as my wife. When you are completely well, we will to go meeting and stand before the congregation to pledge ourselves to one another and to His Word.

Your faithful husband,
Russell

Martha carefully folded the note and shook her head. As much as he seemed to want to reconcile with his wife, Russell Clifford also seemed a tad too arrogant to suit her. "Seven times seventy," she murmured. "The message in the Bible is clear, isn't it? We must forgive others for the wrongs they have done against us, even when it's terribly hard to do so."

Nancy nodded.

Martha let out a sigh. "I'm just a little uncomfortable accepting that the message in that verse is that simple. Just forgive. Always," Martha admitted. "That's my grandmother's fault, I'm afraid. She and my grandfather raised me after my parents died," she explained. "She was Trinity's first midwife, and she was as good a Christian woman as God ever made. She loved and treasured the Word, and she told me over and over again that God expected us to listen to His Word, to believe it with all our hearts, and to act like it."

Confusion clouded Nancy's expression. "If that's true, then I must forgive Russell, go home, and simply pray he won't hurt me again."

"That's only one action. Actually, there are many ways to act and still follow the Word." She smiled. "I remember the first time Grandmother talked to me about that. I'd just had another spat with one of the girls at Sunday school. She was a good four years older than I was. Her name was Ellen something. I don't remember, but they moved away some years back so it really doesn't matter."

"Anyway," she continued, "Ellen was a bully of the first order, and she decided I was her favorite victim. Every time she pulled some nasty trick on me, I'd be a good little girl and turn the other cheek. On this particular occasion, we'd been to a church picnic, and she put something into my drink. I never did find out what it was, but someone told me later they had seen her do it. I got so sick I heaved for the rest of the day and all through the night."

Nancy's eyes widened. "Then what happened?"

Martha chuckled. "Grandmother Poore sat down on my sickbed the next day and told me to listen up. She said the good Lord gave us good common sense, along with His Word. She said she admired me for trying to be a good girl, especially since I'd had some problems of my own playing pranks in the past, but by turning the other cheek time and time again, all I'd done was to make Ellen bolder and more of a bully."

After she wiped away her tears, Nancy caressed the kitten on her lap. "What did you do to make Ellen stop bullying you?"

Martha laughed. "Well, I'll tell you, but only if you promise you'll keep it our secret. I wouldn't want to tarnish my reputation."

Nancy attempted to smile, but winced. No doubt, her bottom lip was being sorely tested by all this conversation.

"The next time I saw Ellen," Martha began, "was a few weeks later. I was coming home from the general store with a basket of eggs. My grandparents built and operated the tavern that used to be at the edge of town where East Main Street meets Falls Road."

"The tavern that burned down last fall?"

Martha nodded.

"I heard about that," Nancy admitted.

"As I was saying, Ellen saw me as I was going home. It had rained earlier that day, and the roadway was just one puddle connected to another by thick, smelly mud. We didn't have the planked sidewalks we have now.

"Ordinarily," Martha continued, "I would have turned around and headed back to cross over the stream by using the bridge near the confectionery, but this time, I kept walking straight at her." She laughed. "I was so scared, I was afraid I'd shake myself right out of my boots, but I kept hearing Grandmother's advice to stand up as a child of God and refuse to be bullied anymore."

"So what did Ellen do?" Nancy asked.

"She stayed true to her nature and thought I'd do the same. She tripped me when I tried to pass by her. I sprawled flat on my face in the mud, dropped the basket of eggs, and broke almost every single one, save for one." Martha chuckled. "Ellen was so sure I wouldn't retaliate, she just stood there laughing at me. Until I took that egg and promptly cracked it right over her head. Fortunately for me, she must have been shocked silent by what I'd done, and I had the chance to tell her if she ever bullied me or anyone else again, I would make sure she regretted it."

Nancy giggled. "Did you get in any trouble?"

A smile lit Martha's heart. "Trouble? Heavens, no. Grandmother Poore was so proud of me, she let me have double dessert that night. She waited for Ellen's parents to show up demanding an explanation, ready to defend me. I don't know what Ellen told them, but they never did."

"And she never bullied you again?"

Martha shook her head. "Never. Of course, I did have to forgive her for tripping me. That took a bit of time."

"I can see why!"

As Martha reminisced, providing more details to her tale, she recognized a strong similarity between Ellen the Bully and Russell the Brutalizer. Each had victimized someone smaller and more vulnerable. Each had counted on the Word, in some perverse way, to give them power over their victims.

She glanced at Nancy and saw, simmering in the depths of her eyes, the truth that Nancy recognized the similarity between Ellen and her husband, too. If so, she might try to stand up to him to try to keep him from hurting her, like Martha had done, but he was much too big and too strong to ensure that that would work.

If anything, Martha was certain she was now prepared to do almost anything to keep Nancy safe — realizing that returning home with Russell was not a good idea.

She patted Nancy's knee. "According to my grandmother, to forgive and turn the other cheek is good advice for when someone speaks sharply to you or cheats you or is unkind to you. So in a way, what Russell is telling you in his note is right. We must forgive others, even though the good Lord doesn't expect us to go out of our way to give anyone the opportunity to be unkind to us.

"On the other hand," she cautioned, "when someone threatens you with physical harm, or repeatedly strikes you, like Ellen did to me or like Russell has done to you, we must forgive, of course, but we must put a stop to the brutalizing or risk losing our health or our very lives."

Nancy bowed her head.

Martha put a finger under the younger woman's chin, tipped her face up, and turned it so they could look directly at one another. "You have turned the other cheek, Nancy. More than once. You have forgiven your husband, time and time again. You must find a way to forgive him again for what he's done, but that doesn't mean you must put yourself back at risk by returning home with a man who has proven himself to be incapable of keeping his promise not to hurt you anymore. Regardless of what Reverend Welsh or your husband tells you to make you feel it's God's will that you return home, I want you to remember this: You are God's child. He loves you. He would never ask you to be faithful to vows you've made to any man who repeatedly brutalizes you. You are too precious to Him."

She paused and took Nancy's hand. "It would take courage to return home, but it will take greater courage to claim your birthright as a child of God and live your life free from terror or pain inflicted upon you by someone who claims to love you."

Nancy's eyes shimmered with tears. "I don't know what's right anymore. I'm so confused. After I heard what Miss Fern and Miss Ivy had to say and saw . . . saw those horrid scars on Miss Fern's neck, I thought I just had to run as far away as I could. Then Reverend Welsh came, not once, but twice. When he came today, he brought me Russell's note, and I thought I had no other choice but to go back home," she cried.

Martha put her arm around Nancy's shoulder and embraced her. "You don't have to listen to anyone. Only God. He'll tell you what to do. If you pray very hard and ask for His help, He'll guide you to make the right decision. He always does. That's what Grandmother Poore taught me all those years ago, and she's never been proven wrong. Not once."

Nancy struggled free. "Even if I wanted

to leave my husband, I have nowhere else to go. I have no way to keep myself."

"There are people who care about you, who will help you," Martha countered.

Nancy tilted her chin just a tad. "I won't know for sure what to do until I speak to Russell. He's not just a friend or a neighbor. He's my husband. Maybe he's learned from this awful experience, just like Ellen did after you taught her a lesson, but I will pray tonight that I will know what to do after we talk."

"If you insist on seeing him tomorrow, then you will, but Miss Fern and I will be here with you."

"All right."

"We'll have to get you ready, too," Martha suggested. "I'm afraid the gown you wore when you arrived still needs mending."

Nancy shuddered. "I don't think I want to see that gown ever again."

"You're about Victoria's size. I'm sure she has a gown you can borrow. There's not much we can do about your bruises, though, but I think Russell should see what he's done to you."

Nancy reached up and touched her cheek.

"I'll send Victoria back in so you two can

decide about your gown for tomorrow, and I'll warn Miss Fern about Snowball, too."

"Thank you," Nancy murmured, "but I thought Victoria said she was tired and going to bed."

Martha chuckled. "I think she's more likely waiting for me to leave so she can sneak back in here to see the kitten."

Martha left the room and slipped out into the hallway. She found Fern dressed in a robe with a nightcap on her head as she sat in the chair with the rolling pin on her lap. "I wouldn't go inside," Martha warned. "Nancy's adopted the kitten."

Fern scowled.

Martha chuckled. "Don't worry. Nancy's well enough to spend time downstairs now so you can still talk with her. I'm going to bed. I'll see you in the morning. We can go to meeting together. Afterward, Nancy wants to see her husband, but she's agreed that we can both be there with her."

Fern shrugged her shoulders. "If the snow keeps up, there won't be meeting. There's nearly another foot on the ground already."

"We'll see, then." Martha went directly to her room, with all intentions of praying for a blizzard that would cancel meeting tomorrow and make even walking about town impossible — if only to give them all a little more time before Nancy and Russell met face-to-face. She was also torn, since Aunt Hilda would be bringing her beloved husband to meeting as a grand surprise for everyone.

There were no easy answers this day. Maybe it would be different tomorrow.

Long after Victoria and Nancy had resolved the question of Nancy's wardrobe for her meeting with her husband tomorrow and everyone in the household had taken to their beds, Martha was still wide awake, sorting through myriad thoughts and emotions.

She punched at her flattened pillow to give it some life, then curled back onto her side again. She was not really worried Russell would try to slip in to see Nancy. She was not worried about Nancy, either. Physically, the girl was really healing well — a benefit of her youth.

Tomorrow, Martha would know whether she would have to go up against Reverend Welsh, as well as Russell Clifford, and support Nancy's right not to be forced back into a marriage that could be deadly, assuming that's what Nancy ultimately decided to do.

Martha was not truly worried about Samuel or Will, either, but she did harbor guilt for interfering in their lives to such an extent that they had run away together. Instead, she tried to be grateful for the strong bond between them. Perhaps one day Samuel would write to her, through Will again, and let her know where they were and how they were faring.

She rolled to her other side, only to be met by more troubling thoughts. Within a day or so, depending on the storm, Victoria would be leaving again, but at least this time Martha would know where her daughter would be going. Martha also knew she could rely upon June and her husband to provide Victoria with the guidance she needed, but could not help wondering if Victoria would have been so anxious to leave again if they had had a home of their own.

To compound her thoughts, Thomas's proposal once again echoed in her mind. With the storm outside, she hoped he had found shelter for the night. A small part of her chafed at his insistence she turn over her patients to Dr. McMillan. Had she been a man, like Dr. McMillan, no one would have suggested setting aside her life's work in order to travel or marry.

The very unfairness of it filled her eyes with tears. She should not have to choose between the man she wanted to spend the rest of her life with and the work that had given her life sustenance and meaning for so long.

Just because Thomas chose to give up his leadership role in the community and leave Trinity to chase some ephemeral idea of how to spend the rest of his life did not mean she could do the same thing. She sniffled and wiped away her tears. For once, she gave herself the gift of self-indulgence and gave herself a good cry, without even the slightest shadow of guilt to spoil the moment.

She had had it all once before with John. Why couldn't she have it again with Thomas?

"Because Thomas is . . . he's . . . Thomas!" She bolted upright, suddenly remembering he had left something for her before starting on his journey. She rose and lit the oil lamp, but kept it low to keep from disturbing Victoria. She scanned the room, visually searching for the note, but saw nothing. . . . There! A thick note was lying on top of Grandmother's diary, which sat on the bottom ledge of a table separating her bed from Victoria's.

No wonder she had not seen it before! If she had made the entry for little Lavinia Stern, she would have found it before going to bed. She reached down and retrieved the note. She'd have to remember to make the diary entry in the morning, but she was too curious about Thomas's note to wait a moment longer.

As she opened the note, her fingers trembled, and a key dropped onto her lap. She wrapped her left hand around the key and quickly read Thomas's short message:

Martha,

In case you need a place to call your own during the next few months, use this.

Faithfully yours,
Thomas

She pressed the key to her heart and closed her eyes, offering a prayer that somehow they might find a way to cross the chasm separating them. She prayed silently for several minutes, refolded the note around the key, and placed it under her pillow.

Her head had no sooner touched the pillow when she heard the most awful commotion out in the hall. She hit the floor at a dead run, charged into the hall, and ran straight into a nightmare.

Chapter 25

Light from Nancy's room poured into the hall. Martha would have had a clear view, but there were so many people clustered in one area that it was hard to tell whether it was Fern or Ivy at the center of the crisis.

"Ladies! What happened?" Martha asked. With Victoria right behind her, she rushed forward to get to the women who huddled together near the empty chair where Fern had been sitting.

Once Ivy turned about, Martha could see Ivy was helping Fern back into the chair. "We need your help. My sister took a bad spill."

Eyes wide, Nancy stood alongside the chair wringing her hands. "I'm sorry. It's all my fault," she whimpered.

Fern sat down and leaned back in her chair. Her nightcap had disappeared, and her long, gray-streaked braid hung over her shoulder. Her face was flushed, and she cradled her right hand with the palm of her other. "It certainly was not your fault," she insisted and caught Martha's gaze. "I must have dozed off. I heard Nancy crying out for help. I was still groggy and tripped over my own nightdress when I rushed to help her. I'm nothing more than a clumsy, meddling old woman," she whined.

Ivy clucked over her sister. "Turns out Nancy was just having a nightmare. It wasn't anyone's fault. It was just an accident."

"An avoidable one," Fern added sheepishly. "If I'd been in bed —"

"Let's have a look at you," Martha interjected before Fern could launch into another round of blame-taking. After making sure Fern did not have any open wounds on her head from the fall and discussing her aches and pains, Martha centered her attention on Fern's right hand and forearm. "Move your fingers for me," she urged, while the others gathered round to watch.

Fern pressed her lips together and managed to move each of her fingers.

"Does that hurt at all?"

Fern nodded. "Some."

Martha's gaze focused now on the wrist area, which seemed puffy. "Try making a fist."

Fern complied. Barely. "That hurts a lot more, but the worst pain seems to be in my wrist."

"Can you bend it?"

Fern tried, but quickly stopped. Her eyes widened and filled with tears. "No."

"It may be broken," Martha cautioned.

"It can't be broken," Fern wailed. "How am I going to help Ivy with the baking?"

"I said it *could* be broken. At the very least you have a bad sprain. I can get you something for the pain, but you need to let Dr. McMillan take a look at it in the morning. If it's broken, he'll have to make sure it's set right so it'll heal properly."

Nancy began to cry. "I'm so sorry. If I hadn't carried my troubles to your doorstep —"

"Nonsense," Fern snapped. "You can't always take the blame when something goes wrong. Now you listen to me, girl. I tripped and fell. It was an accident. It wasn't your fault. Now, if you really want to do something useful, close the door behind you before that critter of yours escapes and sends me into a sneezing frenzy."

"I'll come with you," Victoria offered, but looked at Martha for approval. "Unless there's something you need me to do."

"No. You two go on. We'll make sure Miss Fern gets back into her own bed. Ivy, why don't you help me with your sister?"

Victoria and Nancy quickly disappeared into Nancy's room. With Martha on one side and Ivy on the other, Fern managed to walk back to her own room. While Ivy went inside to light a lamp, Martha held on to Fern just outside the door.

Fern stiffened and tried to turn around. "My rolling pin. I forgot my rolling pin!"

Martha held her tight. "You're getting into bed. I'll get it for you once you're settled."

Fern let out a sigh. "If I'd been in bed, instead of sitting outside Nancy's room like an old fool, this never would have happened."

"We can't change that now," Martha crooned. When light flooded the room, she ushered her patient inside and looked around. She had never been inside Fern's room before, and the elegance of the furnishings surprised her. Nearly every fabric, on the two windows, the bed, and the scarves on the twin mahogany dressers, appeared to be the finest lace Martha had ever seen. The entire room was done in white — walls, bedcovers, even the rug on the floor — and the effect was quite dramatic.

Martha tried not to stare as she helped Fern to her bed where Ivy was waiting for them. She had already turned down the bedcovers and leaned the pillows up against the ornate headboard. Concern etched her features. "Come right here and sit. I'll go heat some water for tea as soon as I have you tucked in."

"I can do that," Martha insisted and turned Fern over to her sister. "I have to get something out of my bag anyway to help with the pain."

"And my rolling pin," Fern reminded her.

Martha smiled. "And your rolling pin." She left the two sisters alone, returned to the hallway, and lit the lamp on the table between Fern and Ivy's rooms. She searched the area in front of Nancy's room, but could find no trace of the rolling pin. "The darn thing must have rolled away," she mumbled to herself as she widened her search. When she still had no luck, she decided perhaps Nancy or Victoria must have picked it up.

She could hear the two girls talking and giggling together behind Nancy's closed door. From the sound of it, they were going to be up awhile. Martha did not know what Victoria had said or done to lighten Nancy's mood, but it probably had something to do with a little white ball of

347

fur and decided to make a pot of mimosa tea big enough for everyone to share, along with some sweet birch oil for Fern's wrist.

Martha returned to her room, paused long enough to find her robe and slippers and put them on, and got the bottle of sweet birch oil. The lamp down the hall cast scarcely any light on the staircase, so Martha made sure she had a good hold on the railing. She had only descended two or three steps when her foot landed on something hard and pointy. She yelped, heard something clatter down the steps, and would have fallen herself if she had not had such a strong hold on the railing.

She waited until her heart stopped racing before she turned around and went back to her room to get a candle to light her way. She was almost certain the object she had stepped on was too small to be the rolling pin, and she was curious to see what it was. She stood at the top of the staircase and held the candle up high so the light fell at the bottom of the steps. To her surprise, she saw the rolling pin — or what was left of it. Both handles appeared to be splintered, but intact, and they had separated from the center pin, which lay end up against the wall.

Apparently, this rolling pin had not been

shaped out of a single piece of wood like most, which accounted for the way it had broken apart when it fell down the stairs. "Poor Fern will be so disappointed," she murmured, then held the candle closer to glance at the steps and make sure this time she did not step on any splintered sections that may still have been there.

She gasped in disbelief and blinked several times, but the breathtaking pieces of jewelry littering the staircase remained, sparkling ever so softly in the candlelight. She made her way down the staircase, pausing to retrieve each piece and store it in her robe pocket until she reached the bottom landing. Once she gathered up the pieces of the rolling pin, she carried them to the table where she set down the candle and inspected the center pin. It had been hollowed out to create a most ingenious hiding place for the jewelry.

No wonder Fern was in a near panic about losing her rolling pin! Martha did not miss the irony of Fern using the jewel-packed rolling pin as a possible weapon against Russell Clifford, either. She put a kettle of water on to boil and fixed a large tray with five teacups, spoons, and honey.

Out of concern that Fern might be truly devastated if she knew Martha had discovered the hiding place for the jewelry, she sat down at the table, emptied her pockets, and lined up the jeweled heirlooms she had found. In addition to a ruby pendant, which is what Martha had probably stepped on, there was a pearl necklace, and two very old, diamond-encrusted rings.

An emerald-studded choker sent shiver's down Martha's spine. She would have to be blind not to recognize the similarity between the necklace Fern must have been wearing the night her husband attacked her and the scars she still wore around her neck.

Martha made quick work of sliding the jewelry back into the rolling pin. It took a bit longer to get the handles back on either end and push at them hard enough to make them stay in place so Fern would not suspect Martha had reassembled the entire rolling pin.

When she finally finished, she mopped her brow with the back of her hand and set the rolling pin near the tray. By then, the water had reached close enough to a boil to allow her to fill the teapot. While the tea steeped, she went to the back door and got a cupful of snow, then carried everything back upstairs.

She went directly to Fern's room where

she found her patient sitting up in bed with her back against the headboard and her right forearm and hand resting upon a pillow. "I have tea for everyone and some sweet birch oil for your wrist, along with your rolling pin," Martha announced as she set the tray on top of the dresser.

Fern's worried expression faded the moment she spied the rolling pin. "Put it right here under my pillow, would you, please?" she asked, pointing behind her.

Martha complied. "That should be a safe place to keep it, although I think it'll be a while before you can use it again. For any purpose," she teased.

Fern snuggled her back against the pillows. "I just feel safer having it near."

Ivy rolled her eyes. "I'll pour the tea."

Martha chuckled, got the sweet birch oil, and gently rubbed some on Fern's wrist. "This should help cut the edge off the pain," she explained. When she noted the additional swelling, she placed a towel under Fern's wrist and packed the wrist in snow. She shook her head. "I don't think it's broken, but I'll fetch Dr. McMillan in the morning. He'll know for sure."

Fern caressed her wounded arm. "Do you think he'd come before meeting? I'd hate to miss —"

"You have to miss meeting tomorrow. I won't have you trying to walk through all that snow whether your wrist is sprained or broken. What if you slipped and fell?" Ivy asked. "No. You're staying home. Isn't she, Martha?"

"She is," Martha replied.

Fern pursed her lips. "I thought I'd have one of you take my side. I never expected you'd both conspire against me."

"Consider yourself under orders to stay in bed for a few days. No housework. No baking. And you're to stay inside until that wrist is completely healed."

Ivy nodded. "Exactly."

"And just how do you think you'll manage the baking, the cleaning, the cooking —"

"I'll help," Martha suggested. "Even Nancy is up to performing a few chores."

Fern cocked her head and glared at her sister. "Victoria is leaving on Monday. Martha is bound to be called to duty, and Nancy may end up going home now that I can't do much to stop her."

"The good Lord will provide," Ivy responded. "He always does."

Martha hoped Ivy was right, especially since Martha did not have any quick solutions to offer. With Fern under Ivy's care now, Martha carried the tray to Nancy's room. "Victoria? Nancy? I have tea. Is anyone interested? If so, I need you to open the door."

She heard the scampering of footsteps before the door partly opened. Victoria looked at the tray and frowned, but her eyes danced with mischief. "What? No cookies?"

"In the middle of the night?" Martha huffed. "This isn't supposed to be a snack. It's just to help settle you both down so you can go back to sleep."

"We're not tired now. We've talked ourselves past it."

Martha could hear Nancy giggling, but she could not see past Victoria into the room. "Since you're both wide awake, I guess it wouldn't hurt."

Victoria eased the tray from her mother. "I'll take this and get the cookies from downstairs. If it's all right, I'll sleep in here with Nancy tonight."

Martha nodded. "I suppose."

Victoria gave her a wink. "I'll tell you all about my talk with Nancy in the morning," she whispered and promptly closed the door.

Rather than go back and rejoin the Lynn sisters, Martha decided to take to her bed.

She really did not have any other choice. With Ivy taking care of her sister and Victoria taking care of Nancy, Martha had nothing else to do. She found the whole experience more than a little odd and traipsed back to her room praying tomorrow would be just a little bit calmer.

Chapter 26

By midmorning on Sunday, Martha decided the day could be considered calmer, but only if she compared it to total chaos.

The snowstorm continued, unabated, and threatened a record snowfall, in addition to forcing a cancellation of Sunday meeting for the first time in years. Ivy had also decided not to bake anything new since few people, if any, would be venturing outside today. With an abundance left from yesterday, however, the confectionery remained open, just in case someone got stranded.

It had taken Martha over forty-five minutes to battle her way to fetch Dr. Mc-Millan to the confectionery and another forty-five minutes to return. At least she had been able to see Bird, who was nursing a rebroken wing the doctor hoped would heal correctly so the bird could fly free come spring.

Snowball, better known today as Beast, had escaped from Nancy's room twice. Each time, the kitten had scampered straight to Fern's room, slipped inside, and hidden under the bed, which inspired a series of sneezing spells that betrayed her presence.

Dr. McMillan was upstairs with Fern and Ivy putting a splint on Fern's broken wrist while June Morgan, who had insisted on tagging along with Martha and the doctor, was with Victoria and Nancy discussing the departure for New York City, which obviously had to be postponed.

When Martha heard someone pounding on the back door and someone else knocking at the door connecting the kitchen to the shop, she threw up her hands and accepted the fact that this day was destined to be a total loss. She had spent the past hour racing up and down the steps to rescue Snowball and bring refreshments for their guests. She had no dinner started yet, and at this rate, there was not going to be anything for supper.

She answered the closest door, connecting the kitchen to the shop, first. When she opened the door, she was so surprised, she took a step back. "Aunt Hilda! What on earth are you doing here? You shouldn't be out on a day like this!"

Arm in arm with her husband, Aunt Hilda looked like a snow woman. Even her eyebrows were coated with snow. "I've been waiting for days for Sunday to come so we could surprise everyone at meeting. Since that's been canceled, I wasn't going to let a little snow stop us. I wanted Mr. Seymour to meet Victoria, of course, and Fern and Ivy, too," she insisted, still referring to her husband in a formal way, as had been the custom in her day.

Richard patted his wife's arm. "Fortunately, we're both strong and healthy. Only took us a little better than an hour."

"Come in," Martha said as the pounding at the back door became more insistent. "Find a peg for your coats and get warm and dry by the fire. Let me see who else is foolhardy enough to be traipsing through this storm. I'll be right back."

As she hurried through the kitchen and storage room to the back door, the pounding kept pace with her footsteps. About the only thing this day needed to make it perfect bedlam was for her to be summoned to duty. She said a rushed prayer of apology for being selfish and thinking of herself, instead of one of her patients, and cracked the door open.

Shivering against the cold, she kept most of her body behind the door. The moment she saw who was standing outside, she knew she had been wrong. The only thing this day needed to guarantee bedlam was the arrival of Reverend Welsh and the newest member of his flock, Russell Clifford.

"A good morning to you, Widow Cade," the minister offered. For the first time Martha could recall, he was actually wearing a hat. "May we come in? It's growing awfully bitter now with the wind."

"I'm sorry I kept you waiting. I had someone knocking on two doors at once. Please. Come in." She stepped back to allow them to enter. Like the Seymours, both men were literally coated with snow from head to toe.

Russell did not meet Martha's gaze when she looked at him, but Reverend Welsh did. "Young Russell is anxious to see his wife. You did promise he could see her today."

Martha nodded. "Take off your things. I'll have to take them into the kitchen and drape them near the fire so they'll dry." She left them to remove their coats and rejoined Aunt Hilda and her husband.

Unfortunately, they knew nothing about the Cliffords and their situation, and Martha did not have time to explain. Perhaps it would be better to let her aunt form her own opinion of the young man before she knew all the facts. She was known to be an excellent judge of character, and Martha would welcome her aunt's advice should trouble arise.

"It's Reverend Welsh. He's brought a new member of the congregation, Russell Clifford, to see his wife, Nancy. She's my patient, and she's resting upstairs," Martha explained.

Aunt Hilda cocked a brow. She knew Martha, like her grandmother, always went to her patients' homes to treat them and never took them in. Before Martha could provide any further details, however, the minister and his charge joined them. Martha made all the introductions and hung the men's coats on the chair backs to dry while the minister focused all his attention on Richard Seymour.

"Since I've only been pastor for seven years, we haven't met, but I've heard all about you." He pressed his hands together as if in prayer. "What a joyous day! To see your faith rewarded, Mrs. Seymour, and to see you both together again after all those years, and now," he added, clapping his hand on Russell's back, "to have Russell reuniting with his wife, it's truly a heavenly day, one filled with blessings, despite the abominable weather."

While her husband engaged the minister in conversation, Aunt Hilda concentrated on Russell. Martha joined them, more than a little anxious about whether today would be filled with blessings or difficult lessons or some combination of each.

"I know exactly which farm is yours," Aunt Hilda said. "Used to belong to a man named Winter. Ezekial Winter. He came here right after Jacob Dillon had the lottery and sold off most of the lots in town. Winter never farmed the land, though. He bought it as an investment, but died a few years later. It got sold to another man. . . ."

She squeezed her eyes shut for a moment. When she opened them, they were sparkling. "Jameson was his name. I knew I would be able to recall it. James Jameson. Farmed all by himself. Never married. When he died, oh, some fifteen years ago, that's when the Brunhilde family bought it. They moved further west, I understand. You remember them, don't you, Martha?"

"I do." She smiled at Russell, who seemed surprised, if not also bored, by her aunt's knowledge. "Aunt Hilda has lived here longer than anyone. We never have to worry about forgetting the past. Not as long as we have her with us."

360

He nodded, glanced overhead, and looked directly at Martha. "I'd like to see Nancy now," he murmured.

"I'll go up and tell her you're here, but I'm sure she'll need some time to get ready. With the storm, we really didn't expect you to come. Aunt Hilda, why don't you keep Mr. Clifford company? I won't be long."

Aunt Hilda took the young man's arm. "I must tell you all about the Brunhilde family. . . ."

While her aunt took charge, Martha slipped up the stairs. She met Dr. Mc-Millan in the hallway.

He smiled nervously. "I was just coming down to see you."

Her heart skipped a beat. "Is anything wrong?"

"No. Miss Lynn is resting very comfortably now. I wanted to speak to you about another matter. It's more of a personal nature," he said. He looked a bit pale and perspiration lined his upper lip.

As much as she wanted to accommodate him, she really did not have the time right now, not with Russell Clifford downstairs demanding to see his wife. Briefly, she described all who had arrived. "Can it wait? I need to tell Nancy her husband has come to see her so Victoria can help her to get ready, then I have to get back downstairs."

"Of course." He stiffened. "With what's going on with the Cliffords, if you don't mind, I think I'd like to stay. Just in case that man decides to try to take advantage of the fact that none of you have a male protector and force his wife or any of you to do something against your wills."

Although she doubted Dr. McMillan could prove intimidating to the likes of Russell Clifford, who was much taller and far stronger, she did appreciate the young doctor's support. "Thank you. That might be wise. In the meantime, why don't you go back and tell Fern and Ivy that Reverend Welsh and Mr. Clifford are here and that you're staying to help. If she can, maybe Fern could get herself situated in the sitting room awhile so Aunt Hilda can bring up her husband and introduce him to everyone."

"Consider it done. What about Reverend Welsh? Will he be accompanying Mr. Clifford when he sees his wife?"

She sighed. "See if you can convince him to stay with everyone in the sitting room. I'll send Victoria to join you, too. This is not a reunion I'd like her to see."

"And June?"

"I'll ask her to stay with me and Nancy while Mr. Clifford is there. I think it will make Fern feel better, too, if she knows I have someone with me." It might make Fern feel better, but she had a feeling Russell Clifford would not be happy having his reunion monitored by two women, especially women he could not intimidate or control.

The doctor put his hand on her shoulder and smiled. "We can talk together about my concerns another time. You're a fine lady. I'm sure this will all turn out well today."

"Let's pray you're right," she murmured, and they each went off to see the Clifford reunion into motion.

The reunion was only moments away.

Martha was so nervous her mouth felt like it was stuffed with cotton and her throat was tight. She did have second thoughts about having only women monitor the reunion, but it was too late to change her mind. She made sure the room was well lit, if only to make sure Russell got a good clear look at what he had done to his wife.

Martha glanced around the room one last time before she opened the door. In the far corner, Snowball was curled fast asleep in her basket. Wearing a pale yellow gown, Nancy sat in a chair, which had been placed at the foot of the two beds. She had her right hand resting in her lap, with the folds of her borrowed gown covering her crooked fingers. An empty chair, some four feet away facing Nancy, was reserved for her husband. Her bruised face looked like a mask a ghoul might wear to frighten mortals, a thought that reminded Martha of Samuel and the serpent tattoo on his cheek. Her eyes, however, were shining bright with anxiety as well as hope.

To Nancy's right, June Morgan, looking as elegant and proper as ever, sat at the end of the bed and held Nancy's hand. Victoria sat at the end of the other bed, providing Nancy with support on both sides. Martha had relented and allowed Victoria to remain, as much to placate Nancy as to recognize her daughter's valuable contributions to the injured woman's progress.

Martha accepted a smile of encouragement from June, sent one to Nancy, and opened the door, confident her figure would block Russell's view of his wife until the door opened wider. To her relief, Russell stood alone waiting to be granted entry. Apparently Reverend Welsh had taken Dr. McMillan's suggestion not to attend.

When Russell glanced past Martha, his eyes lit with surprise. "Mrs. Morgan is a friend. I've asked her to stay with us. My daughter, Victoria, is also present, at Nancy's request."

His eyes flashed with disappointment. "I suppose if Nancy . . . That's fine."

Martha stepped aside and opened the door completely. He took one look at his wife, paled, and rushed past Martha. He fell to his knees at his wife's feet and laid his head on her lap. "Forgive me," he pleaded. "Please forgive me."

Unmoved and unsympathetic to anything beyond Nancy's welfare, Martha closed the door, turned, and leaned back against it to observe the scene. What happened over the course of the next half hour or so would have an impact on everyone here. She braced herself as Nancy wept and stroked her husband's brow.

From the looks on June's and Victoria's faces, Martha had the distinct impression Russell would have a difficult time convincing either of them he deserved anything less than solitary confinement in prison for a few years for what he had done to his wife.

Emotions were bound to seesaw during this encounter on all sides, and she needed to remain objective and clear-minded. She was also prepared to intervene, if necessary, but for the moment, she stood back.

When he finally rose and stood before his wife, Martha got a few steps closer so she could see both Nancy's and Russell's faces and drew in a deep breath. To her surprise, Nancy was gazing up at her husband with such love and tenderness, there was little doubt she was weakening.

"Lord, we need your help. We really need your help," Martha whispered, and waited for Clifford to begin the conversation she was certain he had rehearsed for days.

Chapter 27

Russell Clifford might have been a grown man, but at the moment, he looked like a little boy who had been caught red-handed stealing from his mama's cookie jar.

His shoulders drooped. His cheeks were flushed. His gaze was properly penitent, but Martha detected a gleam of bitter resentment. She was not sure which he resented more — having been caught or being surrounded by women who clearly did not take his side.

With his wife and her two companions seated, he literally towered over them, giving him an advantage Martha did not miss. "Please. Have a seat," she urged. "It'll be easier for Nancy to be able to talk with you."

He looked over his shoulder, grabbed the arm of the empty chair behind him, and pulled it forward. When he sat down, he was closer to Nancy than Martha would have liked, but she did not press the issue. He gripped the sides of his chair and cleared his throat. Nancy toyed with her hands, but kept her gaze locked with her husband's. "Reverend Welsh told me he gave you my note," he began.

Nancy nodded.

"Will you? Will you forgive me?" he asked.

She moistened her top lip. "If I want to follow the Word, I must," she responded.

The corner of his lips began to twitch, as if he were holding back a smile. "Then you'll come home with me? As soon as you're able to travel?" Before Nancy could answer, he turned to Martha. "I expect we'll have to wait till the storm dies down, but will she be able to travel in a day or two?"

"Perhaps," Martha responded, grateful Victoria and June were acting simply as silent monitors, just as they had promised. "Before we talk about her traveling, though, I think it would be best for both of you, if you truly intend to have a better marriage, to openly discuss what's happened in the past so you'll be able to forgive and put everything behind you, not just this one incident."

Nancy briefly closed her eyes. "I'd like that," she whispered.

June and Victoria nodded their assent.

Russell straightened his shoulders and

squared his jaw. A tic started pulsing in one cheek. "Dredging up the past isn't necessary. I've admitted my faults and promised never to hurt Nancy again. If forgiveness cleanses the soul, as Reverend Welsh says it does, then there's no need —"

"Forgiveness for what? That's the issue," Martha insisted. "For simply beating your wife because you were angry over your son's death? Is that all?"

He flinched.

With tears running down her cheeks, Nancy caressed the two crooked fingers on her right hand. "You promised before that you wouldn't hurt me again, but you did."

"I told you that was an accident. I didn't deliberately break your fingers. I just didn't know my own strength. I do now," he snapped.

Breathing hard, he pressed his lips together as if fighting for control. "This is very awkward, discussing our private affairs in front of others. I just want us to go home, Nancy. I miss you so much. I need you. I promise. Nothin' like this will very happen again. Ever."

Nancy trembled. "I want to believe you. I do," she whimpered. "But I'm . . . I'm afraid."

He reached out and gently caressed her

uninjured cheek. "You don't have to be afraid of me anymore. I've changed. Truly, I have. If you don't believe me, talk to Reverend Welsh again. I'll do anythin' you want. Anythin'. I spoke to Mr. Pitt down at the sawmill. He says I can work there in exchange for supplies so I can fix up the cabin."

Clearly wavering, Nancy glanced at Martha, then looked to both Victoria and June, who offered silent disapproval for any plans Nancy might entertain about going home with her husband.

"And I talked to Mrs. Welsh, too. She's awfully nice. She said she had some curtains and other things that were donated to the church. You can alter them to fit. It'd make the cabin really homey. Come spring, I'll be able to put in our first crop, then things will really get better for us," he promised.

He paused and lowered his voice. "Come spring, maybe we'll be able to start again on that family we both want. My heart's broken about little Peter. I know yours is, too. Once we have another child, everything will be better for us."

As he droned on, he used his words to paint a picture of a loving husband, a comfortable home, and children to love, which matched the dream of every young woman; Martha feared he was very close to winning the battle to reclaim his wife. She also feared the dream he promised. If he brutalized Nancy once, he would brutalize her again. What would prevent him from one day turning against their children and hurting them, too? He had misjudged his strength, to use his words, before. If he did it again, he could spark a tragedy from which Nancy might never recover.

By the time he finished talking, Nancy was holding his hands and smiling. "I'd like to come home with you. I truly would."

Her husband grinned from ear to ear. "Reverend Welsh is here. I can't wait to tell him the good news."

Nancy took a deep breath. "I said I wanted to go home with you, Russell. I want that more than anything, but . . . but I don't think it should be right away."

The smile on his face disappeared behind a mask of confusion. "What's that supposed to mean?"

Martha took a step closer.

"It means that I want some time."

He scowled. "Time? How much time? I want you home with me now. I can't stay in town indefinitely, imposin' on Reverend

Welsh and his wife. And frankly, I can't see why it's necessary."

When Nancy tried to pull her hands away, he resisted, held tight, and glared at her three supporters. "Tell me what they've said to turn you against me."

"I haven't turned against you," she countered and yanked free. "I don't want to make a mistake. I'm still confused. I want time to sort out my thoughts so when I decide what to do —"

He stood so quickly he startled everyone, including Martha. "What you should decide is whether you'll honor the vows you took when you became my wife or be damned for all eternity."

"What about your vows?" she cried. "You promised to honor and respect me. Instead, you've hit me, time and time again, and each time, you promised it would be the last."

His arm rose as if to strike her.

"Stop!" Martha cried and rushed forward to place herself between them. Victoria and June rose, too, creating a protective shield around Nancy. With her heart pounding, Martha raised up her hand defensively as his arm loomed over her.

He grabbed her hand so hard she had to blink back tears of pain and swallowed a scream. They were locked in a battle of wills, as well as physical strength, but Martha had the sheer power of righteousness to sustain her. "Get out. Now," she ordered.

He dropped his hand. "I'm sorry. I didn't —"

"Now," she repeated, ignoring the painful throbbing in her fingers.

"I said I was sorry! You have no right to interfere between a man and his wife." He hissed.

Martha took a small step forward.

To his credit, he backed up. His chair kept him from moving more than a few inches, but the symbolism of his action spoke louder than anything he could say or do to indicate his acquiescence.

"This isn't finished," he warned. "Under God's law, a wife must obey her husband, and I am telling her she must come home with me. Nothin' you can do or say can change that. I'll be comin' back for my wife to take her home. When I do, there won't be anythin' you or anyone else can do to stop me."

He turned, kicked the chair out of his way, and started to leave. To Martha's horror, the chair landed near the basket where Snowball was sleeping. Frightened awake, the kitten instinctively ran — straight into the path of Russell, who was storming his way to the door.

He caught the kitten with the toe of his boot and sent her sprawling. She landed, back first, against the leg of the dresser and started meowing pitifully. Russell nearly fell, cursed under his breath, and grabbed the door handle. "Make sure you get rid of that mangy critter before I come back, or I'll do it for you," he spat. He opened the door and stomped from the room without bothering to close the door behind him.

Martha stood very still and waited for her heartbeat to return to normal. The chaos of the day paled to the bedlam that quickly erupted. Weeping, Nancy raced to the kitten, dropped to her knees, and cradled the kitten in her arms like a babe, with June hovering over both of them.

Victoria, also weeping, put her arm around Martha. "Are you all right? Did he hurt you?"

"I'm fine," Martha insisted, finding it odd to have their roles reversed yet again.

Dr. McMillan's ample form filled the doorway as he frantically scanned the room. "I heard loud voices. Where's Mr. Clifford?"

"I sent him away. Would you please be

kind enough to make sure he's left the confectionery?"

June looked over her shoulder. "Please take the minister with you. That young man needs help. We don't. At least not right now."

The doctor disappeared, only to be replaced by Ivy. She took in the scene and frowned. "I take it Russell wasn't pleased by Nancy's answer?"

Victoria sniffed. "He's a fiend. I hope he falls outside and freezes to death."

Martha patted her daughter's arm. "You don't mean that. Go help Mrs. Morgan and Nancy with the kitten," she suggested. "I need to talk to Miss Ivy."

Reluctantly, Victoria let go of her mother. "What are you going to do about Mr. Clifford?"

"I'm not sure," Martha admitted.

"We'll think of something," Victoria said. She kissed her mother on the forehead and went to help with the kitten.

Feeling more than a little proud of Victoria's mature handling of this sorry episode, Martha went out into the hallway with Ivy and shut the door. "Nancy is fine. Let's go into the sitting room. I want to tell both you and Fern what happened. Then we need to develop a strategy. Aunt Hilda should be able to help us, too."

Ivy's brows knitted together. "A strategy?"

Martha nodded and looked up and down the hall to make sure they were alone and would not be overheard. "We need to figure out how we're going to help Nancy escape. I think she's ready now."

Ivy fanned herself. "Mercy, that's good to hear. Fern's been in a real snit ever since she heard that brute was in the house again."

They walked toward the front of the hall, passed the front staircase that led to the shop foyer, and neared the sitting room that overlooked West Main Street. "Dr. McMillan went downstairs to make sure Clifford left. Did Reverend Welsh —"

"He tore down the steps a few minutes ago," Ivy interrupted. "Honestly, I don't think there's been so much activity in this old building since we changed it from an old boardinghouse into a confectionery."

Martha chuckled. "Think about it, Ivy. A boardinghouse? Here in Trinity? Jacob Dillon made few mistakes when he planned out this town, but building a boardinghouse was one of them. I doubt there were ever more than one or two rooms in use at the same time after the lottery was over. Most folks come here to homestead, not live in a boardinghouse."

Ivy laughed with her. They reached the sitting room where Aunt Hilda was waiting for them with Fern. "Mr. Seymour went downstairs with the other men," she explained. "Sit down, Martha. You're as pale as a winter moon."

Martha did not argue and took a seat in a chair facing the hallway so she could see any activity that might take place. Ivy sat next to her sister, and the three women listened, without interrupting, while Martha gave an accounting of what had transpired in Nancy's room. "I haven't spoken with Nancy about it yet, but I have no doubt she understands she can't go home again with her husband. Not ever. She has no family, so it looks like we need to help her."

Fern's expression was sober and determined, but she was still sniffling from her encounter with the kitten. "He won't let her go. Not without a fight."

Ivy nodded. "She'll be in great danger."

"Agreed," Martha murmured and flexed the fingers he had nearly crushed. She leaned forward in her chair and spoke directly to Aunt Hilda, who was sitting with her hands folded in her lap, much like a dowager queen waiting to be asked for advice. "You spoke to him. What did you think? Do you agree he'll become violent again if she tries to leave him?"

"I only had a short time to get to know him," she began, "but I can tell you this much. He has no respect for the past and no interest in anything in the present, unless it relates to him. He wants his wife back. He'll fight for her the same as he'd fight for a horse that had been stolen from him. She's his property. Nothing else matters much to him."

"So it's clear, or at least I think we all agree, that it would be too dangerous for Nancy to stay in the marriage, but it would also be too dangerous for her to remain in Trinity," Martha said. She looked around at the others' faces and found consensus.

She was sorely disappointed Nancy could not stay in Trinity. Fern and Ivy had already suggested Nancy could board with them and work as a helper in the confectionery, an offer ever more important now that Fern would be unable to do any significant work until her wrist healed. Martha thought immediately of Annabelle Swift, the young girl who had helped out in the tavern while Victoria was gone. Although that might help Fern and Ivy, it would not do anything about resolving Nancy's dilemma.

"We really do have our work cut out for us," she murmured. In her mind's eye, she saw the line of people making an exodus from Trinity: Victoria, Thomas, Samuel, Will, and now Nancy. Martha would love to have replaced Nancy with her husband in that line, but he would never leave — not unless he either took his wife with him, which Martha feared he might do, to isolate her from her supporters, or he left to follow Nancy when he learned she had escaped from him.

Martha's major task, as she saw it, was to make sure he left town, very definitely in the opposite direction from where Nancy would be going to start a new life.

Aunt Hilda stood up. "I don't know about anyone else, but I'm hungry enough to eat my way through the goodies in the shop downstairs. It's well past dinner time, too." She sniffed the air. "I don't smell anything cooking."

Martha cringed. "I'm sorry. I didn't have time. I kept getting interrupted."

Ivy's eyes began to twinkle. "We could, you know?"

Martha narrowed her gaze. "Could what?"

"Try to eat our way through the shop. It's an emergency. Sort of," she countered.

Fern sniffled. "Just eat sweets? That's ridiculous. I think there's some cheese and a little cooked chicken —"

"We'll serve that to the menfolk," Aunt Hilda suggested. "Let's go, ladies. I know we'll all think better once we've had some sweets."

Chapter 28

At her own insistence, June Morgan served Richard Seymour and Dr. McMillan their dinner in the kitchen while Martha and Ivy carried down some chairs from upstairs. They transformed one of the serving tables in the shop into a dining table and arranged yesterday's baked goods in the center.

Nancy helped Victoria to set the table and pour tea, while Fern sat at the head of the table directing the work around her. When everything was nearly ready, she sent Nancy and Victoria into the side room to fetch a tin of crispy pretzels.

While the two younger women were gone, Fern slapped the tip of her spoon against the table and got everyone's attention. "Listen good. I have something to say before Nancy comes back. We should keep the conversation easy while we're eating. Afterward, we'll make sure she agrees with us about leaving. Then we'll ask her to go upstairs while we think of a plan. If she stays to listen and Russell gets to her somehow, she'll tell him about it for sure, and we can't have that. Agreed?"

All heads nodded.

Within moments, everyone was seated around the table. Conversation, at first, was a bit stilted, but once the baked goods were sliced and shared, the sound of gay laughter and the young women's giggles chased away the clouds of tension and fear that had shadowed the day.

An hour later, Martha polished off the last bite of cherry pie left on her plate. She surveyed the remains in the center of the table. They had actually demolished an entire cherry pie and apple cobbler, half a tin of crispy pretzels, nearly eight sugared doughnuts (there was half of one left), and too many butter cookies to count. Oddly, the fruitcake had gone untouched.

She eased her chair back from the table for the second time. "I'm finished this time! Please don't let me sample anything else."

Victoria snatched the last half doughnut. "This is the best dinner I've ever had!" she pronounced before nibbling at her doughnut.

"Me, too," Nancy admitted. She took two butter cookies and laid them on her plate. "You said this was a tradition?"

Aunt Hilda nodded. "I declared it so."

Chuckling, Martha dabbed at her lips with a napkin. "As the town matriarch, I suppose Aunt Hilda is entitled to all sorts of privileges. Like starting traditions."

"That's right," Aunt Hilda added. "As of today, every big snowstorm calls for a sweet supper at the confectionery. With the bad winters we've had over the years, I wonder why I didn't think of this sooner." She picked up her teacup and raised it to eye level with her arm extended. "A toast. To the good Lord for all His blessings, to the Lynns for all their sweets, and to each of us, for coming together as sisters in faith."

Everyone, even Fern, managed to raise a teacup and they clinked them together to affirm Aunt Hilda's toast.

When Nancy yawned, Fern caught Martha's gaze and nodded ever so slightly.

"I think maybe you've had enough for one day, Nancy. This is only your second time downstairs. Why don't you let Victoria take you back upstairs so you can nap while we clean up from dinner?" Martha prompted.

Nancy bowed her head for a moment. When she looked up, her eyes shimmered with tears. "I am a little tired. I . . . I want to thank you. All of you," she added as she glanced around the table. "Thank you for helping me. I had hoped today would have turned out differently. For Russell and me."

Aunt Hilda patted the girl's arm. "Hope is a treasured gift. It's not one we give up easily, is it?"

Nancy shook her head. "I know now I was only being foolish to think Russell would change. I know . . . ," she paused to take a deep breath, visibly struggling to keep from crying. "I know I can't go home again. I can't be his wife anymore. I . . . I just don't have anywhere else to go. As much as I want to stay here, I know he'll cause trouble for everyone."

Ivy stood up, walked around the table, and put her hands on Nancy's shoulders. "That's what we're here for — to help you," she promised. "We'll make sure you get situated somewhere far away where you'll be safe."

Nancy sniffled and wiped a tear from the corner of her eye while Ivy went back to her seat. "I can't ask you to do that. Russell will be very angry when he finds out you helped me. I should just . . . just run away. Then no one else —"

"You'll do no such thing," Fern demanded.

Aunt Hilda tilted up her chin. "Now you listen to me, young lady. We have lots of traditions here in Trinity. Some are for holidays and some are for snowstorms. As ladies of Trinity, we have some traditions that are all our own. You're still new to Trinity, so you don't know about all of them," she said, casting a warning glance to all the others to remain silent.

"Traditions just for women?" Nancy asked.

"For one, we call a midwife when we're sick, rather than a doctor," Martha offered with a grin.

"We have sewing bees and apple bees," Victoria added.

Ivy narrowed her gaze, then smiled when she offered her contribution. "We make wedding quilts when one of us gets married."

"We become watchers and keep folks company when they're getting ready to pass on to the next world," Fern murmured.

Aunt Hilda nodded solemnly. "And we help other women out of difficulties. Always. We don't boast about it, though. Most of the time, the menfolk don't even know what we've done. We just see a need and address it."

"That's right," the others said in unison.

Aunt Hilda smiled at Nancy, who still looked so fragile and vulnerable. "So you see, you simply must let us help you. It's tradition. If there's anything I've learned all these years, it's to respect tradition."

As her aunt continued to put the young woman at ease, Martha marveled at the compassion and understanding each of the others had brought to the table in Nancy's time of need. Her aunt also reminded Martha that there truly was a sisterhood here in Trinity, perhaps everywhere that women gathered in communities, with an undeclared, but very real bond between the women, which helped all of them to sustain and survive the troubles life often brought home to them.

Lately, more often than not, Martha had overlooked the other women and tried to find solutions alone, mistakes she now regretted. Maybe if she had consulted with other women, they might have come up with different options to help Samuel and Will, and they might still be here in Trinity. Maybe, if Martha had not acted like the only one who could solve someone's problems or if she asked for other's opinions, she might have had more time to spend with Victoria.

Or Thomas.

She heard the echo of his proposal and her arguments against accepting it, but this time, she saw other possibilities. Some made her heart race just a little faster.

"Martha? Martha!"

She flinched. "What?"

Aunt Hilda scowled at her. "I asked if you'd like to take Nancy upstairs now for her nap."

Martha felt her cheeks warm. "I'm sorry. I must have been woolgathering. I thought Victoria was going to take Nancy upstairs."

"Actually, I'd prefer to stay here," Victoria said firmly.

Confused, Martha searched the faces around the table, but found no supporters for herself.

"Another tradition, unfortunately, is a legal one," Fern said quietly. "Whatever arrangements we make for Nancy must be kept secret, especially from the menfolk. Even though the law dismisses us by not letting us vote or serve as jurors or even testify in court most of the time, there is one exception."

Martha swallowed hard. "For midwives."

"Your status as a midwife gives your words the credibility we don't have," Aunt Hilda reminded her. "They probably won't think it important to question us much, but Nancy has been your patient. If she suddenly disappears and Russell gets the sheriff involved, you'll be the first one he'll want to see and talk to."

"Then there's Reverend Welsh to consider, too," Ivy added.

Their arguments made sense, but Martha did not take being excluded from the planning session easily. Her feelings were hurt. Unjustifiably, perhaps, but it was probably a necessary lesson in humility for Martha that was long overdue. "You're right," she admitted.

When Martha rose from her seat, Nancy followed suit and glanced around the table. "I don't know how to thank you all for being so kind."

Aunt Hilda winked at her. "Why, you'll have to continue the tradition. That's how. Sooner or later, others will need help wherever you go. Helping them is how you'll thank us."

As Martha escorted the young woman toward the kitchen to get to the back staircase, Fern called her back. "Use the front stairs. It's faster. Besides, no sense giving the menfolk any idea what's going on in here."

Martha retraced her steps and led Nancy through the room to the foyer area and the door that kept the front staircase closed off from the public. She stepped aside to let Nancy go first and followed her up the steps. "I can take a look at Snowball for you, if you like," she offered.

"I think she's fine, but maybe that's a good idea. She landed so hard, I was afraid she might. . . . Anyway, after what happened today, I renamed her. I think Lucky suits her better, don't you?"

"Another name?" Chuckling, Martha shook her head. "Cats and kittens have nine lives. Lucky still has eight left."

Nancy giggled. "Not after getting into Miss Fern's room twice today. She used up two right there."

"Then six." Martha stopped at the top landing, held Nancy back, and peered into the sitting room and down the length of the hall. No one appeared to be upstairs, and they continued to Nancy's room where they found Lucky sleeping on Nancy's pillow.

Martha checked the kitten, pronounced her fit, and tucked them both into bed for a nap. "You probably won't be able to take Lucky with you," she murmured. "I'm sorry."

With the kitten nestled into the crook of her neck, Nancy stroked the kitten's head.

"I know. Victoria thinks Mrs. Morgan might let her take Lucky to New York."

"Maybe she will," Martha responded, already trying to think of someone here in Trinity who might be willing to take the kitten. She pulled the window curtain aside a little bit, peeked outside, and let the curtain drop back into place with a sigh.

Nancy yawned. "Is it still snowing?"

"I'm afraid so."

"Good. That means Victoria won't be leaving tomorrow."

Martha cocked a brow. "Yes, it does. In fact, I'd be surprised if they'll be able to leave much before the end of the week." She looked out the window again. Since it faced south, she did not have a view of Main Street, but she could see a corner of the covered bridge. The gully surrounding Dillon's Stream was nearly filled with snow.

In all likelihood, there would not be any wagon traffic for days, if not weeks. Sleighs, of course, would have a better chance, as long as the horses pulling them were as sturdy and surefooted as Grace. Individual riders, however, would be foolish to venture out on any kind of journey. She prayed, this time unselfishly, that any babes about to enter this world would wait until the weather cleared — for the safety of the fathers who would be risking life and limb to fetch the midwife.

A knock at the door interrupted her prayer. When she answered the door, she found June Morgan standing in the hallway. Clearly distressed, she was wringing her hands.

Martha slipped out of the room and closed the door behind her. "What's wrong?" she asked, fearful Russell might have already returned to try to claim his wife.

"There's a man downstairs asking for you. Devon Harper. He says his wife is about ready to deliver."

Martha's heart dropped down to her knees and back up again. Apparently, her prayer had been offered too late. "Tell him I'll be right down. I need to get my things."

"But the storm! You can't possibly —"

"Their farm is just outside of town. It isn't far. I've been out in worse." She tried to ease June's worry. "Sometimes I think these babes have a sense of humor after all."

June's eyes widened. "I'm afraid I fail to see any humor in your venturing out into a storm."

"If you could see what I look like by the

time I get there, you'd laugh, just like those babes probably do. I need to change into my split skirt, too, so if you could see that Mr. Harper gets something warm to drink while he's waiting, I'd appreciate it."

"Of course."

The admiration in June's gaze made Martha uncomfortable, especially after she realized how self-centered she had become lately. "It's nothing you wouldn't do, if you were the midwife," she murmured and went to her room to get ready for one very cold, very wet, very treacherous ride — one that would be forgotten the moment she held a precious newborn in her arms.

Chapter 29

"A girl! You have yourselves a beautiful baby girl!"

From her position on the floor at the new mama's feet, Martha cradled the screeching infant on her lap, cut the umbilical cord, and cleaned the babe up for her proud mama and papa. Joy and awe warmed every chill remaining in Martha's bones and erased any fear left from the harrowing ride that had brought Martha here several hours ago, just as she knew would happen.

Unfortunately, Martha had but one assistant, yet Carrie North was exceptionally good and the most trusted assistant Martha had. The fact that Carrie lived less than two miles away and could get here, even before Martha, was indeed a blessing for all concerned.

The infant gradually began to quiet. "There, there, sweet one," Martha crooned. She used the tips of her fingers to smooth the mass of dark ringlets capping the baby's head. After swaddling the babe in a soft blanket, Martha handed her to her anxious mama.

Genevieve Harper, who was seated on her husband's lap with the birthing stool supporting them both, put the newborn into the crook of her arm. "Oh, look, Devon! She has your chin. See? There's a little dimple, just like yours."

To Martha's right, Carrie stood, gazing at the new family. At twenty-nine, she was a wife and mother who had a particular gift for helping other women give birth and assisted Martha frequently, much like Martha had done at that same age for Grandmother Poore. Carrie was unusually tall for a woman, nearly six feet, and she had the stamina, as well as the will, to one day make an exceptional midwife. Since Victoria would not be following family tradition by becoming a midwife, which Martha now accepted, she could think of no finer replacement, when the time came, than Carrie North.

Martha noted the subtle change in Carrie's expression, heard Genevieve whimper, and got up from resting on her haunches to kneel up straight.

Carrie took Genevieve's free hand. "Hold on to them now," she urged the new father.

"It's just the afterbirth. It won't be as painful. Just take a deep breath and ride out the pain," Martha prompted.

Genevieve yelped and began panting the moment the pain ended. "Something's . . . something's wrong. It hurts. It really hurts," she cried as she arched back and pressed her head against her husband's chest as another pain wracked her body.

"Try to relax. You're only adding to the pain. It's almost over," Martha promised. The most exciting births, from her standpoint, were the ones where a couple welcomed their first child into the world. That's why little Peter Clifford's passing had been extra hard to accept.

Women delivering their first child, however, were often frightened and bewildered, even prone to panic, since giving birth compared to nothing they had ever experienced. Martha's task then became more of teacher than anything else and required great patience.

Carrie looked down at Martha and nodded. "Here comes another pain. This should do it, don't you think?"

"Very likely." She slipped her hands beneath Genevieve's nightdress and placed them at the entrance to the birth canal. "Push this time, Genevieve, and you'll be done. Now push!"

Genevieve screamed.

Devon looked frightened.

Carrie held her hand tight.

Martha felt a warm gush of fluid, then something solid began to emerge. Her heart began to thump against the wall of her chest. Fearing a tumor or mass of some sort, she edged closer. "Lift up her nightdress," she requested, trying to keep her voice from shaking or frightening her patient.

Using her free hand, Carrie scrunched up a section of Genevieve's nightdress and tugged it up to the woman's knees. With the opportunity to see what was happening now, Martha looked, blinked hard, and looked again. Both stunned and alarmed, she had no time to waste. "Push, Genevieve. Push hard!"

"I . . . I can't," she wailed.

"You can and you will. Right now. Push. Push!" Carried ordered.

After one push, Genevieve collapsed against her husband. Martha felt the mass slide free. Her hands trembled as she turned in place and brought the silent treasure to her lap, out of the direct view of her parents.

With her heart racing, Martha snipped

the umbilical cord, cleared the silent, tiny baby girl's airways and massaged her little chest. "Come on, angel. Take a breath. Please," she whispered, dismayed by the blue tinge of the baby's lips.

Nothing. No sound. No movement.

Then Martha saw a twitch, ever so slight, in the baby's neck. She massaged harder, but was careful not to do any damage to the fragile bones beneath the cool flesh. She closed her eyes briefly and offered a prayer, begging for this baby's life. Several heartbeats later, the baby began to cough and sputter. "That's right. Fight, little one. Your big sister would be so lonely without you."

The babe opened her little mouth, filled her lungs with air, and emptied them with a fit of crying that told Martha all would be well. Trembling with happiness and gratitude, Martha bowed her head. "Thank you, Lord," she whispered, quickly wrapped the baby to keep her warm, and handed her to Carrie, whose eyes were as big as melons. "It seems you're twice blessed today," Martha told the parents, who had been shocked into total silence. "You were right about those pains. Much too hard for the afterbirth. You have a second daughter! She's a mite, compared to her big sister, but she'll catch up in no time."

"Twins? We have twins?" Devon Harper turned paler than his wife, who wept openly, unable to speak.

"You do!" Carrie crowed. "I've never seen the birth of twins. This is amazing!" She placed the second newborn into Genevieve's other arm and put a hand under the infants to help their mother support them.

Genevieve looked thoroughly exhausted. Poor Devon looked a bit worse for wear himself. "We still have the afterbirth to contend with, but we'll get you to bed as soon as we can," Martha promised. "You need to get as much sleep now as possible. I have a feeling you're going to need it. Do you have names for these little girls?" she asked to distract Genevieve during the last part of the birth process.

Genevieve sighed. "We were both sure we were having a boy."

Martha chuckled to herself. Twin girls. What a surprise for everyone, including herself. And what a perfect ending to the day!

To welcome two angels into this world together was a rare privilege indeed. She had not helped to deliver twins since the

Matthews' girls, also future members of the sisterhood of all women, had been born some three years ago.

Thinking of that sisterhood, she wondered what was happening back at the confectionery. Had they all decided on a plan to help Nancy escape? If so, where would they send her and how? Martha suspected Fern and Ivy would probably help finance Nancy's escape, but Martha did have a few funds set aside she could offer. She also had the key to Thomas's cabin, in case they needed a place for Nancy to hide temporarily, although the cabin was so far from town it might prove to be very dangerous should Russell discover the hideout.

Samuel's cabin, now empty, would be a more logical hideout. It was so close they could easily watch over Nancy. Most folks did not think twice about the recluse, especially now that he had gone. Even if they did, they would not venture near his cabin for fear he might return. Russell Clifford, a newcomer, would probably have no idea the cabin even existed.

Anxious to get back to the confectionery to offer her suggestions to the others, Martha helped Carrie get Genevieve into bed with her twin daughters and finished the rest of her duties. There would not be a groaning party this time, since no one else had been summoned due to the weather, but there was going to be one very special prayer offered in a few moments to express their gratitude for these two baby girls.

Just past midnight, Martha joined Carrie at the kitchen table to share a pot of tea. "She's resting now," she explained in response to the unspoken question in Carrie's gaze.

"Is this common in twin births?" she asked, clearly curious and as anxious to learn as always.

Martha added honey to her tea and stirred the mixture. "Having twins is uncommon enough that I'm not really sure, but unusually heavy bleeding after delivery is always cause for concern. The Lady's Mantle should help, though."

Carrie let out a sigh. "I wish I could stay longer, but I really do have to go home in the morning. There's been such a rush of babes lately, I've barely seen my own."

After swallowing a long sip of tea, Martha nodded.

"I remember feeling the same way when Oliver and Victoria were little."

"Maybe Mrs. Seymour will be able to come. She lives right in town, so it wouldn't be as difficult for her to get here in this weather as it would be for someone living above the falls."

Martha shook her head. "I'm afraid she won't be able to come. She has a . . . guest," she responded. Unsure whether Aunt Hilda still wanted to keep her husband's arrival home a surprise for next Sunday's meeting, Martha decided to err on the side of caution.

As a first-time mother, especially with twins, Genevieve very definitely needed an afternurse. Martha needed to get home, what with all that was happening, assuming she could get Genevieve's bleeding under control.

Carrie's face lit. "What about Lucy?"

"She's attending Miriam."

"Oh." Carrie's expression filled with disappointment.

Martha went through a mental list of women who usually served as afternurses, but as far as she knew, they were already on duty elsewhere. "I can't think of anyone," she admitted. "That's what happens when you young people settle so far from home and family. If Genevieve's mother lived nearby —"

Carrie slapped the table. "That's it! That's who we can ask."

Martha eyed her skeptically. "Surely not Genevieve's mother. She lives in Maine! By the time she got here, little Martha and Carrie would be crawling," she argued. It still sounded strange to refer to the twins, who were now their namesakes, by their actual names.

"Not Genevieve's mother. Mine!"

"Elaine? As far as I know, she's never been interested in being an afternurse."

"But she has lots of experience," Carrie argued. "She's stayed with me after my babes were born, and she stayed with Anna and Rose, too. Now that Papa's gone and mama's living with David and Anna, I think mama would like to get away from time to time."

Martha chuckled in spite of herself. David and Anna's four boys were famous, at least locally, for being the most rambunctious brood ever born and bred in Trinity. Elaine might very well want to take a breather. "She'd be perfect. Do you think she'll come out in this weather?"

Carrie's grin widened. "With everyone there stuck inside? She'd probably crawl here if she had to. I'll have Mr. Harper stop at David's after he takes me home in

402

the morning. David's place isn't that much farther up Falls Road."

"I'd better wait to leave until after she gets here," Martha suggested, "just in case she's not able to come for some reason. I don't want to leave Genevieve alone, even if the bleeding's slowed."

"She'll come," Carrie insisted.

"I don't know what I'd do without your help," Martha said sincerely. "You'll be a fine midwife on your own one day. Nothing would make me prouder than to have you take over when I'm no longer able to continue."

A flush started at the base of Carrie's neck, spread up her throat, and stained her cheeks. A fine line of perspiration dotted her upper lip. "Actually, I've been meaning to talk to you about . . ." Her eyes misted. "We had a letter last week from Joseph's parents. His father isn't well and . . . we're moving to New Hampshire as soon as the weather permits. Joseph is going to take over his father's mercantile business. He's an only son. He has no other choice," she murmured.

Disappointed to the very depths of her spirit, Martha was also shocked beyond measure. She had become very fond of Carrie, and she would miss her immensely.

In her mind's eye, she saw Carrie and Joseph, along with their three children, joining the exodus leaving Trinity, and her heart trembled with sadness.

"Of course he has a choice," Martha countered, hoping to ease the younger woman's obvious distress, "but he's choosing well. He wouldn't be the man I've come to respect since he arrived if he turned his back on his parents when they've asked for his help. I'll miss you. All our patients will miss you, too."

Carrie sighed and wrapped her hands around her cup of tea. "I'm so torn. I never thought I'd move from Trinity. My entire family is here. My friends are here."

"It won't be easy, but you'll be fine. You'll make new friends, I'm sure. You'll come home for visits, won't you?"

"Joseph promised I could."

"We'll see each other then, and we'll write, too. In the meantime, let's not waste a moment we have left. Tell me all about this mercantile store."

Three days later, Elaine finally arrived.

By then, Genevieve was well on her way back to full health, although it would be months before she got a complete night's rest. Twins Martha and Carrie were getting cuter by the hour, and the proud new father had a good start on building a second cradle.

With the promise of a substantial reward after harvest next fall, Martha finally headed home. By now, whatever contribution she might have made toward planning Nancy's future was no doubt moot.

Nevertheless, she urged Grace to carry her home as quickly as possible, if only to still the worries in her heart that Russell Clifford might have caused trouble while she had been gone.

Chapter 30

Loaded down with her bag of simples and her birthing stool, Martha trudged through the knee-high snow covering East Main Street as best she could and wished she had had a place to stable Grace closer to the confectionery on the other side of the street.

Only four days after the snowstorm hit, the business side of town had undergone quite a transformation. Wagon traffic, including the mail wagon that normally arrived each Tuesday, had packed down the snow in the center of West Main Street so the roadway was now passable. The planked sidewalk had been cleared, creating a mountain range of snow lining the roadway below. Folks were gathered in small groups, either enjoying a break from their errands or simply a chance to see neighbors and friends after being stuck inside their homes for days.

The covered bridge was only a few yards away from her now and offered not only a respite from the wind, but surer footing. She had scarcely stepped inside when she heard footsteps thumping behind her.

"Widow Cade! Wait! I'll walk with you."

Martha turned toward the familiar voice and waited for Dr. McMillan to catch up to her.

"Mrs. Andrews isn't feeling very well, so I offered to go to the confectionery to purchase the bread today so she could rest a bit," he explained as he got closer. "It's nothing serious," he added when Martha lifted a brow. He took her birthing stool. "Here. Let me help you. I take it you're just returning from a call?"

She smiled. "Genevieve Harper. Twin girls! Beautiful babes," she responded and shifted her hold on her bag before they started off together.

"All are well?" he asked.

"The new mother is a little over-whelmed, but Widow Snyder is staying with her. The babes are doing very cleverly, although one is notably smaller than her sister," she responded.

"That's fairly common, I believe," he suggested.

Martha shrugged her shoulders. "After all these years, I've learned not to judge anything as common. As soon as I do, I'm proven wrong." As much as she might enjoy discussing the birth of twins with him, she was more anxious to speak to him about what Russell Clifford had been doing since she ordered him out of his wife's room. She also remembered the doctor asking to speak to her about a personal matter, but she had been called out to the Harpers and had never had a chance to talk with him.

When they reached the confectionery, the young doctor followed her into the foyer. The rooms on either side both held several patrons and offered no privacy. "You mentioned the other day you had something to discuss. I have time now; then perhaps you can tell me what's been happening with Mr. Clifford while I've been gone. We can use the sitting room upstairs," she suggested, careful to keep her voice low.

"Yes, I'd like that."

"Follow me." She opened the door to the front staircase that led up to the sitting room. Once upstairs, she left him in the sitting room while she took her things to her room and stored away her cape as well. With all the bedroom doors closed, she could not tell if anyone else was upstairs, but all was quiet and she assumed they were alone.

When she returned to the sitting room,

she found him standing with his coat still on and his hat in his hands. "This must be a short discussion you've got planned." When his brows knitted together, she pointed to his coat.

"Oh. Actually, I . . . I didn't think it would take very long at all, but . . . ," he let out a sigh. "This is harder than I thought it would be. You're right. Maybe I should take this off."

After he removed his gloves and coat, he handed everything to Martha. She laid them on a chair. "Shall we sit down?"

He nodded and took a seat across from the settee where she sat down and waited for him to begin, with no small measure of anticipation pounding in her heart.

He sat very stiffly with his hands gripping the chair's arms and took a deep breath. "As you'll recall, we didn't start off on a very positive note when we first met."

"True," she admitted. At their very first meeting, the night she returned from searching in vain for Victoria, she and the doctor had both been summoned to the same delivery — one Martha ultimately handled. "You were quite arrogant, as I remember," she teased.

His chubby cheeks turned a deeper shade of red. "Yes, well, I recall a certain level of disdain on your part as well."

She chuckled. He was being kind. They had squared off as bitter combatants, each vying for the same patients, each a symbolic representative of outspoken proponents who took sides, either for doctors or midwives, in the raging debate over who better served a teeming woman. "You recall correctly."

"Since then, we've seemed to reach some sort of . . . truce. I'm indebted to you for your help, especially with the sketches and essays you've prepared."

She cocked a brow. "I was under the impression we had developed a friendship, as well as mutual respect," she ventured.

"Yes, well . . . that, too." He dropped his gaze for a moment, and his fingers drummed the ends of the chair's arms.

"Whatever it is that's bothering you can't be that awful," she prompted. "Spill it out. We'll discuss it."

He took another deep breath. "I owe you a great deal for helping me, on a personal as well as a professional level, and for doing so confidentially. Even though you didn't accept my offer of a place to stay or a room you could use as an office after the tavern burned down —"

"What is it you're trying to say?"

"I've made an offer on your brother's property, and he's accepted. Through Micah Landis. He's handling the land transfer for Mr. Fleming —"

"What?" Martha's heart nearly leaped out of her chest. Her mind froze, and she struggled to understand what he meant. "What are you talking about?"

He paled. "I told him you'd be upset, which is why I insisted on telling you first, before any papers were signed."

"Papers? What papers?" Her mind still refused to function. "What property? James doesn't have any property here in Trinity other than the land for the tavern."

"Precisely. The land for the tavern. That's what I'm talking about."

Images of her room at the tavern, with healing herbs strung from the overhead rafters to dry, blurred with images of the kitchen where she and Lydia had worked side by side and collided with the harsh reality that come spring, there would be no tavern and no room for her. "I — I didn't know James had finally decided to sell the land," she whispered.

"I'm sorry. Truly sorry. I never would have discussed this with you if I thought you didn't know. According to Micah, Mr. Fleming wrote to you weeks ago to tell you he had decided to sell the property. You never got your brother's letter?"

"No," she murmured. The doctor's distress was so genuine and his discomfort so real, Martha did not doubt his words or his intentions. "I never got James's letter, but that's not your fault. It's not James's, either. It's just that you caught me by surprise."

He sighed. "I feel awful."

"It's not your fault."

"It's only because I respect you so much, as a . . . as a healer and as a friend . . . I just wanted to talk to you about this before I signed the papers. I know the property has been in your family for several generations. If you find it objectionable for me to buy the property, then . . . then I won't. There are several other parcels of land that would be nearly as suitable for investment. June looked at them with me when we went for a sleigh ride. Victoria was with us, although she had no inkling of my true mission that day. I wanted to be prepared. In case you objected," he added.

Though stunned by the very real prospect of being without a home for good, Martha had a sudden inspiration burst through the fog that clouded her brain. Micah Landis was Thomas's son-in-law.

Did Thomas know about James selling the land? Is that why Thomas proposed again? Because he knew she would be forced to accept the Lynn's charity indefinitely? Why hadn't he mentioned anything about James selling the land that day at the cabin on the lake? Was it because he knew how upset she would be, or because he simply did not know about the sale at all?

Too many questions, about Thomas, about her future, begged for answers she did not have, but there was no reason for Dr. McMillan to feel uncomfortable. In fact, she was quite impressed that he had thought to consult her first. "If James is selling the land, then someone will be buying it. It's not my place to approve or object, but I appreciate your telling me about this yourself," she began. "I'd like to hear all about your plans, but I'm also anxious to hear about Mr. Clifford."

Dr. McMillan folded his arms across his wide paunch. "My plans are still very tentative, but I can tell you I hope to have a partner. I'm afraid nothing is settled yet, so I can't divulge his name to you. Naturally, our plans are to rebuild the tavern. We'll hire someone to operate the tavern and split whatever profits are left. It's one way to supplement my income while my practice is young and show my commitment to the town and the people here as well."

He paused. His hands clenched into fists. His gaze hardened. "As for Mr. Clifford, I'm afraid there's trouble brewing, especially for Mrs. Clifford."

Martha edged forward in her seat and tried to keep her heartbeat from racing so fast she would get dizzy. "What kind of trouble?"

"Apparently, neither Sheriff Myer nor Mayor Dillon were able to sway that brute's determination to take his wife back home with him. Reverend Welsh still holds out hope for the couple, but even he agrees they need time apart until Russell can get his temper in check. That's probably why Russell moved out of the Welshes'."

"Where is he now? Mr. Clifford, I mean."

"Word's spread about what happened to his wife, and he's been spotted all over town. By more than just a few folks. I wouldn't have thought he'd find any kind of welcome with anyone, but he must have. If his wife leaves the confectionery, he follows her. If she doesn't, he goes into the shop and buys something, just to let her know he's close by."

"He thrives on intimidation," she

snapped. Like the doctor, she suspected no one in town would harbor Russell Clifford now that they knew what he had done. As unlikely as it might appear at first glance, the possibility that Russell had found Samuel's cabin, claimed squatter's rights, and was temporarily nesting there, felt logical the longer she thought about it.

And the vulture was probably just waiting for the right moment to swoop in and snatch up his wife.

Martha was more than a little concerned about Nancy, and she knew Fern and Ivy were, too. Why did they allow Nancy to go outside at all, especially in this weather? Her bruises were bound to invite questions, which obviously must account for word spreading so quickly. Without knowing the plan that had been hatched to help Nancy to escape, however, Martha withheld judgment.

"I'm afraid something has to be done. And soon," the doctor advised.

She could not have agreed more. She only prayed her friends would act before Russell Clifford did.

Dr. McMillan promptly took his leave by the front staircase. Martha followed him down and locked the staircase door from the inside, then went back upstairs and used the back steps to go looking for Fern and Ivy to make sure they were going to do something soon.

Very soon.

Chapter 31

When Martha reached the kitchen, she found Victoria and Nancy clearing sewing notions off the kitchen table while supper, obviously unattended, boiled over on the cookstove.

"Mother!" Victoria cried and rushed over to give Martha a hug, with a rather large, cumbersome sewing basket crushed between them. "We were wondering when you'd get home. Is everything all right?"

"Fine. Everyone is fine." Martha returned her daughter's embrace and turned toward the cookstove. Using thick cloths, she quickly maneuvered the pot of stew to a cooler place on the cookstove. "Mrs. Harper had twin girls so I needed to stay a bit longer than usual," she murmured, reluctant to be overly enthusiastic out of consideration for Nancy's recent loss.

She glanced at both girls. "It looks like you've both been busy," she noted as she approached the table where a plate of sugar cookies looked tempting.

Nancy blushed, and the pink coloring

added an odd hue to the yellowish bruises that remained on her face. Her lip, however, had nearly healed. "We . . . well, we just finished. I'm sorry we didn't notice the stew."

Victoria opened the sewing basket she was still carrying. "Look! Mr. Sweet had several boxes of ribbon he was giving away. For free!"

Martha peered inside and saw half a dozen spools of ribbon. Nearly three-quarters of an inch wide, the ribbon was bile green with a thick stripe of sunflower yellow running down the center. It was simply hideous, and Martha crinkled her nose. "What could you possibly be doing with that ribbon? It's garish, to say the least."

Victoria's smile widened. "You may think it's garish, but others might argue it's the height of fashion in New York City to wear such bright colors. I have some upstairs for you. I think there's a dozen spools, but if you don't want them. . . ."

"No. I'll . . . I'll think of some good use for them," she responded. She was always in need of some type of twine to hang her herbs to dry. Come spring, she would have to start replacing all she lost in the fire, but just the thought that she would have to see this awful ribbon hanging overhead sent shivers up and down her spine, until she remembered she would still be here at the confectionery in the spring. "What did you do with yours?" she asked the girls.

Nancy giggled. "We put ribbon trim on our drawers."

"Nancy even decided to add some color to her cape and trimmed the whole thing, even the hood. Among other pieces we decided looked plain or drab," Victoria added.

Martha chuckled and shook her head. "I probably shouldn't ask what you mean."

Victoria's eyes twinkled. "You probably shouldn't."

Martha snatched a sugar cookie from the plate. "I just spoke to Dr. McMillan. I understand you two have been out quite a bit while I've been gone."

"Just running errands," Victoria answered.

"For Miss Fern and Miss Ivy," Nancy added before she dropped her gaze and toyed with the scissors in her hands.

Martha polished off her cookie and brushed the crumbs from her fingers. "He tells me Russell has been around town as well. Perhaps it would be wiser if you stayed inside, at least until —"

"Martha! You're back! Finally!"

Fern ambled into the kitchen with a broad smile on her face. Her broken wrist, still protected by a splint, rested in a sling. "All finished, girls? I'm so impressed. Why don't you take the sewing basket and the rest upstairs, then go see Miss Ivy in the shop? She needs a little help. And be careful not to let that critter out, or I'll be sneezing all day and half the night."

"Yes, ma'am," the girls replied in unison, then quickly left.

Fern eyed the pot on the stove and frowned. "I had a feeling they might forget to watch it." She headed toward the cookstove, but Martha intercepted her.

"I'll take care of this. You're supposed to be resting that arm," she cautioned.

Fern sniffed. "I have another. I'm not totally helpless."

Martha almost rolled her eyes, thought of Will, and caught herself. She stirred the stew, checked the fire, and moved the pot back closer to the center before setting the thick cloths aside again. "Don't tell me you had the girls use some of the ugly ribbon to trim your drawers," she teased.

Fern's eyes widened, then narrowed defensively. "Actually, I had them trim a petticoat for me and a few other things, too.

It's not exactly the ribbon I'd choose, but —"

"But it was free. And wearing that ribbon will remind you that Wesley Sweet had to admit to making a business mistake by ordering such awful ribbon."

Fern grinned. "Half the women in town have gotten some free ribbon already. The other half will be sure to take the rest. I do so love it when someone like young Sweet gets what he deserves. The man has no heart. Not even for folks troubled by hard times. To see him have to take a loss and give something away just brings a smile to my heart."

"Speaking of someone getting what he deserves, Dr. McMillan told me what Russell Clifford's been doing while I've been gone. Do you think it's a good idea for Nancy to be out and about? Given the man's apparent obsession with his wife, how long are you all going to wait to get Nancy to someplace safe?"

Fern chewed on her bottom lip, looked around the room, and leaned closer to Martha. "We only need a few more days to get everything ready. That's more than I should say, but I know you'll keep this very quiet. If Russell even gets a whiff —"

"You know I wouldn't breathe a word to

anyone," Martha insisted.

Fern patted her friend's arm. "I do. In truth, we may need your help."

"Anything," Martha said, anxious to be part of the scheme, if only to reassert her place as a member of the sisterhood.

"I'll let you know. In the meantime, maybe you can tell me what you think about my plan to resolve my own situation." She retrieved the plate of sugar cookies from the table, added more, and nodded toward the staircase. "We can talk more privately upstairs. Ivy will be back to check on supper once the girls arrive to take over in the shop."

Intrigued and duly tempted, Martha followed Fern upstairs. Once they were settled in comfortable chairs in Fern's room, with the door closed and locked and the plate of cookies resting on Martha's lap, Fern let out a sigh. "I took your advice and talked to Mayor Dillon. He's offered to help me."

Stunned, Martha's hand, with a cookie halfway to her lips, froze in place. "You did? He . . . he did?"

Fern made a face. "I don't know why you act so surprised. You're the one who said I should talk to him. You said he would be helpful, remember?"

Martha laid her hand down, but held tight to her cookie. "Yes, I know I did, but I just didn't expect you'd act on my advice at all, let alone so quickly, and especially considering your injury. Besides, Thomas left days ago."

"He had to turn back when the storm hit," Fern offered. With a shrug of her shoulders, she sampled a cookie, which she chewed thoughtfully.

Martha followed suit and ate her own.

"After fifteen years, I suppose you're right to wonder why I've suddenly decided to do something about my situation. Maybe I just don't want to worry for the next fifteen years. We're leaving for Philadelphia on Sunday, right after meeting."

Martha choked, coughed, and eventually managed to swallow the piece of cookie that had caught in her throat. "You're traveling to Philadelphia? With your arm in a sling? Is that wise?"

"I'm not much help here," Fern countered. "Dr. McMillan said I could go, and Mayor Dillon promised he'd make the trip as comfortable as possible. He was planning to leave for Philadelphia anyway. Since Eleanor is due to deliver next month, he's coming back here before continuing on to New York so . . . so we're making this into a bit of a holiday, too."

Martha struggled to find her voice while her mind latched on to the memory of Thomas's invitation to accompany him on his trip as his bride. Fern and Martha were close in age, and she wondered if either Fern or Thomas had given any thought to the propriety of traveling alone together. The subject, however, was a delicate one, and she was loath to introduce it for fear of putting a damper on Fern's plans. "What about Ivy?" she ventured. "Is she in favor of your plans?"

Fern cocked her head, knitted her brows together, and stared at Martha like she had grown a second nose. "Ivy? She's coming with us, of course! You didn't think I'd go off with the mayor alone, did you? People would surely talk!"

"No. I didn't. I just . . . If Ivy goes with you, what about the confectionery?" she asked as the exodus of folks leaving Trinity grew ever larger in her mind's eye.

"Closed. For renovations. We've been meaning to make some changes anyway, so while we're gone, Luther Phipps is going to do some work for us. When we're in Philadelphia, we're going to look at some new display cases, maybe even some new furniture for the sitting room. We'll be back before folks hardly notice we're gone."

Martha polished off another cookie. "I doubt that. I'm not sure I can survive a full month or more without one of your cherry pies, and Dr. McMillan will be upset, too."

Fern chuckled. "It's cold enough to store some treats outside. You'll just have to make them last till we get back."

"You're not afraid of confronting your husband? Not even a little bit?"

Fern let out a deep sigh. "Like I told Nancy, I'm just plumb tired of being afraid. Besides, I can hardly expect that girl to have the courage to start her life over again if I can't face my past, now can I?"

June Morgan arrived unexpectedly just after the shop had closed for the day. Martha ushered her into the kitchen. "Fern and Ivy are upstairs packing. Victoria took Nancy back to the general store to get more ribbon, so I have to keep a close watch on supper," she explained, although she still felt uneasy about letting Nancy go out. "Would you like something hot to drink? Or some cookies, perhaps?"

June shook her head. "I can't stay long. Mrs. Andrews will have supper ready soon, too."

"How are you feeling?" Martha asked as she stirred the leftover stew.

June removed her gloves, but only opened up her cape instead of removing it. "Very well. Thank you. I've been hoping to talk to you privately about a matter I think . . . I hope you'll find appealing," she suggested.

Curious, Martha led her to the two chairs resting in front of the fireplace where they each took a seat. "I presume this would concern Victoria."

June blushed. "Actually, no. It concerns you, rather the sketches and short essays on different herbs and treatments you've prepared for Benjamin. He shared them with me. I hope you don't mind."

More befuddled than curious now, Martha shook her head. "Mind? I shouldn't think so, but why would you have any interest in them?"

June toyed with her gloves for a moment before she gazed at Martha with great intensity. "May I speak frankly?"

"Of course."

"With Benjamin here now, how much longer do you think you'll be able to continue your work?"

Martha's spine stiffened. "We've managed to find a way so we can both provide for our respective patients without infringing —"

"That's now. What do you suppose it will be like in five years or ten? Midwives have all but disappeared from the largest cities, save for the few who tend to the desperate or the very poor. New laws are being written, even as we speak, limiting what midwives can and cannot do. Doctors are taking over, leaving women no choice but to accept their care, as well as their treatments, no matter how debilitating or dangerous they might be."

"That won't happen here," Martha protested.

June's gaze softened. "Benjamin is a good doctor, and he's better than most because he listens to his heart as well as his head. Unlike many other doctors, he has respect for the work midwives do and the treatments they use — treatments that have been passed down from one generation to the next. All because of you."

Martha felt her cheeks warm. "That's very kind of you, but you overestimate —"

"Little by little, his practice will expand and yours will diminish," June continued. "Women here in Trinity will grow to rely upon him more and more, just like most women have done back East, where midwives are scrimping for ways to survive. In the end, all of the knowledge you and women like you have acquired will be lost or appropriated by doctors for their exclusive use."

Martha wanted to argue that June was wrong. Completely wrong. Maybe doctors had replaced midwives in large, Eastern cities, but she hoped Trinity would always have room for both a midwife and a doctor. But change, it seemed, was as inevitable as the shift in seasons each year. She could see it in the town's landscape. She could see it in the shifting tide of people who came to Trinity to make new futures for themselves and the people who were leaving to do the same. She could even see it in the faces of women who were turning to Dr. McMillan to deliver their babies. Although that number was small now, it would increase. She had the feeling she would not have to worry about finding her own replacement. He was the town doctor, already in place, and as age slowed her down, the number of patients who called for her would also shrink.

She dropped her gaze and steepled her hands atop the table. "What you say rings true, I'm afraid, although I've done my best to deny it to myself." She fought back tears. "I suppose I should be grateful Dr. McMillan has the sense to respect time-proven treatments, enough to try them before resorting to some of the new medicines that mostly put women into a stupor."

June reached across the table and lay her hand on top of Martha's. "But you can do more than just share your knowledge with Benjamin. Other women can learn about the remedies and use them at home, which would limit their need for a doctor. Other doctors, men like Benjamin, might want to learn about them, too."

Martha sighed and shook her head. "I can't see how."

June smiled. "Your sketches and essays. They're a veritable treasure, although the sketches need an artist's touch and the essays need to read more like prose. And if we were to put one or two in every issue of our magazine, hundreds and hundreds of women, perhaps thousands, if our subscriptions continue to increase, would have a reference to guide them at a far more affordable cost when compared to the price of books — which are mostly written by men, I might add."

As she spoke, her voice became more and more excited, and Martha's heart began to race. "You'd put my sketches and essays into your magazine?"

"Imagine the wonder of it, Martha. Women would heed your advice because of your status and experience. You would empower them, give them some sense of control over healing themselves and their families."

"I don't know. . . ."

"Just last year, Mrs. Child published a book," June prompted. "*The American Frugal Housewife* sold six thousand copies in a single year because so many women have either found themselves far from home without an older relative to guide them or they're isolated from other women on homesteads that are stretching further and further west or . . . or they find themselves in reduced circumstances, forced to perform chores they once assigned to servants. Depending on the response we have to the first few issues, your series might very well end up as a book that literally thousands of women would use. My husband has many contacts in the publishing industry. I'm certain he would help to find a publisher who would agree to keep the price affordable to most anyone."

"First in the magazine, then a book?" The idea sounded preposterous, yet deep in the recesses of her very spirit, Martha felt a surge of excitement and joy that spurred new ideas about expanding access to her store of knowledge right here in Trinity — ideas that would acknowledge the very sisterhood she had nearly forsaken.

Until she thought about Victoria.

If Martha did have a series on simples and treatments for common diseases and ailments that appeared as a monthly feature in the magazine, she would be intruding on every hope and dream in Victoria's heart. Writing and publishing were Victoria's dreams, not Martha's. She and Victoria had come too far together, as mother and daughter, to risk becoming estranged over something like this.

Martha patted June's hand. "As much as I'd like to accept your offer, I'm afraid I'll have to decline."

June leaned back and narrowed her gaze. "It's Victoria, isn't it?"

"You're a very intuitive woman. Victoria and I have had our difficulties in the past, as you know. Partly because I failed to realize that our gifts are so very different. She's a poet. A writer. She belongs in that world. I know that now, just as I belong in mine. If I accepted your offer, I'd be intruding into her world. She'd resent it, and I wouldn't blame her."

"No. I wouldn't. Truly. I wouldn't, Mother."

Victoria's voice, as much as her words, startled Martha. She clapped her hand to her chest, looked over, and saw her daughter standing in the doorway to the storage room. "Victoria!"

"I'm sorry. I didn't want to startle you," she said as she walked toward them. "Nancy's upstairs putting the extra ribbon away, but I decided to come downstairs and make some tea." She dropped her gaze for a moment. "I didn't mean to eavesdrop, but . . . but I did. I think it's a grand idea. You should accept."

Martha rose and faced her daughter, but June remained seated. "Are you certain you wouldn't mind?"

Victoria nodded. "We could work on the essays together. I could even polish them up a bit. I think if we make them read more like a story, instead of an article in a scientific journal, women wouldn't be able to resist them."

Martha cocked a brow. "You've read them?"

"Just one. Dr. McMillan left it lying in the sitting room."

Blinking back tears, Martha took several deep breaths. "I'd like it very much if we could work on them together, but you're going to be in New York while I'll be here."

Victoria walked right into her mother's arms and hugged her. "There's an amazing thing called the post, you know."

Martha sniffled. "The only amazing thing I can think of right now is you."

"I'll make sure to remind you of your own words when I begin to edit some of your essays. We have a few days left before I'm supposed to leave. Maybe we could start now and get several done."

Martha kissed Victoria's forehead. "I'll have to get them all back from Dr. McMillan, so you can help me decide where to start this . . . this series."

She turned back to June, ever more aware of the role this amazing younger woman had played, not only in reuniting Martha with her daughter, but also in helping them both to reestablish strong bonds. "Thank you," she murmured. "It seems I'm going to accept your offer after all. Actually, we're both accepting your offer to submit a series of essays and sketches. Since Victoria and I will be working on these together, then we should share the credit as coauthors."

June smiled. "You're very welcome."

"Have you made all the arrangements to return to New York?"

"I spoke to Sheriff Myer just this morning. Apparently, he has some business in Sunrise and he's agreed to escort us there. After Victoria has a visit with her aunt and uncle, we can hire a driver to take us back to New York. If that's agreeable, we can leave on Sunday after meeting."

"Sunday would be fine," Martha responded. Was everyone going to leave together on Sunday? If so, there was going to be a caravan, similar to those that often passed through Trinity heading west, but this one would be heading east, toward the very regions the earliest settlers in Trinity had once called home. "Sheriff Myer will get you there safely," she added, making a mental note to tell Victoria about James's plan to sell the tavern property rather than rebuild.

When June rose to leave, Martha held up her hand. "If you'll wait, I'll walk you home so I can pick up those sketches and essays. That way Victoria and I can start working together tonight."

Martha had scarcely donned her cape when there were a series of harsh knocks on the back door. Instinctively, she sensed yet another call to duty that would obliterate her plans to spend the evening, if not the next few days, with her daughter.

She hurried to the back door and opened it partway. The moment she recognized her caller, she braced the bottom of the door with her foot to keep it from opening any further. Instead of relief that the caller was not summoning her to duty, fear raised the hackles on the back of her neck and flooded through her body.

Russell Clifford reeked of cheap rum, and she nearly gagged at the stench on his rumpled clothing. His bloodshot eyes flashed with impatience. "I want my wife back. Now." He belched and swayed sideways, nearly losing his balance.

Martha took advantage, nudged the door halfway closed, and edged her body partly behind the door. "She isn't home. Even if she were, she has no intention of speaking to you. Now be off. And don't come back, or I'll be forced to send for the sheriff."

He lunged at her so quickly, he caught her off-guard and managed to catch her by her right shoulder. His grip was powerful, but he was so addled, he lost his footing and had to let go to regain his balance.

Martha pulled back, slammed the door,

and dropped the bar into place to prevent him from charging in. Her chest heaved as she drew in gulps of air, and her heart whacked hard against her rib cage. As much as she did not want to wish away her last few days with Victoria, she knew Sunday could not come quick enough — for everyone, but most especially, Nancy.

Chapter 32

By late Saturday night, the shop looked more like a train station than a confectionery. Tables once loaded with hearty breads or sweet treats sat empty and forlorn, like abandoned pieces of track. The curtains on the front window had been removed, and Luther Phipps had already covered the window with a sheet of wood to prevent the curious from getting a peek at the renovations once they began.

A sign on the front door, facing outward, informed customers the confectionery would reopen by the end of February and promised new fare to complement old favorites. In the vestibule, three trunks sat end to end, one destined for Philadelphia with the Lynn sisters, one destined for New York with Victoria and June Morgan, and one for some secret destination for Nancy.

On top of Nancy's trunk, filled with her few meager pieces of clothing, which the sheriff had secured from her home, a small lidded basket lined with a piece of heavy blanket sat ready for Lucky. She had become so attached to the kitten, no one had the heart to deny her. Similar baskets on top of the other two trunks held an assortment of sweet baked goods, a tin of pretzels, and candy to enjoy on their journeys.

Martha lay in bed, dreading the morning, yet urging it to come faster. The anticipation of saying good-bye to Victoria had literally formed a knot in her stomach, which kept her awake long after the rest of the household had gone to sleep.

For the next month, she would be living here alone. She had never, ever lived completely by herself, like Aunt Hilda, a reality that troubled her. She thought of Bird. He was still at Dr. McMillan's, recovering from the doctor's efforts to reset that damaged wing. Rather than live alone, she decided she might bring him back to the confectionery while he recuperated, just for the company.

Without warning, she heard the rustle of bedcovers, followed by several quick footsteps before she felt Victoria slip into bed beside her. Martha wrapped her arm around her daughter's shoulders.

"Mother? Did I wake you? I'm sorry."

Martha chuckled. "It was easier to sneak into my bed when you were little. What's the matter? Having trouble sleeping?"

"I'm too excited about tomorrow to sleep. I'm a little frightened, too," she admitted.

"Frightened?"

"For Nancy. What if our plan fails? What if her husband tries to stop her . . . and succeeds?"

Martha let out a long sigh and stroked the top of her daughter's head. "Well, it's hard for me to say for sure, since I don't know the particulars of the plan to help Nancy escape him, but I suspect all of you came up with a plan that would be hard to defeat. In which case, the best thing you can do is ask the good Lord to bless your plan and keep Nancy safe by giving her His protection. I like to think He's got some angels trained for that very purpose. They protected you, didn't they?"

Victoria snuggled closer. "I . . . I could tell you the plan. Nothing could happen between now and tomorrow —"

"I don't need to know the plan," Martha assured her. "I trust you. I trust the others."

"If our plan fails, then we'll just have to think of another, I suppose."

"It's not going to fail." Martha yawned. "I do have some news from Uncle James I wanted to share with you before you left."

Victoria stiffened. "He's not going to re-build the tavern, is he?"

"No. Apparently not, but that shouldn't truly be a surprise to either one of us. Your uncle has been talking about selling out and moving up to Candle Lake for more than a few years. I'm sure he'll tell you all about his plans when you're in Sunrise visiting."

"But that means . . . What are you going to do? You're truly going to be without a home," she whispered.

"We're both welcome to stay here for as long as we like," Martha ventured. "But I'd like to pray on it a while. I have this craving for my own home again. For our home," she added. "We have time. You won't be home till fall. By then, the good Lord will have decided where we should be."

"But what if —"

"Now don't you worry about a home for us. Not now. We only have a few hours left together." She pressed a kiss to her daughter's brow. "I hope I've told you how much it's meant to me to work with you on the essays these past few days."

A giggle. "Only a hundred times."

Martha returned the giggle. "I guess I've overdone it."

"Just a little."

"There's so much I thought about saying while you were gone. I was actually writing everything down in a daybook I bought in Clarion, but the fire claimed it, along with everything else. I decided later it would be better to just tell you how I felt, rather than have you read something."

"I would have liked the daybook. Can you tell me what you wrote?"

"There was so much, but basically, I wanted you to know that I admire you for many reasons, but most of all because you are the kindest person I've ever known, besides your father, and second, because you have such a strong commitment to the truth. You're an exceptional person, dear heart, and I can hardly believe I am so blessed to have you as my daughter."

Martha continued, and the words poured straight out of her heart. By the time she finished, both she and Victoria were weeping, and the tears of joy and love that flowed between them strengthened their bond even more.

Victoria cupped her mother's face. "I still have so much to learn, but I will be forever grateful to God for giving me such a good mother."

Martha's heart swelled, but her stomach ached anew with the anticipation of bidding farewell to her daughter after meeting tomorrow. "September isn't so very far away. You'll be home before I know it," she murmured.

Victoria yawned. "Perhaps sooner," she whispered.

As Victoria drifted off to sleep, Martha held her close and tried to capture the memory so she could revisit it often during the coming months.

After an extra early breakfast in the morning, the dishes had been cleared away and the kitchen tidied. All five women retired upstairs to dress for meeting amid an aura of excitement blended with sadness that heightened the moment they reassembled in the kitchen and sat together around the table.

"There's still about two hours till meeting, but we need to go over the plans again, just to be sure we all understand the roles we each have to play," Fern announced, clearly more assertive than Martha had ever seen her.

Certain and utterly pleased that she would finally be included, Martha leaned forward in her seat.

"Martha, Russell Clifford has made no effort to hide the fact that he expects to attend meeting and make a plea to be reunited with his wife. We want you to make sure he doesn't attend."

Martha flinched. "Me? Stop Russell Clifford? I was lucky he was addled when he tried to force his way inside a few days ago, or he would have been successful. I'm not even sure where to look for him, even if I thought I could try to keep him from attending."

Ivy dismissed Martha's argument with a wave of her hand. "You were right to suspect he was staying in Samuel's old cabin. He's been living there. With any luck, he'll still be sleeping, especially if he drank all the honey wine we left for him."

Martha's heart began to race. "You know he's staying there, and you left him some honey wine?"

Fern clucked an admonishment. "We're not at liberty to reveal anything beyond what Ivy's told you."

Martha got a glimpse of the determination that darkened Fern's blue eyes and knew better than to press for more information, but using honey wine certainly confirmed Aunt Hilda's participation in the plot. "So just exactly how do you suggest I keep him from attending, assuming that's necessary. He's a powerful man. I'm hardly able to tie him up. Not unless he's completely unconscious."

Victoria shook her head. "You don't have to force him to stay home. Just delay him so he'll arrive late. Once Reverend Welsh shuts the meetinghouse door, no one gets in. We all know that, but Mr. Clifford is new. He probably doesn't know that."

"Delay him," Martha repeated. "If I delay him, then I'll be late, too, and I won't be able to attend services, either. This is an important day for everyone to see Victoria and hear about her plans, for Aunt Hilda and her husband, so everyone can welcome him home. . . ."

Nancy's eyes welled with tears. "I'm sorry. I never meant to cause so much trouble. After all you've done to help me. . . ." She looked around the table at the other women. "There must be another way."

Martha swallowed a large lump of guilt that lodged in her throat. "No. If this is the plan, it's too late to change it now. I'll think of something to delay your husband."

Nancy brightened. "You're sure?"

"Absolutely." She rose from the table. "I'll be waiting outside when services are

444

over so I can bid you all farewell. I'll be able to do that, won't I?" she asked with a glance of longing at her daughter.

Fern nodded. "And if Russell is there, too, all the better. In fact, we'd like you to make sure he's there."

Martha closed her eyes briefly and took deep breaths to keep her frustration under control — frustration she would not be experiencing if she knew more about the plan to help Nancy to escape. "Let me make sure I understand this. I'm to delay Mr. Clifford so he can't get inside to attend meeting, but I also need to make sure he's still there, at least two hours later, waiting outside in freezing weather, when services finally conclude."

All heads nodded, but it was Fern who spoke up first. "Today's service won't last quite an hour."

Martha cocked her head. "You're certain? Reverend Welsh tends to —"

"Absolutely positive," Ivy insisted. "We have it on the highest authority."

"You spoke to Reverend Welsh about this?"

Fern gasped. "Of course not. We spoke to Sarah Welsh. She's going to make sure her husband's sermon just happens to disappear. He won't be able to remember most of it. Preaching isn't his gift, re-member?"

Apparently, the bonds of sisterhood re-inforced the day of the snowstorm when today's plan had been hatched, had been extended to include Sarah Welsh. Of all people, Sarah was about the finest woman ever to be a minister's wife, which was no easy lot. Martha knew Sarah well enough to be fairly certain she would never sabo-tage her husband's preaching efforts. Not when he was only too aware preaching was his nemesis.

Sarah might have told the Lynn sisters she would help, but Martha suspected Sarah had simply used her considerable in-fluence over her husband to convince him to keep today's sermon very short so folks could spend time welcoming Richard Sey-mour back home and talking with Victoria.

Being excluded still pricked at Martha's pride, and she had the distinct feeling she might be the only woman, other than June Morgan, who had not been made aware of today's plan. Without further comment, she strode to the storage room to retrieve her cape and gloves. She noted Nancy's cape, adorned with that garish ribbon, and went back into the kitchen.

"Regardless of your plan, ladies, I'd suggest you convince Nancy to remove that ribbon from her cape or her husband will be able to spot her the instant she steps out of the meetinghouse," she cautioned and took her leave before anyone could argue with her.

Her steps were quick, but did not move quite as fast as her mind, which raced from one approach she might take to delay Russell Clifford to another. As she rounded the confectionery and headed toward the covered bridge, she said a very desperate prayer, begging for some sort of reinforcements, preferably with wings and lots of good ideas.

Chapter 33

Martha approached Samuel's cabin, reminded of her failure to help Samuel and Will, as well as her smug approach which had led them to flee. She prayed her encounter with Russell Clifford would be more successful, although she wanted similar results — Russell's absence from Nancy's life.

Smoke suddenly belched from the chimney, and a weak trail of smoke began to twirl upward. Any hope Russell might be addled and unconscious immediately faded. With both windows shuttered closed, she could not even peek inside. At the same time, the shuttered windows prevented him from seeing her approach his doorstep.

Whatever angels had been sent to help her, in response to her desperate prayers all the way here, had yet to arrive. She knocked on the door, using the signal knock she had used with Samuel out of pure habit, but she still had absolutely no idea what she would say or do when Russell Clifford answered the door.

No response.

She tried again, knocking only once.

Still no response.

At this rate, she would not be able to do anything to delay him except stand helplessly outside while every bone in her body froze solid as she waited for him to leave for Sunday meeting. Fortunately, she was familiar enough with the cabin to know there was no back door. He would have to pass by her when he finally did leave, which gave her no choice but to stand and wait.

That idea appealed to her even less than confronting the brute, who may not have been addled enough the other day to forget how she had slammed the door in his face at the confectionery. She tugged on the sides of her hood to nearly cover her face and protect her skin from the cold wind, one of the decided benefits to using a hood instead of a bonnet during winter.

She thought wearing a hood might compare to a horse forced to wear blinders, which is why she never used them with Grace because it was disconcerting being unable to see. Or to be seen, for that matter.

Actually, with her features almost completely hidden, Russell would have to get right up to her face to be able to identify her. She could use that to her advantage and surprise him, if she ever got him to answer the door.

Mercy, it was cold! She pounded at the door again with both fists and added a kick for good measure — a painful mistake that nearly stole her breath away.

"Go away!"

She pounded again. "It's urgent that I see you," she shouted, without any idea of what she might claim to be urgent if he believed her.

Heavy agitated footsteps clomped toward the door. She held her breath and bowed her head until the door swung open. With one quick, sudden movement, she had her foot inside, resting against the doorframe. She offered a silent prayer. If he decided to use all his strength to slam the door closed, she would wind up with one very sore foot.

"What?" he snarled.

She detected no odor of honey wine, which meant part of the sisters' plan had not worked, and lifted her face. With his face freshly shaved and his dark hair slicked back, he had also cleaned himself up. "I've come to . . . apologize," she blurted.

He leaned closer. When his gaze finally lit with recognition, his hands balled into

450

fists, despite her claim to have come to offer an apology. He glared at her so coldly, her heart nearly stopped beating.

"I . . . I can't go to meeting with my heart so deeply burdened by the wrong that's been done to you, so . . . so I came to apologize and . . . and offer my help." She caught her breath. Where were those angels anyway? She needed help and she needed it now!

He returned her words with a smirk. "I don't need your help."

"I think you do," she countered. When the wind gusted and tore at her cape, she tried to hold it closed. "If I could come inside, maybe I could explain."

He cocked a brow. "After all you've done to destroy my marriage and poison my wife and the rest of the town against me, give me one good reason why I should listen to anythin' you have to say."

Drat. Still no angels!

"Because . . . because I know the others are planning to help your wife to escape, and you'll never be able to stop them. Not unless I help you," she said, praying all the lies she had already told and would have to create during the next hour or so would be forgiven because they were well-intentioned.

He continued to glare at her. Disbelief filled his gaze and held it steady. Until a flicker of doubt, ever so small, appeared.

"I'll only take up a few minutes of your time," she prompted. In that very heartbeat, she felt a distinct pressure in the small of her back, almost like a shove, tripped on the hem of her cape, wrenched her ankle, and fell — straight into the enemy's arms.

The angels had arrived. Pushy, but effective cherubs.

Caught off-guard, he apparently reacted instinctively and grabbed her shoulders to keep her from knocking him off his feet. "You are one ornery, stubborn woman," he snapped as he set her back on her feet.

"So I've been told." She winced the instant her right foot held the slightest pressure and went down on her knee. She held her breath until the sharp pain gentled into mere throbbing. "I'm afraid I've twisted my ankle."

"Nice excuse. You can turn right around and take your leave. You've done everythin' you're goin' to do to ruin my life. I'd be a fool to give you any more opportunity than you've already had."

She tried to get up and nearly toppled over. This time, he left her to her own devices and offered no help. She latched on to the edge of the door for support. "I'll limp all the way home, if that's what you want, but you'll just make it harder on yourself."

He laughed at her. "I doubt that."

"Suit yourself," she snapped, thoroughly disappointed in both the timing and the manner of her so-called reinforcements. "All the good Lord requires is that I tried to make amends. I can go to meeting now and not be judged a hypocrite. If and when you ever decide you want to hear more, let me know. I wouldn't wait too long, though. For every moment you wait, Nancy will be that much further beyond your reach."

With her head held high and her backbone stiff, she pivoted on her left foot, grabbed the doorframe, and limped forward. The pain was surprisingly bearable, although she could literally feel her ankle swelling. She scanned the area just beyond the front door, but the snow covered up anything she might have used for a makeshift crutch.

More than slightly irritated, she looked back over her shoulder and cast him a withering look she had not used since she used it to castigate Will for his bad language. "You might offer me something to use for a crutch, considering I hurt myself attempting to reconcile our differences."

Finally he had enough left in his sorry spirit to respond like a man with some character. "I just started a fire. You may as well sit down and warm up for a few moments before . . ."

She eyed him suspiciously.

"Just come in. Before I lose the little heat I've got left, since you've had me keep the door open for so long."

She limped inside, more certain than ever she had not imagined that none-too-gentle nudge in the small of her back. She even accepted Russell's help so she could make it to one of the chairs in front of the Franklin stove. She sank into her seat, shook the hood back and off her head, and slid her hand into her pocket to check her watch while he went to the corner of the room for more wood.

Still an hour and a half until meeting.

Well, she had gotten inside. Now all she had to do was keep him so preoccupied that he lost track of time and it would be too late to get inside the meetinghouse to attend services. Beyond that, her town sisters would be in charge.

She hoped they had been assigned angels who were a tad more gentle.

Nearly an hour and a half later, using a tree branch for a crutch, Martha made slow, painful progress as Russell Clifford led her through a trail in the woods toward the meetinghouse. Apparently, he had been using this trail, for the snow had been packed down on the pathway, a decided blessing considering Martha's weakened ankle. She had wrapped it tightly, grateful the injury only appeared to be a mild sprain that should heal within a few days.

She deliberately slowed her pace and allowed him to get a few yards ahead so she could check her watch. Three minutes until services began. She looked around and realized they were just passing the rear of Dr. McMillan's property, which meant they would never make it on time, even if Russell abandoned her and ran the rest of the way.

The tension that had stiffened her shoulders and wrapped a tight band around her forehead so her head ached literally melted away. Until Russell stopped and turned around. "We have to go faster than this or we'll be late."

She stopped and waved him on with her crutch. "Go ahead, then. I can meet you there."

"You'd like that, wouldn't you?" He closed the distance between them and glared at her.

She nearly took a step back, but locked her knees and refused to let him intimidate her. "What are you talking about?"

"If I go ahead and leave you behind, what guarantee do I have that you'll eventually show up and talk to the congregation on my behalf like you promised?" He hooked her arm in his and never gave her a chance to answer him. "We're goin' together."

She trembled. "It's getting colder. If you insist on escorting me, then let's not waste time arguing or we'll both get a good dose of frostbite."

With his support, she actually did make faster progress. The moment they approached the rear of the meetinghouse, she could hear the congregation, their voices lifted in the opening hymn. She offered a quick prayer of thanksgiving and another asking for protection when he realized the door was locked from the inside.

"There's no door in the back. We'll have to go around to the front."

He paused to stop and stare at the back of the log structure and shrugged his shoulders. He did not seem the least bit upset they were late. Victoria had been right. He was indeed too new to the congregation to know the minister's habits.

They made quick time walking along the side of the meetinghouse. When they rounded the corner, he rocked to a halt and forced Martha to do the same.

The yard in front of the meetinghouse was literally packed with wagons and sleighs, all oddly parked side by side to form two large circles with the horses and mules huddled together in the center. She had not seen this before; neither had she seen this many vehicles at meeting since . . . since ever!

He grinned. "Must be packed inside."

She could almost see his mind working, anticipating the moment she would step forward, endorsing his redemption, as well as his reunion with his wife, as she had promised. It had not been easy convincing him of her change in heart, until he heard her tale of Nancy's plea for a reunion. It would be far more difficult for both Nancy and herself to escape his wrath once he realized he had been played for a fool.

"You're sure Nancy is at meetin'?" he asked as he changed his position and gripped her upper arm.

She yanked free. "Of course I am. I

spoke to her right before I left. She's expecting you to be there, too."

When he turned her toward the door and hooked her arm again, her heart began to pound. "Let's not keep her waitin'," he suggested.

Before she had taken a single step, a familiar, beloved voice rang out. Not exactly an angel's voice, but one that reassured her that gentler, more competent reinforcements had arrived.

Chapter 34

"Martha? Is that you?"

She turned to look back over her shoulder, nudged her hood back, and flashed the biggest smile of her life. "Thomas!"

When Russell Clifford turned about, he also loosened his grip, enough to allow Martha to free herself so she could face Thomas. As he hurried toward them, she leaned on the branch for support.

He locked his gaze with hers. Concern etched his face. "What happened?"

"Just a silly accident. I turned my ankle."

"You shouldn't be walking on it," he countered. He took her arm to help support her and acknowledged Russell with a cold stare.

Clifford offered a curt nod, but did not extend his hand. "Mayor Dillon. Looks like Widow Cade and I aren't the only ones arrivin' late for meetin'."

"Indeed. And properly locked out as well," Thomas noted.

"Locked out?" Clifford turned and

tested the door. With a grunt, he put his shoulder to the door, but it would not budge. He raised his hand to knock.

"Don't," Thomas cautioned. "Apparently Reverend Welsh is not having one of his better days. You knock and interrupt the service, and he'll have you down in front listening to a diatribe so fierce you'll wish you had listened to me."

Clifford kicked the door and spun around. He glared at Martha, but dared not approach her with Thomas as her protector. "I have to get inside. We both have to get inside."

"Obviously, that's not going to happen now," she argued. "We can . . . we can slip inside the moment the service is over and catch everyone before they leave. Or . . . or if not, don't forget that Nancy will have to come out that door. When she does, we'll both be here waiting for her. I know it's not exactly what you wanted, but . . . but at least you'll be with your wife again. Isn't that what you want more than anything?"

Before Russell could respond, Thomas scooped her up into his arms and nearly stole her breath away. "I have to wait for the Misses Lynn. We're leaving for Philadelphia as soon as the services end. If you insist on staying, then you'll wait in the sleigh with me. At least there are blankets to keep you warm and you'll be off that ankle. Mr. Clifford, you wait by the door. As soon as Nancy comes out, bring her over. Widow Cade is in no condition to stand and wait, especially in this weather."

He gave Clifford no time to argue, or Martha, for that matter. He simply carried her off toward his sleigh and left the younger man standing at the door. She snuggled close and laid her head on his chest. "Thank you."

He looked down at her and smiled. "I had a feeling you might need rescuing. Is your ankle really sprained or is that just a ploy, part of the ladies' plan, too?"

"Plan? What plan?"

When he chuckled, again and again, the sound in his chest rumbled against her ear.

She swatted his arm. "No, it's not part of the plan. I fell and twisted my ankle," she admitted, although she was careful not to tell him she thought an angel had pushed her.

When he reached the sleigh, she saw that the sisters' trunks, as well as one apparently for Thomas, had been strapped to a platform attached to the back. Their treat basket sat on the second seat. Thomas settled her up front, layered several blankets

461

over her lap and legs, and got in beside her.

He nodded toward Russell Clifford who stood with his back braced against the door. "I have a feeling he's about to feel the full wrath of the sisterhood here in Trinity."

Her eyes widened, and she tilted her chin. "Did you say sisterhood? That's an odd term."

He chuckled again. "I overheard Eleanor talking to Mrs. Clark about it. After I got a glimpse inside that meetinghouse today, I got an inkling of what she meant. When I found out you weren't inside, I suspected you might need some assistance when you arrived."

"You are a blessing to me," she whispered. "Truly a blessing."

He took her hand. "Does that mean you've reconsidered my proposal? The congregation is assembled. I'm sure Reverend Welsh wouldn't mind —"

"No. I mean yes. But no . . . not . . ."

He cocked his brow. She realized the stitches had been removed, leaving only a thin scar that sliced through his brow. "I've never known you to be indecisive. Which is it going to be? Yes. No. Or not?"

She closed her eyes briefly and took a

deep breath before gazing into his eyes. "Yes. I've thought about your proposal. A great deal. There are certain . . . certain possibilities I'd like to discuss with you."

The corners of his lips began to shape a smile.

"They're just possibilities, mind you. I can't marry you today because . . . because I want some time to think them through."

His lips stretched into a small smile, but he did not interrupt or offer her any assistance as she struggled to explain herself.

"When you come home in February, I'd . . . I'd like for us to talk again."

He caressed her cheek. "About these . . . possibilities."

Her heart began to race. "Yes."

"And if we can reach some sort of accord, then you'll marry me?"

She swallowed hard and tried to ignore the sweet sensations on her cheek that he was creating with just the touch of his fingertips. "Yes."

"Yes. Yes what?"

She cocked her head. "Yes. I'll marry you. If we reach —"

He kissed her silent. It was just a gentle kiss. Enough to let her know he would wait for her to be sure. Enough to let her feel the power of his enduring affection.

463

Enough to reassure her that the obstacles between them were not insurmountable. And just enough to let her know his patience would be stretched thin by next month when he returned.

When he ended the kiss, he looked at her with his gray eyes twinkling. "Now that wasn't so bad, was it?"

She felt a blush that started in her toes and traveled to the tip of her nose. "Actually, I thought that was quite . . . lovely," she admitted, although if anyone had seen them kiss, she would have been hard-pressed to control the gossip that would follow.

He chuckled and pulled her into his embrace. "I was talking about making the decision to accept my proposal. Even if it is conditional."

"I'm not sure I can marry a man so smug and so sure of himself," she teased as she relaxed in his embrace. "Rather than simply basking in the glory of your triumph, maybe you could tell me about your plans to help Fern."

The next hour passed quickly enough.

Despite the mound of blankets, the cold was sorely aggravating Martha's ankle. To keep her mind from focusing on the pain, she tried to imagine Aunt Hilda's great joy today, as well as Victoria's, as she greeted old friends and shared her future plans with them.

Sitting next to Thomas, enjoying his protection and companionship, as well as his account of the plans he had for helping Fern, Martha could scarcely believe she had actually questioned the idea of spending the rest of her life with him. Whatever the future held, whatever changes took place, she knew she could face it all with Thomas by her side and her faith to sustain her.

When the congregation once again rose voices in song, she recognized the closing hymn. Apparently, so did Thomas. He stiffened, too. "Should we get down so we can get closer?" she asked.

He still held on to her hand. "We'll have a better view from here."

He was right. His sleigh was parked at such an angle they would be able to see everyone as they emerged from the meeting-house. Also, being seated in the sleigh provided the added advantage of height so they would literally have a panoramic view.

The moment the door opened, she caught her breath for a moment. "What are you going to do when he brings Nancy over to us?" she asked. She was not even certain Nancy would agree to come over or if that was part of the plan.

Thomas grinned. "Just watch."

She looked back at the meetinghouse. Several children, as usual, piled out first, followed by several men she recognized as farmers from up on Double Trouble Creek. To her surprise, the first woman she saw was Nancy. Her hood was pushed fully forward. Martha could not see Nancy's face, but she recognized her by that awful, garish ribbon trimming her cape.

Clifford immediately rushed forward to speak to his wife. Martha turned back to Thomas. "I told them to take off that ribbon!" she whispered. "He found her right away."

"Look again," Thomas suggested.

She glanced back, blinked to clear her vision, and blinked again. But the images remained the same. Only then did she realize that the sisterhood in Trinity was much larger, and much more powerful, than she could ever have imagined.

Chapter 35

Amazed, Martha watched as two more women emerged, then a third. And a fourth. All with their hoods pitched forward and held in place to cover all but their eyes. All with their capes trimmed in bile green and sunflower yellow ribbon.

Her heart began to race, but she was too surprised to do anything more than watch the scene unfold. One by one, the congregation emerged into the outer yard. Each woman was escorted and protected by a husband or son, uncle, male cousin, or neighbor. They scattered to different wagons, each ready to carry away a woman who might be Nancy.

Some women were obviously too short or too tall, whereas others appeared to be too heavy, although Martha granted a few pillows would create the same image for Nancy. One by one, the women climbed into the wagons and presented onlookers with only a view of their backs.

Clifford frantically charged toward one wagon after another, only to meet a solid wall of resistance as the menfolk stood side by side, with righteousness their greatest weapon.

When two women turned and began to approach Thomas's sleigh, Martha thought they were Fern and Ivy. As well as she knew them, though, she could not be sure. They may have disguised Nancy with pillows to make everyone, including Martha, think she was either Fern or Ivy. Thomas got out of the sleigh to meet them. He directed them to the sleigh, but stayed behind to greet a number of people, including Sheriff Myer. Moments later, Thomas caught up with the two women and helped them into the seat behind Martha. She promptly turned in her seat to face them as they got comfortable and stored the basket of treats between them.

"You did a good job!" Fern whispered.

"He's got to be furious!" Ivy offered.

Martha recognized both their voices and grinned. "How did you ever get the whole town to cooperate?"

Fern leaned forward as Thomas got back into the sleigh. "It wasn't hard. After Nancy started going out on errands, folks saw what her husband had done to her with their own eyes. I had a feeling they'd look forward to making a stand together to help her."

"Russell helped, too. By being so obsessive and making a nuisance of himself in town," Ivy added. "He'll never know which woman is Nancy, and he'll have no way to follow her. Not with all these wagons going off in every direction. He'll simply have to leave town. Alone."

"I'm so proud of you both," Martha whispered. "I wish I could stay and talk, but I have to find Victoria, so I'll wish you both Godspeed."

When she went to climb down, Thomas caught her elbow. "Enoch told me Victoria forgot her basket of treats, so they're going back to the confectionery. I told him I'd drive you there so you can say good-bye."

Relieved, yet still awed by the spectacle still taking place, Martha relaxed against the back of the seat. Thomas urged the horses forward as soon as the wagons blocking him moved out of the way.

Now that she was fairly certain Nancy was on her way to a new life, without any fear Russell would follow her, the full reality of bidding Victoria farewell hit hard. Fighting back tears, she hung on to the thought that September would be here soon, bringing a bountiful harvest to all,

Lord willing, and her daughter home to Trinity.

When they reached the confectionery, the wagon and sleigh traffic was heavy along both West and East Main Street. Sheriff Myer had parked his sleigh in front of the shop. June was still seated, but Victoria was just climbing out onto the sidewalk.

Even wearing a ribboned cape, Martha recognized her daughter. "Victoria!" She did not wait for Thomas to help her down, but clambered to the walkway as gracefully as she could and grabbed hold of her makeshift crutch.

Victoria's hood blew back as she raced to her mother's side. "Mother! What happened?"

"I slipped and hurt my ankle. It's nothing serious."

"Widow Cade!"

The sound of Russell Clifford's voice sent tremors down Martha's spine. She turned and placed herself in front of Victoria. Both Thomas and the sheriff disembarked and stood on either side of them before Clifford arrived.

"You tricked me! You *all* tricked me," he shouted. When he took a step closer, both Thomas and the sheriff closed ranks while

June, Fern, and Ivy watched silently.

"You can't win this time, Mr. Clifford. It's time you moved on. You have no friends here," Thomas warned.

Clifford snarled. "I want my wife, and I want her now!"

"She's gone. Someplace safe, where you won't be able to hurt her," Thomas countered. He handed Clifford an envelope. "It's a fair price for your farm. Stop by my house on your way out of town to sign the bill of sale. My son-in-law and several of my friends will be waiting for you."

Russell shoved the envelope into his pocket. "And if I don't?"

The sheriff snickered. "Under the circumstances, I suggest you do as the mayor suggested, or else I'll be forced to place you under arrest and see that your sorry soul rots in prison before it roasts in Hades."

Russell Clifford paled. "Arrest me? On what charges?"

Thomas shrugged. "I don't think it matters, does it, Enoch? There isn't a man who'd serve on the jury who would vote Clifford innocent, regardless of the charge. Men in Trinity tend to be hardminded when it comes to protecting their women. And they'd be hard-pressed to accept your claim that the signature on the bill of sale is a forgery."

Russell backed up. "You're a lunatic. You're all lunatics! You want me gone? So be it. That mindless twit isn't worth it," he spat. He stormed off, only to take up a position just inside the covered bridge to watch them from afar — as if he still expected Nancy to suddenly appear.

"He won't cause any trouble now," Thomas assured her. "Micah and the others will make sure of it."

Martha let out a sigh of relief. "Thank you," she whispered to both men, turned, and embraced her daughter. "I don't think I'll ever be more proud of you than I am right now. And I'm relieved to know you really didn't like that ribbon," she added, if only to lighten the moment.

Victoria returned her mother's hug and chuckled. "Me, too."

The sheriff cleared his throat. "We really should be leaving. I'd like to be in Sunrise before dark."

"I just need my basket. I'll only be a moment," Victoria promised and hurried into the confectionery.

While she waited for her daughter to return, Martha gave Fern and Ivy a farewell hug before limping over to bid June farewell. Her voice choked with emotion. "There's so much I want to say," she managed.

June smiled. "It's been my pleasure. I'll write soon and tell you all about the trip. Don't forget to work on that series of articles."

"No. I won't."

When Victoria returned, with her hood tightly bound again and her basket on her arm, Martha gave her a farewell hug. "Godspeed, child. I love you."

Apparently, Victoria was so overcome with emotion, she could not speak or look at her mother. Instead, she returned the hug and quickly climbed aboard. Thomas helped Martha to the confectionery door and pressed a kiss to the back of her hand. "I intend to hold you to your promise."

"I expect you to do just that," she teased. She watched him get back into the sleigh and waved to Fern and Ivy as the sleigh started forward, heading south toward Philadelphia. Martha waved to June and Victoria as the sheriff guided them north, toward Sunrise and eventually New York City, and saw Russell Clifford shake his fist at Thomas before turning and stomping back across the bridge.

Martha waited until both sleighs were

out of sight before going into the confectionery, uncertain whether her heart would ever recover from such an emotional day. Her ankle ached mercilessly, and she was near total nervous exhaustion. She made her way through the vestibule, stopped, and crinkled her nose.

The tantalizing and unmistakable aroma of freshly baked cherry pie hung in the air. Bless their hearts, Fern and Ivy must have known how sad and lonely Martha would be and had baked it for her, knowing cherry pie was her absolute favorite.

She limped as fast as she could, entered the kitchen, and gasped. She dropped her crutch. Her heart nearly leaped right out of her chest. Stunned senseless and rendered speechless, she stared straight ahead at the images of three people who awaited her.

Tears blurred her vision, but in that very instant, when she looked into Victoria's eyes, she knew exactly where Nancy had gone.

In point of fact, she would have collapsed, if her daughter had not rushed forward to help. Victoria led her to the table where the other two waited for her, along with a half-eaten cherry pie that they had helped themselves to. "Sit down and rest that ankle while I tell you all about —"

"That was Nancy who just left with Thomas, wasn't it? Little wonder she didn't look at me. Wh-what are you doing here?" Martha turned to the others. "And you. And you!" She addressed all three of them before easing into her seat.

After Victoria left the room to find a stool so Martha could prop up her ankle, Samuel spoke first. "I'm here to show you this." He pulled a paper from his pocket and laid it on the table. "Read it."

Will grinned. "Got myself a new name now. William Samuel Meeks. I know Will's short for William, but you can call me William from now on."

Martha scanned the paper. "You *adopted* Will?" she asked, completely astounded that any court would consider letting a man of seventy adopt a child.

"Everything's official, so don't go tryin' to meddle again," he teased. "Even hired us a housekeeper of sorts. Fancy's an old salt who served with me for some twenty years, though he claimed the galley as his domain. He had enough with livin' on handouts in Clarion. He's out to the cabin now, gettin' it all cleaned up. Man can't leave for a few weeks without worryin' about some squatter movin' in!"

Martha tried to imagine what Russell Clifford's reaction would have been if he had met up with Samuel or his cohort and chuckled. Before she could do more than think to offer both Samuel and Will an apology, Victoria returned with a footstool, knelt down, and helped Martha get her foot situated. "And you?" she asked. "Did you really let Nancy take your place?"

Victoria looked up at her mother with tear-filled eyes. "As much as I thought I wanted to go back to New York, I knew Nancy needed to go even more."

Martha's heart skipped a beat. "You only thought you wanted to go? You weren't sure?"

Victoria smiled. "I thought I was sure, but the longer I stayed home, the more I realized how much I wanted to stay here. I . . . I can write anywhere. I know that now, but there's only one place where I can be with you. And that's here. In Trinity. Although I probably should hide for several weeks, just to be sure Mr. Clifford is long gone and doesn't find out Nancy switched places with me."

Martha thought of the key from Thomas that she had upstairs and knew exactly where to hide her daughter. She cupped Victoria's cheek. "I was wrong earlier when

I said I couldn't ever imagine being prouder of you because right now, I am."

As they embraced and wept together, Martha offered a heartfelt prayer of thanksgiving to her Creator. He had truly guided her daughter home. To Trinity. To her mother. And for good measure, He had led Samuel and Will back into Martha's life, too, along with another retired seaman named Fancy, of all things.

As for Thomas and the future they might soon share together, Martha could only offer yet another prayer that would grant Thomas a safe and successful journey and bring him home to her in Trinity, too.

Amen.

Author's Note

Modern midwifery has made significant advances since the nineteenth century. Readers who are interested in modern midwifery techniques and their advantages are encouraged to refer to contemporary literature for information and advice rather than applying any historical midwifery practices explored in this novel. Readers are also advised to contact their physicians and modern-day midwives so that any decisions to be made regarding pregnancy and labor/delivery are based on sound, professional, up-to-date information.

The interest in alternative medicine, which includes herbal supplements and/or treatments, has grown enormously in the past few decades. The treatments used in this novel may be historically accurate, but they are not suggested for modern use; instead, readers should combine research of contemporary herbal medications with standard medical advice from their physicians and other trained health-care providers.

My hope is that *Home to Trinity* will place midwifery and herbal treatments in historical perspective and give readers a peek at the beginnings of modern medical techniques and medications. I also pray this novel will help to document the crucial role our foremothers played in guiding new generations into this world and caring for them when they became ill, as well as the very real existence of sisterhood that bound women to one another for the good of us all.

Many blessings.